THE
SUICIDE
EXHIBITION

THE NEVER WAR
Book One

THE
SUICIDE
EXHIBITION

Justin Richards

DEL REY

1 3 5 7 9 10 8 6 4 2

First published in the UK in 2013 by Del Rey, an imprint of Ebury Publishing
A Random House Group Company

The Random House Group Limited Reg. No. 954009

Addresses for companies within the Random House Group can be found at
www.randomhouse.co.uk

A CIP catalogue record for this book is available from the British Library
The Random House Group Limited supports The Forest Stewardship
Council® (FSC®), the leading international forest-certification organisation.
Our books carrying the FSC label are printed on FSC® -certified paper.
FSC is the only forest-certification scheme supported by the leading
environmental organisations, including Greenpeace. Our paper procurement
policy can be found at www.randomhouse.co.uk/environment

Designed and typeset by Steve Tribe
Printed and bound in Great Britain by Clays, St Ives PLC

ISBN 978 0 091 95596 0

To buy books by your favourite authors and register for offers
visit www.randomhouse.co.uk

For Toby – who loves this sort of thing

SHINGLE BAY

REPORT INTO INCIDENT ON 30TH AUGUST
1940

DOCUMENTS ENCLOSED:
- Official Statement (Ministry of War, 1940)
- OS Map of Shingle Bay and Environs (September 1940)
- Report of Colonel Brinkman (September 1940)
- Memo from Prime Minister (September 1940)
- Classification Review Minutes (February 1957)
- Ditto (July 1973)
- Ditto (December 1998)
- Request for file disclosure under Freedom of Information (2001) DENIED
- Ditto (2005)   DENIED
- Ditto (2011)   DENIED

THIS FILE IS CLASSIFIED
Level Z
NOT TO BE OPENED UNTIL
1 September 2040

BY ORDER

[signature]

(Original signed by Winston S. Churchill)

CHAPTER 1

Officially, on 30 August 1940, nothing happened at Shingle Bay. The government records that prove nothing happened were classified for the next hundred years.

It was a day of heavy air raids on the south east of Britain. The sky was filled with noise and death. If there had been anyone to see Sergeant Green and his troops at Shingle Bay, the chances are their eyes would have been turned instead to the heavens. Their attention would have been drawn by the distinctive grumble of the Rolls-Royce Merlin engines that powered RAF Hurricanes and Spitfires against the might of the Luftwaffe.

As the evening drew in, so the skies emptied. Britain held her breath, not knowing that the next day would bring RAF Fighter Command her heaviest losses of the war so far. Unaware of what would happen that night.

'You sure about this, Sarge?' Private Goodall asked.

'This is war, son,' Sergeant Green told him. 'No one's sure about anything.'

'You got the shivers?' Private Wood asked, grinning.

'I ain't got nothing.'

Wood's grin widened. 'That's true enough.'

'Shut it, both of you,' Green said. *He* had the shivers even if the other two hadn't.

They made their way back up the steep cliff path, and took

up position behind a screen of bushes and grass, sheltered by the bulk of the nearby church.

'We really going to stop an invasion?' Wood asked.

Green stared out through the curtain of vegetation, binoculars clamped to his eyes. 'If we have to.'

'Just us, Sarge?'

'You've got the radio. If it gets hairy, call it in.'

'How will I know?' Wood wondered.

Goodall had been at Dunkirk. 'You'll know,' he said.

'Just you be ready at that valve,' Green warned.

The pipeline was like a huge, dark snake curling past their position and down the side of the cliff. It split into smaller pipes on the beach below, spreading out like a black spider's web across the shingle before disappearing under the water.

The three soldiers settled down to wait. It could be a long night. For now the only sound was the waves dragging back over the pebbles on the beach below.

Dusk was drawing in before anything happened.

'What's that?' Wood hissed.

'Can't see anything,' Green told him.

'Nor me. But I can hear it.'

'Me too,' Goodall agreed. 'Plane I think.'

Green scanned the sky. Finally he spotted it – flying high and approaching along the coast from the south.

'Got it. It's all right – it's one of ours.'

It was a large transport plane, lumbering its way on some logistical mission under the cover of approaching darkness.

The note of the aircraft seemed to change as it approached. It became deeper, discordant, and then resolved into two different sounds. Green scanned the sea, peering out as far as he could into the gathering dusk. There they were – he just hoped the aircraft didn't spook them...

'Ready, lad?' Green was whispering, though there was no way the men in the approaching boats could hear him. 'Do it now.'

Wood nodded nervously, reaching for the metal wheel jutting from the side of the pipeline. It squeaked as it turned.

Beside him, Goodall shouldered his rifle, scanning the beach below.

Holding the binoculars steady with one hand, Green scrabbled for the flare pistol with the other. 'Not a moment too soon,' he breathed.

There were three boats, each containing half a dozen men. He could make out the individual soldiers now. He could see their grim, determined faces, their field grey uniforms and their rifles. At the prow of the last boat, one man stood staring towards the beach. His pale, hollow features and his wispy blond hair were clear in the binoculars despite the fading light. He seemed to be staring back at Green through dark, sunken eyes – challenging him to do his worst.

Well, thought Green, that was a challenge he was happy to accept. With gallons of petrol flowing rapidly down the pipeline and bubbling up into the bay, Green raised the flare pistol.

In a stone-built room lit only by the flickering light of burning oil, Number Five was drawing, oblivious to his surroundings and the two men watching. His pencil scratched frantically across the paper, sketching outlines, impressions rather than details. As soon as the drawing was finished, he pushed it across the stone desk, and started on the blank sheet of paper beneath.

The sound of pencil on paper mingled with the guttering of the lamps. One of the two men standing beside the desk lifted the latest drawing and angled it towards the nearest wall sconce.

'They are almost there.'

The other, shorter man, nodded, taking the drawing. The light glinted on his small, round spectacles as he examined the picture. Two boats, heading towards a curving beach. Pale cliffs rose up above banks of shingle. The men in the boats were barely more than silhouettes, guns at the ready. The scene was pictured as if from a third boat, just behind the first two.

The spectacled man placed the drawing on a stone table beside him, aligning it carefully and exactly with the stack of pictures beneath.

Number Five stared into the distance, not seeing the men standing in front of him. Not seeing the drawing evolve on the paper. Intent only on the images in his mind's eye.

The new drawing was similar. The boats closer to the beach now. Perhaps a hint of restlessness in the posture of the men. And high in the sky, a point of light like a blossoming star.

The shorter man frowned. 'What is that?'

The flare lit up the sky like an elongated burst of lightning. Green had aimed long, so that it was still burning incandescently as it fell towards the sea. As it reached the water in front of the boats. As it touched the film of oil slicked across the sea.

The single point of brilliant light burst into a fireball spreading out over the water. A wave of flames, crashing down on the shoreline and rushing out towards the approaching boats. In a moment, it engulfed them.

It was like a painting of hell. The whole sea was ablaze. Green could hear the shouts and screams of the men in the boats. Between the sheets of flame, he caught confused glimpses. Burning men diving into the water. The skeletal carcases of the fire-eaten boats. The man in the prow of the third boat – still standing staring towards the shore. Unmoving even as the flames licked at his smouldering uniform...

Goodall's rifle tracked back and forth as he waited for a target. If any of them made it to the beach, they'd be easy pickings. But Green could tell that none of them would.

'You can shut off that valve now,' he told Wood.

The man's face was shining with sweat as he turned the wheel. They could all feel the heat coming off the sea. Slowly, the flames died down, the smoke thinned, and the screaming faded into the cries of the frightened seagulls.

It was a drawing of hell. Number Five's hand jerked painfully across the page, the pencil almost ripping the paper. The heavy metal bracelet round his wrist scraping against the stone desktop. Jagged spikes of flame. Shaded smoke. The distorted suggestion of men's agony.

And through it all, Number Five was screaming. Mouth open, head back, screaming in pain.

His skin seemed to shrink back from his cheekbones, blackened and dry. Blistering, peeling, smoking from the heat of the fire. His hand was a mess of charred bone, pushing the paper aside and starting on the next sheet. By the time he slumped forward in a smoking heap, all he had drawn was a mass of flames.

But still he was screaming. The last skin was seared from his skull. Eyeballs ran with tears of their own molten flesh. His body convulsed. Number Five clawed at the table. There were blackened scorch marks across the surface where his fingers had gripped it. The pencil clattered to the floor.

The two men watching said nothing. The shorter man snatched up the final drawing – a pencilled mass of flame and smoke. He stared at it for a moment, the fire from the nearest wall sconce reflecting in his glasses. Then Reichsfuhrer Heinrich Himmler screwed the paper into an angry ball and threw it across the room.

The paper hit the wall, and dropped into the sconce below. It rested intact for a moment in the pool of burning oil, then burst into smoky flame.

CHAPTER 2

By late April 1941, the Battle of Britain was over. The price of the Allies' first victory was high. Nazi Germany had suffered its first defeat.

But in the mind of Standartenfuhrer Hans Streicher of the SS the war was practically won. How long could a tiny island continue to hold out against the might of the Reich? Some of Streicher's men were afraid Britain would surrender before they saw action. Streicher knew that Hauptsturmfuhrer Klaas in particular resented not being at the forefront of the struggle.

'When the Wehrmacht marched into Poland, we were excavating in the Austrian Alps,' Klaas said. 'When Paris fell, we were digging through Roman ruins in Northern Italy. Now, we're stuck here in France when the battle's over and we should be fighting the British.'

Streicher sympathised. But he had no such reservations himself about their work. 'You've been with me since '34, Gerhardt,' he said quietly, glancing across at the third man with them. 'You know how important our work is to the Reich. For us, the front line is here.'

Klaas looked round, peering into the gloom. 'An ancient chamber hidden beneath a churned-up field in the middle of nowhere?' He sighed and nodded. 'I'm sorry, sir. I know you are right of course. It's just... frustrating. Everything takes so long.'

'Check on the progress,' Streicher ordered. 'And remember, however long it takes, however frustrated we might get, the work we are doing here could determine the future not just of Europe but of the entire world.'

Streicher took pride in that. He was a man who took pride in everything he did, never giving less than total dedication, commitment and loyalty. Even the tiniest things were important to him – like the fact that his own English was more precise and grammatical than that of the American standing beside him.

Together they watched Klaas talking to the soldiers tunnelling through the unforgiving ground. It had taken three weeks to dig their way this deep. Three weeks of unrelenting, backbreaking work. Anything less sensitive, less important, and Streicher would have rounded up able-bodied men from Oulon and the surrounding villages and used them as slave labour. But not for this... Two years of research had led Streicher here. The imminent results were for the eyes of a select few within the SS only.

And the American. He was useful, and just as the United States as a whole maintained a studied neutrality, so the American seemed supremely unconcerned about what happened in Europe. Just so long as it did not interfere with his own researches or with sites of historic interest.

The American certainly agreed that this site was of historic interest. *Pre*-historic, possibly. Despite his lazy drawl, and the scraggy beard, Professor Carlton Smith evidently knew his subject.

Streicher was wary. America might be neutral but she was no ally. That said, Smith did seem genuinely immune to the increasing tide of pro-British feeling that was flowing over the United States.

'Hell,' he'd told Streicher when they first met, 'you guys can blow each other to Kingdom Come far as I'm concerned, just so long as you leave me to my digging and notes.'

Smith could see for himself, he told Streicher, that the Reich was by no means the all-conquering monster that the warmonger Churchill and his cronies made it out to be. In fact, Smith's politics, on the rare occasions when he ventured an opinion or betrayed a belief, seemed refreshingly in line with Streicher's own.

Of course, Streicher had checked as soon as he met him that Carlton Smith really was a professor of Archaeology at Harvard University. His credentials, it was confirmed through the Reich's sources in New York, were impeccable. His political leanings were indeed slanted in the right direction.

For all his arrogance and brash tone, Smith had offered invaluable advice on the dig and useful insight to some of the finds. It was a lucky coincidence that he had been touring the area making notes on local churches and chateaus for a proposed book. Especially lucky for the men who would have died with Sturmmann Hagen if Carlton Smith hadn't seen the iron spike set in the ground under the wall and shouted a warning.

It was a simple enough mechanism, little more than a lever primed to bring down a ton of rubble on anyone digging through the entrance of the burial mound. Perhaps the most surprising thing was that it still worked, even after thousands of years.

They tunnelled in from the other side after that. Smith's advice had been to abandon trying to get through the tomb's entrance. 'Who knows what other traps the cunning old bastards laid? But you cut your way in from the back, and it's a whole different ball game.'

Now they were digging deep underground, their work lit by electric lamps on metal tripods and by bare bulbs strung from cables fastened to the walls that ran back to the generators at the edge of the dig. Makeshift wooden props shored up the tunnels. The soldiers had worked their way through three caverns, each littered with artefacts all of which were catalogued and crated up ready for later shipment.

Two more men had been killed by hidden traps getting this far. One fell through a thin flagstone that shattered under his weight, the second was crushed by a slab that swung down from the roof. Several others had lucky escapes.

Now, finally, they had reached what seemed to be the final chamber. Streicher's men were scraping the mud and dirt from the last wall. Once through that, the long hard work would be justified…

The project was overrunning. Streicher was under pressure to get into the chamber and recover what he was sure was inside. He was cautious, wary of making rash promises, but everything pointed to this being the place. He tried not to raise the expectations of his superiors. Even so, they asked daily for the impossible. He was aware of one of the Enigma operators pushing through the narrow tunnel behind him and into the cavern where they stood. He could guess what the message said. It would be from Reichsfuhrer Himmler, or possibly his lackey Hoffman. The wording would be clear and short and direct.

Streicher took the flimsy message paper without looking at the operator. Glanced at it. 'No reply. Just acknowledge receipt.'

'More words of wisdom and encouragement from the Fatherland?' Smith asked, his smile masked by the beard.

'Something of the sort,' Streicher said in English. The American spoke no German, and hardly any French. It was a miracle he'd survived in France at all before meeting Streicher.

So the Standartenfuhrer made no effort to conceal the message slip as he handed it back to the operator. If Carlton Smith had bothered to look, he'd have seen a single line of text:

HAVE+YOU+SECURED+THE+UBERMENSCH

In fact, Carlton Smith did understand some German and his French was more than passable. But he knew that the less he seemed to know about what was really going on, the more likely Streicher was to keep him involved. He was under no illusions that he was dealing with the SS. If they thought he'd found out something he shouldn't, they'd shoot him. So he smiled and nodded and feigned complete ignorance, and offered as much help and advice as he thought would be well received.

He played a similar game with his politics – venturing only rare opinions or thoughts, and always carefully clouding what he really thought of the Third Reich and what was happening in Europe.

As well as the historical interest of the site, Smith was fascinated by Streicher's involvement. The Standartenfuhrer's men, while no doubt efficient and brutal soldiers, were evidently also veterans of previous archaeological digs. They worked with care and diligence, and at least some appreciation of the past they were unearthing.

Klaas returned, raising his arm in an abrupt *Heil* which Streicher reciprocated. The wall was clear – they were ready to break into the tomb.

Smith kept his expression neutral. The beard helped. He saved his excited enthusiasm for Streicher's translation.

Armed with heavy torches, the two of them followed Klaas across the cavern to the exposed wall. Two more soldiers, stripped to the waist, stood ready with pickaxes.

'Let me see, let me see.' Smith pushed past. He ran his hand over the rough stone surface of the wall, nodding. 'Yeah – this is absolutely typical of the ninth century. See the way the stones have been interlaced? Looks like you've got yourselves the tomb of an ancient chieftain.'

'Much more than that,' Streicher murmured in German. He nodded for the men to start work on the wall.

The stone was brittle with age. There was no mortar to hold the wall together, and in minutes the soldiers had torn a ragged hole large enough for a man to get through. Streicher stepped forward, determined to be the first to see what lay beyond the wall.

But Smith caught Streicher's arm. 'Be a bit careful there.'

It was sensible advice. Streicher stepped cautiously through, testing the ground on the other side before he committed his full weight to it. It seemed firm enough. Once through, he waited for Smith to join him, several of the SS soldiers clambering after the academic. Two of them still carried their pickaxes.

The torches illuminated a narrow passageway sloping downwards ahead of them.

'So, not quite at the main chamber yet,' Smith noted. 'Can't be far, though.'

Streicher's impatience got the better of him and he set off along the passage. If they didn't find the chamber soon, the messages he received daily from Wewelsburg would become more insistent. He knew only too well that in the Third Reich in general and in the SS in particular you could be transformed from hero to pariah in a matter of hours.

Again, Smith caught Streicher's shoulder.

'Take it easy. There could still be surprises.'

As he spoke, something moved in the shadows ahead of them. A trick of the wandering torchlight, perhaps. But it seemed like a patch of darkness scuttled back from the edge of the shadows and buried itself deeper against the wall. Streicher moved his torch, following the motion. But there was nothing. Just a dark, narrow gap where the stone-flagged floor of the passage didn't quite meet the rough, crumbling brickwork of the wall.

'Is that the end of the tunnel?' Smith wondered. 'We must be nearly there.'

Streicher nodded. It was a shame – the American had saved lives and helped them get this far. But depending what they found at the end of this passage, Smith might become a liability. Streicher would do it himself. He owed the man that.

'Wait!'

Smith's warning shocked Streicher out of his thoughts. He froze – one foot raised. Smith gently helped him step back.

'What is it?'

'Not sure.'

Professor Smith stooped down, shining his torch at the stone slab where Streicher had been about to put his foot. The edges seemed darker than the slabs around it.

'Pickaxe.' Smith held his hand out behind him, not turning to look.

Streicher repeated the instruction in German to the nearest soldier, who handed Smith the short-handled pickaxe he was carrying.

Smith positioned the handle of the upright pickaxe on the slab of stone, and pressed down hard. There was a grinding sound – stone on stone. The ground shuddered, and Smith pitched suddenly forwards as the slab dropped away. Smith stumbled as he fought to keep his balance. In front of him, the whole section of floor had disappeared.

The soldier who had carried the pickaxe staggered, and fell. He pitched sideways with a cry. Another soldier made to grab him, but was too late. His hand closed on empty air. The falling soldier disappeared over the edge and into the darkness. His shout echoed round the passageway – the sound of hopeless terror.

Streicher had firm hold of Smith's arm, pulling him up and back from the brink.

Ahead of them was a gaping hole, about ten feet across. The section of floor had pivoted on the far side, tilting away. Below was darkness. The cries of the falling soldier faded into the distance.

Smith handed the pickaxe to another soldier and took a deep breath. 'A bit more extreme than I was expecting,' he admitted. 'Sorry about that poor fellow. But thanks for the helping hand.'

'My pleasure.' Streicher smiled grimly. It might have saved a problem later if Smith had fallen. There again, it looked like they might still need the man's help. The loss of another soldier was regrettable, but Streicher was used to death.

The jump was made more difficult by knowing the consequences of not making it. No one asked if the ground on the other side would be secure, but everyone was wondering. Streicher went first.

He took a short run up, and leaped across the abyss, landing heavily on the other side. The ground was firm. Smith followed, taking a longer run up, moving clumsily, arms flailing in the air as he made his ungainly journey across. He landed close to Streicher with a loud sigh of relief followed by a nervous laugh. The others crossed without incident.

'I think this could be it,' Smith announced, aiming his torch down the passage.

A short way ahead, what Streicher had taken for more shadows and the continuing passage was now visible as a huge barrier. It was caked in mud and grime. Smith rubbed his hand over it.

'Metal,' he announced with surprise. 'Bronze, perhaps? Or iron. Difficult to tell in this light. Not what I was expecting, though, whatever it is.'

The door – and there was soon no doubt that it was a door – was embossed with a series of circles and lines. It was hinged on one side. A heavy latch slid into a socket on the other side. It took two of the soldiers to slide the latch back out of the socket. It finally gave in a shower of dirt and rust. The door creaked on its hinges as if it too was sighing with relief.

The two soldiers leaned back, using their whole weight to drag the door open. It moved slowly at first, the metal screeching in protest. Once it was free of the frame, it swung ponderously outwards. Then it jammed on the uneven floor leaving a gap just wide enough for a man to squeeze through. Behind it was a gaping maw of darkness.

Streicher stepped towards the darkness, Smith at his side. The torch beams disappeared into the void, as if it was swallowing up their light.

'Best send one of your men first,' Smith said quietly. 'I mean, hell, I'm guessing they're more expendable.'

Streicher did not reply, but motioned for one of the soldiers to lead the way. The man took a torch from one of his colleagues, and struggled through the opening, almost immediately calling back that it was safe.

Smith squeezed through the gap after Streicher, the other SS men following behind. He was fascinated, but wary. Most

22

of them had been lucky – he himself had been very lucky – with the collapsing floor. But they couldn't rely on luck for ever. Smith, more than most, understood the importance of proper planning and meticulous research. This place, by its very nature, denied them that.

Beyond the door was a small, empty antechamber. Ahead of them was another wall. The stonework was more regular, tighter fitting than the other walls they had breached getting this far. Smith glanced back past the door behind him, out into the passageway beyond. The small chamber they had just entered made no sense. It was like a watertight compartment before a vital section of a ship or a submarine. Watertight and airtight.

Airtight.

The first man through raised his pickaxe. Streicher and the others stepped back to allow him room to swing at the wall.

'No – stop him!'

But Smith's cry was too late. The pickaxe bit into the wall. Nothing happened.

Not until the man levered it out again.

There was a sudden, loud hissing sound. A white mist, like smoke, curled from the hole in the wall. Smith pulled his handkerchief from his top pocket and jammed it over his nose and mouth. He pulled Streicher away, struggling to get him back through the doorway.

The man was coughing and spluttering – choking on the pale mist. The whole antechamber was full of it. Through the thickening fog, Smith saw men staggering into each other, clutching their throats. Falling. Their faces blotched with bursting pustules.

One of them blundered in front of Smith. The whole side of the man's face was peeling away, like it was drenched in acid.

Smith shouldered the poor man aside, and with a final effort he dragged Streicher back through to the passageway. He pushed at the door, but it was jammed open. The deadly mist curled out after them, like a smoky finger stabbing towards Smith as he half dragged, half carried Streicher away. Something brushed against his leg, and Smith almost fell.

He caught a glimpse of a dark shape lingering for a moment against Streicher, then scuttling into the shadows, like a huge spider. A trick of the light. An artefact of the drifting mist that swirled towards him…

There was barely room for them both as Smith staggered back along the tunnel, holding his breath for as long as he could, lungs bursting with the effort. He had to breathe through his handkerchief, hoping the air out here wasn't poisoned. Streicher was a dead weight against him.

In the panic and the swirling mist, he almost stumbled over the edge where the floor had dropped away. Smith teetered for a moment on the brink, staring down into the blackness in front of him. He managed to take a step backwards. But what now? Streicher was in no fit state to jump. The man was practically unconscious, and retching and choking as Smith supported his weight.

Deciding this was no time for playacting, Smith unceremoniously hoisted the SS officer onto his shoulders in a fireman's lift, taking care not to drop his torch. He backed down the passageway, straightening up as he bore the other man's weight. In the gloom of the tunnel he seemed taller, more confident.

The torchlight juddered, cutting through the mist and dancing over the walls and floor as Smith ran towards the abyss. Despite the near-dead weight over his shoulders, there was none of the awkwardness of his earlier jump. But it was a hell of a distance for a man carrying another.

The darkness rushed past below. The far side of the pit flew towards him. Before he was halfway, Smith knew he wasn't going to make it.

He fell short, his chest slamming into the top edge of the abyss. Streicher's body was jolted from his grasp. Somehow Smith managed to heave it over the lip and onto the floor of the passage. The SS officer rolled away, groaning.

The torch skidded after Streicher, its beam pointing straight back at Smith. Dazzling. Then he was falling, dropping into the bottomless pit.

He scrabbled desperately, arms stretched out along the tunnel floor, fingers searching for the slightest purchase. Smith's nails ripped as he tried to force them into the tiny gaps between the slabs. Finally, with an excruciating jolt, he caught hold with his right hand. He worked his fingers deeper into the crevice he'd found, scraping with his left hand to find a similar grip.

It was a slow and painful process, but somehow Smith managed to haul himself back up. He was holding his breath, his lungs bursting, though all the air must have been knocked out of him by the impact on the side of the pit.

He gathered up the torch and his handkerchief from the ground, then heaved Streicher over his shoulders again. The man grunted, but there was no other sign that he was even alive.

Aching and exhausted, Smith stumbled down the passageway towards the broken wall into the next chamber. The heavy mist drifted after him.

At last they were out of the tunnel, through the final chamber and into the warm afternoon sunshine. Smith let Streicher fall on the grass beside the trench leading down into the mound. He gasped in great lungfuls of fresh air, before yelling for help.

He grabbed the first soldier to arrive, miming putting on a gas mask. The soldier glanced at Streicher, and understood, shouting to the others.

'We'll be OK,' Smith told them in rasping, painful English. 'You go help the others.'

They seemed to understand, and soon Smith and Streicher were alone. Smith felt for a heartbeat. Weak and erratic, but Streicher was still alive. Smith looked round, checking again that none of the remaining soldiers were within sight. Certain that they were alone, he undid Streicher's tunic and emptied the man's pockets. Carefully and neatly, he laid out everything. He unfolded letters and papers, placing them so they caught the brightest sunlight.

Then he took out a packet of cigarettes. The packet seemed

25

full, but that was because most of the space inside was taken up with a miniature camera. Smith slid back the hidden cover to expose the lens then quickly but systematically photographed Streicher's possessions, including the letters and orders. When he was done, he replaced everything exactly as he had found it in the SS officer's pockets.

Finally, he took a cigarette from the pack and lit it.

'I may live to regret saving you,' Smith said quietly, his accent now more Eton than Harvard. 'But we all have our iron cross to bear.'

CHAPTER 3

Major Guy Pentecross dived to one side as the bullets raked through the sea where he had been. His arm exploded with pain. His mouth filled with blood and saltwater. His nostrils absorbed the stench of fuel oil and death. Someone was screaming.

The scream was the blast of the engine's whistle as the train entered a tunnel. The windows were suddenly opaque, and Guy found himself staring at his own pale, haunted face. Over his trembling shoulder, another face watched with unfocused concern.

'Are you all right, young man?'

He forced a smile, and turned to reassure the elderly woman. 'Bad dream. Sorry if I…'

She waved away his apology. 'We all have bad dreams these days. It's the bombing.' She hesitated before adding: 'You're not in uniform, I see.' There was just a hint of accusation.

'I work at the Foreign Office.'

'Oh.' More than a hint this time. 'Well, I'm sure that's very… useful.'

'I'm sure it is,' Guy agreed. 'Though I'd rather be back in uniform, I have to admit. I made the mistake of getting shot up at Dunkirk.'

He left it at that, turning back to the window. They were soon out of the tunnel and rattling through the fields again.

'All charging along like troops in a battle,' he murmured, recalling a poem he'd learned at school. A lifetime ago. Before Cambridge, before joining the army back when a war seemed possible but not likely. Mother had expected him to follow his father into the Foreign Office and become a diplomat. He had tried – joining the staff of the FO straight from Cambridge.

But the military had always appealed more to Guy. He soon left the civil service and joined up, soon making the rank of captain. Even if his mother didn't, he knew how bored his father had become with the whole diplomatic round, with never knowing quite which part of the world he could end up in next year or even next month. When Guy was growing up, they never seemed to stay long in one place before moving on. 'Each a glimpse, then gone for ever.'

The army meant travel and uncertainty too of course, but it was so much more invigorating. The thing that had kept Guy sane as he grew up was the challenge of learning the languages. He found he had an aptitude for it, a natural ability. Another reason why mother thought he should become a diplomat. The irony was, of course, that the Foreign Office was exactly where he had ended up after being injured at Dunkirk. As soon as Guy was declared unfit for active service – even temporarily – the Foreign Office intervened. Someone had remembered his aptitude for languages, and he was seconded to the government offices he had been so keen to escape.

Guy was fit again now – fighting fit. But he was too good at his job. They'd let him go once, and they weren't about to do it again. His uniform had become a pinstriped suit, and Guy hated it. He'd rather face the nightmares every night than the mundane monotony of Whitehall every day.

Painted stations whistled by. Guy dozed, read the paper, stared out of the window. Planes passed high above, too distant to make out details, like houseflies against a pale blue ceiling. Clear weather was not a good thing.

It was sobering to walk through London from the station to the office. Some streets seemed perfectly normal, untouched by the bombing. Others had collapsed into a wasteland of devastation. Volunteers shovelled debris from the road. A fire engine charged past, bells ringing. It should have impressed on Guy how important his role was, how vital that he play his part. But instead it made him angry and impatient. He wanted to be out there *doing* something. Not sitting on his backside in an office sifting through reports, or travelling round the country interviewing people who invariably turned out not to be enemy spies.

As a linguist, he was a valuable resource. He understood that. He also appreciated that it was important that any foreigners arriving in Britain needed screening. He just didn't think it should be him doing it. The most cursory check by anyone with an ounce of common sense would have saved him the previous day's journey down to the south coast. The local police had three men in custody who'd arrived in a small boat. They spoke reasonable English, and claimed to have fled from Poland. But the police were convinced they were spies.

Guy had suggested he could talk to one of them on the telephone, but the police sergeant insisted he should come and see them in person on the grounds that 'they look German to me.'

So he had wasted the best part of a day. When he finally got to see the three men it took Guy less than a minute to verify that they were indeed Polish. They spoke the language – better than their hesitant English or halting German. They obviously had first-hand knowledge of Danzig, where they claimed to have come from. And when Guy asked them what they thought of the Germans, they all three displayed a knowledge of Polish slang that considerably expanded Guy's own rather meagre vocabulary.

'They're not German spies,' he told the police sergeant with exaggerated patience.

The sergeant nodded. 'But they could have been,' he said.

And that was the problem – Guy had to admit the man was right. They *could* have been German spies. And while every 'could have been' was a frustration, it was also a relief. Every wasted journey was in fact not a waste of time at all. His work was necessary, but it was boring and it was frustrating.

Talk at the office was of the evacuation of British forces from Greece following the Greek army's surrender. It reminded Guy of his own experiences at Dunkirk. The Greek government had already been taken by submarine to Crete and it was generally thought to be only a matter of days before the Germans marched into Athens. Another maddening reminder of his distance from the real action, especially as Guy knew Athens well from when his father worked at the embassy there.

By the afternoon, the Whitehall offices were stifling. The warmer weather that came with the transition from April to May seemed to suck the air out of the building. Combined with the paperwork and translations which had built up in the time he was away, this made Guy desperate for any excuse to leave. If the Foreign Secretary Anthony Eden had an urgent message to be handed to Air Vice Marshal Keith Park in person, and no one else was free to go, then Guy was happy to see that as an invitation.

'You sure you want to go all the way to Uxbridge?' Sir James Chivers asked for the third time. Chivers' tone implied that he thought his subordinate could be better employed.

'I've got nothing urgent this afternoon,' Guy assured him. 'And I could do with a break from the paperwork.'

'You see this as a break, do you?'

Guy sighed. 'Tell you what, I'll stay late to make up the time. I just need some air, if I'm honest.'

'Not much of that if he's down in the bunker, Guy. Rather you than me.'

If Chivers' family had a motto, Guy suspected it was 'Rather you than me'. Quite probably in Latin.

The ministry car threaded its way between piles of rubble now cleared to the roadside from the previous night's bombing. The gutted, broken facades of buildings made some areas of London seem like a ghost town.

The Air Vice Marshal was indeed down in the bunker. This

housed the Operations Room for RAF Number 11 Group, responsible for defending London and the south east. Here, data from what was now called RADAR as well as other observation posts was recorded on a vast gridded map table. The colour-coded counters that the girls of the Women's Auxiliary Air Force moved round the map with magnetic rakes kept track of the position and timing of each enemy raid.

'The Dowding System', named after Air Chief Marshal Dowding (retired the previous October) was hugely effective. It provided up-to-date information that could be absorbed at a glance, enabling the Fighter Controller to deploy his forces quickly, accurately and with devastating effect.

But to Guy, it always just looked like a mess. A well-organised mess, but chaotic nonetheless.

Air Vice Marshal Park was in conference, so Guy had to wait at the side of the room. He could see Park on the gallery above the map table, staring down at it while engaged in a hushed and urgent conversation with a Wing Commander sporting a healthy moustache – the duty Fighter Controller.

While he waited, Guy too examined the map table. There were relatively few markers on it today – and all Allied flights. He had been here during a major raid a few months back, and watched the calm efficiency of the women as they moved counters over the board as if this was a vast, complicated game of chess. In a way, he supposed, it was.

Somewhere a telephone rang. The phones were ringing almost constantly, so there was no reason for Guy to remark this one. But he watched across the room as a WAAF lifted the receiver, cutting off the sound. Her face etched into a frown as she scribbled notes on a pad, then put the phone down.

'I have a sighting in Sector D,' she called across the room. The general noise faded. 'Possible UDT.'

All noise stopped. The woman tore a sheet off her pad and handed it to another WAAF.

'What's a UDT?' Guy asked a girl with dark bobbed hair standing close to him.

31

'Don't ask.'

'You mean you don't know what it is?' He meant it as a joke.

But she answered him seriously. 'It's an *Unknown* Detected Trace. None of us knows what it is.'

Park and the Fighter Controller he'd been talking to were rapt, looking down at the map as a new counter was swept into position. It was jet black, and right in the middle of the board. Guy wondered how a plane could have got there without being picked up sooner.

All eyes were on Park now. He nodded to the Fighter Controller. 'It's been a while. But you know what to do.'

The Fighter Controller cleared his throat. 'All right, we have a possible UDT, so we track it as long as we can. McAuley – scramble the nearest fighters, for all the good it will do. All non-essential personnel will please clear the Operations Room now.'

Guy found himself caught up in the general exodus. It looked like he'd have to wait a while longer to deliver his message.

Behind him he heard the calm, efficient voices of the girls at the table and manning the phones.

'Three Hurricanes airborne from Hornchurch. Moving to intercept.'

'UDT now moving west at approximately 400 knots.'

'Sir – there's another plane already up there. Hornchurch is trying to establish radio contact. Looks like it's an Air Transport Auxiliary flight.'

'Then it probably doesn't have a radio,' another WAAF replied.

'Call Station Z,' Guy heard Park order. 'They'd better send someone over.'

Then the door closed, and the sounds of the Operations Room were cut off.

There was nothing to do but wait. Most of the other personnel drifted away – perhaps to their offices, or to find the canteen.

But Guy needed to deliver his message. He felt duty-bound to wait. That was the story of his life, he thought – 'duty-bound'. Maybe just once he should forget about 'duty' and do what he thought was *right*. But he was past the point where he could just run away and re-join his regiment.

In fact, he didn't have to wait long.

As abruptly as everyone had been cleared out of the Operations Room, they were let back in. The black counter was gone from the map board. Park was talking urgently to someone on the gallery. The newcomer had his back to Guy, but he was surprised to see that the man wore the uniform of an army sergeant, not RAF.

Guy made his way over, waiting where Park could see him over the soldier's shoulder. All he needed to do was hand over an envelope and wait for any reply.

Park glanced across, acknowledging that he'd seen Guy, and gesturing for him to hand over the envelope he was brandishing.

He continued speaking as he opened it and scanned the brief letter inside.

'Only one other plane in the vicinity. I'll get you the details... Is he serious?'

It took Guy a moment to realise this last remark was aimed at him.

'Er, I assume so, sir.'

Park refolded the letter and stuffed it back into the envelope. 'I've barely enough aircraft to do the job here, and Eden wants me to back his request to divert new deliveries to North Africa?' Park's New Zealand accent was more pronounced when he was angry.

Guy felt he ought to say something. 'I believe it's pretty urgent, sir. They've got just thirteen Hurricanes left to defend the whole of Egypt.'

'My heart bleeds.' Parks reached past the soldier to return the envelope. He sighed. 'Tell him I'll do what I can. But I won't compromise on our own requirements. He should know that, after France.'

'Of course, sir. I'll pass that back.'

As Guy spoke, the soldier turned and glanced at him. For a moment, their eyes met. It took Guy a moment to place the man, though if the sergeant recognised him, he didn't show it but turned immediately back to Park.

'Don't worry,' Park said to the sergeant. 'Colonel Brinkman will get the tracking data and reports. And good luck to him.'

Guy made his way out of the bunker and back towards daylight. The car was waiting where he'd left it, and he climbed into the back.

On the way back to Whitehall, he stared out of the window. Rain was starting to fall, spattering across his view and running down the glass. But he didn't see it.

All he saw was the events of eight months ago playing out again in his memory, and one of his first tasks for the Foreign Office after recovering from his wounds.

CHAPTER 4

When Guy Pentecross had stepped off the train at Ipswich station eight months earlier, the weather was very different. Summer was fading but not yet gone as the September of 1940 arrived. It was a warm day, and rather than find a taxi he decided to walk to the hospital. From the directions he'd been given, it wasn't far.

It was a pleasant change to walk through streets that weren't strewn with rubble. Just that morning he'd seen the wardens and the firemen pulling broken twisted bodies from the remains of a house. In the mid-afternoon sun, this place almost seemed normal. Except for the distant drone of bomber engines and the angry buzz of fighters heading out to intercept them.

The front of the hospital was insulated with sandbags. Guy presented his identity card to a flustered nurse and asked where he could find Doctor Hugginson.

'They're still bringing people in from Felixstowe,' she said. 'I don't know where we're going to put them.' There were dark rings under her tired eyes. 'Doctor Hugginson will be doing what he can for them. Try Ward Three.'

He tried Ward Three, doing his best not to stare at the patients. Trying not to think back to his own time in hospital. It was only a couple of months since he had been discharged and assigned to the Foreign Office. More than anything else, the antiseptic smell of the place brought it back to him. Eventually Guy found Hugginson hurrying along a corridor. The doctor made no effort to slow down as they spoke.

'I haven't got time for you now.' There was a trace of apology, but it was really a statement of fact.

'It's not you I came to see.'

That earned a short laugh. 'Good. So why are we talking?'

'I'm here to question the German.'

There was a break in his step. 'Then you'll have to be quick.'

Hugginson grabbed a nurse who probably had better things to do. She led Guy to a small room that contained a single bed. There were bars across the window.

'Not that he's going anywhere. Not in this world, anyway,' she said. 'We have to keep him separate.'

'Security?' Guy guessed.

'The other patients won't have a German in the same room. Not fair to ask them really. Most of them would rather we dumped him back in the sea. There's probably a few in the ward that his bombs put there.'

'I doubt it,' Guy told her. 'He's not a flyer. That's army uniform. What's left of it.'

'We can't take it off him, the skin would come too,' the nurse said, sounding sympathetic for the first time. 'It's melted right into his flesh.'

That went part way to explaining the different smell in here. Like burned meat. Guy forced himself to look closer at the man on the bed. One eye stared bloodshot at the ceiling. The other was gone, the whole of that side of the face a waxy mass of charred tissue.

'It wasn't just a fire,' the nurse went on. 'Doctor Hugginson says the man was covered in some sort of accelerant. Petrol, most likely. Maybe a burst fuel tank, something like that.'

'I wish I could say I've never seen anything like it,' Guy said.

'Me too.'

The only signs that the man was still alive were the shallow rise and fall of his shattered chest, and the dry rasp as he struggled to draw breath.

'If he's army, how did he get here?' the nurse asked.

'Good question.' It was what Guy had been sent to find out.

'Was he a passenger on a plane?'

Guy shrugged. 'Where was he found?'

'Washed up at Bawdsey.'

That meant nothing to him, but Guy nodded. He could look it up later. 'Can he speak?'

'Only in German.' She smiled, and instantly looked younger. Probably just out of school. 'I have to go, I'm sorry.'

He nodded, turning away before she was out of the room, attention focused on the blackened body.

'Who are you?' he asked gently in German. No response. 'Where are you from?' Nothing to indicate the man could even hear him. 'Have they given you anything for the pain?'

That got a reaction. Just a blink of the single eye, and a breath that might have been: 'Ja.' Then, slightly more clearly: 'Danke.'

'How did you get here?'

The man's head turned slightly. The skin of his neck stretched and tore, oily liquid leaking out.

'Why did you come?' Guy asked. His own voice was husky and raw.

The answer was barely a whisper. A single word that was almost lost in the sound of the door opening.

Guy spun round angrily. 'What the hell are you doing?'

'I could ask you the same thing, sir.'

The man was tall and broad, with close-cropped dark hair and a nose that had been broken several times. He was wearing the uniform of an army sergeant, and had the gruff no-nonsense tone to go with it.

'Pentecross, Foreign Office,' Guy told him. 'I'm here to speak to the patient.'

'Sergeant Green, sir. And I'm here to secure the prisoner. My orders are that no one is to have contact with him.'

Obviously some local officiousness, Guy thought. 'I doubt that applies to me.'

'I doubt you're an exception.' Then, almost as an afterthought: 'Sir.'

Green's assurance annoyed Guy. 'What unit are you with? Who gave you these orders?'

If the sergeant was intending to answer, he was interrupted as the man on the bed struggled to sit up, hand clutching in the air in front of him. His whole body was shaking. His breath was a ghastly wheezing sound, ragged and desperate. Then he slumped back. The noise stopped. His body was deathly still.

Guy and Sergeant Green stared down at the bed, united by another's death.

'Did he say anything?' Green asked.

'Not really.'

'So what *did* he say?'

'It'll be in my report,' Guy told him.

'There's no need for a report, sir. You can tell me.' When Guy didn't answer, Green went on: 'I'll make sure the Foreign Office knows the man was already dead when you got here.'

'But that's not true.'

'What did he say? Colonel Brinkman will want to know.'

Guy had had enough. He'd wasted his time coming here, and now a sergeant was ordering him about. The sooner he got out of this stifling death-room the better.

'He only said one word, apart from "yes" and "thank you". And it didn't make any sense.'

Green nodded. 'And the word was?'

'The word was "Ubermensch". It means—'

'That's all right, sir.' Green turned away, looking back at the body. 'Someone else can worry about what it means.'

'Like Colonel Brinkman?'

No reply.

'Who is Colonel Brinkman, anyway?'

Green turned, stepping closer to Guy. 'If you need to ask, then you don't need to know. Sir.'

Guy was seething as he left the hospital. He had several

questions, and no hope of getting an answer to any of them. The first was who was Colonel Brinkman? Then, who was the German, and how had he died? Why had he come here, and how?

And when Sergeant Green stood close to Guy, why did the man's uniform smell of smoke and petrol?

CHAPTER 5

Heinrich Himmler never tired of showing off his castle. It was rare that he had a visitor who was technically of a higher rank than himself, and he seemed determined to make the most of it, shunning the bright sunshine of early May for the cold stone interior of the edifice. An observer who knew neither man would have assumed that Himmler was the one in charge.

His guest seemed happy to allow the misconception. In fact, Deputy Fuhrer Rudolf Hess knew very well that it was best to humour Himmler. The man deferred only to Hitler, and occasionally not even to him.

'There has been a castle here at Wewelsburg since the ninth century,' Himmler said proudly as he led the way out of the cellars.

Although he was still reeling from what he had just seen, Hess was willing to bet that nothing of the original remained. He knew that Himmler had signed a hundred-year lease on the castle at a cost of a hundred marks, back in 1934. Since then he had in effect rebuilt it, if not in his own image then to his own design.

'There is a very real possibility,' Himmler went on, 'that the original castle was the *bastion*. You know about the bastion, of course.'

'The fortress that legend foretells will stand fast against the forces of the East in the final confrontation,' Hess said. He was familiar with the myth. In fact he was relieved that for all his delusions and credulities, Himmler accepted that war with Russia was inevitable.

'Initially we used this castle as a training centre for the SS,' Himmler went on, apparently ignoring Hess's words. 'A place where the elite can become versed in history, archaeology, astronomy, art and culture. Now it is much, much more than that.'

Hess was aware of this too. Wewelsburg had become the Reichsfuhrer's centre of operations – a shrine and a cathedral for the quasi-religious order that Himmler had created. But to Hess, though he said nothing, the whole castle reeked of pretence and affectation.

Hess himself was a committed occultist, a member of the Thule Society who believed that Hitler was the German Messiah; an astrologer who thought that our faults lie not in ourselves but in the stars. The Thule Society believed that German Aryans were the true descendants of a race of Nordic 'supermen' from a long-lost landmass akin to Atlantis. Hess subscribed fully to this theory.

But what Himmler had just showed him at Wewelsburg caused him to question everything he thought he knew.

It was a disappointment to Hess that Hitler distrusted occult thinking and put little store in things that could not be proven. But once the Fuhrer saw what Himmler had at Wewelsburg, Hitler would have the proof he needed to believe. For the first time, the Deputy Fuhrer was forced to consider what that would lead to, and what reaction it might provoke from Hitler...

He could not let Himmler see what he truly thought, but Hess was appalled.

He mopped his heavy brow with a handkerchief, his dark eyebrows knitted together as they emerged into the light. Himmler gestured for the door to be sealed behind them before leading the way along a corridor. The only light came from flickering sconces where pools of oil burned and sputtered.

The only sound Hess could hear was his own racing heart.

The final meeting of his visit took place in the Hall of the Generals in the castle's North Tower. Beneath the high vaulted ceiling, twelve stone seats were arranged in a perfect circle around a green and gold symbol of the sun inlaid in the marble floor.

Himmler sat facing Hess across the circle. He was an unimposing man, dwarfed by the room and even the chair he sat on. Everything about him was slight – his close-cut hair, the shadowy moustache, the almost-invisible frames of his round glasses. You could pass him in the street, Hess thought, and not notice the man. Except that here, like the spider at the centre of its web, Himmler exuded an aura of absolute control. Here, despite his appearance, there was no mistaking who was in charge.

The others present were Himmler's assistant, Hoffman, and various generals and other high-ranking SS officers, as well as several white-coated scientists. No one took or spoke from notes.

The unease and anxiety Hess felt grew with every report he heard. His brain was in a whirl, his senses numbed. Himmler listened intently to everything. He nodded and frowned, murmured corrections and asked for occasional clarification. It was exactly like a hundred other briefing meetings that Hess had attended – except for the extraordinary surroundings and the terrifying subject matter.

'How sure are you of this?' he asked at last. 'Of *any* of this?'

'You have seen the Vault,' Himmler said. The light reflected off the lenses of his glasses, hiding his small, dark eyes. 'You know the legends. Some of what we have told you is speculation. No,' he corrected himself with a thin smile. 'Not speculation. It is *extrapolation*. Theorising from the facts. Probabilities rather than certainties, I will admit. But there is little room for error, isn't that right, Sturmbannfuhrer?'

Hoffman had sat still and silent throughout. Now he nodded. 'It would seem so, Herr Reichsfuhrer.'

'It would seem so,' Himmler echoed, his voice quiet and reedy compared with Hoffman's gruff response. 'You see, even the sceptical Sturmbannfuhrer Hoffman is a convert to our cause. And you, my friend, you with your knowledge and background and connections...' He waved a hand in the air as if dismissing the last vestige of doubt.

Hess shifted uneasily. The stone seat was cold and hard and uncomfortable. 'The Fuhrer will want to see the process in action. As well as the...' He hesitated, unsure of how to describe what he had been shown. 'As well as the *artefacts*, and the film. He will want proof that these people are not just... artists.'

Himmler turned to Hoffman. 'What news of Streicher?'

'Standartenfuhrer Streicher reports that his work is going well,' Hoffman said. 'Despite the, er, setback and the loss of eleven of his team when they broke into the main chamber.'

Himmler leaned forward. A pale tongue licked out over his bloodless lips. 'Do we have a replacement? Has he found it?'

Hoffman nodded. 'He is confident that he has. The inner chamber is just like the first site. They need to proceed with caution. It will be a few days before the air has cleared and they can bring out—'

'Details,' Himmler snapped. 'Urge Streicher to make all speed. Obviously we cannot afford to damage the discovery. But I want it back here as soon as possible.'

Hess's mouth was dry. 'What has Streicher found?'

'A burial chamber, just like the original site. And inside...'

In his mind's eye, Hess could see the film replaying again and again as if on a loop. The burial chamber. Streicher and his men opening the casket. The light shone inside, illuminating the contents. And the later footage, back at Wewelsburg.

Himmler was still speaking, his tone eager, confident, triumphant. 'We shall soon have another Ubermensch.'

Hoffman escorted Hess through the castle and back to his waiting car. The Deputy Fuhrer's heavy eyebrows were knitted together in thought.

'You seem troubled by what you have seen and heard,' Hoffman said as they emerged into sudden sunlight.

'No,' Hess said quickly. 'I see only opportunities.'

'You would not be the only one who appreciates the inherent danger in what we are doing,' Hoffman said quietly. He glanced round. 'Some might say that the potential risk outweighs the possible reward.'

'Is that what you think, Sturmbannfuhrer?'

Hoffman smiled grimly. 'It really isn't for me to have an opinion, sir. But I am sure that whatever the Fuhrer decides will be for the best. And I'm sure he will value your judgement and advice.'

Hess gave a snort of amusement. 'I'm not.' He said it before he could stop himself. But once said, it hung in the air between them.

'The Fuhrer, no doubt, has many things on his mind,' Hoffman said. 'Many opinions whispered in his ear. I know that the Reichsfuhrer-SS spoke to him by telephone only yesterday.'

Hess did not reply. He didn't know Himmler had spoken to Hitler. What had they said? Was his visit here redundant? No doubt that brute Bormann had listened in, poisoning the Fuhrer's thoughts with his own view of things.

'I do not know the Fuhrer,' Hoffman was saying. 'Not as you do. We met when I received this, of course.' He tapped the Iron Cross with Oak Leaves and Swords at his throat. It was one of the highest bravery awards the Reich presented. 'But,' Hoffman went on, 'I think he is perhaps very focused on the current military and political situation. I wonder if we should not be taking a longer-term view.'

'What do you mean?'

Hoffman smiled apologetically. 'The military benefits of the work we are doing here and the discoveries we have made are obvious. But the implications are worrying. More than that. May I confide in you, Deputy Fuhrer?'

Hess nodded. His chest tightened as he listened to Hoffman's words.

'I have stared death in the face, and felt nothing but determination and anger. I have waded ankle-deep in the blood of my comrades, and not so much as blinked. But what we are doing now, what might happen as a result of our work here – to us, and to the whole world… It terrifies me.'

Hess felt the blood drain from his face. He was suddenly light-headed.

'I sense that we are of a similar opinion, sir,' Hoffman went on. 'I pray that the Fuhrer will listen to you.'

'He must,' Hess breathed.

'Or if he does not,' Hoffman said, 'then I pray that *someone* will. There is no distinction between the Reich and her enemies in this coming war. There is only our world and the forces ranged against it.'

Hess stared at him, not daring to speak. Fearful of what he might say. Afraid of the thoughts that were creeping into the back of his mind. If the Fuhrer would not listen to his warnings, then who would? All his doubts – about the war with Britain, the coming conflict with Russia, the future of his country… They all aligned behind this new danger.

The silence was broken by the sharp crack of Hoffman's heels clicking together. His salute was crisp and smart. 'Heil Hitler.'

Rudolf Hess, Deputy Fuhrer of the Third Reich, did not reply.

CHAPTER 6

The Greek politician spoke good English. But he seemed grateful to Guy for making the trip nonetheless.

'I am sure there are some nuances – is that the word? Some *nuances* that might cause problems, Major Pentecross,' he said with an apologetic smile. He shook Guy's hand warmly as the meeting ended.

The Greek minister's words mitigated the frustration of another long journey. It was approaching midnight on 10 May 1941 and the plane was waiting to take the politician back to Crete. Guy was faced with the choice of a spare bed somewhere on the base at RAF Crosby-on-Eden or the prospect of a long ride back to London if he could beg a lift with one of the high-ups who'd attended the meeting.

He got neither.

As he handed his notes from the meeting to one of the secretaries to be destroyed, an RAF officer came up to him.

'Major Pentecross? Telephone. Whitehall. Urgent.' Then, as an afterthought. 'Sorry.'

'Chivers here,' the voice at the other end of the phone announced. Guy would have recognised the plummy tone anyway. 'You still at Crosby?'

'So it would seem.' He was tempted to add: 'That's why I'm answering their phone.'

'Good... Good. Got another little job for you.'

'You want me to hang on here?' His heart sank.

'Not there exactly. Want you to cut along to Maryhill Barracks. Seems they've bagged themselves a German flyer. Need help with the debrief. Bit sensitive really.'

'Maryhill?' Guy had never heard of it. 'Is that in Carlisle?'

'Not quite, no. But you're the closest man we've got. I'll have someone ready to brief you as soon as you arrive. I've already arranged for the base to provide a car and driver to get you there. The chap you'll be interrogating is...' There was a distant rustle of papers. 'Hauptmann Horn, apparently. Probably nothing, but you never know.'

'Fine.' Guy sighed. It would mean an early start. 'I'll get over there first thing.'

'Um, tonight actually. If you would. The car should be waiting.'

'Tonight,' Guy echoed. 'To Maryhill Barracks, was it?'

'Spot on.' Then the inevitable: 'Rather you than me. It's, er... It's in Glasgow, actually.'

They found him a staff car rather than a jeep, so at least Guy could sleep on the journey. He was too tired to be annoyed, and at least it seemed this was unlikely to be a false alarm. More than that, if they wanted him there tonight, then the German must be important.

'Hauptmann' translated roughly as 'captain'. It was a Luftwaffe rank, and Chivers had described the man as a flyer. He'd probably bailed out after being shot down. Pentecross wondered where they had picked him up. No doubt the briefing would make everything clear, he thought as he slipped into a mercifully dreamless sleep.

Guy was instantly awake as the car pulled up at Maryhill Barracks. A corporal was waiting. He introduced himself as Matthews and looked about nineteen. His accent was from closer to London than Glasgow.

Corporal Matthews led the way to what looked like an admin block. The first light of dawn was yellowing the sky, and there was a chill in the air that made Guy shiver.

'Plane crashed, apparently. Bad weather.' Corporal

Matthews gestured for Guy to enter an office. 'Farmer found the pilot. Apprehended him with a pitchfork.' He shrugged. 'That's what they say, anyway. It'll be in the report.'

Matthews nodded at the single desk in the middle of the room, where a plain folder lay. There was a chair either side of the desk. Another stood against the blank white wall. The room was lit by a single bare bulb.

'You need a few minutes, sir? Or shall I send in the prisoner?'

'Send him in,' Guy decided. 'I doubt this will take long, then you can cart him off to whatever internment centre or POW camp is nearest.'

Sitting at the desk, Guy found that the folder contained a single sheet of paper. It was a carbon-copy of a typed report.

```
At 22:08 hours on May 10th (1941)
Station Ouston north of Newcastle
detected a RADAR (formerly RDF)
trace 70 miles from the coast
and heading for Lindisfarne. The
sighting was designated HOSTILE
RAID 42J. Since such a course
makes no strategic sense, the
base commander initially listed
the craft as an 'Unknown Detected
Trace' in line with standard
operating procedure, and Station
Z was informed.
    However, unlike previous UDTs,
this trace continued on a straight
path at a speed consistent
with standard aircraft. Ouston
continued to track it, and the
craft lost altitude as it crossed
the coast.
    It was next sighted visually by
a Royal Observer Corps position
near Chatton at 22:35 hours, and
identified as an enemy Bf110
```

flying at approximately 50 feet.
This is well below the safety
margin. Having identified the
craft as a Hostile rather than
an Unknown, two Spitfires from
602 Squadron were scrambled. A
Defiant was also sent from RAF
Prestwick, but all three aircraft
failed to intercept RAID 42.

Contact was lost, until the
Operations Room at RAF Turnhouse
reported a crash south of Glasgow
at 23:09 hours. The remains of
a Bf110D were duly discovered,
although the pilot had parachuted
to safety before the crash.

The pilot was subsequently
apprehended by a farmer near
Eaglesham. He had sustained
an ankle injury and identified
himself as Hauptmann Alfred
Horn. He claimed to have vital
information for the Duke of
Hamilton, whom he demanded to
see.

The prisoner was handed over
to the Home Guard, and is now
being held at Maryhill Barracks
in Glasgow pending interrogation
by an FO Translator Officer.

Guy was amused to see his description as a 'Translator Officer'. The report seemed very full, and right up to date, but perhaps such efficiency was normal. Guy recalled hearing 'Station Z' mentioned when he was at Uxbridge, down in the RAF bunker with Keith Park. 'Unknown Detected Trace' as well, although it seemed to be a term that just meant the observers didn't know what they were looking at...

He didn't have time to ponder further because, while Guy had been reading, Corporal Matthews had returned with the prisoner. The man was tall and broad, dark-haired and with a heavy forehead and prominent eyebrows. He limped across to sit on the other side of the desk, waiting while Guy finished reading the report and returned it to the folder.

When Guy looked up, he saw the man's dark eyes staring intently at him.

'You are not the Duke of Hamilton,' the man said in German.

From the report, Guy knew that the man had asked for Hamilton before. 'You know the Duke?' he replied, also in German.

'We have met, just the once. A few years ago.' The man leaned back in the chair, elbows on the armrests, tapping the tips of his fingers together. He seemed not at all nervous or disconcerted.

'Your plane crashed. Were you lost?'

'No. The bad weather was to blame.'

'You don't seem to have had an escort. And you couldn't have had enough fuel to get back home.'

'What makes you think I planned to return to Germany?'

Guy wasn't sure what to make of that, so he tried a different tack. 'You think the Duke can help you in some way? Maybe put in a good word?'

The man laughed. Standing in front of the closed door, Corporal Matthews frowned. He evidently didn't understand a word of the exchange.

The prisoner leaned forward across the desk. 'I do not need a good word, as you put it. I have information that I shall share only with the Duke of Hamilton. He will know who to pass it on to.'

'What is the nature of this information, Hauptmann Horn?'

'It is classified. And "Hauptmann Horn" is merely the name I gave my captors. I wasn't sure whether to be relieved or disappointed when they didn't recognise me.'

There *was* something familiar about the man, Guy realised.

51

They had not met before, he was sure of that. But he'd seen a picture of the man, perhaps. Or newsreel footage... It came to him in a dizzying flash just as the man spelled it out:

'If I tell you who I really am, perhaps that will smooth the wheels and you will summon the Duke. My name is Rudolf Hess, and I am the Deputy Fuhrer of the Third Reich.'

It was like he was in a different room, watching the scene unfold. Guy was aware how startled he must look. Corporal Matthews was looking on in bewilderment. Hess seemed amused at Guy's surprise.

'But – why?' was all Guy could eventually stammer.

'Why come here? Oh there will be a story, I am sure. Bormann will already be working with Goebbels to denounce me. He's been after my job for years, you know. No doubt they'll say my nerves deserted me and I came to sue for peace or some such rubbish.'

'Whereas...?' Guy prompted. He still could not believe that he was sitting opposite the Deputy Fuhrer in an ill-furnished office in a Glasgow barracks.

'Whereas, as I told you, I have vital information for the Duke of Hamilton.'

'Why the Duke of Hamilton?'

'As I say, we have met. Once. Briefly. He is well-read. We share certain... interests. I think, from what I know of him, that he will understand the importance of my information.'

'But you won't tell me.'

Hess leaned back and folded his arms. His small eyes narrowed to slits as he stared back at Guy. 'Are you familiar with the work of Lord Lytton?'

'Is he a colleague of the Duke of Hamilton?'

Hess sighed. 'Hardly. Perhaps you know him better as Edward Bulwer-Lytton?'

Guy shook his head. 'I'm afraid not. Perhaps I don't move in the right circles.'

'Or read the right books.' Hess nodded, as if coming to a decision. 'Lord Hamilton – it must be him. His Grace will know who in your government should be informed.'

Guy was obviously getting nowhere. Maybe the man was mad, driven over the edge by the war and the weight of responsibility. Did he have a guilty conscience? Yet he seemed very much in control.

'You think Hamilton will talk to you?' Guy asked.

Hess nodded. 'But tell him this. Tell him I wish to speak of the Vril. Tell him it concerns the Coming Race.' He stood up, putting his weight on his good leg. 'Now I am tired. I will rest until His Grace arrives.'

Lord Hamilton, it transpired, had already been contacted. But he had no idea of the real identity of the captured German. Having spent an intense half hour with the barracks commander, Guy had just ended an urgent phone call to Chivers in London when there was a knock on the door of the room he was now using as an office.

'Hamilton,' the newcomer announced, shaking hands with Guy. He looked as if he was on his way to a funeral, dressed in a black suit and carrying a dark hat. 'I'd only just got home and changed out of uniform,' he said. 'Ironic, really, as I'm the head of air defence for Scotland so it was me who despatched the planes to shoot this blighter down. Anything I should know before I speak to him?'

'You mean apart from the fact that he is actually the Deputy Fuhrer, sir?'

Lord Hamilton laughed. But the smile froze on his face. 'My God – you're serious, aren't you?'

'It's Hess all right. I recognised him from newsreels and the press. But he made no secret of it to me. Do you know him, sir?'

The Duke shook his head. 'Rudolf Hess. Dear God... Did he tell you why he's here?'

'Refuses to talk to anyone but you, sir.' He summarised what Hess had told him. 'He said he wants to talk about the Vril, if that means anything?'

Hamilton frowned. 'Possibly.'

'And he said it's about the Coming Race, which I assume is

some Aryan Nazi propaganda.'

Hamilton's frown deepened. 'You would think so, wouldn't you. But I'm not sure. It is also the title of a novel. Very well.' He turned to go.

Guy made to follow, but Hamilton shook his head. 'I speak passable German, Major. I'll see him alone. At least to begin with. We have met once before, back in '36, I think. Once I've gained his trust...'

'Then I'll wait outside. In case you need me, sir.' Guy did his best to hide his disappointment. He was intrigued, he couldn't deny it. What the hell was really going on here?

Hess was brought back to the room. He nodded to Guy as Matthews led him inside. A moment later, Matthews emerged again.

'Doesn't want you in there either?' Guy said.

'There's a colonel on his way up from London,' Matthews said. 'Looks like I get all the meeting and greeting jobs, sir.'

'You must be good at it.'

He leaned against the wall by the door, straining to hear what was going on inside the room. But all he could make out was the faint burr of indistinct conversation. He replayed what Hess had said in his mind, but it still made little sense. Why had the man come here – to the enemy? Whatever the reason it was important to him. It wasn't a step he has taken lightly.

Guy stepped back sharply as the door opened. Through it he could see Hess still sitting at the desk. The man did not turn round.

The Duke of Hamilton's forehead was filmed with sweat, and he was deathly pale. His eyes had a startled, haunted look about them. He stared at Guy, opened his mouth to say something. But then he looked past him, along the corridor.

Pentecross turned to see Matthews returning. With him was a colonel – tall and thin with narrow features and close-cut dark hair.

Hamilton dabbed at his face with a folded handkerchief. 'I have to talk to Whitehall,' he said. His voice was shaking as much as his hand. 'Someone in authority. The implications...'

'You can start with me, sir,' the colonel said. 'Perhaps then my journey won't have been a complete waste. I'm Colonel Brinkman.' He obviously knew who the Duke was, presumably from Corporal Matthews.

Hamilton was getting some colour back in his features and his relief was obvious. 'Of course, Colonel. Perhaps you can make sense of what I've just heard.'

'Perhaps.' Brinkman glanced at Guy. 'And you are?'

Guy straightened to attention. It felt strange not being in uniform. 'Major Pentecross, sir. Foreign Office.'

Brinkman's mouth twitched as he considered. Then: 'You won't be needed, Major. Dismissed.'

In something of a daze, Guy allowed Matthews to lead him back through the base. He was angry and tired, but also intrigued and mystified. When he got back to London he was going to demand that Chivers tell him what the hell was going on.

They emerged into the morning light at the edge of a large parade ground. Matthews said something about organising transport to the station and how often the trains ran to London. But Guy barely heard him.

He was staring at a soldier leaning against the wall close to the door, smoking a cigarette. His mind was in a whirl. It was the same sergeant he had seen in the RAF bunker at Uxbridge, and before that at the hospital in Ipswich.

'Major Pentecross.' The man took a last drag, then flicked away the butt end. 'Good to see you again, sir.'

CHAPTER 7

The Fuhrer was white with rage. Hoffman stood at the back of the room, doing his best to blend into the wall. Hitler's fist crashed down on the desk again, scattering papers. Behind him, a half-smile edged on to Bormann's face.

Himmler was impassive and silent. He let Heydrich do the talking, and take the lion's share of Hitler's rage.

'You are in charge of Reich security,' Hitler shouted. His finger jabbed at Heydrich. '*You*. How can this have happened? How could you *let* this happen?'

'We none of us anticipated this,' Heydrich admitted. 'Even...' He hesitated as the Fuhrer stared up at him through pale blue eyes with pin-prick irises. 'Even the Reichsfuhrer, who was with him just a few days ago.'

Hitler turned towards Himmler, who spread his hands apologetically.

'There was no indication, no sign of this imbalance of the mind when he was at Wewelsburg. Though I did think he seemed a little...' He paused as if to select exactly the right word. 'Preoccupied. I sent you a report, of course.'

'You did?'

'But events have moved so fast that perhaps you have not yet seen it.'

Hoffman made a mental note to have the report sent as soon as they left the Fuhrer's office. If necessary he would type it himself in the anteroom. Interesting, he thought that no one mentioned that Hess had spent four hours alone with Hitler the day before he flew to Britain. There were no notes from the meeting, no witnesses – Himmler had already had Hoffman check.

Hitler wiped his hands down his face. Doing so, he seemed to wipe away his fury. He sat down at the desk and stared back at the men standing the other side. 'Why?' he asked quietly.

Hoffman suppressed a shudder. Hitler was at his most frightening when he was like this. The aftermath of his rage was more dangerous than the initial sound and fury.

'The Deputy Fuhrer – former Deputy Fuhrer,' Heydrich corrected himself, 'feared a war on two fronts. That's how it looks from the letter he left behind and from what others have said.'

'Britain should have made peace with us,' Hitler said. 'They had their chances.'

Himmler nodded. 'If we had been dealing with a reasonable man like Halifax instead of that madman Churchill...'

'The campaign against Russia cannot be deferred,' Hitler snapped, interrupting Himmler. 'Hess knew that.'

'Exactly,' Heydrich agreed. 'Which is why he went to England.'

'Scotland,' Himmler corrected him quietly.

'To sue for peace before the glorious war against the Communists begins.'

'The Reich asks no one for peace,' Hitler said. 'Though Britain and her Empire should be our natural allies.' He leaned back in his chair, arms folded, brooding. 'Once Stalin is crushed, Britain will truly be isolated and then they will come begging for peace.'

'We must consider what damage has been done,' Himmler said. 'I believe it can be contained. This is more of a propaganda problem than a military one. Herr Hess was not privy to the planning of Operation Barbarossa.'

Hitler sniffed and waved a hand in the air. He seemed suddenly bored with the whole discussion. 'Goebbels can handle it.' He leaned forward suddenly, eyes fixed on Himmler. 'But Hess knows other things. He has seen Wewelsburg. He knows what you are doing there.'

'A glimpse, no more. We showed him very little, and as I say he was distracted. Now we know where his mind really was – planning this flight to Britain. He saw little and understood less. Besides,' a smile cracked across Himmler's round face, 'if he tells the British what he has seen they will think he's insane. They will not believe a word of it.'

Hitler nodded slowly. He dismissed them all with a wave of his hand, and started to rearrange the papers on his desk into neat piles.

Outside, Himmler waited until Heydrich and the others had gone, then turned to Hoffman. 'You will organise the report I mentioned.'

'Of course, Herr Reichsfuhrer. And the Vril project?'

The light glinted on Himmler's glasses as he turned abruptly to look at Hoffman. 'What of it?'

'I appreciate you did not wish to confuse or worry the Fuhrer with details, but the Deputy Fuhrer was uneasy at Wewelsburg. He saw... everything. He understood the implications – the potential risks as well as the benefits. It unsettled him. It is possible that this insane mission of his—'

'Yes, yes,' Himmler snapped. 'But there is nothing we can do about it now.'

'Perhaps we should delay the project. Slow down.' Hoffman swallowed. He was on dangerous ground here. 'At least until we can be sure the allies know nothing.'

'Slow down? *Now?*'

'As a precaution, nothing more.'

Himmler considered for a moment, staring down at the floor. Then he looked up, grasping Hoffman's shoulder. 'You are right, we cannot simply proceed as if nothing has happened.'

'A little caution—' Hoffman started to say.

But Himmler was not listening. 'If the Allies believe even a fraction of what Hess might tell them, then speed is essential.'

'Speed?'

'We must redouble our efforts. The Vril Project cannot be compromised. Write my report for the Fuhrer, and then signal Streicher in France.'

Himmler had made up his mind, and Hoffman knew he could not be persuaded to change it. 'Of course, Herr Reichsfuhrer.'

'Tell Streicher he must finish his excavations now. Tell him to bring the Ubermensch to Wewelsburg immediately.'

CHAPTER 8

They sat in a gloomy corner of the café, away from the windows, drinking hot, black coffee from small cups. Smith knew the man only as 'Jacques'. They had met several times before, never in the same place and never for more than a few minutes. This was already their longest encounter.

'Streicher thinks you've left the area,' Jacques said. 'He's sent messages to other local forces to find out where you are. But he's not really interested. Just covering himself in case anyone else asks where you went.'

Smith nodded. 'I left word that my nerves couldn't take it after that last accident in the excavations,' he replied in excellent French. 'Gone back to my churches and castles. He'll accept that. After all, it solves a problem for him.'

'You think he'd have killed you if you'd stayed?'

'It's possible. Not a theory I'd like to hang around and test. Better that he thinks I'm out of the way and know as little as possible.'

'Streicher won't be here for much longer. They're packing everything into crates ready to move out.'

That made sense after what had happened. 'So the painstaking, methodical business of archaeology has become an exercise in hasty evacuation.'

'My colleagues are watching,' Jacques said. He took a sip of his coffee. 'They're definitely clearing out. They have a train waiting at Ouvon.'

'When does it leave?'

'Some time the day after tomorrow, according to the station master.'

'So tomorrow they transport the crates to the train.'

'You want us to intercept the trucks?' Jacques asked. 'It will be risky. Heavy casualties. I hope whatever you are after is worth it.'

'So do I.' Smith drained the last of his coffee. There were bitter grounds in the bottom of the cup that grated on his tongue and caught in his teeth. 'But I don't want Streicher to know he's been robbed. Not for a while, anyway.'

'How do you propose to manage that, my friend?'

Smith rubbed his beard as he considered. 'A little deception,' he decided. 'But not on the way to the station. How do you feel about blowing up a railway line?'

They laid the charges under cover of darkness. The fact that the Resistance made a habit of destroying railways and other communications across occupied France would allay any suspicion. There was no reason for Streicher and his men to assume they had been singled out for special treatment.

Jacques also passed word that Streicher's shipment was not to be interfered with at the station. A 'low-level' but effective form of resistance was for the railway workers to deliberately mislabel German supplies or change the cargo manifests so that supplies ended up in the wrong place. The last thing Carlton Smith wanted was to find that his own subterfuge had been pre-empted.

The spot they chose was about seven miles out from Ouvon. The track ran through a cutting before emerging close to a lane. The lane was screened by a line of trees and an area of dense undergrowth. The two men with the detonator watched for the smoke that would show the train was nearing the end of the cutting. The light was fading as evening became night, but the sun was low behind the smoke, making it easy to see. Out of sight, Smith and Jacques waited on the lane with two more of the Resistance – a young man called Pierre, and a woman who gave her name as Mathilde.

The sound of the approaching train was drowned out by the blast of the explosion. The noise melded into the screech of metal on metal as the driver hit the brakes.

Moving through the undergrowth, Smith watched the train slowing. Its wheels spat sparks. Doors were sliding open along its length as Streicher's men tried to see what was happening ahead. Several of the soldiers leaped down, guns ready. They ran on ahead of the train, disappearing into the drifting smoke and steam.

As soon as the soldiers were clear, Smith and Mathilde made their move. They ran, crouching, to the back of the train. Mathilde disappeared beneath the back wagon. She emerged again a few moments later, giving Smith a thumbs-up. In moments, she had disappeared into the fog of smoke that spewed from the canister she had placed. The whole of the back of the train was soon swirling in acrid smoke and steam.

Smith was wearing a long, dark coat. In the thick haze it might pass for an officer's greatcoat, and he was hoping no one would get close enough to make out any more than his vague outline. As soon as Mathilde was out of sight, swallowed up by the smoke, he hammered on the door of the back wagon.

'Come on, come on!' he shouted in German. Smith's accent was a good approximation of Streicher's voice. He had learned and practised the simple lines he needed as if for a command performance. 'I need you out here.'

He could barely see the door opening, let alone the two soldiers guarding the crates.

'They've blown up the line ahead of us. There's a pile of supplies back at the end of the cutting. Bring two rails.' He didn't give them time to reply. 'Quickly – now, now, now!'

'Sir!' one of the soldiers responded.

Smith was aware of them pushing past and hurrying back down the track. The smoke was already beginning to clear, so he would have to act fast.

Jacques, Pierre and Mathilde appeared out of the gloom and the four of them clambered into the wagon. Two more men arrived – the ones who had set off the explosives – and climbed in after them.

Smith and Jacques needed the torches they had brought.

'One large crate, or several smaller ones,' Jacques said quietly. 'There is no time for more than that.'

'It's a large one I'm after.'

Smith quickly found the crate he was looking for – one of the largest. He tore the packing label from the side of the crate and handed it to Pierre. Mathilde and the others were already stripping labels from other crates and swapping them round. Pierre positioned the label from the large crate on another that was just slightly smaller, pressing it firmly into place.

'If they start to peel off, they'll just stick them back on again,' Smith said. 'German efficiency.'

Jacques checked outside the wagon, looking both ways into the smoke. It was thinning considerably, but the sky had darkened as the sun dipped below the horizon.

'We need to go,' he announced.

They heaved the crate to the edge of the wagon. Pierre and Jacques climbed out to take the weight from the outside. It was about ten feet long and very heavy but, with Mathilde and one of the other men helping, the four of them managed to carry it away from the train.

Inside the wagon, Smith and the other explosives expert moved the large crate of similar size to where the missing crate had been. They shuffled a few others round to fill the space, so that it was not immediately obvious that anything had gone.

Smith looked towards the engine as he clambered out. Figures were silhouetted against the glow from the firebox, wreathed in steam. One of them was obviously Streicher, standing with his hands behind his back as he watched his men working. The two who had found the rails to repair the track would probably get a commendation, Smith thought. Until someone realised what had happened, but that could be days if not weeks away. He hurried away from the train and pushed his way through the undergrowth.

The crate had already been loaded into the back of the waiting lorry. Mathilde gave a wave as she cycled off down the lane. The two explosives experts followed close behind. Pierre waited to shake Smith's hand.

'We make a good team, eh?'

'We do. Thank you.' Smith slapped him on the shoulder. 'Now get going before the Bosch come looking for us.'

'They won't come looking,' Jacques said confidently. He climbed up into the front of the lorry next to where Smith was now behind the wheel.

'Let's hope you're right. You got my transit permits?'

Jacques handed over a sheaf of papers from his inside jacket pocket. 'You can drop me at the farm. I need to see Jean.'

They sat in the lorry, Jacques smoking a thin but potent-smelling cigarette. The sounds of metal being hammered into place echoed through the night. But they waited until the train had moved off again before starting the engine. Smith drove without lights until they reached the narrow track up to the farm.

'Drop me here, I'll walk the rest of the way,' Jacques said. He leaned across to shake Smith's hand.

'You take care of yourself,' Smith said. 'Thanks for your help. And for the truck.'

'Happy to oblige,' Jacques said, lighting another cigarette.

He jumped down from the cab, looking back through the open window, as if there was something else he wanted to say.

'Yes?' Smith prompted.

'I was just wondering...' He paused to take a drag on his cigarette.

'Wondering what?'

'I spent some time in London before the war.'

'It's a great city.'

Jacques nodded. 'Indeed it is. I very much enjoyed the theatre, and the movies.'

'Did you?' There was a slight wariness in Smith's voice.

'And I was thinking... Has anyone ever told you that

without that beard you would look very like Leo Davenport –
you know, the British actor.'

Smith's expression did not change. 'No,' he said levelly.
'No one else has ever mentioned it.'

It took Smith almost two weeks to complete his journey.
Jacques had arranged contacts along the way from whom he
could get new travel papers and fuel for the truck. He avoided
the main roads and towns, but even so he was stopped on
several occasions. Each time he was allowed to continue once
his papers had been checked.

Eventually he crossed into Portugal, and the going got easier.
The country was technically neutral, but it was generally pro-
fascist so he still needed to be careful.

It was not until he was safely in Lisbon, with his crate full
of 'sugar' booked onto a cargo ship to Britain that he began
to relax. He would travel on by plane, which was safer. Even
if his cargo did not make it, he had at least deprived Streicher
of his prize.

An hour before the flight, alone in the men's room at Lisbon
airport, 'Carlton Smith' peeled off his beard and dropped it
into the rubbish bin.

CHAPTER 9

The inevitable paperwork had piled up while Guy was away. Most of it was routine, and just took time. But between the routine and the boring, he found a few moments to think about what had happened in Glasgow.

Chivers was not interested. 'Way above our heads, old boy,' he told Guy, while subconsciously dry-washing his hands. 'Way above. Shouldn't touch it with a barge pole, if you ask me. Best leave it to others. Rather them than us, eh?'

But Guy was not about to leave it alone. It might be 'above his head', and he understood the necessity and value of secrecy, but the strange conversation he'd had with Hess haunted him. Now when he slept, as often as he recalled the flames and horrors of Dunkirk, he saw Lord Hamilton's gaunt, pale, frightened face and Colonel Brinkman striding down the corridor towards him.

The sergeant's name was 'Green'; he remembered that from their first meeting. But that was of little help – it was hardly an uncommon name or rank.

Tracking down information about Colonel Brinkman proved more fruitful. Pentecross told himself his curiosity was justified – the Foreign Office should know what was happening, what information Hess had been so desperate to pass on.

He called in a couple of favours. Finally, after a month

getting nowhere by being discreet, Pentecross phoned a girl from Army Records. He'd met Mary Creasy at a party his mother had dragged him along to, and even Mother had noticed the girl was sweet on him.

Mary didn't need a lot of persuading to take a look at Brinkman's file. She'd probably have done it without Guy's rather flimsy story about informally checking the colonel out for a Foreign Office assignment. The agreement that they should meet for a drink once she'd looked at his file seemed incentive enough.

At last he was making progress, Guy thought. A drink with Mary was a small price to pay. Until she told him that Colonel Oliver Brinkman's exemplary service record ended abruptly in January 1940 with a handwritten note simply saying: 'Transferred to special duties'.

After hearing that, it was hard to maintain the pretence that he was interested in talking to Mary. She made a better job of pretending not to notice.

'Oh Guy, I do hope you find what you're looking for,' Mary said as they stood outside the pub. 'I'm sorry I couldn't help.' She wasn't talking about Brinkman's file. She tiptoed up to give Guy a kiss on the cheek, and he managed a smile.

'Do call me,' she said.

They both knew it was unlikely.

The air raid warning made up his mind for him. Guy had considered walking while the evening was clear and safe. But with the siren, he headed for the nearest tube station.

The platform was already packed with people settling down for the night. It was midsummer's day tomorrow, and the evening was warm which didn't help the smell emanating from the crowd. Some people had brought food and bedding. While not relaxed, the atmosphere was calm. Guy picked his way through the sheltering people to the platform's edge. There were not many people waiting, so chances were he'd just missed a train. He might have a long wait for the next one, especially if the raid had started.

Beside him a tall man with thinning red hair and a round, freckled face nodded a greeting and offered a cigarette. Pentecross smiled a thank you but declined. Apart from the hair the man looked far younger than he probably was. He was carrying a leather briefcase, hugging it under his arm as if afraid it might escape.

'Pity about the raid,' the man said. His voice was cultured and assured despite his schoolboy looks. 'It was shaping up to be quite a pleasant evening.'

'It was,' Guy agreed. 'I was just thinking I might walk to London Bridge.'

'You work round here?' the man asked. 'I have an office a few streets away, on the edge of Whitehall. But I end up all over the place these days. Some of the chaps I work with even have desks down here.' He looked round. 'Well, not here exactly, but in unused tube tunnels.'

Guy had heard of some government departments and even protected businesses being relocated underground for safety.

'I've got a boring office job,' he said, vaguely.

The man smiled knowingly. 'Me too. David Alban.' He juggled the briefcase to shake hands.

Guy was surprised how firm the man's grip was. But he smiled and introduced himself. Chances were they'd never meet again. The tracks were humming which meant a train was coming. A crowd of people had built up behind them, pressing forwards as the train approached.

'Going to be a bit of a crush,' Guy said loudly to Alban as the train drew in.

'Oh, I'm not waiting for the train.'

'What?'

Alban smiled, and again looked like an overgrown schoolboy. But his words sent a chill through Guy. 'I just wanted to talk to you.'

The train squealed to a halt and the doors opened. People were pushing past as they got out on to the platform. Alban stepped closer to Guy to leave them room. His voice was clear in Guy's ear:

'You really should drop this Brinkman thing, you know. It's not doing you any favours, and it's best to have nothing to do with those jokers from Station Z. Between you and me, their time will come.'

The office was in turmoil when Guy arrived for work next morning. There was more than the usual rush and bother. Messengers came and went at a run, and the phones seemed to be ringing constantly.

'Drop whatever you were planning to do today. Going to need your help with the latest translation, there's so much stuff coming in,' Chivers told Pentecross. 'How's your Russian?'

'Passable,' Guy admitted.

Chivers gave a snort of laughter. 'Is there a language in which you are not "passable"?' he asked.

Guy smiled. 'Oh yes, plenty. I'm saving them for my retirement.'

'Rather you than me.'

'But why are we getting intercepts in Russian for God's sake?'

Chivers dabbed at his forehead with a grubby handkerchief. It was 21 June and the heat was building in every sense. 'Because the glorious armies of the Third Reich are even as we speak preparing to march into the Soviet Union.'

Guy felt the blood draining from his face. 'How do we know what's happening?'

Chivers raised an eyebrow. 'I was told not to ask. Enough said, eh?'

'Does Stalin know?'

'I'm told he's been warned it's imminent. But whether he believes us is another matter.'

'But...' Guy was struggling to understand the implications. 'That's got to be a good thing, hasn't it?'

'Best news we've had all year,' Chivers agreed. 'But for the moment it makes things bloody hard work. So all hands to the pump.'

*

The invasion of Russia – Hitler's 'Operation Barbarossa' – started the next day. Once the tanks were rolling across the border, things actually calmed down. But Chivers was wilting under the stress and the midsummer heat. Guy found him in his office, head in hands and sweating profusely.

'I haven't been home for three days,' he confessed. 'God alone knows what the wife thinks I'm up to. Can't remember when I last slept. Now they want me at some emergency meeting at the War Rooms. Spirit's willing, but the flesh... Well that's another matter.' He stood up, wobbled slightly and immediately sat down again.

It hadn't occurred to Guy before that the stress actually affected Chivers. But now he began to understand that the man just hid it well. They all dealt with it in their own way – Chivers' apparent jovial disinterest was his way. He stood up again, and forced a smile.

'Needs must when the devil drives,' he said, with a sigh. 'And at the moment the devil is driving towards Moscow. Mainly, I gather, in equipment taken from the French when they threw in the towel.'

'This meeting,' Guy said. 'Can I go?'

Chivers looked surprised.

'I've finished the latest batch of translations,' Guy told him. 'Not much to do that's urgent.'

'I doubt they want spare bodies clogging the place up. Precious little air down there as it is.'

'I meant instead of you. As your representative. I've done that often enough before, though maybe not at this level. But, I mean, if you're not...' His voice faded.

'Not up to it?' Chivers finished for him. 'I'm up to it, never fear. But...' He stared down at the papers strewn across his desk. 'I could do without the distraction. It'll just be a glorified pep talk from on high. So...' He looked up at Guy and nodded. 'Good idea. I'll have Maureen write you a chitty in case anyone asks.'

Guy smiled back, though he was already wondering what he'd let himself in for.

'Ten o'clock sharp, down in the War Rooms.' Chivers nodded his thanks. 'Rather you than me.'

Deep under the New Public Offices building in Whitehall lay hidden the nerve centre of Britain's war effort. Guy had been to the War Rooms several times before. He found it even more claustrophobic and airless now. He had never seen it so busy.

The meeting was little more than an update on the situation in the Soviet Union. Guy already knew most of it. Churchill sat at the end of the room in a fog of cigar smoke. He said little until the end of the meeting when he hauled himself to his feet and addressed the assembled officers and civil servants.

'Herr Hitler has made a grave mistake,' he announced. The glint in his eye was visible even through the smoke. 'He has opened a second front in the war. He is not a man to learn the lessons of history. Either he is impatient, or he considers us merely a thorn in his side. But make no mistake, this thorn will bleed him dry.'

Guy slipped out of the room during the inevitable military updates. It was the diplomatic side of things that would interest Chivers, and that had already been amply covered. He made his way through the narrow corridor, squeezing past messenger girls and military personnel. Pausing at a junction of another corridor, he glanced to his left and saw a distinctive head of thinning red hair above the other people.

The man from the underground station – David Alban. Guy eased his way closer. He wasn't sure if he wanted to talk to the man, or just to let Alban see he was here. But as he got closer, he saw that Alban was speaking with an army officer. It was Colonel Brinkman.

Guy took a step back, colliding with a woman carrying a message flimsy. He apologised profusely, earning a smile as she hurried on her way. She passed Alban and Brinkman, who were now walking slowly as they talked.

The corridor cleared slightly, and Guy could make out some of the conversation ahead of him. Brinkman's voice was calm and quiet. But Alban was more animated – loud and angry.

'… poached their best agent, SOE won't be happy.'

Brinkman made some comment. It didn't calm Alban. Guy caught snatches of his reply.

'They're already screaming blue murder at us for not getting enough involved. Smash bang wallop is the SOE philosophy… No idea about intelligence gathering…'

Again Brinkman's reply was lost in the general noise of the bunker.

Alban stopped, and Guy was close enough to hear the man's response.

'Too right it's your concern,' Alban said. His voice was lower now, but no less angry. 'Or it soon will be. SOE are all right, they're Churchill's baby and still the blue-eyed boy. But we need to up our game in eastern Europe now that the second front has opened. That means MI6 needs more funding. Everyone knows how vital our work is at MI5, and if SOE is sacrosanct then the only place that funding can come from is Station Z. Close you down, and that frees up funds and personnel. It's only a matter of time.'

He didn't wait for a reply, but turned and stalked back down the corridor. Alban's shoulder brushed against Guy's as he went past, but he gave no sign of recognition.

Guy watched him go, then hurried after Brinkman. He kept the colonel in sight, but was careful not to get too close. The whole place was a maze of passages and rooms. It was now three times the size it had been when first completed just days before the German invasion of Poland.

When Brinkman stepped into one of the offices, Guy decided that enough was enough. What was he doing, following an army officer about the place just because he didn't understand the man's role?

But it was more than that. There was something important going on here. Chivers didn't know about it, Guy was sure. And twice now Brinkman's intervention had interfered with Guy's ability to do his job. He wasn't especially happy with the work he had to do, but he was determined to do it as best he possibly could.

Brinkman emerged from the office almost immediately, now carrying a cardboard folder. He headed on down the corridor, towards the exit stairs.

Guy was on his way out too, so he found himself again following. He turned away quickly as Sergeant Green appeared and Brinkman handed him the folder. Guy kept back as the two men spoke. Then Brinkman set off down another corridor, away from the exit.

So now Guy was following Green. The man walked briskly to the stairs and out of the War Rooms. Guy was close behind, but Green never once looked back.

Out on the street, Green paused to look round. Guy stepped back quickly into the shadows. But the sergeant had already spotted who he was looking for.

A woman emerged from the shade of a doorway where she had been keeping out of the glare of the sun. She was wearing a long dark blue skirt and a white blouse with a short jacket over it. It was hard to tell how old she was – probably not as old as she looked, with her dark hair tied up severely behind her head, and black horn-rimmed spectacles.

Green and the woman greeted each other quickly and with the ease of people who knew each other well – as friends or colleagues. They set off along the pavement, heading into Whitehall.

Instinctively, Guy followed. Chivers wouldn't expect him back at the office for a while yet. In fact, if he didn't make it back in for the rest of the day, Chivers would just assume that he was stuck in an interminable meeting down in the War Rooms.

Quite why he was following, Guy wasn't sure. Maybe he would find out where Green worked – what Whitehall department was home to the mysterious Station Z. Assuming they were heading for an office in Whitehall.

He became less certain of their possible destination as he became more certain of something else. He glanced back several times. He made a short detour round a square and back again in time to hurry after Green and the woman. It wasn't long before Guy was sure that as he was following them, so someone else was following him.

He waited until he was passing a narrow alley, and ducked down it. Pressing himself against the wall, he waited. He had caught only glimpses of the figure behind him, so he was surprised when a woman's voice called round the corner. He was surprised too by the American accent.

'I know you saw me, but I wasn't following *you*.'

There was obviously no point in pretending, so Guy stepped back out on to the street.

She was probably in her late twenties, tall and slim, wearing a belted mackintosh despite the warm weather. Her fair hair was cut short, curling away from the collar of her coat, and her features were thin and slightly angular.

'So what's your game?' the woman demanded. 'Why are *you* interested in Sergeant Green and Miss Manners?'

Guy considered denying it, but she had been following him for long enough to know the truth. He glanced down the street – it was empty.

'It's all right,' the woman said. 'I know where they're going. Tell me who you are and what you're up to and I'll let you in on the secret.'

'You work with them?' Guy asked.

She laughed, and folded her arms. 'That's not likely, is it. Well?' she prompted.

'Guy Pentecross.' The 'Major' might just intimidate her – though she didn't look like she intimidated easily.

'Sarah Diamond,' she responded.

Guy gestured across the road. 'There's a pub just down there. The Red Tavern. Let me buy you a drink, and I'll tell you what I can.'

CHAPTER 10

'I'll have a half of bitter, thank you.'

Guy thought he made a good job of hiding his surprise. But when he returned with his own pint and Sarah's half, she smiled.

'Developed a taste for it trying to keep up with the other flyers.'

That surprised him even more. 'You're a pilot?'

'I'm with the Air Transport Auxiliary.'

Guy nodded. He knew that the ATA was responsible for delivering new or repaired planes to where they needed to be. It was a huge logistical exercise to make sure the right planes were in the right places when they were needed.

'Isn't that part of the RAF?' he asked.

'No, we're technically civilian. That means the ATA has to recruit pilots who aren't suitable for frontline duties.'

'Like women.'

She put down her beer and glared at him. 'It's a matter of opinion,' she said levelly, 'but yes. Also pilots who've been invalided out of the RAF but can still fly a plane, and citizens of countries that are neutral but who want to do their bit.'

'Like America?'

'Don't be fooled by my accent. I might sound like a Yank, but I'm as British as you are. Well, half as British – on my dad's side.'

Guy tried to imagine the woman sitting opposite him in the cockpit of a plane rather than in the corner of a crowded pub. The hint of anger and steel he'd just seen from her made it easier. Yes, he thought, this was a woman who had the determination, skill and courage needed to be a pilot.

'Sorry if I've been making assumptions.'

Her expression softened. 'People do. Don't worry about it. But I guess you're wondering how being an ATA pilot got me following Sergeant Green and Miss Manners.'

'Is that the woman's name?'

She picked up her beer, looked at it, then put it down again. She was looking past Guy, though he could tell she wasn't focused on anyone or anything else. She was staring back into her memories.

'I guess it all started a few months ago, back in early May…'

Sarah loved flying. She could fly anything.

Almost all the aircraft in service with the RAF had the same basic instrument layout, so any pilot could fly any plane. But that didn't mean they handled the same. She didn't care. Even the twin-engine Avro Anson she was currently delivering could get Sarah Diamond into the sky, and the sky was where she loved to be.

One day, she promised herself, she'd fly fighter planes. For the moment, though, Hurricanes and Spitfires were the preserve of the ATA's male pilots. But yes, one day… For now, she sacrificed the speed of nimbler aircraft and made do with the exhilaration of flying through a clear blue sky, of feeling alone in the world, of seeing her father's native England spread out beneath her like an eiderdown of quilted fields and hedgerows.

The Avro Anson was used mainly as a training aircraft for pilots of the larger Avro Lancaster bomber, though it could carry a decent cargo and also played a role in maritime reconnaissance. It performed well enough, and the conditions generally back in early May, and especially today, had been ideal for flying. She had the sky above Essex to herself.

The first she saw was the shadow. It crept over the cockpit canopy like a dark cloud edging across the sun. But, glancing up, Sarah saw that the shape was too solid, too regular to be a cloud. It had to be another plane.

Sarah dipped the nose of the Anson, losing height. Until she could see what was above her she was going to assume the worst. Friendly aircraft tended not to come at you rapidly out of the sun.

Very rapidly. The Anson was hardly the fastest of aircraft, but the dark shape kept pace, matching every turn as Sarah pulled out of the dive and looped round. All the time she tried to make out what was following her so closely.

Nose up now – a rapid climb. For a moment she seemed to throw the pursuer. Caught a glimpse of the dark shape. It didn't look like a plane at all – stubby, almost a disc. Prehensile fins erupted from the back section. Light shone out from beneath.

Then, in a blur, it was behind her again. Sarah twisted and turned the plane, feeling the fuselage judder under the strain, hearing the metal creak. The two 350-hp Armstrong engines roared in protest.

She pulled out of a steep turn and climbed into a loop. Somehow she was behind the other aircraft. Its shape was still indistinct. All she could see was a black silhouette like the stern of a warship. Hard and brutal rather than elegant and aerodynamic.

If the plane had been armed, she'd have had a perfect shot. But even when the planes Sarah flew had guns fitted, there was never any ammunition. Her role was strictly – and forcibly – non-combat.

The dark shape in front wouldn't know that though, so she pressed home the 'attack'. She'd heard that a pilot had rammed his unarmed training Anson into an enemy Heinkel bomber over Gloucestershire last year – destroying both planes. For an insane moment, she considered the same manoeuvre. But then, suddenly, the 'target' was gone.

Sarah was flying into a blaze of light that streaked away from her, carrying the dark aircraft with it and disappearing into the distance. In seconds, Sarah was alone again, with the sky to herself.

If the plane had been fitted with a radio, she'd have been screaming into it by now. As it was, Sarah was talking to herself. Her American accent was more pronounced when she was angry. 'Someone down there had better have a bloody good explanation for what just happened.'

Pauline Gower, head of the female branch of the Air Transport Auxiliary, was quite severe-looking, until she smiled. She wasn't smiling now.

'What have you got yourself into this time?' she asked.

Sarah Diamond was sitting in the common room of the ATA Women's Section at their base not far from Maidenhead. A cup of tea sat cooling on the table in front of her.

'I haven't gotten myself into anything.'

Gower sat down opposite, staring intently at Sarah. They contrasted almost perfectly. Gower was dark-haired with a roundish face, whereas Sarah was blonde and thin-featured. Gower was organised, ambitious, determined. Sarah was certainly determined, but she was impulsive and lived in the moment.

Both of them were passionate about aircraft, though. Both were women who had made their way in a very male world. Both of them knew nothing more exhilarating than flying, and each secretly imagined they would die doing it.

'So why do I have a colonel no less phoning to tell me you're confined to barracks?'

'We don't have barracks,' Sarah pointed out.

'I did mention that. I don't think he was amused. Anyway, you're grounded until someone from London talks to you.'

'What about?'

'You tell me. Or actually, don't,' Gower added waving her hand. 'I don't want to know. Colonel Brinkman said that until his people get here you're not to talk to anyone. So he obviously doesn't know you.'

Now she did smile, and Gower's whole face changed. The

cares of the world seemed to melt from it, and Sarah imagined this was how she looked when she was alone in the sky.

'You're off for a few days, aren't you?' She knew full well this was true. Gower knew every detail about her girls and their roster.

'I was about to drive into town.'

'Soon as these people have spoken to you, you can go. But please wait for them. I don't need any more grief than I'm getting already. You all right for petrol?'

'Should be all right for getting to London.'

'Yes.' Gower stood up. 'Well, make sure you've got enough to get back again.'

The man was in army uniform – a sergeant. He was broad-shouldered with close-cropped hair and a flattened nose. The woman looked more like a secretary, in her navy skirt, white blouse and dark jacket. Her dark hair was gathered up and she wore horn-rimmed spectacles. All of which made her look older than Sarah Diamond suspected she really was.

The man introduced himself as Sergeant Green. The woman said nothing and sat slightly apart with a notepad and pencil as Green spoke to Sarah.

'I didn't catch your name,' Sarah said pointedly.

'Miss Manners is here to observe and take notes,' Green explained.

Miss Manners glanced over the top of her glasses before returning her attention to whatever she had written.

'You're American,' Green said.

It wasn't a question, but Sarah had no hesitation in denying it. 'No, I have a British passport.'

'You *sound* American.'

'You *look* like a boxer.' She let that hang for a moment before explaining. 'All right, so my mother is American. Her father was at the US embassy for a while, and she came over with him. Met my dad, and they got married. Moved back over to New York when I was four years old.'

Green nodded, and Miss Manners made a short note.

'I don't believe you came here to quiz me about my ancestry,' Sarah told them.

'Where did you learn to fly?'

'Dad had a freight business. Couldn't keep me away from the planes. Eventually he gave in and taught me. Mother was furious. It's not very ladylike to fly planes.'

'So you flew for the company?'

'No, I ran away and joined a flying circus.'

She could tell he thought she was joking. But it was the truth.

'What did you see today?'

They both leaned forward as he asked – this was why they were here, as if she hadn't guessed.

'Well, you tell me,' Sarah said.

He smiled thinly. 'I'm afraid I can't do that. But it would be useful to know what exactly you saw.'

Sarah took her time. She lit a cigarette and blew out a long stream of smoke.

'An aircraft,' she said at last. 'Dark, no markings that I saw.'

'Shape?' Green prompted.

'Strange. It didn't have wings, well not to speak of. More of a disk, or a foreshortened fuselage. I only caught glimpses.' The cigarette wasn't doing anything for her, and she leaned forward to stub it out. 'It moved at a hell of a lick, though, I'll tell you that. Experimental, is it?'

The sergeant's eyes narrowed – obviously it was. They didn't want word getting out. Well, that made sense.

'Are you married?' Green asked.

She laughed. 'Why, Sergeant Green, we only just met. I don't even know your first name.'

He blushed and looked down.

'It's a serious question.' Miss Manners' voice was as prim and precise as her bearing.

'I believe it always is.'

The woman's eyes were hard as flint behind the lenses. 'He is asking so we know whether or not you are likely to confide in your husband when we tell you that you cannot speak of what you have seen.'

'I don't talk about my work,' Sarah assured her.

'You don't talk about today either,' Green said. 'Not to your colleagues. Not to Miss Gower. Not to anyone. Not ever.'

'Even my husband?'

'You're not married,' Miss Manners said.

'How do you know?' Sarah snapped. How dare this secretary make assumptions about her personal life.

But the woman seemed unperturbed by Sarah's angry tone. 'I can tell.' She closed the notepad and tucked it together with the pencil into her shoulder bag as she stood up. 'This interview is over.'

Green tried to gloss over it. He assured Sarah that they appreciated the fine work she was doing. He told her that it was in everyone's best interests if she said nothing of today's events. He told her that her country – her father's country at any rate, though he didn't say that – would be in her debt.

But none of this disguised the intriguing fact that Sergeant Green was the assistant, and that the mysterious Miss Manners was actually in charge.

'There's a war on,' she told herself as she drove to London. 'There's a bloody war on.' But even so, she didn't like the idea of being told what she could and couldn't tell anyone. Was this any different to the secrecy surrounding her work for the ATA? Well, yes it was – that was her job.

And, Sarah realised, she didn't really object to being told to keep quiet. She was more annoyed at the thought she would never know exactly what she had seen. What *was* the aircraft – why had it come at her, and how fast could it go? The thought that she would never get to find out, let alone fly something like that, drained her.

There was some comfort to be had from gunning the SS100 Jaguar along the more deserted stretches of road. She longed to get it up to the hundred miles an hour its name boasted the 3.5 litre engine could achieve. But that just drank the precious petrol. So she contented herself with a more modest speed, enjoying the throaty purr of the engine. Jaguar was a great name for a car, she thought.

Reluctantly, Sarah left the car in the garage that went with her flat in Hammersmith. She didn't go into the flat, but continued on into central London by bus and then underground train. Normally she would have treated herself to a bath and something to eat, but she was still tense after the meeting with Sergeant Green and Miss Manners. She needed to keep on the move, to be *doing* something.

Sarah doubled back on herself several times, taking an indirect route to her destination. Only when she was absolutely sure that she was not being followed did she approach Grosvenor Square. She walked round the whole square twice before heading into the large imposing building that was Number 1. The United States embassy.

'My name is Miss Diamond and I have to see Mr Whitman,' she told the woman at the front desk.

'I'm afraid Mr Whitman sees no one without an appointment. He's a very busy man.'

'Just tell him I'm here,' she said sharply.

CHAPTER 11

Sarah Diamond blinked. She sipped at her half pint of bitter. 'And that's about it really.'

Guy realised he'd not touched his own drink, he had been so involved in her story. And, if he was honest, in watching her tell it.

'Whitman is a friend of Mother's,' Sarah said. 'He owes me a few favours, so I asked him to track down Sergeant Green. It took him a while to find the right one.'

'Seems you had more luck than I did tracking down Colonel Brinkman.'

'So how did you manage it, then? Come on.' She leaned forward across the table. 'Your turn to spill the beans.'

But now that it came to it, he was reluctant. He couldn't tell her about Hess, that was classified. But she'd confided in him. He hadn't actually said he'd tell her anything, but she'd obviously assumed his agreement.

'You're not going to tell me, are you?' she said when Guy said nothing. 'Bloody typical. I show you mine and you won't show me yours. I wish I could say that's the first time it's happened to me.'

Guy felt the blood rising in his face. 'No, it's not that,' he said quickly. 'I was just... just wondering how you came to be following the Manners woman if it was Green that you tracked down.'

85

She leaned back and folded her arms. 'I got an address. Government office near St James's Square. I kept watch and Miss Prim-and-Proper Manners came out before I saw Green. So I knew I had the right place.'

Guy was going to have to tell her something. He *wanted* to tell her something. But how much?

Before he could decide, she leaned forward again. 'It was the weirdest thing, though. Well, maybe not the absolute weirdest given everything else, but even so.'

'What?'

'Well, I followed her, OK?'

Guy nodded, wondering what was coming now.

'About ten o'clock this morning, she headed off to the tube. Took the Northern line right down to Morden, then walked for ages. She had a bag with her, like a holdall.'

'So where was she going?'

'Just some house. An ordinary house on an ordinary street. Not bombed out or anything. A woman answered the door, they talked for a moment and then she went inside.'

'A friend maybe. Or a relative.'

Sarah nodded. 'That's what I thought. I was a bit disappointed, I don't mind telling you. She was there for about half an hour. I watched from a little park just down the road. I was going to give up and head back to the offices to look for Sergeant Green, but then she came out. And off she goes to another house on another ordinary street. She had a list, I think. She checked a piece of paper before she headed off.'

'And she went inside there?'

'But only for a minute. This house was set back from the road with a little front garden. Quite nice. She came out with the woman who'd answered the door and a dog. Labrador, I think. And then...' She shook her head as if she still couldn't quite believe it. 'She had a camera in the holdall. A proper one with a flash gun and everything.'

'She took a picture?'

'Several – of the woman, and of the dog. Then of them both together. Then she's off again.'

Sarah paused to finish her drink. 'I followed her to three more houses and a flat. And at all of them she took pictures – of the women there. One of them had a baby, one had a small girl. One had a cat. She took photos of them all.'

'A hobby?' Guy wondered.

'But there wasn't any pattern to it. Just random houses in south London. And it didn't seem like she knew any of the people, but they were happy for her to snap away at them. Then she headed off back to Whitehall, and that's where I saw her meet up with Green.' She leaned forward again. 'What's the place he was coming out of? Just some office?'

Pentecross forced a smile. 'Just some office,' he lied.

Luckily, she didn't pursue it. 'Oh, I nearly forgot. Before that, after all the photos, she went somewhere else on the way back. Just down from Clapham High Street.'

She waited, obviously expecting Guy to ask her where Miss Manners had stopped off. He didn't disappoint her.

'The YMCA,' she said. She nodded vehemently before he could react. 'Yeah – that's what I thought. Why the hell does someone like that call into the YMCA?'

'Maybe she's been bombed out and has a bed there.'

'No. She was only there for a couple of minutes. Five at the most.'

If Guy had hoped to get some answers from talking to this woman, he was just getting more and more confused. 'In the scheme of things,' he said, thinking out loud, 'I think we can probably leave aside the photography and the YMCA, given everything else.'

He told her about the burned German in Ipswich hospital. So many people must have known about him that Guy didn't think he was giving anything away that he shouldn't. He glossed over the fact that it was eight months ago, but he told Sarah how he'd been intrigued by Green's presence and the mention of Colonel Brinkman.

'There have been other things too,' he said, hoping she wouldn't push him for more details. 'I saw Green at an RAF base when I was delivering a message. Ran into Brinkman when I was following up on a… a downed German airman. A guy on a tube station who tried to warn me off. Each time I felt I was missing something, something important – something I should know about and be able to help with, only it's just out of reach.'

'I know the feeling. You just want to know what the hell's going on, right? Even though you know, deep down, that you shouldn't ask.' She gestured at a poster pinned to one of the pub walls: 'Be like Dad – keep Mum.'

'We should drop the whole thing,' Guy said. 'There's so much going on that the likes of you and me know nothing about anyway. One more shouldn't matter to us.'

'No,' she said. 'It shouldn't.'

The building was bland and nondescript – just one of a row in a Regency street. If the street had a name, it was probably lost in the rubble where the end block had taken a hit from a bomb. The only thing that marked out the building where Sergeant Green and Miss Manners worked was the pile of sandbags outside. The windows were shuttered, and the stone façade was stained with age and London smog. It looked just like any of a number of offices or government departments across the city. It could, Guy thought, have been chosen for precisely this reason.

'So that's Station Z,' he murmured, examining it from the other side of the unnamed street.

'Station Z?'

'Just a name I've heard mentioned.'

'So what now?' Sarah asked. 'Is this it? We just walk away and leave well alone?'

'We should,' Guy conceded. Before she could respond, he caught her shoulder and pulled her back into the shade of a doorway.

'Why, Mr Pentecross – we only just met.'

He nodded at a figure on the other side of the road, striding towards the building they'd been watching. 'That's Colonel Brinkman,' he said quietly.

As Brinkman went inside the building, Guy caught a glimpse of a uniformed soldier just inside the door. Slightly embarrassed, he realised his hand was still on Sarah's shoulder, and he was standing rather close to her.

'Sorry,' he said, stepping away. He tried to ignore the way she was smiling at him.

They stood in silence for a few minutes. Eventually, Sarah said: 'You need to be anywhere this afternoon?'

Guy shook his head. Was she going to suggest they go for another drink? Or maybe lunch – it was past one o'clock. He wouldn't mind. Perhaps she wanted him to ask her. 'What about you?'

'A couple of days leave.' She tilted her head to one side, looking past him. 'Brinkman's back. You going to grab me again?'

He was tempted to say yes, but Guy hadn't really got the measure of Sarah Diamond yet. He wasn't sure quite how serious she was about anything. Instead he stepped back to stand beside her in the doorway.

Brinkman was walking briskly away from them, Miss Manners by his side. Brinkman was carrying a briefcase.

'Stopped off to pick up some papers or something,' Sarah said. 'Let's see where they're going.'

'I'm not sure that's wise.' Now they'd got this far, now he'd seen where Green and Brinkman worked, Guy wasn't sure how far to push this. He was past the point where he could pretend it was part of his job to know what the mysterious Station Z was doing.

'I thought you said you were free this afternoon.'

'I am.'

'Then come on.'

Because some of the roads were still closed off after the previous night's bombing, it was impossible to tell where Brinkman and Miss Manners were heading. It wasn't until they arrived at their destination a good half hour later that Guy realised:

'They're catching a train.'

'Then so are we,' Sarah told him.

She didn't wait for him to argue, but followed Brinkman into Euston station. When Guy caught up with her she was biting her lower lip and staring across the concourse.

'What is it?'

'I was going to queue behind them for a ticket,' she said. 'Listen out for where they're headed. But…' She pointed to where Brinkman was disappearing onto one of the platforms.

'He'll have a travel permit,' Guy said.

'So we're scuppered.'

'Not really.' It would be easy just to agree and walk away. But it was also a chance to show her he wasn't a complete fool, and that he was as committed to this as she was. 'Check the departures board and see where the train from that platform is headed. Then we buy tickets to the end of the line.'

Five minutes later, Guy was buying two returns to Denbigh Hall. 'Is your journey really necessary?' a poster beside the ticket window demanded. It was a good question.

Sarah was already on the platform. She pointed out the carriage where Brinkman and Miss Manners had boarded, then suggested they find a nearby compartment. 'We'll need to check at each station to see if they get off.'

The train was quiet enough that they had a compartment to themselves, two down from Brinkman and Miss Manners. At each stop, Sarah pulled down the window and leaned out to see if they were leaving the train. She closed the window again as the train pulled away, to keep the smuts from the smoke out.

'So what aren't you telling me?' she asked.

'What do you mean?' Guy shifted uncomfortably on the seat.

'There must be something. I mean, what you've said is hardly enough to get you on a train with a strange woman heading God knows where. Following Green? Maybe, at a pinch. But why are you here now? It's not because of some dying Kraut in a hospital or feeling snubbed by a sergeant.'

Guy was saved from answering as the train slowed again. Sarah gave him a look that suggested she still expected an answer, then pulled down the window again.

'Quick – they're leaving!'

She pushed past Guy and hurried down the corridor.

'What station is it?' he asked.

'God knows.'

The sign opposite the door as they left the train said 'Bletchley'.

'Never heard of it,' Sarah said, pulling a face. 'Where are we – Bedfordshire?'

But Guy knew the name. 'Bucks, I think. And I know where Brinkman's going.'

'Clever man. Glad I let you come.'

He didn't rise to that. 'He's changing trains. Depending which way he goes, it's either Oxford or Cambridge – this is the Varsity Line, it links the two university cities.'

But he was wrong. Brinkman and Miss Manners were heading out of the station altogether. Guy and Sarah followed, turning right along the main road and keeping well back. Two other men and a woman in WRENS uniform were heading the same way, so it was easy to keep out of sight.

They'd gone almost no distance, just a few hundred yards, when Brinkman turned into a wide driveway. The other passengers followed. Sarah hurried after them, Guy close behind. He almost walked into her as Sarah stopped abruptly.

She was behind the woman in uniform, who was waiting behind the two men. There was a barrier lowered across the road, and two soldiers were checking passes.

Guy tapped Sarah on the shoulder. 'Maybe discretion is the better part of valour right now,' he said softly.

But as he spoke, another man arrived in the line behind him. If they turned and left now it would be obvious they weren't supposed to be here – wherever 'here' was.

The soldiers nodded through the two men and the WREN. More people from the train were arriving behind Guy now, nudging him forwards. The nearest soldier turned to Sarah.

'Got your pass ready, miss?'
She didn't move. The soldier's eyes narrowed.
The second soldier reached to unsling his rifle.

CHAPTER 12

Guy stepped forward, pulling out his Foreign Office pass. 'Sorry,' he said, showing the pass. 'We're with Colonel Brinkman. He just went through with Miss Manners.' He nodded to where Brinkman and Miss Manners were walking up the main driveway.

Ahead of them, in the distance, Guy could see a large house. To either side were trees and concrete driveways leading to what looked like wooden-boarded temporary huts.

Sarah seemed to have recovered her composure, and showed her ATA pass. The guard took both passes, inspecting them carefully before turning to his colleague.

The other soldier shrugged. 'Brinkman brings all sorts.'

'You should have been booked in,' the first soldier told Pentecross.

'I know, I'm sorry. It was a bit of a rush. Last-minute thing. You know what it's like.'

People in the queue behind were shuffling impatiently.

'You need to catch up with the colonel,' the soldier said. He handed their passes back. 'You won't get into any of the secure locations unless you're with him, not on these passes.' He waved them through and turned his attention to the man waiting behind.

'That was close,' Guy breathed as they hurried up the driveway.

'What the hell is this place?' Sarah asked.

'Somewhere we shouldn't be, that's obvious. We stay just long enough that they don't get suspicious when we leave, then we're out of here, all right?'

Sarah nodded. From her expression Guy guessed that like him she was beginning to think they should never have come. Some things were best left well alone. He silently cursed his curiosity.

Ahead of them, the house was now clearly visible as they approached. It looked, Guy thought, a bit of a mess, as if sections had been added haphazardly over the years. The result was an unsymmetrical structure that didn't quite look 'right'.

But this was not Brinkman's destination. He and Miss Manners turned off along a narrower roadway that led between several of the temporary wooden buildings. The place was busy – people walking or on bicycles. Many were in uniform, but a lot of them were in civilian clothes. The number of women suggested to Guy that it was some sort of administrative centre.

Wherever they were, it was apparent that the work done here was sensitive. Sarah nudged Guy as they passed a noticeboard by the side of the drive. In amongst notices of social events and concerts was a foolscap poster:

```
REMEMBER
Do not talk at meals
Do not talk in the transport
Do not talk travelling
Do not talk in the billet
Do not talk by your own fireside
Be careful even in your Hut
```

Anywhere else, Dr Henry Wiles might have cut a rather odd figure in his threadbare tweed jacket, ancient waistcoat, and wire-rimmed glasses. But here at Bletchley Park, staffed with the most brilliant and eccentric academics and thinkers, Wiles fitted right in.

'Colonel Brinkman is due in a few minutes, sir.'

Wiles couldn't recall if he'd ever been told the girl's name, but she reminded him vaguely of his niece Deborah. He should probably find out what she was called, since it was always the same girl who brought the messages to this Hut. At least, he thought it was.

'Thank you. What was your name again?'

'It's James, sir.'

'James?' Wiles pushed his glasses further up his nose.

'Eleanor James.' She was smiling. 'I've asked the Gate to send the colonel straight up when he arrives.'

Wiles nodded. 'He sent another of those weird transmissions last week, this one originating over south east England. Damned if I know why he's coming here himself, though.' He cleared his throat, realising he had said that out loud. 'Um, sorry, Debbie.'

'Eleanor,' she corrected him.

Wiles nodded without really hearing. He needed space to work, he needed to talk to Fredericks and arrange time to examine this latest data from Brinkman. The colonel would want answers – he always wanted answers. Wiles bundled together the papers he had been working on, shuffled them into a neat pile, and dumped them on the floor. He still had to provide the data needed for a run on the bombe machines used to try to derive the day's Enigma rotor settings. But there would be time for that later. For the moment, the German Enigma codes could wait – this was far more worrying.

Immediately, he was absorbed in the problem. He didn't hear the knock on the door of the small hut. Didn't look up when the door opened and Colonel Brinkman came in. Didn't react when the colonel cleared his throat. Not until the girl who wasn't Debbie tapped his shoulder and said quietly:

'Colonel Brinkman's here.'

'Thank you,' Brinkman said to her. 'You can leave us now.'

'Sir.' Eleanor James nodded to Brinkman and the woman with him, and let herself out of the hut.

Wiles straightened up. 'I'm giving it all the time I can spare.

You really don't need to check up on me, you know.' He nodded deferentially to the woman. She had been before, but Wiles didn't immediately remember her name either.

'I'm not checking up on you,' Brinkman assured him. 'Though I have brought you more data.'

'Another trace?' Wiles peered over his glasses excitedly. 'Excellent – data is what we need. The more the better. We can compare and contrast, look for patterns, clues, fragments...'

Brinkman opened his briefcase and removed a folder. Wiles all but snatched it from him. He opened the folder and tipped out the papers inside, spreading them across the desk. He pushed his glasses up his nose again as he inspected them.

'This is tracking information?'

'From the Observer Corps,' the woman said. He remembered her name now – Manners. 'The other sheet gives RADAR traces.'

'What do you think?' Brinkman asked.

Wiles answered without looking up. 'I think you're a very impatient man. I shall have to study these for a long time before I know whether there is anything to be learned from them. Gleaning that knowledge will take even longer. And with the amount of other work that Fredericks and his lackeys are foisting on me I wouldn't hold out too much hope for a swift response.'

'Don't worry about Fredericks,' Brinkman told him.

Wiles snorted. 'Easy for you to say. It's not your neck he's breathing down. Proverbial dragon, that one.'

'You no longer work for Fredericks,' Brinkman said.

Wiles looked up sharply. 'Does *he* know that?'

Miss Manners checked her watch. 'He should have been informed just a few minutes ago.'

'From now on, the UDT transmissions are your number one priority,' Brinkman said. 'In fact, they are your only priority.'

'But what about my other work?' Wiles protested. He kicked at the papers he'd earlier dumped on the floor. 'Enigma? And the other stuff? I've got a bombe run scheduled in about half an hour, you know.'

'Not any more,' Brinkman said. 'From this moment, you work exclusively for Station Z, you understand?'

Wiles sniffed and frowned. 'Well... I can't deny it's a challenge.' He smiled suddenly. 'Yes, a real poser, this one. But to be honest, even working full time it will take a while to crack the transmissions. Even if we *can* crack them. I say!' He looked suddenly startled as a thought occurred to him. 'Do I have to move out of here?'

They all looked round the hut – papers piled precariously on every surface. A blackboard was covered with tiny chalk calculations, some underlined and others crossed out. Books lay where they had toppled across and from shelves.

'You don't have to move out,' Brinkman said, to Wiles' evident relief. 'And you can choose your own team.'

'Team?'

'Within reason,' Miss Manners said quickly. 'Three assistants and a runner. Maximum.' She glanced at Brinkman, and he nodded.

'And Fredericks has agreed this?' Wiles shook his head in disbelief.

'I'm not sure "agreed" is exactly the word,' Brinkman said. He turned as the door to the hut slammed open so hard it hit the wall behind. 'Ah, looks like you can ask him yourself.'

When Brinkman and Miss Manners disappeared inside the hut, Sarah made to follow. But Guy stopped her.

'They'll spot us straight away.'

'Maybe that's the best thing.'

'That and a court martial.'

'We've come this far. I want to know what's going on.'

'Me too,' Guy told her, though he was no longer sure it was true.

The door of the hut opened again and a woman in WRENS uniform emerged. She glanced at Guy and Sarah as she passed, but made no comment.

'Let's try round the back,' Guy suggested.

He led Sarah round the side of the hut. They were hidden

from the path here, and Guy risked a quick look through the window. It was dusty and he could barely make out the inside. Several people stood in the middle of the small hut – Brinkman, Miss Manners, and another man. More than that it was difficult to tell. He ducked out of sight again quickly.

'Well?'

'They're talking to someone,' Guy whispered.

They both strained to hear. Through the window came the faint buzz of conversation, but it was impossible to make out anything coherent. They persevered for a few minutes before Sarah sighed and shook her head.

'This is a waste of time,' she said. 'We might hear more through the door.'

'That won't look at all suspicious,' Guy muttered. But he followed her back to the front of the hut.

As soon as Sarah had turned the corner of the hut, she was back again. 'Someone coming!' she hissed.

They both pressed against the side of the hut, out of sight.

'Man in a crumpled suit,' Sarah whispered. 'He doesn't look happy.'

As she spoke, they heard the door of the hut slammed open.

'What the hell are you playing at, Brinkman?'

The words reached them clearly through the open door. A moment later, it slammed shut again. Sarah and Guy stepped out from behind the hut. They could still hear the voices from inside, and Guy saw that the door wasn't quite closed – the newcomer had slammed it so hard it had sprung open again.

They crept closer, listening, but also trying to look as if they had just stepped out of the hut for some air. As if they had every right to be there.

'You can't just commandeer my staff like this.'

'Actually I can, Mr Fredericks.' Guy recognised Brinkman's voice. The colonel's calm manner obviously did not have a soothing effect on Fredericks.

'Dr Wiles is one of my senior analysts. I won't have him diverted onto your... your... Onto whatever it is you people do,' Fredericks finished lamely.

'I'm afraid it's not your choice. Dr Wiles and whoever he chooses to serve on his team—'

'His *team*?'

'I do hope you're not going to make this any more difficult than it needs to be.'

Fredericks sounded almost incandescent with rage. 'I shall fight this at every level, believe you me.'

'Michael…' another voice said, evidently trying to calm the man. 'I didn't ask for this. But for what it's worth—'

'You keep out of this, Wiles. It's nothing to do with you.'

'Um, well – actually…' the hapless Wiles started.

But Fredericks wasn't listening. 'I'll take this right to the top. We'll see what Mr Churchill has to say!'

Guy glanced at Sarah, and saw that she was already watching for his reaction. She raised her eyebrows.

'I can tell you exactly what Mr Churchill will say,' Brinkman countered. His tone was conversational. 'Miss Manners, do you have the letter?'

'Of course.' Her voice was so quiet they had to strain to hear her.

'What is this?' Fredericks demanded.

'If you read it,' Miss Manners said, 'you'll see that it is a letter of authorisation. It gives Colonel Brinkman carte blanche to recruit or requisition whoever and whatever we need.'

'That's ridiculous.'

'You are welcome to take it up with the authors of the letter,' Brinkman said. 'You'll see that it is signed by General Ismay on behalf of the Prime Minister.'

There was silence for several moments. Guy found he was holding his breath as he waited for Fredericks' response. But there was none.

Instead, he heard Miss Manners say: 'We'll let you know if we need anything else.'

The door was yanked open before Pentecross or Sarah could move. A man in a crumpled dark suit, his face so red with anger that he could only be Fredericks, strode out of the hut. He pulled the door shut behind him, glaring first at Guy, then at Sarah, before he marched off.

'He must think we're with Brinkman,' Sarah whispered as they took cover behind the hut once more.

A few moments later, they heard the hut door open again. Guy risked a quick look round the corner, and saw Brinkman and Miss Manners heading off in the same direction as they had originally come.

'They said his name was Dr Wiles,' Sarah said.

'That hardly helps,' Guy said.

'It does if we want to talk to him.'

'If we—' He broke off as Sarah pushed past. 'Now, hold on – you can't just...'

But she could and she did. Sarah opened the hut door and stepped inside. Guy took a deep breath, and followed.

Wiles sat at his desk staring into space. He needed to think carefully who he might need to help with the transmission decryption. The trouble was, without knowing more of the nature of the problem, it was difficult to decide who was best able to help.

Wiles didn't want to antagonise Fredericks any more than he had to. It was a question of getting the right balance between who was best for the job, and who could be spared from their other assignments. An added complication was that secrecy was so strict Wiles didn't actually know what most of the people at Bletchley did or where their expertise lay. He was rather restricted to those he had worked with before.

'Better the devils you know,' he murmured.

He was about to return his attention to the latest documents Brinkman had brought when two more people came into the hut. A man and a woman, neither of them familiar to Wiles. The man wore a suit that had seen better days, the woman was smartly dressed in skirt and blouse.

'Can I help you?'

'We're with Brinkman, Dr Wiles,' the woman said. He caught the American accent.

'Are you here to help, or to add further entreaties for me to do the impossible?'

'We were supposed to be here for the briefing,' the woman told him.

'Briefing?'

'The meeting,' the man said quickly. 'Just now. We got delayed.'

'Hardly a briefing,' Wiles said. 'Anyway, Colonel Brinkman's been and gone. You missed him.'

'Maybe you could just tell us what he said?' the woman asked.

Wiles frowned. 'Why not ask the colonel?'

'Like I said, we missed him.' The man smiled apologetically. 'So, if you could just fill us in.'

'I'm not sure what you want to know, but you'd better show me your passes and I'll tell you what I can.'

The man and woman exchanged looks, before offering their passes. Wiles glanced at them and forced a smile. 'Fine, fine. Not that I can tell you much. Colonel Brinkman gave me the latest UDT intercepts from the Y Stations along with tracking data. I gather it's a priority.'

The man nodded. 'Absolutely. Top priority.'

'Thank you, Dr Wiles,' the woman said. 'That's a great help. We'd better be on our way. It was good to meet you.'

'The pleasure's all mine,' Wiles said, but he was talking to the closing door. They were in a hurry to get out. A man from the FO and a woman from Air Transport. Brinkman was pulling strings in all directions it seemed.

Assuming things *were* what they seemed.

Wiles watched through the window as the man and woman disappeared back down the path towards the main driveway. Somewhere in amongst the books and papers there was a telephone. It took him a few moments to unearth it. He raised the receiver and listened. It was dead.

The door opened to let Eleanor James back in. Wiles waved her over with relief.

'How do I get an outside line on this thing?'

She took it from him, dialled, and handed it back.

'Thank you. Oh,' he added, 'and you just got promoted. From whatever you are now to something else.'

Wiles ignored her reaction and dialled a number. He might not have much of a memory for faces, but numbers were his business. The phone was answered on the third ring.

'I wonder,' Wiles said, 'if I could leave a message for Colonel Brinkman?'

CHAPTER 13

Brinkman got the message when he returned from Bletchley – a pencil scrawl on a scrap of paper left on his desk. He called Wiles back, and was still on the phone when Sergeant Green came into the office.

'He didn't get the woman's name,' Brinkman told Green. 'But the man is Pentecross, from the FO.'

'Persistent bugger, isn't he, sir,' Green said. 'The woman could be that ATA girl, Diamond. I saw her in Piccadilly the other day. Thought it was a coincidence.'

'Remind me,' Brinkman said.

'She had a run-in with a UDT, couple of months ago. Miss Manners and I spoke to her about it. Warned her off.'

'Or not, perhaps.'

'If it's her.'

'It seems likely,' Brinkman decided. 'I don't believe in coincidence.'

'You want me to do anything about it?'

'Yes. But I'm not sure what. Need to think about this one,' Brinkman said. He tapped the tips of his fingers together as he considered. 'Is there anything else?'

'Yes, sir. Mr Alban is here. Miss Manners won't let him past the front office, but he's insisting he needs to see you.'

Brinkman sighed. 'That's all I need.'

*

David Alban sat down without being invited. He stretched his legs out and yawned. Brinkman pretended to be involved in paperwork, refusing to spare the man more than a glance. He knew what MI5 in general thought of Station Z, and Alban in particular was more than sceptical. He was downright hostile.

'You're ruffling feathers again, Colonel,' Alban said at last.

Brinkman closed the cover of the file he'd been examining and fixed Alban with a stare. 'Oh?'

'Friend Fredericks at Station X has been on to us.'

'I'd hardly call him a friend. And as you say "us" I assume that's someone higher up the chain than you.'

Alban grinned like an annoying schoolboy. 'Assume away, old man.' The grin faded, and Alban leaned forward. 'But he's not happy. Making waves. He's a man of considerable influence, and rightly so, given what his people have achieved.'

'He's an administrator,' Brinkman countered. 'He's not even that important at Station X.'

'Then he has important friends.'

'Don't we all,' Brinkman snapped.

Alban ignored the comment. 'Fredericks says that you've commandeered one of his top men. "Poached" was the word he used, actually. Like an egg. First SOE and now Station X, you're overreaching yourself, Colonel. And if you keep pinching – "poaching" – other people's prize personnel, it's only a matter of time before the gamekeeper comes after you.'

'And you see yourself as the gamekeeper, do you?' Brinkman asked.

Alban grinned again. 'Oh I'm just an errand boy, I've no illusions about that. But even an errand boy can wonder what gives you the right to behave in such a cavalier manner.'

'My authority comes from the Prime Minister himself,' Brinkman said quietly. 'And I will not have it questioned by a self-confessed errand boy.'

Alban seemed unimpressed. 'Well good for you. Enjoy it while you can, I say. Because, you know what Winston's like. He has six impossible ideas before breakfast each and every day.'

'*Mr Churchill* knows how important our work here is,' Brinkman said. For some reason Alban's use of the Prime Minister's Christian name irritated him more than anything else the young man had said.

'Implying that I don't?'

'I know you don't.' Brinkman opened the file again, staring down at it. 'You have no idea what we do here.'

Alban's shadow fell across the desk as he stood up and leaned over, hands pressed down either side of the file. 'I don't want to know. But I'll tell you what I *do* know.'

Brinkman looked up, and was surprised at Alban's grim expression. The man suddenly looked much older, and Brinkman wondered if perhaps he had underestimated his ability and position as well as his age.

'I know that your Station Z is a passing fad of the Prime Minister's. I know that you've upset SOE, which he really does care about, and you've upset Station X which Churchill knows is vital to the war effort. And I know that your own security here is a joke.'

Brinkman said nothing.

Alban straightened up. A nerve twitched for a second under his left eye. 'You were followed to Bletchley, you know.'

'Yes, I do know.' Brinkman watched for a reaction, but there was none. 'And it wasn't our security that the two individuals in question breached to get into the site.'

'They were following *you*.'

Brinkman stood up, angry. 'Which you could only know if you were following me as well.'

The grin was back. 'Just doing my job, Colonel.'

'Then kindly get out of here and let me do mine.'

'With pleasure. As it happens, I have an appointment at Euston station. There are a couple of people coming in on a train from Bletchley that I have to arrest for breaching the Official Secrets Act.'

'Errand boy promoted to policeman?' Brinkman said. It was a cheap jibe and he regretted it as soon as he'd said it. But he was not about to apologise.

Alban's expression didn't change. But there was a tremble of suppressed anger in his reply. 'I don't know what exactly your department does, Colonel,' he said. 'But you're not very good at it, and it's costing us funds and resources that could be better used elsewhere.'

'Goodbye, Mr Alban. If you could see yourself out, I have important things to do.' Brinkman turned back to his file.

Alban watched him for a moment before he left. As he turned to go, he said: 'You're an expensive luxury, Colonel. And this war isn't about luxury – it's about austerity and thrift. First chance I get, I'm closing you down for good.'

CHAPTER 14

The ship docked at just after three in the afternoon, and Leo Davenport was there to meet it. If the captain noticed that 'Carlton Smith' had lost his beard since leaving Lisbon, he didn't mention it. He also pocketed the folded banknotes that Davenport gave him without comment.

Having got his cargo this far, Davenport was determined not to lose it now. He watched as a crane lifted the large wooden crate and lowered it gently onto the back of a flat-bed truck that Davenport had arranged. As soon as it was secured, he gave the crane driver and the dockers a cheery wave and clambered up into the lorry's cab to sit beside the driver.

Every time he came back to London, it seemed to Davenport that there was less of the city standing. They drove past burned out cranes and warehouses, through streets lined with rubble swept to the pavement edges. Several times he had to stop while the driver worked out a new route because the way was blocked. Roads were closed, or the way impassable because of fire engines and military vehicles. Everywhere smelled of dust and ash.

Although Davenport was in no particular hurry, he did glance skywards every now and again, hoping that the Luftwaffe would hold off at least until he reached his destination. It would be just his luck if he managed to smuggle his cargo across France and into Portugal, ship it across the hostile seas only to see it bombed to bits on a London street almost within sight of its destination. Doubly annoying if he himself got blown up with it.

Eventually they turned in through imposing iron gates and drew up outside an even more imposing building. The classical façade stood proud and defiant in the evening sunshine, though Davenport knew that much of the interior had been burned out by incendiary bombs back in May.

'Here you are, guv,' the driver said. 'The British Museum.'

Davenport told him to wait and he'd send someone to help unload the crate. He descended from the cab, and hurried up the wide steps to the main entrance where he found a uniformed official. Davenport briefly explained that he had a delivery to go to Mrs Archer. He waited while the crate was unloaded and carried round to the back of the museum.

With four men carrying the crate, hoisted up on their shoulders, it looked rather like a funeral procession, Davenport thought. He went ahead to hold open the door, standing back to let them through.

'Hey – aren't you…?' one of the men started to say as they passed.

'I get that a lot,' Davenport told him. 'I gather he's not so handsome in real life.'

'Not so handsome on the big screen, if you ask me,' the man grunted as he helped manipulate the large crate through the narrow doorway.

Davenport sniffed. 'That's a matter of opinion,' he murmured.

With the crate safely deposited in a storeroom off one of the main galleries of the museum, Davenport made his way down a narrow corridor. Halfway along, he let himself through a doorway marked 'Strictly Private'. Along another corridor, and he reached a solid metal door. It was locked, and Davenport spent almost a minute with a piece of wire and a narrow-bladed instrument before he managed to open it. He locked it again behind him, and descended a flight of stone steps.

The steps emerged into a large area beneath the Great Court – a cavern of unpainted brick and rough stone. An area that few people knew even existed. Illuminated by electric lights strung from the vaulted ceiling high above, the whole area was almost filled with shelves and cupboards, crates and boxes and tea chests. Soon, Davenport knew, another crate would be added to the collection.

He made his way through narrow paths left between the boxed artefacts and shelves. He always went the same way, a route he had memorised long ago. But even though he passed the same display cases and shelves, crates and boxes, he always saw something that he couldn't recall ever seeing before. This time it was a large earthenware jar with a lid in the shape of a jackal's head. Ancient Egyptian, he thought – a canopic jar. He must have seen it dozens of times and just not noticed it before. But then this place and the things gathered together in it never ceased to amaze him.

Davenport's destination was at the heart of the maze through the collection. Several of the pathways met in an open area. In the middle of it was a single desk, surrounded by several filing cabinets. A woman sat at the desk, intent on a large book open before her. She was old – her face lined and ancient, her steel grey hair tied up severely. Sensing she had company, she glanced up, peering over her gold-rimmed reading glasses. Her eyes were greyer than her hair, but alert and unblinking.

'Oh it's you,' she said, and returned her attention to the volume in front of her. 'I do wish you wouldn't just let yourself in like that. Where have you been, anyway?' Her voice was stronger and younger than one might expect. 'Gallivanting?'

'Always gallivanting, Elizabeth,' Davenport admitted. There was no spare chair, so he perched on the edge of a packing case and watched her until she sighed, took off her glasses and looked up again.

'Well?'

'I brought you a present. From France.'

She raised an eyebrow. 'What sort of present? I should

warn you that my yearning for silk stockings and perfume has long since passed.'

'I'm sure that's not true. But actually, I don't know exactly what it is. A prize of opportunity, you might say.'

She leaned back, amused. 'Yes, well, you were always the opportunist, Leo.'

'The Nazis were excavating a site. Bronze Age, I think. Ancient, anyway. It was... interesting.'

'Then you must tell me all about it.'

'Oh, I will,' he promised. 'But when they cleared out I managed to get hold of one of the larger artefacts. I'm hoping, if I liberated the right crate, that it's the coffin and mortal remains of a chieftain. It's in a storeroom off—'

She waved a hand, interest evaporating. 'I don't care where it is now. Tell young Edward. He can have it brought down here.'

Davenport nodded, amused. Young Edward might be younger than Mrs Archer, but he was probably in his seventies. The two of them had run this place for as long as Davenport had known about it.

'You haven't been tempted to move out then?' he asked.

'Ship some of this stuff out to Wales or dump it down the Aldwych Tube tunnel with the other exhibits and artefacts and I'd be lucky ever to get it back. It's safe enough down here. We had a bomb in Prints and Drawings last September. It got through four floors to the sub-basement, but still didn't penetrate this far.'

'Must have done some damage,' Davenport guessed.

'Didn't go off. Four days later another bomb fell through the hole the first one made. What are the chances of that, do you suppose?' Mrs Archer stood up, pushing the book she had been examining to one side. 'Now, let's find an atlas and you can show me where exactly in France you've been.'

He followed her over to a bookcase. After a glance, she moved on to another.

'The trouble with this place is that's it's almost impossible to find anything that's less than a few hundred years old.'

'Does that include the staff?' Davenport said.

That earned him a glance that was half amused, half resigned. But before she could comment, a telephone began to ring. Elizabeth Archer made her way back to her desk, uncovered the phone lurking beneath a pile of papers and answered it abruptly.

'Yes.' She listened for a moment, then said: 'Yes, he is.' She held the receiver out to Davenport.

He took the phone. He could guess who it was – there were not many people who knew this number. Even fewer could have known that he might be here.

After a brief conversation, he hung up.

'You're leaving?' Elizabeth guessed.

'Sorry. But I shall return to tell you all about my adventures and the mysterious crate.'

'But first?'

'But first, someone's in trouble. And as usual, it's up to me to get them out of it.'

The journey back from Bletchley was a nervous one. Both Guy and Sarah were desperate to talk about what had happened, what – if anything – they had discovered. But before they got the chance, a man let himself into their compartment and settled on the seat beside Guy. He nodded a greeting, then unfolded a copy of *The Times*.

They sat in silence for most of the journey, exchanging only the blandest comments to pass the time. Several times Guy thought he saw the man with the paper staring at him or Sarah. He was probably being over-anxious, he thought. And of course, Sarah was well worth staring at.

He was relieved when the train finally pulled into Euston. The man with the paper waited politely for the two of them to leave before following. When they stepped down from the train to the platform, the man continued to follow closely behind as they made their way towards the main concourse.

'Is he following us?' Sarah hissed as they pulled ahead of the man.

'It's probably nothing,' Guy replied quietly.

'I thought he was staring at me,' Sarah said.

'Me too.'

Her mouth twitched into a half smile. 'That's all right. I don't mind *you* staring.'

'That's not what I meant.' He realised she was joking as soon as he'd said it. 'Sorry.'

Sarah glanced back. Guy resisted the urge to look back too, but he could see the man reflected in the glass of a window as they crossed the main concourse.

'Probably heading for the underground, like us,' he said.

'Or not,' Sarah added as they approached the wide steps leading down.

Standing at the top, also holding a newspaper, was a man in a long nondescript raincoat. His hat shadowed his face, but Guy could see that his attention wasn't on the paper so much as the people passing by. Did he imagine it, or was there a flash of recognition as he and Sarah approached?

Guy took Sarah's elbow and steered her gently aside, past the steps.

'Let's see if there's a cab.'

He sensed rather than saw the man at the top of the stairs following them.

'Two of them now,' Sarah said, confirming his fears.

Another man in raincoat and hat stood by the exit to the taxi rank.

Sarah had seen him too. 'They probably know who we are anyway. Even if we get away from them now...' she didn't need to finish the thought.

They paused at a paper stall. 'If we can get to my office,' Guy said, thinking out loud, 'then I might persuade Chivers, my boss, that I was following up a legitimate lead. Get him to call this lot off, whoever they are.'

'And what about me? Am I following up a legitimate lead too?'

'We'll think of something.'

'Who are they anyway?' She looked round. The three men

were walking slowly towards them, confidently unhurried. 'Police.'

Another figure had appeared from the exit to the taxis. A figure that Guy recognised at once – the man from the tube station, Alban. He stood watching, hands in his jacket pockets and a thin smile on his ruddy face.

'MI5. Christ!'

'Is that better or worse.'

'Yes. No. Maybe – I don't know.'

The acrid smell of smoke announced the arrival of another train more clearly than the station announcer. It was a busy train, and people streamed out from the platform and across the station concourse.

'Now!' Guy said, grabbing Sarah's arm.

They disappeared into the mass of people, losing themselves in the middle of the crowd. Guy caught glimpses of the MI5 men looking into the mass. One of them pushed through, staring round as he tried to see where they had gone.

The tide of people swept them past the news stand back towards the exit. There was a narrow gateway past the main exit. As they reached it, Guy pulled Sarah out of the crowd and they hurried through. Her heels clacked so loudly on the flagstones that Guy was sure everyone in the station must be turning to look. He risked a glance back over his shoulder.

Nothing.

No one was following. He breathed a sigh of relief.

'Taxi?' Sarah suggested as they emerged into the dying rays of the evening sun.

He shook his head. 'They might have someone watching.'

They set off briskly round the side of Euston and down a narrow alley that led away from the thoroughfare of the Euston Road and towards Cardigan Street.

'We can cut through St James's Gardens, take a back way to Whitehall and find Chivers.'

'You really think he can help?'

'I don't know,' Guy admitted. 'You got any better ideas?'

'I know a chap at the American embassy. Friend of mother's.'

113

'You said,' he remembered. Was that an option? Maybe he could call Chivers from the embassy.

He was still considering the alternatives as they reached the gardens. They turned in at a narrow gate, past a low wall drilled with holes where the iron railings had been removed to be melted down for the war effort. Not that they were much use, but it was another way of showing that Something was Being Done.

A man coming the other way stepped back to let them through. Guy nodded a thank you, and the man acknowledged with a smile.

'Keep walking,' Sarah hissed as they entered the gardens.

'What?'

'That man – I've seen him somewhere before. He must be one of them.'

There was something familiar about him, Guy realised. He turned back to look.

And found the man was walking close behind them.

'Looks like you're going my way,' the man said. His voice was cultured – almost plummy. He had a round, handsome face, with bushy eyebrows and dark eyes and looked to be in his early forties, with slicked back dark hair. 'No, no, don't run.' The man glanced down, and Guy followed his gaze. The man's right hand was in his coat pocket.

'I really wouldn't advise it, Major Pentecross,' the man said. He smiled apologetically. 'I promise you, I can shoot both you and Miss Diamond in less than a second and vanish into the evening in less than a minute. Or we can all go for a little stroll through the gardens, which I have to say are looking very fine despite everything. Now then, which would you prefer – smelling the roses, or pushing up the daisies?'

CHAPTER 15

The sun was dipping below the shattered London skyline. It bathed the ruined streets with an orange warmth that belied the destruction. Barrage balloons shimmered in the evening sky. An elderly lady picked her way through rubble balancing herself with a large bag in each hand.

Perhaps it was all she had left in this world, Guy thought. He wondered if, under different circumstances, he might have waded through the debris and offered to help. But right now that wasn't an option. At some point Sarah had taken hold of his hand. Or perhaps he had taken hold of hers.

The man behind gave them terse instructions about which way to go. Guy had assumed it would be towards Piccadilly. MI5 had offices in St James's Street, identified to those who knew – and disguised from those who didn't – by a large 'To Let' board outside. But they seemed to be heading instead towards the lower end of Oxford Street.

'Nearly there,' the man said as they turned onto High Holborn.

There were more people around here, and Guy wondered if he should make a run for it. Could he and Sarah lose themselves in the crowd? Or would the man fulfil his boast and shoot them both within seconds? But even if they did get away – where could they go? The more he thought about his plan to get Chivers to intercede, the more he knew it wouldn't

115

work. Chivers was relatively unimportant, even if he could be persuaded to stick up for Guy Pentecross. More likely he'd shake his head sadly and offer his universal mantra: 'Rather you than me.'

Sooner or later both he and Sarah would have to account for themselves. Running for it now could only make things worse.

Guy was used to buildings not being what they appeared from the outside. There was no 'To Let' sign, but a polished brass plaque announced that the imposing building the man had led them to was 'The Atlantean Club'. Sarah gave him a quizzical look as she too read the sign, and Guy shrugged. Inside, it was likely to be offices and desks.

Except that it wasn't. A tall, thin man immaculately dressed in a dark suit stood inside the door.

'Are you members?' he asked, peering suspiciously at Sarah.

'It's all right, Charles,' the man behind them said.

Charles was immediately deferential. 'I'm sorry, I didn't see you there, sir. Will you be dining with us tonight? The chef has, I believe, managed to acquire some mutton for a casserole.'

'That sounds ideal.' Their captor pushed past Guy and Sarah. 'Don't worry, you won't need your ration books here. It's all right, Charles, I'll sign them in. Then if you could find us somewhere quiet?'

It felt more like a weekend party at a country house retreat than an interrogation. Guy and Sarah were shown into a large wood-panelled room, and invited to sit in small leather armchairs round a low coffee table. The man who had brought them here took a third chair, from which he had a good view of both his prisoners. He kept his jacket on, and his hand in his pocket.

'What is this place?' Sarah demanded. 'Why have you brought us here? Who are you anyway?'

The man nodded. 'Fair questions. In strict order of asking, this is my club, and I've brought you here for dinner.' He smiled, and settled himself comfortably into his chair. 'I'd offer to shake hands,' he said, 'only…' He smiled apologetically, his jacket twitching as what Guy knew was a gun barrel jutted against the material. 'Harry Heslington-Smythe,' the man went on. His voice was as affected as his name.

'I suppose you want some answers,' Guy said. Maybe if they cooperated things might not go so badly.

'I suppose I do.'

Guy looked at Sarah. She gave a quick nod, then looked away. 'We went to some crummy little village in the middle of nowhere,' she said without looking at either of them. 'That's all there is to it. It's a free country isn't it?'

'Well,' Smythe said, 'I'm not sure we really have long enough to debate that one. What people will give up to preserve their freedom, eh?'

'Look – what do you want to know?' Guy demanded. 'Can you just stop being so damned affable and get on with it?'

'I'm sorry if I've ruffled your feathers,' Smythe said, his smile undercutting the apology. 'But really I'd just like to know why you're so interested in Colonel Brinkman and his merry men. What would induce a former officer now highly regarded in the Foreign Office and a young lady with a penchant for aeroplanes and fast cars to infiltrate a highly secret establishment?'

There was something in his manner, something in his voice which again made Guy think they had met before. It was more than just his appearance – he knew how the man sounded, recognised his voice.

'Do you work in the FO?' he asked.

'Alas, no.'

'But I know you from somewhere.'

'So do I,' Sarah said. 'Have we met before?'

'I'm sure I would remember. Perhaps I just have one of those faces. Now, are you going to answer my questions?'

'Why should we?' Sarah demanded.

'Well, I did just save you from getting arrested.' He glanced down at the hand still in his jacket pocket. 'Amongst other reasons.'

'You're not going to shoot us,' Guy said. Though even as he said it, he wasn't at all sure. There was an underlying coldness about the man, despite his façade of good humour and cordiality.

'It would be a shame to get blood on the floorboards,' Smythe admitted. 'Though I suspect it wouldn't be the first time. This place has quite a history. I do hope you won't be adding to that history in an unpleasant way. And I would hate to be barred. Now, you were going to tell me about your interest in Colonel Brinkman.'

'What do you want to know?' Sarah said with a sigh. She seemed suddenly deflated, and Guy guessed she was as tired and hungry as he was. He hoped the offer of casserole wasn't an idle one.

'Assume I know nothing. Tell me why you've been following the colonel and his colleagues.' He leaned forward in the chair, hand still in his jacket pocket, eyes gleaming with sudden interest. 'Tell me what you have found out, and what you think is going on.'

Again, Sarah told her story first. She gave a shorter account of events than she had treated Guy to in the pub. But she covered the essentials. Smythe listened attentively, nodding now and then, asking the occasional question.

'You're curious,' he summed up when she paused, having reached the point in her narrative where she met up with Guy. 'I can understand that. I'm a curious man myself. So then the two of you followed Brinkman to Bletchley and fell rapidly out of your depth.'

'I guess so.'

Smythe was silent throughout Guy's account. He again omitted any mention of his trip to Glasgow and his meeting with Hess. When he was finished, Smythe frowned.

'Is that it?'

'Pretty much. I'm curious too.'

'I don't think so.'

'What do you mean?' Sarah asked. 'He told you what happened, how he got involved. You think Guy's lying?'

118

'Because I'm not,' Guy insisted.

'Oh I'm sure you are veracity incarnate,' Smythe said. 'I'm quite prepared to believed you've told the truth and nothing but the truth.' He considered for a moment before going on: 'Only, it isn't the *whole* truth is it? There's not enough in what you said to merit what you've done. I mean – an RAF interception you didn't really understand, a burned German soldier, a rather vague warning from someone who you think works for MI5, and… Well.' He smiled. 'That's about all there is, really. So what aren't you telling me?'

'He's told you everything,' Sarah said.

'In that case I apologise and revise my question. What aren't you telling *us*?'

For the first time Sarah seemed uncertain. She looked at Guy. He could tell from her expression that there was something in his own manner that gave him away. Rather than prolong the process he raised his hands in mock surrender.

'All right. There was something else.'

Sarah's expression hardened. She looked away. That upset Guy more than Smythe's knowing smile.

'I met Brinkman, just briefly. In Glasgow, back in May.'

'What were you doing in Glasgow?' Sarah wondered.

He was in too deep to stop now, so Guy told them. 'I was there to interrogate a German pilot who'd crashed his plane. Except…'

'Except he wasn't just an ordinary German airman, was he?' Smythe prompted. He must have guessed what was coming from the coincidence of the place and the date.

'No. It was Rudolf Hess, the Deputy Fuhrer.'

When Guy had finished there was silence for several seconds.

Then Sarah shook her head sadly. 'And you couldn't tell me this before?'

'I'm sorry. But there's not really much to it. I saw Hess. He spoke to the Duke of Hamilton, not me. Whatever he told Hamilton evidently affected the man. Then Brinkman turned up and I was sent packing.'

'But you think it significant?' Smythe asked.

Guy nodded. 'So now you know everything. Are you going to charge us? Or do you hand us over to the police for that?'

Smythe was all sympathy. 'Before you've had your dinner? I promised you mutton casserole, I think. In any case,' he added, 'I can't charge you with anything or hand you over to anyone.'

'But – ' Guy was confused. Confused and annoyed. 'Look – who the hell are you, then?'

'I know,' Sarah said quietly. 'I recognised you just now. Something you said, the way you said it, your expression.'

Smythe was smiling encouragingly. 'Go on.'

'I saw you in some Shakespeare play on Broadway back in '37. You're Leo Davenport – the actor.'

As soon as she said it, Guy could see that she was right. How could he not have recognised the man? He'd seen him on stage several times, and in more films than he could remember.

'Perhaps I'm less impressive in the flesh,' Smythe – or rather, Davenport – said, as if guessing Guy's thoughts.

'If you're not MI5 or Special Branch, why are you keeping us here?' Guy said. His anger was tempered with curiosity.

'Just because I am an actor doesn't preclude me from working as a policeman,' Davenport retorted.

'Are you a policeman?' Sarah asked.

'Actually, no.'

'Yet you're holding us here at gunpoint.'

He seemed outraged. 'I'm doing no such thing. I invited you to join me at my club, you're welcome to leave at any time.'

'But...' Guy looked again at Davenport's jacket, his right hand thrust into the pocket.

Davenport pulled his hand out. He was holding a fountain pen. 'In case of autograph hunters. Although I suspect you're not after my autograph?' He raised a hopeful eyebrow.

'Hardly,' Sarah said.

'Pity.'

'You said you were pointing a gun at us,' Guy said. The

anger was winning out now, helped by Davenport's unflappable good humour.

'I beg your pardon, but I said nothing of the sort. It was *you* that mentioned a gun.' Davenport opened his hands in apology. 'I might have said that I could shoot the two of you in less than a second, and I stand by that boast. As a hypothetical statement. Obviously I have no intention of shooting anyone just at present.'

'Then we're free to go.'

'Of course.'

Guy stood up, Sarah mirroring him a moment later.

'Although,' Davenport said affably, 'my offer of dinner was quite genuine and the casserole does sound rather tempting, wouldn't you say? So here's the deal...'

Guy hesitated. 'Go on.'

'Let's adjourn for dinner, and I will tell you *my* story. I can promise you, even compared with your own, it's quite a tale.'

CHAPTER 16

The casserole was hot and watery, thin strips of meat eked out with Oxo and carrots. It was better than Davenport had expected, and his guests were positively enthusiastic, despite the circumstances.

Davenport waited until the food had thawed their attitudes a little before he launched into his narrative. He was vague about how he had come to be in France but spared no detail of his courting Streicher and wheedling his way onto the expedition.

'Streicher's group seem to be associated with the Ahnenerbe,' he explained.

'The what?' Sarah Diamond asked.

Davenport scooped up the last of the stew before setting down the spoon and dabbing at his lips with his napkin. 'It's a group within the SS that is responsible for finding evidence that pureblood Germans are the descendants of Nordic gods.'

'You're joking,' Guy said.

'Simplifying a little, but no, I'm not joking,' Davenport told him. 'It's all to do with establishing the credentials of the Aryan master race. But actually, Streicher's group has a rather different remit. They are looking for something else entirely.'

'Which is?'

'Ancient knowledge that will help them win the war.'

The other two lapsed into silence as Davenport described

the archaeological dig in France. He was a good storyteller, though he was careful not to embellish the facts. He described the excavations, breaking into the central chamber and dragging Streicher away to safety. He didn't go into the details of how he got the man clear, and neglected to mention photographing his papers and possessions.

'The mist – what was it? Some sort of gas?' Sarah asked.

'I don't know. But it was lethal, whatever it was. I was lucky to get Streicher out.'

'And then you legged it while he was unconscious?' Pentecross asked.

'That would probably have been the sensible thing to do,' Davenport admitted. 'But no. I thought that since I had saved his life, the Standartenfuhrer might be grateful. Oh, I didn't imagine it would make him any less likely to have me shot when his mission was completed. But I reckoned it might just make him a little more, what shall we say – loquacious?'

'Meaning?' Sarah asked.

'Meaning I took him down to the village and plied him with local wine and cognac for the evening in the hope he'd open up a bit. I thought that even Streicher might feel a little guilty knowing he was going to have to kill his saviour, and that might loosen his tongue. You'll tell a dead man things you'd never dream of mentioning to anyone who might live to repeat it.' He paused to take a sip of water. 'I assume.'

'And were you right in your assumption?' Guy asked. 'Did he tell you what they were really after?'

'Yes and no. He wasn't as explicit as I'd hoped, but he was certainly forthcoming. I told him I could tell he was a veteran of these sorts of excavations, that he was no ordinary soldier. Rather than appeal to a better nature I doubt he possesses, I majored on his vanity instead.'

Sarah nodded. 'Often the best approach.'

Davenport stifled a smile. 'Thank you. It certainly worked for Streicher. He was rather in his cups by the time we were finished, so how much of what he said was due to the drink, how much was him trying to impress me, I don't know. But he told me he'd been all over the world for Himmler in the past ten years. He mentioned Finland and Sweden, a few other places – even Antarctica, though he clammed up about that straight away. But there were two expeditions he did describe in a little more detail. To say that I was intrigued is an understatement...'

'And are you about to intrigue us too?' Guy asked.

Davenport leaned forward in his chair. 'Let me tell you about his expedition to Tibet, back in 1934...'

... The only paths were worn by goats, and the clouds hung low over the snow-covered peaks like smoke.

'Can we trust him?' Hauptsturmfuhrer Klaas asked, nodding at the Tibetan guide as they paused for a short break.

Streicher shrugged. 'There's no one else.' None of the other villagers had even spoken to them. They had all seen the looks of contempt the villagers gave the old man when he led them away. But with the promise of the Nazis' gold he need never return.

Perhaps sensing they were talking about him, the guide smiled across at Streicher. His face was rough and lined like old stone. What teeth he had left were blackened stumps. He said something in his incomprehensible language, and Tormann translated:

'He says it is not far now. The entrance is just a small hole, barely wide enough for a man to enter. We'll be there soon.'

'He's told us that before,' Klaas muttered.

This time he was right. Another hour and they were trudging through shallow snow. The air was thin and it was getting harder to breathe. The hole was a narrow opening in the side of the mountain, partly hidden behind a rock fall. Snow had blown into it, and the guide knelt down to scoop it out with his gnarled hands, gesturing for Streicher and his men to help.

'He might fit through there, but we won't. Not with all our kit,' Klaas pointed out.

'We don't need to,' Streicher told him, shielding his eyes

from the sun with his hand. He was looking up at the rock formation above the opening.

'You think we can dig in from above?'

'Not dig, no.'

The guide was chattering away rapidly to Tormann, who held up his hands to stop him. The man seemed agitated, pointing to the opening in the rock, and then to the men in the expedition.

'He says this is as far as he goes,' Tormann said. 'He wants his gold now. He'll stay and lead us back if we want, but he's not going in there.'

'Why not? Is he scared of the dark?' Klaas laughed, and some of the others joined in.

'No, he says it's… I guess "bad magic" is the closest I can get.'

'Magic?' Streicher said. 'It's supposed to be a burial chamber, not a conjuring show. Does he mean ghosts?'

'I don't know what he means. But he says the reason it's still here, still intact, is because no one goes inside. No one at all.'

Tormann turned back to the guide, who was talking excitedly again, fast as a machine gun.

'Anyone who does go inside,' Tormann said, 'never comes out again. To enter the tomb is to die, or so he says.'

Streicher nodded. 'Well you can reassure him that we aren't going in there.'

The guide listened, forehead creasing in puzzlement before he gabbled his reply.

'He wants to know why we came here. How will we get the treasure if we don't go inside?'

'Tell him he'll find out in a few minutes.' Streicher turned to Klaas. 'Get Schmidt and Huber to dig shallow holes along that ridge.' He pointed up to the area above the opening to the tomb. 'Work out how much explosive we need to put in them. We're not going through the front door of this place. We're going to blow our way in.'

Once he realised what Streicher's men were doing, the

guide became even more agitated. He grabbed Tormann's arm, jabbering away rapidly, hardly letting Tormann reply.

'What's he saying?' Streicher demanded.

Tormann tried to shake the little man off, but the Tibetan clung to him, still talking. What had started as anger now seemed like pleading. The man was scared.

'He says we'll bring down the wrath of the gods,' Tormann said. He had to speak loudly over the guide's guttural barrage. 'We'll wake the... I don't know – it's like the great man. Some tribal king. We'll desecrate his tomb.'

'Fine, we'll desecrate his tomb,' Streicher snapped. 'If the guy wants his cut of the treasure, tell him he can shut up and let us get at it. If not, then shoot him and be done with it.'

The guide finally lapsed into silence, encouraged by the fact Tormann had drawn his Luger and jabbed it into the man's ribs. He sat on a rocky outcrop, watching as Streicher's men finished laying the explosives. He'd shown no sign that he was even aware it was cold on the journey up from the village. Now he was shivering and pale. The Tibetan continued to mutter under his breath, shaking his head. Perhaps he was praying.

Schmidt and Huber finished their work, hurrying back down the mountain, unrolling a thin cable behind them. They all took shelter behind the outcrop where the Tibetan was sitting. Huber took a small detonator from his pack and connected the cable. He had to take his gloves off to tighten the screws holding the stripped wire, blowing on his hands to stop them freezing.

'Better get your friend down from there,' Klaas said.

'He's not my friend.' But Tormann patted the Tibetan's shoulder and spoke to him. The man didn't move, gave no sign he had even heard. So Tormann dragged him back over the rock and down to join them behind it.

'When you're ready, Sturmann Huber,' Streicher said.

Huber nodded. He counted down from three, then twisted the switch on the detonator.

The sound of the blast echoed round the mountain. Debris

ricocheted off the rocks above the soldiers. Streicher barely waited for the sound to die away before he stood up to see what had happened. A deep hole had been scooped out of the side of the mountain, cratering the snow, and leaving a dark opening. He caught a glimpse of stone walls leading back into the darkness.

At first he thought it was snow, thrown up by the detonation. A mist drifting across the opening torn in the landscape. But then he realised the mist was coming from inside the mountain. Like smoke, wafting out – thinning in the air, slowly dissipating.

'What was that?' Klaas asked. 'Did you see it? It looked like fog.'

The Tibetan was standing staring up at the ruptured ground. He was no longer shivering, but his pale eyes were wide. He said something, then slumped down to sit despondently at the base of the rocks.

'What was it?' Streicher asked.

'He says you have disturbed the spirit of the mountain,' Tormann said. 'Its soul is awake and angry.'

'Nonsense,' Streicher said. He saw that the guide was looking up at him. 'It was just… snow,' Streicher told him. 'Or low cloud.'

Tormann translated the Tibetan's mumbled reply.

'Once you let the genii out of his prison, you can never get him back inside.'

Streicher shivered. He looked again at the hole in the side of the mountain. There was no sign now of the smoke or mist or whatever it had been. It was just superstition he told himself. But if they had just released a genii, they'd done it by breaking the bottle.

'That was in the winter of 1934,' Davenport said.

They'd all finished eating. Sarah and Guy were enthralled by Davenport's retelling of Streicher's story.

'They had uncovered a chamber, rather like the one we found in France. That's why Streicher was happy to talk about it, I suppose. He didn't tell me what they found inside, but whatever it was they shipped it back to Germany for analysis.'

'Forgive me,' Guy said. 'This is fascinating, but how is it relevant?'

'Yes,' Sarah agreed. 'What's it got to do with Colonel Brinkman and whatever he's up to? You're not suggesting he's working for the Nazis?'

'Heavens no. Perish the thought.' Davenport smiled. 'But the connection will become clear, I promise you.'

'You mentioned two expeditions that Streicher described,' Guy reminded Davenport.

'I did. Though he was a bit vague about the second.'

'Sounds like he was a bit vague about the first,' Sarah said.

'Indeed. I confess, I'm not sure about the relevance of the other expedition. Or rather, excavation because it was in Germany. Near Freiburg, wherever that is.'

'It's in the Black Forest, I think,' Guy told him.

'Ah, then perhaps I do see the relevance. Or begin to.'

'Yes?' Sarah prompted.

'The fruits of the 1934 expedition were shipped to a castle at Beetlesborg,' Davenport said. 'And that is also in the Black Forest. It could be a coincidence, but...'

'So tell us about this expedition or excavation,' Guy said.

'Don't know much. As I said, Streicher was rather vague, and by that stage rather drunk. But he did tell me that some time in 1936 he and his team were sent to a part of the forest near Freiburg, to assist with an aircraft crash.'

'You mean to find out what caused it?' Guy asked.

'No, Streicher has no expertise in that sort of thing. From what he said, they were told to treat the area round the crash like an archaeological site, and excavate the remains of the plane. They didn't want to know what caused the crash – perhaps they knew that already. But they were keen to discover everything they could about the aircraft itself, and what was inside it.'

Sarah leaned forward. 'And what *was* inside it?'

'I'm afraid I have no idea. Our discussions rather petered out at that stage.'

'Shame.'

'Yes. Though I can take a guess at what they found in Tibet.'

'Go on,' Guy urged.

'Well, at the French site they were most interested in the burial chamber, and in particular the sarcophagus containing the body of the chieftain.'

'You think they found something similar in Tibet?' Guy said.

'I do.'

'And they shipped the French sarcophagus back to Germany, just like the one from Tibet,' Sarah assumed.

Davenport sucked air through his teeth. 'Well, yes and no. That is, they think they did.'

'What do you mean?'

'I mean that someone removed the crate from the train it was on and sent it somewhere else.'

'You?' Guy guessed.

Davenport made a point of inspecting his fingernails. 'I really couldn't say. But I can't help wondering, as they obviously went to a lot of trouble to find that sarcophagus...'

'What's really inside it?' Sarah asked.

'Of course. But I also wonder what they'll do when they find they no longer have it.'

CHAPTER 17

The sun was setting behind the western towers of the castle. Standing on the battlements, looking across the main courtyard, Hoffman thought it was a strange contrast. The stark blackness of the castle wall silhouetted against the diffuse red of the sky.

Beside him, Streicher wiped his forehead with a handkerchief. It was unlike Streicher to show nerves, Hoffman thought. But then standing with the Reichsfuhrer at a time like this was enough to make anyone nervous. Hoffman was aware his own hands were curled into tight claws behind his back.

The distant rumble of the approaching trucks jolted them all out of their reverie. Hoffman fancied he heard the faintest exhalation of relief from Streicher.

Himmler checked his watch. 'A few minutes early,' he said. It sounded more like a criticism than a compliment.

'They have come a long way,' Streicher said.

'Through space and through time,' Himmler said. 'is that not so, Sturmbannfuhrer Hoffman?'

'As you say, Herr Reichsfuhrer.' He forced a thin smile. 'As we examine these artefacts, we will also be looking back into history.'

'And forward,' Himmler said. 'To the glorious future.' The setting sun was reflected in his glasses as he turned, staining them for a moment blood red. 'Now we can build on the work

131

done at Beetlesborg, the discoveries from Freiburg and Tibet and…' He broke off to watch the convoy enter the castle.

There were four trucks in all. They drew up alongside each other in the vast courtyard. SS soldiers jumped down from inside, lowering the tailgates of the trucks and starting to unload the crates.

'Very well,' Himmler decided. 'It is time to unpack our destiny.' He led the way along the narrow walkway to the nearest tower, and then down winding stone steps.

'You think the training will take as long this time?' Hoffman asked as they descended. 'Almost two years last time…'

'But last time, we did not know what we had. We were still learning its secrets.'

An area had been cleared in one of the storerooms close to the main laboratory. Several large crates had already been brought in. Himmler and Hoffman watched as more arrived. Streicher had a sheaf of papers. Together with one of the SS soldiers, he went from crate to crate marking them off on the papers.

'Is that all?' he demanded when the last crate had been brought in.

'That is all of them, yes, sir.'

Streicher frowned, checking the manifest again.

Himmler stepped forward. His voice was worryingly quiet. 'A problem, Standartenfuhrer?'

'We are short of one crate. I'm certain it will turn up. Or perhaps it is an error in the paperwork.' Streicher double-checked the papers. 'It is not important. Some minor artefacts unearthed near to the site. I suspect we would have discarded them as superfluous anyway.'

'Then this saves us the effort,' Himmler said, bloodless lips curling into the merest hint of a smile. 'Now – where is the Ubermensch?'

'Of course.' Streicher snapped to attention. 'Crate A-17.'

The SS private next to Streicher also snapped to attention before hurrying to find the crate. Other soldiers helped, checking the labels pasted to the wooden sides.

'Here!' one of them called.

Himmler hurried over, his eagerness evident in every step. Hoffman followed, picking his way round the other crates and boxes. One of the soldiers had produced a crowbar and stood ready to prise the top off the crate. At a nod from Streicher, he forced the end of the crowbar under the lid, and heaved down on the other end.

The crate looked, Hoffman thought, unnervingly like a coffin. The wood creaked and then splintered as the lid was forced off. Another soldier grabbed it and pulled. Nails screeched in protest as they tore loose. Straw spilled out.

'We use the straw to pack the artefacts securely,' Streicher said unnecessarily as a soldier pulled away handfuls of straw to reveal the contents nestled beneath.

A metal door, removed from the main entrance to the burial chamber.

Streicher frowned. Himmler's eyes narrowed behind his glasses before turning accusingly towards Streicher.

'Apologies, Reichsfuhrer...' Streicher was leafing quickly through the papers. 'A-17, that's right.'

Hoffman stepped forward to tap the label on the side of the crate. 'A-17,' he agreed. 'Your list must be wrong.'

'But that door should be in...' Streicher turned several sheets. '... B-09.'

'Perhaps that's where we shall find what we are looking for,' Himmler said. There was no mistaking the edge to his voice.

'B-09, sir,' a soldier called from nearby.

'Too small,' Streicher said. His forehead was sheened with perspiration.

'Open it anyway,' Himmler ordered.

The crate was the size of a small suitcase. Again, it was full of straw. Streicher had already turned away, but Hoffman pulled away the straw to see what was inside. Broken pottery, a tarnished brooch, two silver goblets.

He lifted out a bronze bracelet. It was heavy, inlaid with an intricate tracery of silver lines. Unlike the other artefacts in the crate, it was in pristine condition. There was no sign of rust or tarnish. It could have been made just days ago. The inside of the bracelet was studded with small indentations. A hinged clasp allowed it to open in half and then close round the wearer's wrist.

'Ah, well done, Sturmbannfuhrer.'

He had not been aware of Himmler watching him. He handed the bracelet to the Reichsfuhrer without comment. Himmler examined it, nodding slowly. He too was careful to hold the bracelet by the edges.

Across the room, Streicher was supervising the opening of another crate.

'The French Resistance make a habit of changing shipping labels,' Hoffman said. 'They alter timetables, swap manifests... Anything they can to disrupt the smooth running of the Reich.'

Himmler walked over to join Streicher at the latest crate. 'May I suggest that rather than trying to make sense of your list, you simply open all the crates. Start with the largest – we can see that the Ubermensch isn't in most of these.'

'Perhaps it isn't in any of them,' Hoffman offered. 'It's a small step from disruption to theft.'

Himmler nodded thoughtfully. 'Then let us hope they do not know what they have.'

'It's here somewhere,' Streicher insisted. 'It has to be. There are half a dozen crates large enough. It must be in one of them.'

It became increasingly obvious that the crate they wanted was not among the others. Streicher's men were almost quaking as they opened the last of the larger crates. Hoffman might have found their discomfiture amusing if the situation wasn't so dangerous. Who knew what Himmler would do, deprived of the replacement Ubermensch.

In the event, to Streicher's obvious surprise, the Reichsfuhrer waved a hand in the air as if to say: 'These things happen.'

'We do have the bracelet,' Hoffman said.

Himmler nodded. 'The delay is unfortunate, but as you say,

we have the bracelet.' He held it up, so that the light from the bare light bulbs hanging from the ceiling reflected off the bronze and silver.

'Forgive me, Reichsfuhrer.' Streicher dabbed at his forehead again. It seemed more than nerves – Hoffman wondered if perhaps he was coming down with a fever. 'I don't know what could have happened.'

'It is no matter,' Himmler said. 'With this we can track down the Ubermensch.'

'With a bracelet?' Streicher asked.

But the Reichsfuhrer had already turned away and was striding from the room.

Streicher turned to Hoffman. He rubbed at his own wrist through the sleeve of his jacket, an instinctive, nervous movement. 'Is he serious?'

'Completely,' Hoffman said. He wondered how much Streicher actually knew of what he had been searching for. What he would make of the events about to unfold. 'But first, we need to hold a séance.'

The coffee was hot but very bitter.

'How did you become interested in Colonel Brinkman?' Guy asked Davenport. 'I don't see the overlap between our stories and yours.'

'Don't you?' Davenport sipped at his own coffee, and made a face before setting it aside. 'Someone told me they make this stuff from acorns now. I can believe it. So what do you think Brinkman's team is doing?'

'Something secret, obviously,' Sarah said. 'They warned me not to talk about the aircraft I saw. But whether it's ours or theirs...'

'Theirs,' Guy said. 'I think that's what a UDT is. That's what they were tracking at Fighter Command when they threw us all out of the Ops Room.'

'Could still be a secret plane of ours, couldn't it?'

'Then they'd have known it was going to be there and cleared the area. You'd never have been allowed to fly there.'

Davenport was nodding, like a teacher encouraging his class. 'That seems logical.'

'You mentioned a crashed aircraft, that this Colonel Streicher excavated in the Black Forest.'

'But why would they excavate their own aircraft?' Sarah asked. 'And what's it got to do with Brinkman? Or that base at Bletchley?'

Guy counted off what they knew on his fingers, thinking aloud. 'Experimental German aircraft. One crashed back in 1936 and they wanted to find out why. We detect these craft. Bletchley is some sort of tracking station, I guess.'

'But then why doesn't everyone know about them?' Sarah said. 'If it's an experimental plane why was one over Britain? And if it's in service, how can it still be a secret?'

'And what's it got to do with Hess?' Guy added. 'If Brinkman is responsible for, what – finding out about German secret aircraft? Then why's he interested in Hess?'

'Would Hess know about the project?'

'He didn't mention anything about aircraft. Just some old book.'

'*The Coming Race*?' Davenport asked.

'That was it,' Guy said.

'Have you read it?'

'I'd never even heard of it.'

Davenport sighed. 'Pity. There is one possibility you've not thought of.'

'And what's that?' Sarah asked.

'That this experimental secret aircraft, if that's what it is, wasn't developed by either us or the Germans.'

Sarah frowned. 'It's American?'

Davenport smiled. 'I suspect you are still missing the point. You're thinking too narrowly.'

Guy was going to ask him what he meant. But before he got the chance, there was a commotion outside the room. The sound of heavy footsteps. Raised voices. The steward, Charles, still dressed immaculately but looking flustered, hurried in.

'Mr Davenport, sir!'

Davenport got to his feet. 'What is it, Charles?'

'I'm sorry, sir – I couldn't stop them.'

Behind him, several more figures entered the room. Guy recognised the first of them immediately – it was David Alban.

'Oh, how tiresome,' Davenport said. 'That's all right, Charles. You can leave this to me.'

Alban spared Charles the barest glance as he pushed past. His expression was somewhere between anger and satisfaction.

'Well you two have led me a merry dance, I must say. But now it's time to face the music rather than dance to it.' He gave an exaggerated sigh. 'And please don't try to make a run for it. You'll only increase the trouble you're in.'

Guy looked at Sarah. She was very pale, but she looked determined. He hoped he was showing as much resolve, but he could feel his stomach dropping away. If they were lucky this would end with them locked up. How had he let things go so far? How had he got her involved in this? They should have backed off, let things lie. Damn his curiosity!

Davenport was still standing in front of Alban. He made a point of clearing his throat, then waited until Alban turned to him. There was a flash of recognition in the MI5 man's eyes. Maybe something more than that, Guy thought through his fog of self-recrimination. Anxiety, perhaps?

'I think you've made your point,' Davenport said, his voice calm, quiet, reasonable. 'We're all suitably impressed. Now why don't you run along.'

'You keep out of this,' Alban snapped. 'I've no argument with you. Let's keep it that way. But these two are under arrest.'

Sarah made to stand up. Davenport shot her a look that told her to stay put, and she sank back on to her chair. Guy wasn't sure his legs would take his weight right now.

'May I ask the charges?' Davenport said.

Alban glared. 'Treason, I should think. They followed a senior officer in pursuit of his duty. They infiltrated a secure facility – '

'You mean they went with Colonel Brinkman to Bletchley,'

Davenport cut in. He turned to gesture at Guy and Sarah. 'These two people are with me. As of this morning they are working for Station Z, reporting direct to Colonel Brinkman.' He pulled a folded paper from his coat pocket and thrust it at Alban. 'Read this, please.'

Warily, Alban took the paper, unfolded it, and read it. The colour drained slowly from his ruddy face. 'This can't be right,' he said.

Davenport reached out and took the paper back. 'That is Colonel Brinkman's signature. You can phone him if you need confirmation, though I doubt he'll be very impressed to learn you can't read.'

Alban stared back at Davenport for several seconds. Then without a word, he turned on his heel and stamped from the room. The other men followed without comment.

The sound of their footsteps on the stairs outside had died away before Guy found his voice. 'Thank you. That was some bluff.'

Davenport seemed amused. 'Who said I was bluffing?'

'Well, you sure convinced them,' Sarah said. 'But how did you get that forged paper?'

'Forged paper?' he seemed scandalised. 'I can assure you it is quite genuine.'

Pentecross felt as if the world was spinning around him. 'But – that would mean...'

'It means I work for Colonel Brinkman, yes,' Davenport said. 'He asked me to have a little chat with you both to see if I thought you could be useful. You're certainly tenacious, but he wondered if it would be advantageous to bring you into the fold rather than have you trying to sneak in under the fence, as it were. For what it's worth, my assessment is that it would. Miss Manners will have your transfer orders out by breakfast tomorrow, so if you could both report to Station Z at oh-nine-hundred sharp, that would be helpful. You know where it is. We'll be expecting you.'

CHAPTER 18

Everywhere was stone. The pillars that held up the vaulted ceiling, the floor, the circular table in the heart of the chamber. Dark smoke curled from the flame of a black candle that stood in the round recess at the centre of the table. Other candles nestled in niches set into the pillars and the walls. Flickering lights and pools of shadow conspired to hide the dimensions and shape of the chamber.

The table was huge – large enough for twelve figures to be arranged round it. They lay on low metal-framed beds, their feet close to the table and heads angled away from it so that if they were somehow raised up, they would be looking at the black candle.

But they barely moved. Eyes closed, faint breath misting the cold subterranean air and susurrating like a faint winter breeze. Candlelight glinted on the glass vessels upended on metal stands beside each bed, reflections distorted by the clear liquid that dripped down tubes and into the left forearm of each of the sleepers. The right arm of each sleeper was folded across the chest, over the single thin sheet that covered but didn't disguise the nakedness of the figures. Six male, six female. Several were elderly, one was a boy of about twelve. Most were white, fair-haired, discovered in the ranks of the Hitler Youth and its associated League of German Girls or recruited from the SS itself.

Georg Kruger wore a white coat over his black uniform. As he moved, the candles cast broken shadows of him across the floor and the table. Angular and sharp, like his features – slightly hooked nose, high forehead, thinning grey hair. He went from each bed to the next, checking the drip was properly in place, gently opening an eyelid with his thumb to see if the pupil was dilated, listening to the rhythm of the breathing...

Satisfied, Kruger paused for a last look at the sleepers, then nodded and strode quickly from the room.

Hoffman stood with Himmler at the back of the chamber. The acrid candle smoke caught in Hoffman's throat, and he struggled not to cough. They watched but took no part in the ceremony. It never failed to astonish Hoffman that these rituals actually worked. He had not been there when they first linked to the original Ubermensch, but he had read the file. He'd seen the film.

No one filmed it this time, but Hoffman suspected the woman who now entered the room had watched the first ceremony several times in the last few hours. The Seer was old and stooped. The robes she wore looked like a witch's cowl. She shuffled along arthritically, struggling to keep the red velvet cushion she carried level. Making sure the bronze bracelet that rested on it did not slip off.

Behind her, more cloaked figures entered the chamber. They positioned themselves round the outside of the circle of sleepers. The Seer moved slowly from bed to bed, holding the bracelet on its cushion level with her glazed eyes. Mumbling under her breath.

The other figures joined in, quietly at first but louder and louder until the words became a chant that echoed off the stone walls. The words were guttural and harsh, nothing that Hoffman recognised.

'It is interesting, isn't it?' Himmler said quietly to Hoffman, not taking his eyes off the Seer. 'Is the bracelet a charm, to be awoken by the intonation of a spell? Or are we witnessing a technology so advanced it is controlled by voice, and the words of power are no more mystical than the press of a switch or the positioning of a lever?'

The chanting faded. The Seer placed the bracelet on its cushion on the table. She stepped back, intoning one last phrase. The bracelet flickered and shone in the candlelight. As her words died away, the candle flame leaped upwards. Hoffman felt the heat of it even across the chamber. Then the flame went out.

A moment later, the rest of the candles snuffed out as if an abrupt wind had gusted from the central table. Sudden darkness. The only light was from the bracelet – still flickering and shining, as if reflecting the light from candle flames that were no longer there.

Harsh white overhead lamps glared on, a sudden contrast to the guttering candles. In an instant the chamber was transformed from shadowy and inchoate to bright and defined. The robed figures now seemed out of place. They bowed and left, the Seer hobbling after them. She paused in the doorway, looking back awkwardly at Hoffman and Himmler. Her face was wizened, the same texture as the weathered stone wall behind her.

Himmler ignored her. The woman's job was done and he had probably dismissed her from his thoughts already. 'Hoffman,' he prompted.

Hoffman clicked his heels in salute, and marched to the table. 'Do we know which one?'

The answer came from the old woman still lingering in the doorway. 'It could be any of them. Or none of them.' Her voice was as cracked and worn as her features.

Again, Himmler ignored her. Hoffman glanced across to see her shuffle out. The door swung slowly shut behind her.

'Start with the boy,' Himmler instructed.

Hoffman lifted the bracelet from its cushion, careful to hold it only by the edges. Even in the bright room he could see the inner glow, as if light was filtering through the silver tracery. He expected it to be warm, but it was cold to the touch. He sprung the bracelet open, and turned to the boy in the bed beside the table.

Himmler watched impassively as Hoffman lifted the boy's right hand, and closed the bracelet over the thin, pale wrist.

Nothing.

Himmler nodded as if he had expected this. He made no comment, so Hoffman moved to the next bed. A young woman lay beneath the white sheet. Her features were soft and delicate, framed by a mass of blonde curls. Hoffman lifted her hand from her chest, exposing the shape of her body beneath, the sheet moving slightly as she breathed, breasts rising and falling. He hoped it wouldn't be her, holding his own breath as he closed the bracelet round her wrist.

There was a slight stutter in her breathing. But then the rhythm was restored. She slept on, oblivious.

Hoffman repeated the process with the elderly man in the next bed. His wrist was dry and bony, like a brittle stick.

Himmler stepped closer to watch. 'He was a farmer, you know.'

No reaction to the bracelet. Hoffman moved to the next bed.

'His wife came to us, or rather to the Gestapo. She said he was a witch because he always knew what the weather would be like the next day, even the next week. The experience of a good farmer, you might say... But someone was alert enough to give him the test. And here he is.'

The woman in the next bed was almost as old. Still nothing.

'Ah now this man is interesting,' Himmler said. He stood at the end of the bed, by the young man's head. The sleeper's hair was dark and longer than the other men's. He was unshaven, a stubbly beard sprouting from his chin. His eyebrows were dark and heavy.

'Not a volunteer,' Hoffman guessed.

'An Italian, I forget where from exactly. But he was reading Tarot cards in the local bar. When his readings started to come true...'

'He was sent here,' Hoffman said. As he spoke, he felt the bracelet tremble slightly in his fingers. He almost dropped it. 'It could be him.'

'Let us see.'

Hoffman lifted the man's wrist. His forearm was tanned, coarse with dark hair. Hoffman closed the bracelet on the man's wrist, and let it fall back across his chest. His heart leaped in his chest as the man's eyes snapped open. He stared up at Hoffman, his face filled with confusion and terror. His mouth twisted open, letting out a sudden shriek of pain.

The bracelet glowed brighter, clamping tightly round the man's wrist. Sharp spines sprang out from inside the bracelet, curving back inwards to clamp into the man's wrist – digging deep into his flesh. Blood oozed out, running from each incision, soaking into the sheet.

Then the man's eyes glazed over. He sat up, the bloodied sheet peeling away from his chest and pooling round his waist. His right hand jerked and spasmed, moving across the folds of thin cotton, back and forth.

Himmler hurried to an alcove, returning with several sheets of thick cartridge paper and a pencil. He pushed the paper beneath the man's hand, and thrust the pencil between his fingers.

The hand continued to move across the paper. The man stared into space. Blood congealed round the bracelet, smearing over the paper as the man shaded it black and red.

'Just darkness,' Hoffman said. 'No detail. No image. Perhaps the connection hasn't worked?'

'Perhaps,' Himmler said. He watched transfixed, the light from above a glare on the lenses of his spectacles, so that it looked as though his eyes were shining white.

'It might be like a radio wave,' Hoffman went on. 'If the bracelet isn't receiving properly… We had one Viewer who connected to the first Ubermensch without the need for a bracelet.'

'I remember,' Himmler said evenly. 'His images were vague… distorted.'

'Could the bracelet be damaged?'

Himmler shook his head. 'No. It is working perfectly. He draws what the Ubermensch sees.'

'He draws nothing,' Hoffman said. The paper was almost completely shaded.

'He sees darkness. That is good.'

'It is?'

'It suggests the Ubermensch has not yet awoken.'

In darkness so complete it was palpable, the same words echoed in emptiness. The voice was different, but the guttural sounds, the expression, the *shape* of the language was just as when the Seer spoke the litany at Wewelsburg.

A tiny blink of light in the dark. The faintest shape of a symbol glowed into life, like an ancient rune cut out of a black curtain to let light through from another world.

A second shape gleamed beside the first. Then another... A series of runic symbols stretching out as if carved into the darkness itself.

Words... Phrases...

Instructions.

CHAPTER 19

Working far beneath the main building, Elizabeth Archer had no way of knowing what was happening above her, and with no windows she easily lost track of the time. It was not unusual for her to be the last person working at the British Museum. Many of the staff had been shipped out along with the artefacts. Plans had been drawn up for 'evacuating' the museum's contents back in 1934 – which Elizabeth thought was rather forward thinking for an institution dedicated to looking into the past.

It was after midnight when she finally finished cataloguing a set of ancient scrolls unearthed in a remote region of India. She made a token effort to tidy her desk before leaving. The electric lights snapped off instantly at the press of a switch plunging the cavernous space beneath the Great Court into darkness. When Elizabeth first came here, it was lit by gas – a softer, less invasive light that gave the whole place a more moody and dangerous atmosphere. There was something about the bright whiteness of the electric lights that dispelled the feeling of history and age. It reduced everything to the more commonplace and mundane.

But she knew from experience that there was little here that was common or usual. As she made her way carefully up the steep steps, holding on to the metal railing set into the brickwork, she remembered how she used to run up and down these stairs. It didn't seem that long ago. She didn't feel any older, not really. Just slower. But she looked at young Edward – now in his seventies – and she saw in him a reflection of her own mortality. Saw in him memories of younger, happier times before she was widowed...

The muffled thump of falling bombs and the constant drone of aircraft high above grew louder and more distinct as she neared ground level. She had hoped to be away before the bombing started. Now she would have to forget the idea of a taxi and get to the tube. Deep in the cellarage Elizabeth was probably safer than in a shelter, but up here...

As she locked the door to the stairway behind her, Elizabeth became aware of another sound, closer than the bombs. A scraping, banging sound from somewhere nearby – one of the storerooms, probably. It would be just like Eddie to spend the night unpacking the latest acquisitions, keen to see what had arrived. Perhaps it was whatever Davenport had brought in.

A dark figure, barely more than a silhouette, hurried towards her down the corridor.

'Mrs Archer – is it you making that racket?'

It was one of the night staff. Several of them had a rota to keep watch in case a bomb hit the museum, ready to raise the alarm and act as firemen. His features became clear as he moved under a light – receding, dark hair and a stubby nose. Harry, she thought his name was.

'Not guilty,' she said. 'It's probably Young Eddie.'

Harry shook his head. 'Mr Hopkins left over an hour ago.'

The sound started up again – hammering, and then a splintering of wood.

'It's coming from down here...'

Harry hurried to one of the doors and threw it open. Moonlight shone in through a skylight. An orange glow lit the lower edges of the glass as tonight's fires began to take hold.

'No,' Harry said as Elizabeth reached for the light switch. 'Blackout, remember.'

There was enough light streaming in from the moon and the bombings for them to see that the room was empty. Or rather, it was full – of boxes and crates, shelves weighed down by papers and books and artefacts. But there was no one there.

Harry walked over to a wooden packing crate that stood in the middle of the floor. It was about ten feet long, a yard wide and just as high. Large enough for someone to be hiding behind it. Warily, Harry walked round it. He shook his head – no one.

'This wasn't here last night. It's come from Lisbon according to the stamp.'

'Delivered this afternoon,' Elizabeth told him. It was evidently Davenport's artefact.

She made to follow Harry from the room when there was another loud thump from behind her. They both turned back. The crate was shuddering, shaking as something knocked hard against the inside. The wood of the lid splintered.

'What the hell?' Harry put his arm out to stop Elizabeth going closer. 'Better keep well back, miss.'

Another massive blow raised the lid several inches, nails squealing as they pulled from the wood.

'Must be an animal,' Harry said.

'I don't think so,' Elizabeth told him. 'We should get out of here. Lock the door.'

Her words were drowned out by the crash of the wooden lid shattering. Splinters of wood flew across the room. Harry cried out and threw his hands up in front of his face. Elizabeth felt something sharp scrape past her cheek.

Without the lid to hold the crate together, the sides fell away, revealing the plain dark stone of the rough-hewn sarcophagus inside. The heavy lid juddered and scraped. The weight and force of it lifting had been sufficient to shatter the crate – what the hell was inside, Elizabeth wondered.

As she watched, transfixed, the lid moved again, pushed up from the inside, revealing a strip of darkness.

The Italian was designated Number Nine. He sat at a plain stone table in the crypt-like room lit only by the guttering oil lamps. He hadn't moved since he was brought here, which Kruger knew meant that what he saw had not changed. When

147

that happened, he would draw a new picture. If it ever did change.

Kruger stifled a yawn. There was no point in him staying. He would send one of the junior technicians to check every half hour or so. He turned to leave.

And as he turned, he heard the familiar scratch of pencil on paper.

Number Nine was drawing. Again, the image was of darkness. But now there was a strip of light.

The lid of the coffin crashed to the floor. The solid stone split across under the impact. But Elizabeth barely noticed. Her attention was focused on the coffin itself. On the hands that had hurled the heavy lid aside.

Beside her, Harry crossed himself. 'Sweet Jesus.'

'Hardly,' she murmured in reply.

Flashes of light blazed across the skylight. A plane crashed past, engulfed in flames.

In the flickering orange glow, a figure was hauling itself out of the casket. Withered, wrinkled hands gripped the rim of the coffin. Ancient, translucent skin stretched tight across the bones as the fingers scrabbled to get a grip.

Then the face, rising out of the sarcophagus and staring at Elizabeth.

Number Nine's hand worked rapidly across the paper. The next picture showed the moon, almost full, shining down through a casement. It was shoved aside as the Italian started on another sheet.

Hoffman arrived in time to see this next picture.

'The Reichsfuhrer has been alerted,' Kruger told him.

Hoffman nodded, staring down at the picture taking form in front of them. Two figures stared out of the image, their sketched expressions a mixture of fear and disbelief. A man with receding dark hair and a stubby nose, and an elderly woman.

*

The ancient robes had rotted to rags, barely covering the figure's withered, emaciated body. The ridges of ribs thrust through. Bony fingers clutched the air. The remains of leather sandals fell away as it climbed out of the sarcophagus.

But its face was the worst. A sudden burst of flame right above the skylight lit up the room, drenching the nightmare figure in blood red lightning. Flesh the texture of rotten fruit, empty eyes sunken into a head that was little more than a skull. Wisps of grey hair clung to the scalp. Blackened, broken teeth were visible through the cracked, drawn lips.

Elizabeth took a step backwards as the figure shuffled towards them. But Harry remained rooted to the spot. He was incredibly pale, shivering with fear. A withered hand reached out for him, and he let out a cry.

It was choked off abruptly.

A hand clamped on a neck. The man's face screaming above, eyes bulging in terror.

The paper thrust aside and on to the next image.

A body lying on the floor. Bare, skeletal feet beside the man's head. The decayed leather strap of a broken sandal trailing from one foot.

Number Nine pushed the paper away, hardly pausing before starting on the next image. The old woman's startled face – up close. A withered hand punching towards her.

The hand was dry, like forgotten autumn leaves. Elizabeth reeled back from the blow, colliding with the frame of the door. Her legs gave way beneath her and she fell. The shrivelled, desiccated figure loomed over her, moonlight streaming round it. The rhythmic percussion of a stick of bombs growing louder as they approached. Her vision blurred, faded… Died.

The sound cut out.

Everything went black.

The old woman's body was a crumpled heap on the ground.

Number Nine pushed the paper away. Kruger pulled the

pencil from the man's cold fingers, pushing another sharper one into place immediately.

The pencil sped over the paper. The shape of a dimly lit corridor began to form, grey scratches across the paper. Impressions and ideas rather than sharp details as the Ubermensch moved quickly along the corridor. Through heavy doors, the hint of wood grain sketched into place, out into the night and the ruined city.

CHAPTER 20

It was with a mixture of nervousness and excitement that Sarah Diamond travelled into the centre of London the next morning. She couldn't imagine what Pauline Gower would say to her transfer. Her reaction was sure to be extreme – but whether extreme anger and resentment or extreme indifference Sarah couldn't guess.

That was a potential problem for later though – one that Colonel Brinkman could deal with, hopefully. And at the back of Sarah's mind was the possibility that she would return to the Air Transport Auxiliary in due course anyway. She couldn't bear the thought of being away from flying for very long. Perhaps she could continue to fly for the ATA occasionally while working for Station Z.

Once she knew what Station Z was and what it did, she'd have a better idea.

For now, though, she stood across the street from the offices, just as she had when watching them clandestinely. She was expected, she had every right to be here. But she felt as nervous as a schoolgirl on a first date. What would she find? Once through the doors, despite her hopes of continuing to work with the ATA, she knew that there would be no turning back. It would be a threshold crossed in more ways than one.

So she stood and watched, and waited for Guy Pentecross. There was a calmness and sensibility about the man that had touched something in Sarah, even though it was a contrast to her own impulsive personality.

'I wasn't sure whether to wear uniform.'

The unexpected sound of his voice made her heart jump, and she spun round.

'God, you startled me.'

'Sorry.' Guy smiled apologetically. He was wearing his Foreign Office suit, like the day before. Or one very similar. Sarah hadn't even considered putting on her ATA uniform – it was designed for the practicality, and chill, of flying rather than office work.

'I guess you're as wary of going inside as I am,' Guy said.

'No,' she said quickly. 'I was just...' She stopped and laughed. Who was she kidding? 'Yes,' she admitted. 'I have no idea what we're going to discover, what we'll end up doing.'

His eyes glinted. 'Exciting, isn't it?'

'Yes,' she agreed, but hesitantly. Then, more confidently, she decided: 'Yes, it is.'

In the event, they never made it inside. They crossed the road, only to meet Colonel Brinkman hurrying out of the door.

'Come with me,' he said, without breaking step.

Sarah and Guy fell in behind him.

'Where are we going?' Sarah asked.

'British Museum.'

'I didn't know it was open,' Guy said.

'It's not.'

'So if we're not going to see some*thing* we must be going to see some*one*,' Guy said.

'Absolutely right,' Brinkman agreed. 'Leo Davenport just telephoned. He says Elizabeth Archer was attacked last night.'

With no further explanation as to who Elizabeth Archer might be or why Davenport was at the British Museum, Brinkman increased his pace. Sarah and Guy exchanged glances and hurried to keep up. Although it was a little way, it was undoubtedly quicker to walk than to try to drive through the remnants of the previous night's bombing.

*

Brinkman evidently knew his way around the museum. There was a smell of dust and age in the air. Sarah caught glimpses of empty galleries, and of burned out rooms where incendiaries had fallen.

'It's taken a bit of a beating,' Guy said quietly.

Sarah didn't reply. There was nothing really to say. So much of London had 'taken a bit of a beating'. She didn't consider the city to be her home, not really. But she felt for it like it was a living thing, just as she felt for the people who did live here.

The building was a rabbits' warren of corridors and stairways. They descended deeper and deeper below the main structure until they emerged into a vast cavernous space all but filled with crates and shelves, boxes and storage cabinets.

The sound of Davenport's voice drifted to them from somewhere out of sight. Its soothing tone was punctuated by the sharper timbre of a woman's voice. As Brinkman led them through the maze of shelves and cabinets, the words became clearer.

'I am fine, thank you, Leo. Now please stop fussing and let me get on.'

She didn't look fine. Brinkman introduced the elderly lady with Davenport as Elizabeth Archer. She forced a polite smile, but Sarah was sure it was painful, her face was so bruised. Around the purple discolouration, she looked pale. She remained seated behind her desk, and Sarah suspected she didn't trust herself to stand up. What had happened to her?

Davenport answered the unspoken question: 'Elizabeth was attacked last night. As she was leaving here.'

'My God – who by?' Guy asked.

'I keep telling Leo, I'm quite all right. Poor Harry was *killed* by the brute. I was merely... inconvenienced.'

'We need to get you checked over,' Brinkman said.

'No,' Elizabeth Archer told him, 'we don't. I'm a bit shaken, I don't deny it. Bruised, but it looks worse than it is.'

'Should we tell the police?' Sarah asked.

'Absolutely not,' Brinkman said immediately. 'This was no ordinary attack.'

'Then – what?' Guy demanded. 'The poor woman was badly injured, however brave a face she puts on it.'

'"The poor woman" has a name, you know,' she said.

'I'm sorry, Miss Archer.'

'It's Mrs. But I'll thank you to call me Elizabeth.' She turned to Brinkman. 'He should be easy enough to find. The young lady's suggestion of involving the police may not be such a bad notion.' She shook her head. '*I'm* doing it now, I'm sorry. I assume "the young lady" has a name too.'

'You still haven't said who attacked you,' Guy pointed out once Davenport had introduced them.

'The man from the coffin, from the burial site,' Elizabeth said, as if this had been obvious from the start. From Guy's expression, Sarah knew he was no more enlightened than she was.

'It was my fault,' Davenport said. 'I shouldn't have had that thing brought here.'

'You weren't to know he'd suddenly wake up.'

Sarah tried again: 'Who?'

'Oh, I'm sorry,' Elizabeth said. 'A dead chieftain from a hidden Bronze Age burial site in France. Probably about four thousand years old. He certainly looked it.' She shuddered.

'And he – woke up?' Guy said, amazed.

'He certainly did. I take it you've not been with Station Z for very long.'

'Our first morning,' Sarah admitted. What the hell had they got themselves into?

'Well, if he's wandering about in the open, someone should report it soon enough,' Brinkman said. 'Are you sure I can't get a doctor over to check you're all right?'

'Quite sure. The doctors of London have more urgent cases than a bruised old lady who was knocked over and bumped her head, I'm certain of that.'

'This Bronze Age chieftain, whoever he is,' Guy said to Davenport. 'He was in the sarcophagus you shipped back? The one you wanted to stop the Germans getting hold of?'

Davenport nodded. 'That's the fellow. Beginning to wish I

hadn't bothered.'

'Your point?' Brinkman asked.

'Two points, really. First, why did he wake up now?'

'I was wondering the same thing,' Elizabeth said. 'Could be the change of environment, though I think that's unlikely.'

'External factors then,' Davenport said.

'I think so,' Brinkman agreed. 'Someone woke him up, simple as that.'

'What's the second point?' Sarah asked.

Guy shrugged. 'Another question, really. Why did the Germans want him? I mean, did they know what was going to happen?'

'I suspect it may be the Germans that woke him up,' Brinkman said. 'He's been sent his orders.'

'Orders?' Sarah echoed. 'You mean, like they sent him a radio message or something?'

'I doubt it was anything so direct,' Brinkman said. 'Now, since I'm obviously surplus to requirements here, I'll head back to base.' He turned to Guy and Sarah. 'Not you. You can both stay here with Davenport and Mrs Archer. It's as good a place to start as any. Elizabeth – show them what was recovered from Shingle Bay.'

Across the street from the British Museum, a thin figure stood huddled inside an ill-fitting raincoat it had found half-buried in the rubble. It kept to the shadows, features shaded and indistinct. Its bare legs and feet, protruding from the coat, were bony and discoloured, etched with wrinkles and scratches.

It had watched the three people arrive at the museum, had noted the sense of purpose and urgency of step in the tall uniformed man who led them. When the same man emerged again, alone, the Ubermensch followed.

It did not feel the cold, sharp stones under its feet as it picked its way through the remains of a building. All its attention was on the man ahead. It stopped for nothing, pushing aside occasional other pedestrians to maintain its course.

When the man it was following finally entered a large office building, the Ubermensch positioned itself on the opposite side of the road. It stood close to the spot that Guy Pentecross and Sarah Diamond had chosen to keep watch, and waited patiently. It would wait for ever if it had to, or until it received new orders or identified a useful source of information.

A light rain dappled the pavement. The Ubermensch turned to look upwards. It had not felt the rain on its face for so long... Now the moisture soaked into the dry skin, filling it out a little, giving it fresher colour.

Picking her way through the streets, taking a shortcut back to her house, Dorothy Keeling hoped the rain wouldn't come to anything. She had her head down, and didn't see the man until she collided with him.

'Careful,' she chided. 'You wanna watch where you're going.'

The man didn't move. Dorothy peered up at him through cataract-dimmed eyes. She'd seen his feet were bare, and he looked like he was wearing only a tattered coat. His face looked... old. She couldn't really make out his features. But there was something about his deep-sunken eyes that almost made her walk quickly on.

No, she thought. He was down on his luck like she was. So instead, she asked: 'You all right, dearie? You look half done in. Caught in the bombs, I expect, like I was.'

He didn't answer, staring down at her. Perhaps he was in shock. It could happen. Dorothy had stood frozen to the spot for hours, not saying a word, after the bomb hit her house.

'You get bombed out?' she wondered. 'They tried to move me out of my home, but I wouldn't go. Told me it wasn't safe, but where is safe these days? These nights? I may as well get bombed to death in me own home as out on a strange street, that's what I say.'

Still the man didn't reply. But Dorothy persisted. She sensed a kindred spirit. 'You know what you need? A good cuppa, that's what. You come along a me – it ain't far. Get you a nice cup of Rosie.'

Dorothy lived out towards Blackfriars. It was a bit of a walk, but she often wandered a long way. She had nothing else to do after all. The man still said nothing as he followed her to the house. He didn't comment when they arrived – didn't seem at all worried that the whole of the front had been torn off, so that Dorothy's home looked like a opened dolls' house with every room on display.

'You have to keep dusting,' Dorothy said as she led the way through where the front door used to be. Past the stairs, the kitchen was more or less intact, offering some privacy. 'It's dreadful when it rains. Dreadful.' She pronounced it 'dretfull'. 'Just let me put the kettle on. There's no sugar, of course. Unless you've got coupons?' she added hopefully. 'No, I didn't think so.'

She carried the tray with the tea things through to the sitting room. They could look out across the debris in the street at the broken faces of the houses opposite, although Dorothy couldn't see much past the broken wall of her own house.

'There's no one left here now but me, you know,' she said sadly. 'Even Mrs Willis moved out last week. I thought she'd stay at least. Took her cat with her, more's the pity.'

The man watched her sip her tea from a cracked cup before he sipped at his own. If her eyesight had been better, Dorothy might have noticed how he held his cup exactly as she held hers. How his stick-thin little finger curled out just a little, mirroring her own. She might have mentioned that they said Hitler drank his tea like that – little finger extended as if he was proper English, proper brought up. How dare he?

She could see well enough to notice that when the man set down his cup, he lifted a book from the shelf close to his threadbare armchair. She couldn't see what it was – she didn't have much time for the books. Couldn't really focus on the print.

'That was my Teddy's chair, that was. Long time ago now. But I still keep his books there. He liked to take down a book and read a bit, like you're doing.'

Slowly, the man turned the pages. When he got to the end,

he started again. She watched him leaf through the same book four times before she struggled to her feet and collected up the tea things. She fumbled as she reached for the man's cup. Even her hands were giving out now.

The man looked up from his book at the noise. She smiled at him, and put his cup on the tray. She'd make a fresh pot. It was something to do at least. As she made her way out of the room, her foot caught on the edge of the rug and she stumbled slightly, bumping her shoulder into the doorframe, making the cups and saucers on the tray rattle. She glanced back, smiling apologetically. 'I'm all right,' she assured him.

His voice was cracked and dry. 'Careful,' he chided. 'You wanna watch where you're going.'

Hoffman lifted away the paper. It showed a picture of a book, open on the Ubermensch's lap. The text was Greeked and unreadable. Pictures were vague outlines.

The next picture showed the old woman again. She was carrying a tea tray from the room, looking back over her shoulder.

Then the book again.

'It is acclimatising,' Kruger said. 'See how it has been through this same volume several times already. It will go through it again and again until it understands what it is looking at. Until it has assimilated all the data.'

Hoffman nodded. He remembered how it had been last time. 'Just like before,' he said.

'Language will come quickly. The rate of absorption is really quite phenomenal. It will learn. How to read, how to speak, how to behave.'

Hoffman watched Number Nine start on a new sheet. Another image of the book as the Ubermensch began the process of learning. But Kruger was wrong, this wasn't about language or behaviour, at least not in isolation. The Ubermensch was learning how to become human.

CHAPTER 21

The official story was that Harry had been killed in the previous night's bombing – along with a good number of other people, no doubt. Guy was angered that the man's family would never know the truth, but that anger was tempered by the fact that at least they would know he *was* dead. There were so many families who were in limbo, not knowing if their loved ones posted as 'missing in action' were still alive. Hoping for the best, fearing the worst.

He pushed thoughts of the dead man to the back of his mind, and followed Elizabeth Archer as she led the way through the corridors of the museum.

'Have you worked here long?' Sarah was asking.

'Since I was younger than you.'

'An ambition fulfilled?' Guy wondered.

'Not really. I wanted to be an actress. I rather fancied taking to the stage.'

'It's not all it's cracked up to be,' Davenport assured her with a smile.

They passed through a large exhibition gallery. It had been cleared of contents and was just a vast empty space. The walls were blackened by smoke, and the damage to the ceiling was extensive.

'Incendiary bombs,' Elizabeth explained. 'Over a dozen of them hit in one night about six or seven weeks ago. Gutted the place. The museum's been closed ever since. Not sure when we shall open again, to be honest.'

'I'm surprised you stayed open this long,' Guy said. 'Did you lose much of value in the fires?'

'Most of it was shipped out a long time ago,' she told them. 'But we lost the Suicide Exhibition.'

'The what?' Sarah said.

'When the war started, we had a dilemma,' Elizabeth explained. 'On the one hand we had to keep the exhibits and artefacts we held safe. On the other, it would have been bad for morale to close the museum. So the Suicide Exhibition was devised.'

'It was impressive,' Davenport told them. 'Unless you knew, you wouldn't guess, but it was made up of things that the museum could afford to lose.'

'Some were duplicates. I don't mean copies, but spares if you like. Some were artefacts that simply aren't that rare. There were a few facsimiles, but not very many. Hence "Suicide Exhibition".' Elizabeth gave a wry smile. 'Well, perhaps calling it that was tempting fate. And fate intervened when the incendiaries fell. So now we really are closed for the duration.'

'But we've got to the point where that hardly affects the nation's morale,' Davenport said.

'The fact you've taken a hit might even help,' Sarah pointed out. 'Like with Buckingham Palace.'

'But *you* haven't been moved out,' Guy said. 'I'm afraid I don't even know what you do.'

'Whatever she likes,' Davenport said.

'Thank you, Leo.' Elizabeth led them out of the burned-out shell of the exhibition area and down a flight of steps. 'The museum's artefacts are grouped into departments. Most are geographical, like "Greece and Rome", and some are thematic, like "Prints and Drawings". I am the curator of one of the departments.'

'Which one?' Sarah wondered.

'The one that handles things that don't fit into any of the

others, or which no one else wants. The artefacts I care for are defined as *Un*classified.'

'Which is rather ironic,' Davenport added, 'since the department itself is certainly classified. Very few people know of its existence.'

'Why is that?' Guy asked. 'Why keep secrets in a museum?'

'Best place for them,' Davenport said.

They had arrived at the bottom of the stairs. Elizabeth Archer led them down a narrow corridor and into a large room. It was so cold in here, despite the summer heat outside, that their breath misted the air. The room was unfurnished, but one whole wall was taken up with what looked like a huge metal filing cabinet. More than a dozen large drawers, each with a sturdy handle, were labelled with simple combinations of letters.

'Why's it so cold?' Sarah asked.

'Because these drawers are refrigerated,' Elizabeth told her.

She had taken out a small key, and unlocked one of the drawers at about waist level. It was marked 'TQ'.

'The reason my department is kept secret,' she said as she pulled open the drawer, 'is because we store and examine artefacts like this one.'

The drawer squeaked as it pulled out under the weight of whatever was inside. Cold mist rose like steam, obscuring the contents. The drawer was long, sliding out six feet or more. Elizabeth lowered a strut from beneath it which then acted as a prop to support the weight. The sides of the drawer were hinged and she unclipped them and folded them down.

The drawer was now a shelf or slab, covered by a grey cotton sheet. Guy could already guess what lay beneath. He could make out the shape through the material. Despite the cold, he could smell it – reminding him of the day he went to Ipswich. Burned flesh.

Davenport helped Elizabeth fold back the sheet, revealing the body that lay beneath.

It was charred almost beyond recognition. Like a statue carved out of coal. One leg had shattered and broken away.

The arms were twisted in front of the chest, hands bunched into fists, fingers fused together by the heat.

Sarah gasped, and turned quickly away. Davenport, who must have seen it before, looked pale. Guy felt sick, forcing himself to look. Only Elizabeth seemed unaffected, regarding the corpse with the same studied interest with which she probably inspected any artefact.

The face was like something out of a nightmare. The skin had drawn tight over the skull, blistered and pitted, lined and weathered. The eyes were sunken pits. Cracked teeth clung to the gums of a lipless mouth. The ears had burned away and there was no hint of hair.

'Some of the uniform is in evidence on this side,' Elizabeth said. 'German, of course. SS, or so I'm told.'

'Where was he found?' Guy asked. He could hear the strain in his own voice.

'He washed up in Shingle Bay, after the incident.' She evidently expected them to know about the 'incident'.

'Shingle Bay?'

'Middle of nowhere,' Davenport said. 'Just north of Ipswich.'

That made sense, Guy thought.

'It's horrible,' Sarah said. She had turned back, but was not looking at the body. 'But dozens of soldiers and flyers must have been burned to death. Hundreds, probably. Why are you keeping this one?'

'Because this isn't just any burned body.' She gestured for them to look at the shattered leg. It looked like a brittle, snapped tree stump – jagged and ridged. 'It's pretty damaged, of course. But the internal structure of the body is… interesting. Do you know anything about anatomy?'

'Not a lot,' Guy admitted.

Sarah shook her head.

Elizabeth asked to borrow a pen from Davenport, then to his disgust used it to prod at the broken end of the corpse's leg.

'These filaments here, you see?'

Guy nodded. 'I assume they're blood vessels.'

'That's a very reasonable assumption. But they're not. Perhaps they used to be, but not any more. And I don't mean because of the fire.'

'Then what do you mean?' Sarah asked. Her voice was regaining its confident tone, but she still looked pale.

'We opened one up – look.'

'Oh God,' Sarah gasped, stepping back. Guy stepped back too, instinctively putting his arm round her shoulder. Once it was there he didn't like to remove it, so they stood together, in a loose embrace, forcing themselves to look down at the grisly scene.

Elizabeth had run the tip of the pen up the burned leg, lifting back a wide section of burned skin that had been cut away. She folded it back, exposing the tissue beneath. The burning was less extensive inside the body, and the internal structure was revealed – bone and muscle, flesh and tissue.

The colour was what surprised Guy. The inside of the upper leg had an orange tinge. There were areas of more pronounced colour, like patches of moss growing in a lawn. Elizabeth prodded at one of these with the pen.

'This is not normal.'

'I'll take your word for it,' Sarah said.

'In fact,' Elizabeth went on, 'it's more like plant matter than human tissue. The veins are full of the same material.'

'It seems to have grown *into* the body,' Davenport said. 'I'm no expert, but this substance is apparently rather akin to a fungus.'

'Inside someone's *body*?' Guy said. 'While they were alive?'

'Undoubtedly. Though whether they were alive in the sense we usually mean, who can tell,' Elizabeth replied. 'This fungus, or whatever it is, gives extra strength to the body. It's incredibly resilient. Fire is about the only thing that could destroy it short of ripping the whole body apart.'

'Is it an infection?' Sarah wondered.

'Quite possibly. In fact, I think this fungus has grown through the man's body over a long period of time. Certainly weeks, possibly months or even years. It strengthens the body, but it also looks as though it mirrors the nervous system, perhaps making the host's system redundant and replacing it.'

'Host?' Guy repeated. 'You mean this stuff is a form of, what – a parasite?'

'Yes, I think so,' Elizabeth agreed. She flipped the folded skin back into place and handed Davenport back his fountain pen.

Davenport took it rather gingerly, hesitating before returning it to his jacket pocket.

'This material takes over the body, providing its own internal systems. We have no way of knowing how or if it affects the brain. But kill the human host and the secondary systems would just keep going.'

'Like ivy growing through a tree,' Davenport said. 'The tree might die, but the ivy isn't directly affected.'

'And you think this is a German secret weapon of some sort?' Sarah said.

Elizabeth and Davenport exchanged a look.

'Not exactly,' Davenport said. 'Though the Germans obviously have some degree of involvement. As Elizabeth said, he was wearing an SS uniform.'

'If they had an army of near-indestructible soldiers like this,' Guy said, 'then we'd surely know about it by now. So this must be a one-off.'

Sarah stepped away from Guy to look closer at the body. 'A body that keeps going long after it should be dead,' she said. 'Is this connected with last night?'

'It's a very real possibility,' Davenport said.

'The man who attacked me was *ancient*,' Elizabeth said. 'His features were decayed, his face little more than a skull.' She leaned forward slightly, looking straight into the blackened face of the charred man. 'Apart from burns, he looked rather like this.'

CHAPTER 22

Station Z occupied most of the first floor of the building. From what Guy could gather, the ground floor was taken up with some sort of army administration group, while the upper floors of what had been a large Regency townhouse were given over to the storage of files and a few logistics staff.

Davenport led Guy and Sarah through a door into the set of offices that comprised Station Z. There was one large room furnished with four desks. Miss Manners sat at one, surrounded by telephones and piles of papers. The wall beside her desk was papered with maps and charts showing all of Britain and most of Europe. Guy saw that a map of the Soviet Union was pinned up on the adjacent wall, and he guessed it was a new addition.

'There's a small kitchenette through there,' Davenport told them, pointing to a side door. He nodded towards another door at the end of the room. 'Brinkman's office.'

Miss Manners peered at them through her spectacles before standing up and coming over to greet them.

'I've had desks brought in for you,' she said, indicating the two desks nearest the door. 'Decide between you who gets the window and who gets the draught from the door.'

'What about that desk,' Sarah said, pointing to one further in the room.

'Sergeant Green sits there.' She glanced at Guy. 'You might outrank him, Major, but the sergeant and I need to be within shouting distance of Colonel Brinkman. *His* shouting that is, not ours.'

'And I guess the sergeant was here first,' Guy conceded, smiling to show he wasn't too bothered.

'Indeed.' Miss Manners did not smile back.

'Don't you get a desk?' Sarah asked Davenport.

'Lord no,' he laughed. 'What would an interloper like me do with a desk? If I need to do anything cerebral I'll take a room at the Atlantean Club thank you.'

'Where the tea is no doubt rather better,' Miss Manners added.

'The brandy certainly is.'

The area was bigger than it at first appeared. As well as the small kitchen area, the side door also led to a conference room and two more offices. Davenport took them through to the conference room where they waited for Colonel Brinkman to join them.

'Is this all the staff he has?' Guy wondered. 'A colonel commanding a sergeant, a secretary and an actor?'

Davenport smiled. 'He's got a major and a pilot now too, don't forget. But no, Brinkman can commandeer resources as and when he needs. Green's got half a dozen soldiers on call, but when he doesn't need them they do normal duties at the barracks in Knightsbridge. And then there's Dr Wiles out at Station X, who you've already met, of course.'

Brinkman joined them, Sergeant Green just behind him. Miss Manners entered a few moments later, carrying a notepad and pencil.

'I take it you've seen the body from Shingle Bay,' Brinkman said, starting straight in. He made no effort to introduce anyone or set an agenda. 'So – thoughts?'

There was an uneasy silence before Guy and Sarah realised he was expecting them to respond.

'Bizarre,' Sarah said at last. 'Unpleasant. Worrying.'

'All of those,' Guy agreed. 'But we need to know more

about it. I mean, is he something the Germans created. Some sort of experiment. Or a freak of nature – what?'

Brinkman drummed his fingers on the table. 'You're here, both of you, because it's easier and probably safer to have you with us rather than against us. But if you're going to stay, you need to prove your worth.'

'And how do we do that?' Sarah demanded. 'We don't even know what you do here, let alone what you expect of us.'

'None of us knows what we do here,' Davenport said quietly. 'Which is why, although the colonel won't admit it outright, we need help from people like you. People who will worry at a thing until they understand it. People with tenacity as well as insight.'

Brinkman sniffed and folded his arms. He leaned back in his chair. 'You probably know almost as much as the rest of us already. But to spell it out in simple terms, we believe there is a third force in this conflict. I don't mean the Soviets, I don't mean the Italians. But I don't know who I do mean. Maybe it's some faction of the German forces with access to technology the rest of the Wehrmacht doesn't have; certainly the Germans are utilising their resources, although only to a limited extent. But whether as allies or through acquisition...' He unfolded his arms and leaned forward again. 'Whatever the case, there is a potential threat. Our job is to analyse that threat and then neutralise it.'

'The threat being that burned soldier, or people like him?' Sarah said.

'That's part of it. Then there are the UDTs.'

'I've heard the term. But what exactly are those, sir?' Guy asked.

It was Miss Manners who answered. 'An Unknown Detected Trace, called a UDT or an "Unknown" is just that. You probably know that the government publicly admitted just a few days ago that we have a radio-detection system that warns of incoming enemy aircraft.'

'RDF,' Guy said, to show he was aware of it.

'We call it RADAR now, apparently, but yes,' Brinkman

acknowledged. 'Sometimes it picks up aircraft that don't fit the pattern of an incoming raid or reconnaissance. Usually they turn out to be aircraft anyway – our own, or something unexpected like Hess's flight back in May.'

'Oh yes – Hess...' Guy wanted to ask about how Hess was involved.

But Brinkman waved the question away. 'We'll discuss him later. I was in Glasgow, quite by chance because his plane was originally flagged as a UDT.'

'The plane I saw,' Sarah said slowly. 'If it *was* a plane.'

'Another reason you're here. You are one of the few witnesses actually to have seen one of these things. The three Hurricanes we scrambled when it showed up got there too late, there was no sign of it. As usual. But you actually *saw* the thing.'

'I saw *something*. As I described to the sergeant and Miss Manners.'

'And we are working on the assumption that there is a connection between these UDT craft and the body from Shingle Bay?' Guy said.

'We are assuming nothing,' Brinkman told him. 'But neither can we rule anything out. Both remain unexplained, which is enough of a link for now.'

'So what is Shingle Bay?' Sarah asked. 'How did the body end up at the British Museum?'

'Shingle Bay was the site of an invasion,' Brinkman said. 'Or at least, an incursion. We received information that the Germans intended to put ashore a small force that would include what they referred to as an "Ubermensch".'

'Ubermensch?' Guy interrupted. 'That's what the German soldier in the hospital said.'

'It's a term we've come across before,' Miss Manners told them. 'In Ultra traffic originating with the SS, specifically from Himmler's command.'

'Ultra?' Sarah asked.

Brinkman ignored the question. 'The point is, we have reason to connect the word with the UDTs. They've been referred to, albeit in different terms, in communications that also reference Ubermensch. We assumed it was a code word.'

'Is it?' Sarah wondered.

'It's German for "super man",' Guy said. 'In the way that Hitler thinks the Aryans are the master race. Superior, better than the rest of us. So what exactly happened at Shingle Bay?' he asked Brinkman.

Brinkman nodded to Sergeant Green, who told them: 'Several small boats were launched from a U-Boat off East Anglia. But thanks to information received, we were waiting. We had a couple of large petrol tankers concealed on the cliffs above the beach, and ran pipes out into the bay. We had no idea what sort of force we were up against, not much time to react, and under the circumstances it would have been difficult to get cooperation from other units.'

'You burned them,' Guy said quietly. He could remember the charred wreck of the man in the hospital bed. The awful stench of his blistered flesh.

'We did,' Green admitted. He didn't sound proud or remorseful, it was a statement of fact. 'When we saw the boats coming in, we pumped petrol out into the bay. It floated on the water and we ignited it with a flare gun.'

'The whole sea was burning,' Sarah said quietly. 'Like some Biblical catastrophe.'

'Sorry?' Brinkman said.

'Something one of the other ATA girls said. She was describing what she saw below her on a delivery flight. That was somewhere on the Suffolk coast I think. Was this late last summer?'

'There *was* a plane,' Green said. 'We were afraid it would scare off the boats. Anyway, afterwards, we collected up the bodies.' He looked down at the table. 'Not a very pleasant job. They were all normal, though badly burned of course. All except the one that Mrs Archer has in her care.'

'And just the one survivor?' Pentecross asked.

'One more than we intended,' Green said. 'And as you know, he didn't survive long, poor bastard.'

Sarah shook her head. 'I still don't understand how you knew about this raid, or whatever it was, how you knew it was going to happen.'

Miss Manners gave a polite cough. 'I have a friend,' she said, glancing at Brinkman for his permission to elaborate. He nodded, and she adjusted her spectacles before continuing. 'She is part of a group that makes various claims, including that they can divine information from some rather unorthodox sources. But her... employer, if I can call him that, has been right before.'

'But this employer of hers isn't deemed reliable enough to be able to second troops from regular army units?' Guy guessed.

Again Miss Manners glanced at Brinkman before she went on: 'Her employer, though I use the term rather loosely as he's more of a mentor I suppose, well... He's Aleister Crowley.'

There was silence for several moments. Guy was aware that his mouth was open in surprise.

'Who?' Sarah said.

'You've never heard of him?' Guy was amazed.

Sarah shrugged. 'The name sounds familiar, but...' She shrugged.

'The press called him "the wickedest man in the world",' Miss Manners said.

'That's not far off the truth,' Green said. He was smiling and making a point of not looking at Miss Manners. 'Bit of a libertine. Spiritualist. He's into all that occult mumbo-jumbo and talking to the dead stuff.'

Miss Manners coughed again. 'And he *did* predict that the Ubermensch would come ashore at Shingle Bay, Sergeant.'

Green's smile faded. 'He did, yes. Well, after all I've seen – maybe there's something in that nonsense after all.'

'There were also Ultra intercepts, as well as Crowley's rather less orthodox information-gathering,' Brinkman said.

Guy recalled hearing the term 'Ultra' earlier in the meeting. But Brinkman was not forthcoming.

'All you need to know is that we are occasionally allowed

access to information from an unimpeachable – and entirely non-spiritual – source. You've been to Bletchley and met Wiles, I'm sure you can put two and two together. Just keep the answer to yourselves.'

'And how is Wiles involved?' Guy asked, deciding to save the mental arithmetic for later.

'The UDTs emit signals,' Davenport said. He'd been sitting back with his arms folded, watching and listening with amusement to the previous exchanges. 'Transmissions that are picked up and recorded by the Y Stations. They monitor all radio traffic. Dr Wiles is a bit of an expert at unravelling such things. Though he's not made a lot of headway so far.'

'It's been more of a hobby for him up till now,' Brinkman said. 'But I've finally secured permission for him to put together a small team at Station X to work exclusively on the UDT problem. Hopefully we'll get some results.' He leaned across the table towards Guy and Sarah. 'It's a lot to take in, I know. And a very incomplete picture, I'm afraid. Like yourselves, we have more questions than answers.'

'I do have one more question I think you can answer,' Guy said.

'Oh?'

'How does Rudolf Hess fit into all this? Assuming he does.'

'He's on the periphery,' Brinkman admitted. 'Like us, he is worried by what's going on, and I don't mean the war. How much of what he says is reliable isn't clear. How much he actually knows is a moot point. But what he has told us... That is, what he told us before he decided that it was best to shut up and pretend he actually knows nothing... What he told us is...' Brinkman hesitated, searching for the right word. 'Terrifying,' he said at last.

With that, he stood up and strode from the room. Green followed close behind him. The meeting was apparently over.

'I'll see you both later,' Davenport said jovially as he also left.

Miss Manners ushered Sarah and Guy from the room. 'I've put together some briefing papers,' she said. 'You should read

Colonel Brinkman's report to General Ismay, and his account of his meeting with Hess. Again, I'm afraid you'll come away with rather more questions than answers but thus is progress made.'

'Is this progress?' Sarah asked Guy quietly as they returned to the main office.

'I don't know,' he admitted. 'I have the horrible feeling we've opened Pandora's Box. And whatever we've let out can never be put back in.'

CHAPTER 23

Dawn had been breaking across Glasgow by the time Colonel Brinkman and Sergeant Green arrived at Maryhill back on 11 May 1941. Brinkman was disappointed that the UDT had turned out to be a German plane after all. But he was determined to be meticulous about every detail, so Sergeant Green drove them to Glasgow to interview the pilot.

The discovery of the pilot's actual identity lifted Brinkman's mood a little. But it dipped again when the officer in charge of the barracks told him a man from the Foreign Office was already with Hess. The additional presence of the Duke of Hamilton intrigued Brinkman more than anything – not least as technically the man outranked him.

'You mind if I take a break, sir?' Green asked. 'I could do with a smoke.'

Brinkman nodded for him to go ahead. 'I'll send for you if I need you. This Pentecross,' he went on, thoughtfully. 'Same chap as at Ipswich do you think?'

'It's an unusual name,' Green conceded. 'Seems likely. But probably a coincidence. He deals with Germans who turn up on British soil – like at Ipswich, and the same here. Even so...' he added.

'Even so,' Brinkman echoed.

Corporal Matthews led Brinkman through the barracks. They were coming to life now as day broke. But the block where Hess was being held was quiet and empty. Two men stood at the end of the corridor, one looked pale, dabbing at his face with a folded handkerchief. The second man had the bearing of a soldier, even though he wore a civilian suit. Pentecross, Brinkman decided.

'I have to talk to Whitehall,' the shorter man – Hamilton – said. His voice was shaking as much as his hand. 'Someone in authority. The implications...'

'You can start with me, sir,' Brinkman told him. 'Perhaps then my journey won't have been a complete waste. I'm Colonel Brinkman.'

Hamilton was getting some colour back in his features and his relief was obvious. 'Of course, Colonel. Perhaps you can make sense of what I've just heard.'

'Perhaps.' Brinkman glanced at Pentecross. 'Who are you?' he asked, though he already knew, of course.

The man from the FO straightened to attention. 'Major Pentecross, sir. Foreign Office.'

Brinkman nodded. So he still used his rank even though he'd been discharged. Brinkman wasn't sure he approved of that. 'You won't be needed, *Major*,' he said. 'Dismissed.'

Five minutes with Hamilton was more than enough to convince Brinkman that his trip had not been wasted after all.

They spoke German throughout. Colonel Brinkman recognised the Deputy Fuhrer from newsreel footage and photographs. But he was surprised how pale the man looked, how nervous. His hands were clasped tightly on the table in front of him in the small room. So tight the knuckles whitened.

'Hamilton did not understand.'

'No,' Brinkman said. He sat down behind the desk, aligning the pencil neatly across the top of the pad that lay there waiting. 'I spoke to him just now. But I do.'

'You think so?' Hess smiled thinly. It was a fleeting moment. 'I doubt it.'

Brinkman shrugged. 'Convince me.'

'You know what I told Hamilton?'

'Some of it. As you said – he didn't really grasp the implications, though they worried him. He doesn't know that we have been logging what we call Unknown Detected Traces for some time.'

Brinkman leaned back, wondering if he had said too much. Did the Germans know about RDF, or RADAR as they were now calling it? Not that Hess would be going back to Germany.

'For some time?' Hess shook his head. 'They have been coming here for centuries. For millennia. Or rather, they used to come here.'

Brinkman leaned forward again. 'And now they are back?'

Hess did not reply. Brinkman waited, but still Hess offered nothing.

'So why did you come?' Brinkman asked at last. 'You were alone. Your plane was armed with machine guns, but there was no ammunition on board. We know the Luftwaffe tried to intercept your flight.' He didn't know that, but it seemed likely.

'We have done a terrible thing,' Hess said slowly. He unclasped his hands and waved away Brinkman's response. 'Oh, you will tell me that we have done many terrible things. Many you don't even know about. But none of them as terrible as this.'

'And what have you done?'

'We have sought out forbidden knowledge.'

That surprised Brinkman, though he didn't really know what to expect. He needed to draw the information out of the man. Hess had come here for a reason, and it was not a trivial matter. He'd defected from the Fatherland. He'd betrayed the Fuhrer just by being here. Whatever the cause, it was more important to Hess than his reputation, or probably his life. Brinkman waited for Hess to go on.

'The Fuhrer has never been much interested in the occult. But Reichsfuhrer Himmler is another matter. The knowledge of the Ancients has also fascinated him. He sees connections there that, to be honest, I do not. But there is no harm in indulging his interest. Others pander to it. I share it, up to a point. I showed enthusiasm. Or rather, I used to.'

Brinkman knew of Himmler's obsession. It was well documented. 'Himmler believes that the symbols and rituals of the occult are some residue of ancient wisdom, is that it?'

'Knowledge, wisdom, *science* that we have long forgotten. And he has gathered enough evidence to convince the Fuhrer that something of what he claims is true.'

Brinkman shook his head. 'Forgive me, but what has this to do with our UDTs? With these objects we have been... following?'

'I shall come to that.' Hess seemed more comfortable now as he told his story. There was some colour in his cheeks again. 'Could I have some coffee, do you think?'

Brinkman didn't want to break off the debriefing, so he opened the door and called to Matthews for coffee.

'Tell me,' Hess said, 'are you aware of a book called *The Coming Race*?'

Brinkman was not.

'You should read it. It is by Edward Bulwer-Lytton. *Lord* Lytton, in actual fact.'

'He is British?' Brinkman wondered where this was leading.

'He was English,' Hess confirmed. 'Primarily a politician. But he wrote cheap fiction. Few remember him now, but he coined several phrases that have become clichés in your language.' Hess smiled, breaking into English to say: 'It was a dark and stormy night.'

'Hardly the height of literary prowess,' Brinkman said. 'Though evocative, I'll give you that.'

'It might appeal to "the great unwashed" – another of his phrases. Or how about, most aptly, "The pen is mightier than the sword"?'

Now it was Brinkman who smiled. 'I am not sure that Herr Hitler would agree with that.'

'He sees both as a means to an end. He is the author of a bestselling book, don't forget. But we digress. While he was never an enthusiastic devotee of the occult, *The Coming*

Race struck a chord with the Fuhrer. It tells of a man who falls through the earth and discovers a maze of tunnels and catacombs inhabited by an ancient, advanced race. They rely on unknown technology, especially an oil with miraculous properties called Vril – from which they take their name.'

'And Hitler thinks the story is true?'

'Allegorical, perhaps. It is yet more evidence of an ancient, hidden society that has secret knowledge. Knowledge that, encouraged by Himmler, the Fuhrer craves.'

'And I thought Himmler was only interested in the Holy Grail,' Brinkman said sarcastically. Coffee had arrived, but he had been so absorbed in Hess's words that he hadn't even noticed.

'He follows any lead that might render up the secrets. And not without success.'

Brinkman leaned forward to pour the coffee. 'Oh?'

Hess shook his head. 'The details – later. All we need concern ourselves with now is that he has gone too far. He discovered something. Back in 1934, I think. In Tibet. I say "discovered" but perhaps I should say "disturbed".'

'But you don't know what?'

'I only know that there were consequences. Someone – some*thing* – knew of the discovery. It was as if the archaeologists set off an alarm. In 1936, five years ago now, something crashed in the Black Forest, not far from Freiburg.'

'A plane?'

'Not just any plane. The locals described it as a flying disc.'

Brinkman nodded. That tied in with some of the vague eyewitness reports of UDTs. 'What happened to it?'

'The SS took possession of it. What was left after the crash was taken to Wewelsburg – Herr Himmler's residence, if you can call a restored Renaissance castle a residence.'

'And this is what Himmler used to convince the Fuhrer of his beliefs?' It seemed likely.

Hess nodded. 'And now he is closer to Hitler on these matters than I ever was. I confess, even after the Black Forest crash, I dismissed much of it as fantasy.'

'But now you are not so sure.'

'Now I know better. That is why I am here.'

'And what exactly do you know?'

Hess leaned across the table, hands once more clasped tightly together. 'I know that bodies were recovered from that crash. There are rumours of a survivor, held at Wewelsburg. I know that we too have detected objects in the sky that are not aircraft flown by either side in this conflict. I know that Himmler, on the Fuhrer's instructions is using spiritualists to try to contact what he calls "the Coming Race", though whether they come from within the earth or beyond it, I cannot say. I have seen, at Wewelsburg, I have seen... Such things.'

'And why are you telling us all this?'

There was a sheen of sweat on Hess's brow. 'Because it has to stop. Himmler is tampering with forces he does not understand. None of us can understand them. And in doing so, he has provoked the ire of a society far more advanced, far more aggressive, far more dangerous than our own. He and the Fuhrer hope to harness the forces of that race – forces and powers we cannot even dream of. But I fear they will be destroyed by them instead. And it will not stop there.'

Hess leaned back suddenly, staring up at the ceiling. Brinkman waited. He could tell the man had not finished.

'There is a war coming,' Hess went on at last. 'Not the war we are already fighting, but a greater, more dangerous conflict than we can imagine. I have always believed – as I think the Fuhrer believes – that there is an affinity between our peoples, between the Germans and the British. Our two countries should not be in conflict. When the time comes, we should be standing together against the common enemy. And that time is coming fast.'

He leaned forward and thumped the table, making the coffee cups jump. 'They are already here – don't you understand? I'm not concerned about the tiny war between Britain and Germany. I don't care if America or Russia get involved, though God help the Reich if they do.'

178

Hess was breathing heavily, his eyes glistening with tears and his voice trembling with emotion. 'I am talking about a far greater war. And we are already fighting it.'

Brinkman wrote up his notes in the car travelling back south. He barely noticed the passing countryside, hardly registered how far they had come. Before he knew it, they were at the outskirts of London.

He had left instructions that Hess was to speak to no one, though the man had lapsed into a sullen silence. Brinkman guessed he was already regretting his rash flight to Britain, already deciding that he would find little sympathy for his fears here. Brinkman himself wondered just how much of what the man said he could believe. How much could he afford *not* to believe?

As soon as they were back, Brinkman handed his scrawled notes to Miss Manners. What with the motion of the car and his rush to get down everything he could recall, they were barely legible.

'Type these up, best you can,' he ordered. Carbon copy to me, the original to the Prime Minister, accompanied by a memo I shall draft now.'

Miss Manners sniffed as she leafed through the pages. 'You think he'll read it?'

'I hope he will. At the very least, he'll shuffle it on to someone else.'

'Let's hope it's someone perceptive.' She placed a carbon between two sheets of foolscap paper and rolled them into the typewriter.

In truth, Brinkman expected to hear nothing except possibly an acknowledgement of his memo and the usual Prime Ministerial order to 'keep buggering on'.

But two days later, he was summoned to Downing Street.

'MI5 haven't a bloody clue. No idea what to do with the man. For the moment they've sent him to the Tower of London, which I suppose makes some sort of symbolic point. They think he's barking mad, to tell you the truth. But what about you, Oliver – do you think he's genuine?'

'Oh yes,' Brinkman said. 'He's definitely Hess, and he certainly believes what he says. He probably *is* barking mad as well. But more than anything, the man's terrified, though he keeps it under control.'

General Hastings Ismay gave a short bark of laughter. 'That goes for us all. Though I gather he's feeling the pressure now. Clammed up so tight they can't get so much as a peep out of him.' Ismay – known to his friends and colleagues as 'Pug' – swirled the whisky round the inside of his crystal tumbler, letting the ice cubes clink together. He was Chief Military Assistant to Churchill – in effect, the Prime Minister's Chief of Staff. No one was closer to – or more trusted by – the Prime Minister.

'He's still loyal to Hitler and to Germany,' said Brinkman. He won't do or say anything to undermine the enemy's war effort. But he sees these *Vril*, as he calls them, as a separate issue.'

'And you say he's not alone in that?'

'Hess maintains that he has allies who feel the same. Again, they'll do nothing to sabotage their country's war efforts, but they'll do anything they can to help win this separate war they believe they are fighting.'

'My enemy's enemy is my friend,' Ismay said. 'Up to a point, anyway. Yet, they admit Hitler is not allied to these Vril?'

'Hitler will take whatever he can from them. But no, he's not after an alliance. It's more like…' Brinkman paused to sip from his own glass as he tried to think of a good analogy. 'It's like invading Poland. Hitler will happily press-gang the local population into his armies and force them to fight for him. He'll take whatever technology and resources he can find in Poland. But he's not offering any sort of return or alliance.'

'And he thinks he can do the same with the Vril.'

Brinkman nodded. 'Whereas Hess thinks he's bitten off more than he can chew. He's stirred up a hornets' nest, and the hornets aren't particular whether they go after the person who disturbed them or anyone else in the vicinity. In this case, the vicinity is our whole world.'

Ismay was pacing the floor as he thought. 'So what do we know about these Vril? What are their intentions, their objectives?'

'In military terms? Hard to say. They have advanced technology that overlaps with the occult – maybe it even informed occult thinking originally. They have evidently been here before, long ago as Hess maintains. We know that because their artefacts and their philosophy for want of a better word persist.'

Ismay drained his glass. He refilled it from a decanter, before offering Brinkman a top-up.

'Thank you.' Brinkman took a sip before going on: 'According to Hess, Hitler believes that *The Coming Race* was right, that it was some sort of factual treatise, and the Vril live under the ground. There are a few points where their world emerges into ours. The Antarctic seems a key touching point. If that's true, and there's nothing to confirm or deny it, then the Vril agenda would seem to be expansionist. They're running out of space and they think this planet belongs to them. They believe they are, if you'll forgive the irony, the Master Race.'

Ismay nodded, a tight smile on his lips. 'I begin to see why Hitler is both attracted to them and opposed to them. Their existence suggests he is right in his twisted thinking, while these Vril seek to usurp Hitler's own people's rightful place in the order of things – he believes. He wants to be their heirs, not their lackeys.'

'The fact of it is,' Brinkman said, 'we need more information. What Hess conveys is second-hand at best. Much of it is supposition on his part. It may even be contrived to mislead us, though we do know that, at the heart of it all…' He waved his glass in the air vaguely.

'At the heart of it all is some measure of truth,' Ismay finished for him. 'God help us.'

'There is one other thing. One other worrying thing.'

'As if I'm not worried enough. Go on.'

'The Vril have sympathisers. People who know the legends, who follow the occult, who even think they can communicate with them.'

'Like Himmler's female medium, what's her name?'

'Maria Orsic – yes, she's one of the so-called Vril Society. There are several highly placed Nazis in that. Himmler, Goering, Bormann... Hess himself, of course. But this is different. The others all seem to share Hitler's view, this desire to exploit and defeat the Vril.'

'And you're talking about Vril Fifth Columnists.'

'Exactly. Hess thinks it is possible that the Vril may look like us. Or perhaps can make themselves look like us. Remember Shingle Bay? The Ubermensch?'

Ismay slammed his glass down on the mantelpiece. 'Damn it! It's bad enough that we might have Germans or Nazi sympathisers coming over here and trying to conceal themselves. Now you're saying we could have these Vril too.' He shook his head. 'We need more information. More than anything, before we can act at all, we must know more.'

Brinkman had to agree. 'We need to know their origins, their intentions, their strengths and weaknesses. Who they are, what they look like. Their capabilities – both as people, if indeed they are "people", and in military terms.'

'And all we currently have, despite your Station Z being operational for almost a year, are the words of a defector, and logs of these Unknown Detected Traces.'

'We also have the detected transmissions,' Brinkman pointed out. 'We're still trying to make sense of them, but they could be communications traffic.'

Ismay nodded. 'Or they could just be engine noise, or some sort of atmospheric disturbance. The point is, we don't know. So,' General Ismay said, fixing Colonel Brinkman with an intense gaze, 'what do I tell the Prime Minister?'

CHAPTER 24

War happens in fits and starts. Perhaps it was the opening of the Russian Front, or maybe it was because he was away from the constant updates of the Foreign Office, but it did seem to Guy as if the conflict was slowing down. The most immediate reminder of the war was the bombing of London, but since late May even that had eased. By the start of September 1941, a year after it first started, the Blitz seemed to have petered out. The threat was always there, but the bombers came less frequently.

As a soldier, Guy had been in the thick of things – literally on the front line. In the Foreign Office he was a step removed, but still very much caught up in day-to-day events. Now, at Station Z, his work was further divorced from the actual combat. Apart from the bombing, the most effect it had was that he now had to use margarine coupons to buy clothes.

In early July, Sarah told him that she'd heard American troops had landed in Iceland to prevent a possible German occupation. Perhaps after all, the US was about to enter the war. But nearly three weeks later, with America still not committed, the news was less good as the Japanese set up base in Saigon and moved troops into Cambodia...

In the last week of August, Chivers – Guy's former superior at the FO – rang him at home one evening. He had taken to calling, though at increasingly infrequent intervals, to beg

Guy to return to work in his office and get involved in 'real work that will make a real difference'.

'I was asked to recommend someone for a new outfit they're putting together called the Political Warfare Executive,' Chivers said when Guy again turned him down. 'Don't suppose you'd be interested in that either? Unless it's what you're already doing?'

Guy refused to be drawn, though Chivers was obviously curious about what he *was* doing. Even so, Chivers couldn't disguise his upbeat mood.

'So what's happened?' Guy asked.

'I suppose it'll be common knowledge soon,' Chivers said, 'but our lads together with the Gurkhas have taken Iran. Joint operation with our Soviet allies. First of many, we're hoping. A complete success, and almost without loss.'

'Almost' was always the kick in the shins, Guy thought. 'Almost' meant that somewhere a widow was distraught, children were crying for the father they would never see again. 'Almost no loss' for others was total loss for them...

The work at Station Z was unrelenting, though it was difficult for Guy to convince himself it was making any difference. When he shared this view with Brinkman in an unusually candid moment, Brinkman nodded.

'We have to chip away at this until we can see the shape of it. The smallest thing now could mean a huge difference later. Patience must be our watchword, I'm afraid. But I agree – it's a bugger.'

'He's right,' Sarah said when Guy related this conversation to her. 'I was with Wiles at Bletchley the other day. I asked him how he's getting on decoding the UDT transmissions, and he said he'd got nowhere so far.'

'He must be as frustrated as we are,' Guy said.

'Yes and no. He said, you have to do a lot of work that seems to take you nowhere or the wrong way before you find out where you're really going. Then one day some tiny thing, maybe something you discounted ages ago or didn't realise was significant, will just slot into place. Like pulling on a tiny thread in the fabric of the code, and the whole thing then unravels.'

Guy knew what he meant. The trouble was, they didn't know what the tiny, precious, all-important thread might turn out to be. And until they found it they couldn't afford to ignore anything.

Since reading Brinkman's report of his meeting with Hess, Guy had also read *The Coming Race*, and found to his surprise that he quite enjoyed it. Miss Manners supplied a seemingly unending stock of occult literature, some of it quite obtuse and impenetrable. Then there were the UDT reports to follow up – searching for eyewitnesses. Most were false alarms or easily discounted. But some added a little to their meagre stock of knowledge.

Guy liaised with a police inspector about the creature that had attacked Elizabeth Archer. An artist's likeness was circulated, but no one reported seeing a walking corpse. Possibly there were so many emaciated and sleep-deprived Londoners that he didn't seem so out of place. Possibly people had better things to concentrate on, like surviving. Inspector Cartwright was more interested in applying, and reapplying, for a military posting. But, as Guy soon realised, the man was too good at his job to be spared. Guy sympathised.

Much of the work was similar to what Guy had done at the Foreign Office. He attended boring and barely relevant meetings together with Brinkman, and deputised for the colonel at others. He read, wrote, and filed reports.

Most evenings, he walked to the nearest tube station with Sarah Diamond and listened to her similar frustrations, both alleviated and exacerbated by the fact her role seemed to be as Brinkman's main driver. It meant she spent a lot of time with the colonel, so she had a better idea of what was going on than Guy did. But she felt underused and unappreciated. Guy hoped that, like him, she appreciated their time together if nothing else...

A rare joint expedition was a trip Guy and Sarah made to Station X at Bletchley in the first week of September. Sarah drove, and Guy dozed for much of the journey in the passenger seat. He'd spent most of the previous night tracking down a Spitfire pilot who it turned out had seen nothing at all of a UDT that RADAR had put right behind him. Guy had a wire recording of the UDT transmissions as well as the tracking coordinates in his briefcase.

Dr Wiles was enthusiastic. It was unusual for a Y Station to have managed to record more than a few seconds of a transmission. 'The most we usually get is an approximation broken down into Morse code. That gives us an idea of the shape of the sound, but not the pitch, not the intensity, not the *tone*.' He handed the spool to the young woman who seemed to be his personal assistant. 'Let's play it for everyone to hear, please Deborah.'

'I thought her name was Eleanor,' Guy murmured to Sarah.

The young woman heard him. 'It is,' she said, before hurrying off with the spool of magnetised wire.

The two huts Wiles and his team had been allocated were separate from the rest of Bletchley, not geographically but conceptually. Whereas the other huts were numbered, Wiles' team worked in Hut A and Hut B. In common with the other paired huts, 'A' was concerned with decoding, and 'B' with analysis.

Guy and Sarah usually dealt with Hut B. The documents they delivered tended to be reports and accounts unearthed during their seemingly endless task of going through archives for any hint of UDT activity that had been misinterpreted, ignored, or simply not understood. These went to Hut B for further analysis, and to be added to an increasingly large, and increasingly incomprehensible wall chart that Wiles was compiling. Each time Guy saw it, the chart had grown. It now covered two whole walls, papering over the windows with a pattern of text and lines, boxes and circles.

The wire recording was played in Hut A. Here the walls and desks were covered with paper dotted and dashed with Morse code, scrawled with fragments of text – usually suffixed by multiple question marks.

Two men sat in upright chairs. One of them tilting his chair back at an alarming angle as he puffed on a pipe and stared at the ceiling. The pipe did not appear to be lit. The other man was scribbling feverishly on a pad with a stub of pencil.

Eleanor threaded the wire through the heads of a playing machine in the corner. The single large room was soon filled with the hissing, crackling sound of the recording.

'It's someone frying chips,' the scribbling man said without pausing in his work.

There was a polite ripple of laughter, which broke off as the actual UDT transmission began to play through the background noise. It was a series of clicks and whistles without any apparent structure. How it could possibly *mean* anything, Guy could not imagine. He glanced at Sarah, who seemed just as nonplussed.

'Play it again,' the pipe man said as soon as it finished. 'Keep playing it.'

After the third time through, neither of the men apparently paying any attention, and Wiles smiling and nodding as if it all made perfect sense, Guy had had enough.

'We'll leave you to it,' he said quietly.

'What? Oh, rightio.' Wiles nodded again. 'You ever heard dolphins?'

He shook his head.

'Me neither,' Wiles admitted. 'Just wondered.' He whistled in time to a segment of the recording. 'I'll see you off the premises.'

'I hope it's useful,' Sarah said as they walked back to the car.

The trees were slowly turning to their autumn colours, and the cooler evening sunshine filtered through the leaves to dapple the ground.

'I hope so too,' Wiles said.

'You'll just keep... listening to it?' Guy asked.

'That's the way to get started. We'll play it over and over till we can remember every detail. Then we'll play it again, and we'll hear something we missed. We'll play it backwards, in pieces, write it down in different forms of notation, look at it every which way. You always see – or in this case hear – something new.'

'Some clue, you mean?' Sarah said.

'Eventually, one of us will find a way in. It's like a maze we have to navigate. But the first stage is finding the entrance. Once we've done that at least we have a path to start down. It might be a repeated phrase, it might be the fact that nothing seems to be repeated. Could be anything, really.' He smiled. 'But whatever you do, no matter how urgent it is, you can't rush these things. Once you've got your way in, once you can begin to see what you're dealing with, *then* perhaps you can rush.'

As she turned the car out of Bletchley Park, Sarah said: 'What's the most tangible evidence we have? The most comprehensive?'

'The coffin or sarcophagus or whatever it is that Davenport brought back. And the Ubermensch itself.'

'Elizabeth Archer's examining that. I mean, out of what you and I understand. Reports, papers, that sort of thing?'

Pentecross thought through what he'd read. It was all second hand.

'Put it this way,' Sarah said, 'what do we *know*? Out of all this, is there anything we know for sure?'

'That UDTs exist, not least because you saw one.'

'True. Go on.'

'There's Hess, of course. But the more we learn from him the more obvious it is that he's hardly a reliable witness.'

'He doesn't actually know very much,' Sarah agreed. 'And we can't be sure that what he tells us is the truth even as he perceives it.'

'We know about the archaeological dig in France, from Davenport and because he brought back… something. That's real and tangible.' What else, Guy wondered. 'We know that the Ubermensch at the British Museum died in the fire at Shingle Bay…'

'But how does it all fit together?' Sarah wondered.

'Wait a minute,' Guy had thought of something. 'Shingle Bay. That's what we know for sure – that either the Germans or the Ubermensch had a reason to come to Shingle Bay.'

'Or both of them did. But what reason?'

'Exactly,' Pentecross agreed. '*Why* did they come? Why come at all, and why *there*?'

'We should do what Wiles said,' Sarah told him. 'With the Shingle Bay report. With whatever Green can tell us.'

Guy nodded. Wiles' words had struck a chord with him too. 'We go over it all again,' he agreed. 'Look at it over and over, every which way. Forwards, backwards, sideways, whatever it takes. It's not that we've missed something,' he realised. 'But there's always more to find.'

Some things had to be learned from people rather than books. Between visiting libraries and bookshops, reading newspapers and watching newsreels and films, he spoke to people. Or rather, he listened to people.

There was a law of diminishing returns. The same sort of people that he found in the same sort of places tended to provide the same sort of information about the world in general and London in particular. Occasionally, he found someone who could add information, colour, depth to what he already knew. Less frequently he learned entirely new information. The hardest to assimilate was social behaviour – which seemed to embody a mass of contradictory data and advice. But slowly, the Ubermensch was learning.

The Ubermensch was learning to derive information from implicit sources, to make assumptions and test them, as well as simply absorb what he was told or read. But he had to protect himself and his existence. Often he could gather information without giving away anything about himself. But sometimes an information provider learned or guessed too much, or asked too many questions of their own. Or had something the Ubermensch needed – like an Identity Card.

The young man had told the Ubermensch his name was Jeff Wood. He was on leave from the army, he said. But the information he provided about his army life was inconsistent and ambivalent. Conclusion: Jeff was not in the army. Conclusion: Jeff was a liar.

'But if you want to know about women,' Jeff said, putting down his pint, 'I can tell you everything you need to know.'

'I need to know everything,' the Ubermensch replied. For the purposes of this meeting, his identity was Robbie Stone. The real Robbie Stone had been an Air Raid Warden who asked too many questions about the Ubermensch's life and background, where he lived, who he *was*. The real Robbie Stone had told him everything.

Jeff talked his way through another two pints. 'Robbie Stone' barely touched his own bitter. But he paid for Jeff's drinks with money that used to belong to a barmaid, which (he now understood) was ironic.

'Pilot, was you?' Jeff asked at last. They all asked eventually. They all had different ideas about why he looked the way he did.

'You think I was burned?'

'Well, you do look a bit… done over.' Jeff smiled apologetically and slurped more beer. 'Had to bail out, did you? I admire you RAF boys, I really do. Though it ain't easy in the army.'

The Ubermensch was aware that he still attracted attention. The hat worn low and the turned-up coat collar helped deflect attention. But it was impossible to get this close to someone, close enough to ask questions, without them seeing the sunken eyes, the withered skin. Water helped, rehydrating his body. But it would take months before he could truly pass as normal.

'You were never in the army,' the Ubermensch said. A simple statement of fact. He stood up.

'What you saying?' Jeff demanded.

'You are a liar. You have avoided service, ignored the call-up. You buy and sell on the black market.'

Jeff started to stand up, but 'Robbie' put a hand on his shoulder, forcing him back down onto the bar stool. The wrinkled, skeletal hand should have been weak and ineffectual, but Jeff slumped down under its unexpected strength.

'All right, so I buy and sell. No harm in it. What are you after? Coupons? You want coupons? I can get you coupons. Petrol, meat, anything.'

'Tell me how it works. How you get what you want. How you sell it on.'

Jeff's eyes narrowed. If he had drunk less he might have decided enough was enough. But instead, he judged that there was no harm now in telling Robbie a little – just a little of what he really did. He spoke, uninterrupted save for the occasional specific question, for an hour.

'Have you told me everything?'

'Course I have.'

Robbie nodded. 'Good.' He stood up.

To anyone watching, it would have looked like a gesture, a flick of the hand in farewell, nothing more. After the man in the hat and the coat with the high collar left, it would have seemed that the young man who'd drunk too much had simply slumped against the wall, resting his head against the panelling.

CHAPTER 25

The office was deserted apart from Miss Manners. She peered over the top of her spectacles and her typewriter as Davenport hung his coat on the rack by the door.

'Everyone on leave?' he asked.

'Only you, apparently.'

'I don't think I get leave, do I?' He smiled. 'I'll gladly take it if I do.'

Miss Manners returned her attention to the papers on her desk. 'Colonel Brinkman is at the War Rooms. Miss Diamond has taken herself off somewhere, and the others are down there.' She nodded at the door leading to the kitchenette and back offices. 'So where have you been these last few weeks?'

'Some of us have a crust to earn. And a reputation to keep up. Though I doubt I've been doing that.'

'Oh?'

'Propaganda film. Not that they call it that of course. But it will show our exaggeratedly brave soldiers defeating a woefully inept Wehrmacht.'

Miss Manners sniffed. 'How uplifting.'

'I play the dashing captain of a troop ship off to… I'm not sure actually. Somewhere in Scandinavia, I think.'

'Is anyone famous in it?'

Davenport laughed. 'Careful, Miss Manners. I think I detected the hint of a smile just then.'

There was more than a hint as she looked up again. 'Unlikely.'

The smaller of the two spare offices was where Davenport found Guy Pentecross and Sergeant Green. The two desks had been pushed up against the walls, which were themselves covered with typed reports, handwritten notes, maps and photographs held in place with drawing pins.

'We can go over it as many times as you like, sir,' Green was saying as Davenport came in. 'But that won't change what happened.'

'I'm not trying to change what happened, just interpret it,' Guy said. He nodded at Davenport. 'Hello, stranger.'

'Film,' Davenport told them. 'Don't ask. So, what's going on here? You having fun?' He singled out one of the photographs, a view over a curving bay with pebbled beaches. Dark grey clouds hung heavily in the air. 'Shingle Bay?' he guessed.

'Trying to work out what was going on there,' Guy told him. 'I mean, why there in particular?'

'Good thought. And you reckon going over what we know, time and again, looking at it in different ways... You think that might throw some light on the German intentions?'

'It's the approach Dr Wiles takes to his code breaking. I thought it might work here.'

'And does it?'

'No,' Green said shortly. 'If you ask me, we're wasting our time.'

'Only if we have better things to do,' Davenport said. 'And I for one don't, it being a bit early for lunch.'

As he spoke, he walked slowly round the small room, inspecting the papers, maps and pictures. 'The conclusion at the time,' he said at last, 'was that... Ah yes, here we are.' He had found the short report he was looking for – pinned between a photograph of the church on top of the cliffs above the bay and a requisition order for two fuel tanker trucks.

'We thought they were after the RADAR station at Bawsey Manor,' Green said. 'A raid, possibly to recover equipment.'

'There you are, then.'

'Except that it doesn't make sense,' Guy said.

All three of them were standing by the Ordnance Survey map for the area. Davenport located Bawsey with his index finger. He put another finger on Shingle Bay. 'They *are* fairly close, so it seems a reasonable assumption. There's nothing else nearby of any note.'

'That's what I thought,' Guy agreed. 'But then it occurred to me that we're looking at this backwards.'

'How do you mean?'

'He means,' Green said, 'that we're looking at where the raid came ashore and trying to guess where they were going.'

'But if we put ourselves in the enemy's shoes,' Pentecross said, 'and try to think how we'd plan the raid in the first place...'

'Yes,' Davenport said, nodding quickly. 'That's good. That's very good. Worthy of Stanislavski.'

'Thank you.'

'You're assuming that was a compliment,' Davenport told him. 'But let's follow this through. Green – how would you plan a raid on Bawsey Manor?'

'Well, Major Pentecross is right. From Shingle Bay, the only sensible target is the RADAR station. But if I was planning to get a raiding party *to* the RADAR station, I wouldn't choose Shingle Bay as my landing zone.'

'Hoping for the element of surprise, perhaps?'

'I'd have to hope for that anyway. And it didn't exactly work. But I'd put ashore here, or even here,' Green pointed at two other small coves on the map, 'before I considered Shingle Bay. We've been over it several times, and the tides are better, the water is shallower, this cove is further from any military units though they might not know that...'

'There's another thing,' Guy said. 'Why head for Bawsey Manor at all?

'A reconnaissance mission, to find out about the RADAR, possibly take back components and equipment. That was the assumption,' Davenport said.

Guy smiled. 'All right, but take things back another step. If that was the objective, then you wouldn't choose Bawsey as your target. There are other RADAR stations, which we can assume the Germans know about, that are more isolated and vulnerable to a raid. If that was what they were up to they'd never have come to Bawsey, which is right in the middle of an army training area, at all. Never mind Shingle Bay, they'd have targeted a different installation entirely.'

They talked round the problem again, checking the maps and documents.

'Well, I can't fault your conclusions,' Davenport said at last. 'But it doesn't help if we still don't know what their objective really was.'

'And we won't find that out by talking about it,' Green complained. 'We know less now than we thought we did when we started.'

'We need more information,' Guy admitted. 'But I have no idea where we'll get it.'

New information arrived that afternoon with the return of Sarah Diamond. There wasn't room in the small office, so they moved into the conference room next door. Brinkman was still out at meetings, but Miss Manners left her telephone and typewriter to join them.

Sarah had a large envelope which she laid on the table. 'I have no idea if these will help, but it occurred to me that there must be a lot going on in that area that isn't shown on the map.'

'Such as?' Green asked.

'Well, we only know that Bawsey Manor is a RADAR station because we have a list of all the RADAR stations. There's nothing on the map to say that it's of importance. The map doesn't show temporary structures, or anything much to do with the war effort.'

'That's true,' Guy said. 'But whatever they were after, the Germans would have to know about it somehow.'

'Exactly, so I asked myself how they might find out.'

'Spies,' Green said.

'They don't have any spies,' Davenport said. 'Oh they think they do, but...' He smiled. 'Forget I said that. Just take it from me that the Germans aren't getting any useful or significant information from agents in this country.'

Guy was smiling. 'Air reconnaissance. They send planes over, sometimes in amongst the bombers but often on their own to photograph the landscape. They're looking for RADAR installations, airfields, checking what damage they've done.' He glanced at the envelope, then at Sarah. 'That's it, isn't it?'

In reply, she tipped out the contents of the envelope. Photographs spilled across the table.

'The ATA regularly fly over the area on ferry flights, delivering planes. I asked one of the men if he could take some pictures. He was happy to oblige.'

'I bet,' Guy murmured, leafing through the pictures.

Sarah coloured slightly. 'It's not very sophisticated. I think he just leaned out of the cockpit with a camera.'

'These are very good,' Miss Manners said, showing real interest for the first time. 'And actually, that's pretty much how we take reconnaissance photographs of the continent. It's a rather ramshackle operation in that respect. The secret is in interpreting the results.'

'They're just pictures,' Green said. 'Should be easy enough.'

'Oh there's an art to it,' Miss Manners told him. 'Mainly to do with scale. Do we know from what height these were taken? Or what lens was on the camera? No? Then we have to work out the scale some other way.'

'There's a church on this one,' Davenport said as they spread out the photographs. There were about thirty of them. 'Bit of a jigsaw, isn't it?'

'If we know which church it is, that will help,' Miss Manners said. 'We need something, some landmark, to give us a size. If you look at the church tower, for example, from this angle there's no way of knowing how high it is. An expert would look at the angle of the shadow, take into account the time of day and position of the sun, that sort of thing. We need to try to relate these images to the map and see how they fit together.'

'Here's Shingle Bay,' Sarah said, pulling out one of the photographs. 'You said it was like a jigsaw, Leo – well, let's see if we can piece together the area.'

Miss Manners took charge of organising the photographs. Although some photographs showed overlapping views of the same area, the task was complicated by the fact that there were also gaps. But with constant reference back to the maps, eventually they had a patchwork photographic picture of the area.

'Now for the hard part,' Guy said. 'Spotting what the Germans might have spotted. They probably have similar photographs, so what did they see?'

'If anything,' Green said.

'You still think we're wasting our time?' Guy asked. 'Still think there's no reason for them coming to Shingle Bay?'

'Oh there was a reason all right, and I'd love to know what it is.' Green gestured at the photographs spread across the table. 'But I'm not convinced that we'll ever find out what it was. I'll be more than happy if you can prove me wrong, sir.'

'You need to reduce the size of the problem,' Brinkman told them the next day.

Guy was frustrated, wondering if Green was right and they were wasting their time. Davenport had a stack of books and papers he was reading through, occasionally wandering round the table and peering at the photographs. Miss Manners and Green had returned to the main office, leaving Sarah to mark up the map with notes of anything visible in the photographs.

They had made a lot of notes, but little progress.

Brinkman tapped the photograph of Shingle Bay. 'This is the key, fairly obviously. Start from here. You've looked for possible targets for the raid, and you've found reasons why a raid on potential targets wouldn't start from here. So turn it round again.'

'How do you mean?' Pentecross asked.

'Don't look for a target at all. Instead, look for a location. Don't worry about what's there on the map or the photographs.'

'Because it might not be visible?' Sarah said.

'Or it might have gone,' Brinkman told them. 'You're looking at a landscape over a year after the raid took place.'

Davenport frowned, putting down his book and joining them at the table. 'But if they were after, I don't know, a person – someone driving along this road near the headland – then there's no way we could find out about it now.'

'True. But a person is unlikely as they'd have to know precisely that person's movements in advance.'

'But you're saying we can look for things we can't actually see,' Pentecross said. 'Or something like that.'

'Something like that. Work out where they were heading. Then worry about what was there, what they were after.' Brinkman straightened up. 'Just a suggestion. Give it another day, but I don't think it warrants more than that.'

They ringed the areas on the map that seemed prime target locations. From that they moved back to the photographs. Miss Manners sent for the troop and supply movement orders for the area for the week either side of the incident, warning that there would be a lot of information and that it wouldn't give them the complete picture.

'There's a wooded area,' Sarah said, checking one of the circled areas against the corresponding photo. 'Maybe there's something hidden by the trees.'

Davenport looked over her shoulder. 'What's that in the middle of the trees? A clearing?'

'Just raised ground, I think. Small hill.'

He grunted and moved round Sarah to peer closer at the image.

'Important?' Guy asked.

'Looks familiar, that's all. The shape, I mean… It reminds me of something.' He peered at the map. 'Anything on the map?'

Guy checked. 'Something's marked. It just says "Tumulus". What's that mean?'

Sarah shook her head. 'Haven't a clue.'

But Davenport was staring at them, his mouth open in surprise. 'Tumulus? Are you sure?'

'You know what it means?'

'It means we've found what they were after.' He stared back at the map. 'Of course. That's why I recognise the shape of the mound. Looks a bit different from above, of course, but even so...'

Guy looked at Sarah, but she shrugged.

'A tumulus,' Davenport said at last, 'is an ancient burial mound. Like the one Streicher and his men were excavating in France. Like the one where they found the other Ubermensch. And here's a very similar looking mound right next to Shingle Bay. I'll bet you Threadneedle Street to an orange *that* is what they came for.'

There were some things he remembered from before the great darkness, the long sleeping in the tomb. Pain was one of them – what it felt like, and how to deliver it.

But it took time with books on anatomy to understand how pain worked, and a long session with a doctor he waited for outside a hospital to learn how best to inflict it. Pain as a tool was unparalleled. Pain could unlock information from any of the people he sought out. Pain was his friend.

'Have you told me everything?' he would ask. And pain helped him to know when they had. When they were of no further use to him.

He didn't think of it as home – he had no home. But he returned through habit and convenience to Dorothy Keeling in her shattered house near Blackfriars. He sat and listened as she related more of her life history, more of what her friends had told her over the years. He learned something else from her too – that information given willingly was less concise but often more useful, more insightful, more reliable than information taken under duress.

'I lost my brother Tom in the Great War,' she said as she fumbled to find the table for his cup of tea. 'Did I tell you that?'

'You did.'

She shuffled back towards the doorway, relating for the third time exactly how she thought Tom had died. The Ubermensch stood up, walking slowly after her, ignoring the steaming tea.

'Even Mrs Willis has moved out now, did I say?' She paused in the doorway and turned back, shaking her head. Her blurred vision meant she could barely make out the form of the man standing in front of her. 'You're not drinking your tea. I told you, if you leave it too long it'll go cold and won't be nice. I'm sorry there's no sugar. Have I told you there's no sugar?'

The man who had lived in her house, eaten her meagre meals, and drunk her weak tea for several months now put his hands gently on her shoulders. 'You *have* told me. You have told me everything.'

He sat her down in the chair which he no longer needed. He wouldn't be coming back. Beside her, the tea got slowly cold.

The British Museum was an obvious place to return to. Some people had the potential to provide more information through their actions than their words. The old woman at the museum was one of these. He watched her leave the building, and followed her through the streets. She had lived a long time – perhaps there was value in asking her to relate her knowledge and experiences.

She met another woman, outside a building in St James. Connections were useful, and he followed the other woman now. He could always find the old woman at the museum if and when he needed to.

The other woman was younger, with fair hair and slightly angular features. At the end of the street, she turned and almost collided with a man. He caught her arm. He knew her, but she seemed surprised to see him.

*

'Andrew?'

'Did I startle you?'

Sarah had been half-expecting a call from Whitman. But she had certainly not expected to find him in St James's Square. 'You following me?'

'I was looking for you. It's been a while.'

She looked round, checking that no one had followed her from the office. 'We can't be seen together. People might...'

'Might get the right idea?'

She shook her head. 'That's over. You know that's over.'

'That a fact?'

In truth it had never really started. A few fumbled moments and stolen kisses in his office at the embassy. But that was never what she wanted. 'I only saw you because I wanted to do something.'

'Then let's do something.'

'For the war.'

He grinned. 'Whatever reason you want.'

'Be serious.'

'OK, OK.' The grin subsided into a more passive smugness. 'The information you provided, about transport, logistics, all that, it was really useful.'

'Was it?' she snapped. 'Then why hasn't America joined the war?'

'You got lend-lease, what more do you want?'

'What do *you* want?' Sarah demanded. 'I'm not at Air Transport Auxiliary any more, so I don't have access to the information I used to.'

'That a fact?' Whitman said, though he obviously knew this. 'So what do you instead?'

'It's just... office work.'

'I'm sure you have access to a load of useful stuff in this office work.'

'No,' she insisted. 'I don't.'

'Even so, it'd be a shame if your new colleagues thought they couldn't trust you.'

Sarah felt suddenly cold. 'Are you threatening me, Andrew?'

'Hell no,' he said. But his unsympathetic smile suggested otherwise. 'Just don't be a stranger, OK? You hear anything you think would interest Uncle Sam, you look me up.' He reached out and cradled her cheek for a moment in his hand. 'Good girl.'

Sarah stepped away. She didn't reply, but turned and walked back towards the office.

Whitman watched her go, the smile still etched on his face. If he had been concentrating less on how much of Sarah Diamond's legs were visible below her skirt and more on his surroundings, he might have seen the tall, gaunt, hollow-eyed figure that watched him from the shelter of a nearby doorway. That followed him as Whitman turned and headed off towards the American embassy.

CHAPTER 26

Although Sarah was not one to worry about anything for long, the encounter with Whitman unsettled her. Usually by the time she got home, made herself some dinner and perhaps read for an hour, Sarah was exhausted. Her social life, such as it was, had dwindled to the occasional drink at the end of the day with Guy Pentecross or Leo Davenport when he was around. Occasionally Miss Manners joined them, but she said little and drank less.

After her run-in with Whitman, Sarah went back to Station Z, hoping Guy would ask her to the pub. But he was deep in conversation with Davenport, waiting for Brinkman to be free so they could talk about the burial mound in Suffolk. She hung around for a few more minutes, then left.

Sleep came slowly. In her mind she went over the short conversation with Whitman again and again. 'Is that a fact?' he said inside her head, in that annoying drawl she had once found faintly attractive. Would he really tell Brinkman – or worse, Guy – that she was a spy?

It was a blunt word. But it was true. She'd passed on sensitive information that she had been entrusted with despite her background, despite being only half British. Were the other non-British nationals caught up in this war as ambivalent as she was?

That was all nonsense, she thought as she finally drifted off to sleep. She'd acted out of the best of motives – hoping the more they knew, the more likely the Americans were to come to the Allies' help. Though the petrol coupons he'd given her were useful. She hadn't exactly objected to being paid for the information, had she…

She woke early, still exhausted but with an idea of what best to do. She thought she would be in the office before anyone else, but she could hear the clacking of Miss Manners' typewriter before she reached the top of the first flight of stairs.

'You're in early,' Sarah said, trying to sound bright. Her head was pounding, like she had a hangover though she'd not had a drink for days.

Miss Manners paused to give her a sympathetic look. Perhaps she was always in by seven in the morning.

'What time will the colonel be in?' Sarah asked quickly, before the typing resumed.

'He's in already.' There was the hint of a smile at Sarah's expression. 'There's a budget review coming up in a few days. Colonel Brinkman wants to be sure we can make the best possible case for… Well, for continued funding.'

'You mean, we might not?'

'It's possible. MI5 and SOE would both like to see us closed down.'

That was a worrying thought. 'But surely, what we do…'

'As far as they're concerned we don't do anything. Except take resources they'd rather deploy elsewhere. We have precious little to show for our efforts after all.'

'But…' Sarah struggled to disagree with this. Most of what they were investigating was based on supposition and extrapolation. 'Shingle Bay – they know that happened.'

'Just a raid – so they would say. The enemy probing our defences.'

'And what about Hess?'

'Again, to play devil's advocate, do we really want to commit valuable resources, money and personnel to investigating the ravings of a delusional misfit who has defected from the enemy and could for all we know be feeding us all sorts of bogus nonsense precisely to ensure we make those commitments?'

Sarah suddenly felt desperately exposed – could she go back to the ATA after this? What would she tell them? What about the aircraft she had *seen*? 'Surely we don't cost the war effort very much.'

'True,' Miss Manners agreed. 'But the problem is, the war effort doesn't *have* very much.'

Brinkman was making notes as he read through a pile of documents. He didn't look up when Sarah knocked and went into his office. She waited for a while, coughed politely when he still didn't look up, and waited some more. Finally, he glanced at her and gave a small nod.

'We should tell the Americans,' she said. Best to be direct. 'I know someone at the embassy.'

'Why?'

'They can provide funding. We'd be less dependent on the British war effort, not have to worry about MI5 and SOE and the others grabbing our budget.'

'You think the Americans would believe us?' he asked.

She could tell from his tone that he didn't. 'We could try.'

Brinkman grunted and returned his attention to the papers on his desk.

'Is that a "No", then?'

'We're not wasting time and effort telling the Americans. They want to get involved, they can do it properly rather than continually sitting on the fence.'

'But this is different.' Sarah said, exasperated.

'We're still fighting a war.'

'Not if we lose our funding we're not.'

Brinkman sighed. He leaned back in his chair. 'Thank you for the thought, Sarah.'

He usually called her 'Miss Diamond'. She was only 'Sarah' when he was annoyed.

'As in "thanks but no thanks" you mean. But look,' she went on, 'surely things are different now that Roosevelt and Churchill have signed the Atlantic Charter?'

'It stops short of bringing the US into the war.' Brinkman sighed, wiping his hand across his forehead. 'I'm sorry. Sharing information with the Americans would still be difficult under the best of circumstances. I'm sure it will happen one day, but not yet.'

'And American funding?'

'To be honest – not if I can help it. They'd turn this whole operation into a bloody circus.'

Davenport sat in the front and talked to her almost all the way. That at least made Sarah feel she wasn't just there to act as the driver. Guy dozed in the back, and she knew he'd been at the office most of the previous night finishing up paperwork from a fruitless day interviewing fighter pilots. None of them had seen the UDT they had almost intercepted, but it still had to be written up and filed.

'It's on a smaller scale to the French barrow,' Davenport said, once he had exhausted the latest society gossip. 'But the design is very similar. From my notes we were able to dig in, avoiding most of the traps and tricks Streicher's men ran into. Green commandeered a squad from some nearby unit and the ground's firm enough they could dig quite deep and come up into the central passageway from underneath.' He mimed with his hand. 'Clever, eh? My idea, of course.'

'Of course,' Sarah said. She couldn't help smiling.

'False modesty is *so* affected, don't you think?' Davenport said.

'I've not come across it recently.'

Davenport smiled back. 'If Green and his chaps have been putting their backs into it, they'll have broken into the main passageway, just shy of the burial chamber itself.'

'When do they break into that?' Guy asked from the back of the car, stifling a yawn.

'Oh they don't. Green will dismiss the men before that.' Davenport lapsed into uncharacteristic silence, and Sarah guessed he was recalling the ordeals of France.

'Had the devil's own job finding the place last week,'

Davenport said as they drew closer to their destination. 'The road signs have all been taken away and according to Green about half the population has been moved out of East Anglia. So no signs to follow and no one to ask.'

He seemed to know the way perfectly now, and Sarah guessed he remembered a route as easily as he recalled his lines for a play. Certainly it seemed that once he had read something, Davenport could remember it pretty much verbatim.

Main roads gave way to narrow, winding lanes and finally, they turned off the lane and on to a single-track bridleway. They reached a farm gate, and Davenport got out to open it and allow the car through.

As he pushed open the gate, an elderly woman came hurrying up from the other side of the hedge. Her grey hair blew across her face and she pushed it aside irritably before jabbing her finger at Davenport.

'Who is she?' Guy asked, leaning forward in his rear seat.

'No idea. She's not happy, though.'

The woman had turned to glare at the staff car, pointing. When Guy opened his window, her glare turned into a smile for a moment. She hurried forward, and Sarah could make out the details of her weather-beaten face and milky eyes.

'Is that him? It doesn't look like him,' she said, her voice a sharp nasal whine.

Davenport caught up with her. 'No, that's not him. He's very busy, but we're hoping tomorrow. Or possibly the day after.'

The woman turned. 'I shall want to see him.'

'Of course. I'm sure he'll want to thank you personally.'

The woman seemed to stiffen slightly at this. 'Really? You think so?'

'I'm sure of it,' Davenport said.

The woman nodded. 'Very well then. You can drop me by the barn, I'll walk from there.'

Sarah watched in surprise as Davenport opened the back door of the car to let the woman climb in. He raised his eyebrows at Sarah before returning to the gate and waving her through.

'So who are you, then?' the woman demanded as they stopped to let Davenport close the gate behind the car.

'Um, Major Pentecross. And this is Miss Diamond.'

'Hello,' Sarah said, glancing back and switching on a smile.

The woman did not smile back. 'They let women drive, do they?'

Davenport opened the door in time to hear this. 'Oh, indeed,' he said. 'And Miss Diamond is very good at it. She flies aeroplanes too.'

'Does she?' The words were laced with both admiration and disapproval in roughly equal measure.

'This is Lady Grenchard,' Davenport explained as they drove slowly up the track. 'She owns the land, and indeed the burial mound. She has very kindly allowed us to dig a very small investigative trench.' He nodded meaningfully at Sarah and Pentecross.

'They tell me that I can see how it's going when Mr Carter arrives,' Lady Grenchard said. 'Though why the need for all the secrecy I have no idea.'

'Bureaucracy, I'm afraid. The war, you know.'

Lady Grenchard sighed. 'This war is so inconvenient.'

Sarah was about to make a sarcastic comment. But the old woman added quietly: 'They killed my grandson, you know. The Germans.' She wiped her sleeve over her eyes. 'The sooner it's all sorted out and we send them packing the better. I shall be very cross, Mr Davenport,' she went on quickly, 'if your people have dug too close to the mound. We respect the dead here. And the legends. I told you about the legends.'

'Indeed you did.' Davenport ignored Sarah's inquisitive glance. 'And we will be very careful, I can assure you.'

'What legends are these?' Guy asked, ignoring the glare this earned from Davenport.

Lady Grenchard was shocked. 'Hasn't he told you?'

'We're just visiting. Rather short notice.'

'Local stories about the burial mound,' Davenport said. 'Apparently it's cursed.'

'Really?' Sarah said.

'Oh do tell,' Guy said. 'This is all so interesting.'

Lady Grenchard seemed to soften slightly at his request. 'The legends date back longer than anyone can remember. But the mound is said to be the burial place of an ancient chieftain. He was a tyrant – oh, a terrible man if the stories are true. Dreadful. It is said that if anyone opens the burial chamber, they will die the most agonising death and the chieftain will rise again to claim his former kingdom.'

Guy nodded. 'How… fascinating.'

'I put no store in such frivolous stories myself, of course.'

'Of course.'

'But as the landowner I do have a responsibility to history, and to local superstition and feeling. My father was very much a believer that we should leave well alone. He said that the story was probably a load of tommyrot – that was the word he used. Tommyrot. But if there was even the slightest chance that the smallest part of it might have some grain of truth in it… Well.'

'Well,' Davenport echoed. 'Indeed.'

'Just here will do very nicely, thank you.'

It took Sarah a moment to realise the woman was talking to her. She stopped the car beside a stone-built barn, and Lady Grenchard got out.

'You will tell me when he arrives,' she said to Davenport. Her tone made it clear this was an order rather than a request.

'Oh I will, I promise.'

He let out a long sigh as they drove on. 'We'll have to leave the car at the bottom of the hill. The track peters out after that.'

'This Mr Carter she's waiting for?' Guy asked slowly. 'Is he…?'

'Yes. I didn't want to have to order her to make the land available. That would have garnered all sorts of unwanted attention, and it doesn't do to upset the local nobility. Could make things a bit sticky.'

'So you told her Howard Carter was coming to see the excavations?'

'Together with the promise of a couple of tickets to my next West End play. Though God alone knows when that will be.'

'Hang on,' Sarah said. 'You mean Howard Carter as in the chap who discovered the tomb of Tutankhamun?'

Davenport nodded. 'That's the one. Luckily, the formidable Lady Grenchard doesn't seem to be aware of the fact the poor blighter's been dead for a couple of years.'

The track wound its way down the side of a hill towards woodland. At the edge of the woods a truck was parked – having brought Green and his soldiers, Sarah assumed. She parked the staff car close by, leaving room for the truck to turn.

They made their way on foot through the woods to the burial mound. It was strange walking through the landscape that Sarah had examined so closely on the aerial photographs. When they emerged from the small wooded area, it was to see the grass-covered mound rising up in front of them. It looked just like a small hill, the regular shape visible in the photographs indiscernible at ground level.

As they approached. Sarah could hear a low rumble, like a badly tuned engine. A generator, she realised, seeing thick cables running to a dark maw at the side of the mound. To the side, just where the trees started again, freshly dug earth was banked up in huge piles.

'She'll have a fit if she sees this,' Davenport said.

No one needed to ask who he meant. There was a deep trench cut into the ground on one side of the 'hill'. It formed a tunnel, leading down into darkness. Wooden posts and lintels held the ground back, and electric lamps were strung between them casting a pale yellow glow through the tunnel.

'Abandon hope and all that,' Davenport said, leading them into the tunnel. 'Mind your heads, it gets a bit low further along. Oh, and there's a pit we have to get across, no idea how deep it is. Would rather not find out.'

Sarah had visions of having to jump. But the soldiers had laid long wooden boards. They had to cross one at a time so their weight didn't break the planks. Even so, they creaked and bent alarmingly in the middle as Sarah made her way quickly across.

The air grew musty and heavy, cloying in the heat and ever-present dust. They seemed to be burrowing deep into the ground. Sarah couldn't help thinking of the fate of the narrator of *The Coming Race* – his journey underground and what he found there...

'Nearly there,' Davenport assured them at last.

Ahead, Sarah could hear the sound of laughter. The tunnel had been rising for a while, so they were walking uphill. Finally it opened out into a wider area, hollowed out from the earth. How far beneath the burial mound they were, Sarah had no idea. Tools were piled up around the edge of the area – pickaxes and shovels, wheelbarrows and buckets. A group of half a dozen soldiers stood or sat in the middle of the open space. Sergeant Green came to greet them.

'Just got a brew on if you fancy a cup of tea.'

One of the soldiers was pumping the small plunger at the side of a primus stove to build pressure in the metal canister. Once he had done that, he struck a match on the heel of his boot and lit the stove. Water was already starting to boil in a billycan resting on the top of another stove.

'Come to make the tea, love?' one of them called across to Sarah.

She forced a smile. 'In your dreams.'

'You don't want to know about my dreams, darling.'

'Oi!' Green barked. 'Show some respect for the lady.'

The soldiers suddenly leaped to their feet – not in response to Green's words, but seeing the uniformed Guy emerge into the dim light.

'As you were,' he said. 'But the sergeant's right. Miss Diamond maybe a civilian, but you can behave as if she outranks you. Any order she gives – jump to it. You and your team have done a splendid job,' he went on, turning to Green. 'Well done.'

'Thank you, sir.'

Davenport motioned to Green, and the two of them withdrew to the edge of the area where another, wider passageway entered. They spoke in hushed voices for a few moments before Green returned to the soldiers.

'I've told him to send the men back to their base when they've had their tea,' Davenport explained. 'We can take it from here.' He pointed to where the opening ended in a smooth wall caked with dust and dirt. 'The lads widened this whole area. It was just a passageway, leading to that. Through there is what we are after. Assuming it follows the same design as in France, and so far that has been the case.'

'You don't want their help getting through?' Guy asked.

'The fewer people here the better. Both for safety, and security.'

'Security?' Sarah asked.

'We'll break through on our own, well away from gossiping squaddies and interfering landowners,' Davenport said. His eyes gleamed as they caught the light from a nearby bulb. 'We'll do it tonight.'

CHAPTER 27

The only way to tell that the evening was drawing in outside was that it got colder. Green returned after seeing the group of Royal Engineers back to their base. Davenport insisted they wear their gas masks before breaking into the main burial chamber.

'Whatever that mist was at the French burial site, it was certainly toxic,' he told them.

'And we're hoping gas masks will be effective against it,' Guy said.

'German ones were. The troops who went in afterwards suffered no obvious ill effects.'

'Fingers crossed then,' Green said. He handed them torches. 'Obviously the lights only come this far.'

What had looked like a smooth wall was actually a door. It was made of rusted metal, dust and earth clinging to its etched surface. Davenport brushed it away with the back of his gloved hand.

'Through here, there is a small antechamber. We break through the wall, and into the burial chamber. There are other chambers too, but I don't know much about them. After the gas was released, Streicher was a little reticent about letting me see much more.'

'We're assuming this follows the same layout,' Sarah said.

'So far, it has. But I suggest we put our gas masks on before opening this door, in case the internal wall has been breached.'

Green levered the end of a pickaxe between the door and its frame, forcing open a gap wide enough for Guy to get his hand inside. Between them, Green and Guy heaved the metal door open. Sarah and Davenport shone their torches into the gloom the other side. The opening was wreathed with cobwebs. Davenport brushed them aside, revealing the small chamber he has described, and the stone wall.

'So far, so good,' Davenport's voice was muffled by the gas mask. He gestured for the others to stand back while Green picked up the pickaxe again and swung at the wall.

The blade of the pickaxe bit into the wall, finding a point between two of the stone blocks. Again, Green worked the tool like a lever, forcing the handle sideways to ease out the stone block. It crunched out of the wall, standing proud of the other blocks. Green removed the pickaxe and leaned it against the side wall. He gripped the block tight in his hands, looking up at the others.

'Ready?'

Green pulled the block. It scraped forwards a little, then stopped. Guy bent to help, gripping the other end of the block. Together they heaved and the stone block came clear of the wall in a shower of dust and disintegrating mortar. Except the dust didn't stop. It became a fine, white mist, drifting out from the gap left by the stone.

'Is that it?' Sarah asked indistinctly through the gas mask.

Davenport nodded. 'Doesn't look like there's so much this time.'

The gas curled like smoke, thickening the air in the small anteroom. Davenport motioned for Green and Guy to return to work on the wall. They set about enlarging the hole, and the gas was thinning by the time it was big enough to climb through into the main burial chamber.

Sarah's torch picked out a large circular area with a low, vaulted roof. The tattered and rotted remains of some heavy material – tapestries perhaps – hung from the walls like ancient curtains. Further in, cobwebs hung like swathes of decaying silk. Several dark doorways lead off to other areas, and in the centre of the chamber stood a large casket. It was crude, roughly hewn from a single piece of rock. A slab of stone lay across the top, sealing it.

Davenport made his way warily to the casket, walking slowly round it. He beckoned them over.

'I think the gas has dissipated, but best keep our masks on for a while longer.'

They gathered round the casket, examining the stone lid. As the light of one of the torches caught it, they could see a design etched into the surface.

'Is that a Swastika?' Green asked, amazed and appalled in equal measure.

'Not quite,' Davenport told him. 'The Swastika is itself an ancient symbol. This is similar, but see how the "legs" are jointed. A bit like the Manx symbol used by the Isle of Man.'

'Celtic, do you think?' Guy asked. 'The Celtic cross is not dissimilar.'

'Nothing Christian about this,' Davenport said. 'Too early for one thing.'

'You an expert?' Guy asked.

'Hardly an expert, but a well-informed amateur. Elizabeth Archer helped me learn a bit more about the Bronze Age to bluff my way with Streicher. Being blessed with a good memory has its uses. But I must confess I've always had an interest in ancient history, myths and legends, that sort of thing.'

'Do you think we can get the top off?' Green asked.

'Do we want to?' Sarah wondered. 'God knows what's inside, or what state it's in.'

As the men discussed the best way to remove the heavy lid without damaging anything, Sarah examined the rest of the chamber. In amongst the dust and cobwebs, there were urns and jars. They seemed to have been dumped without any order to them, sometimes grouped together sometimes individually. Several were broken – collapsed in on themselves through age.

She shone her torch to the roof. It was difficult to make out the details of the structure, but it seemed to be composed of slabs of stone resting on long ribs, also of stone. She hoped whoever built it knew what they were doing – how many tons of earth must the structure be holding up?

Sarah turned her torch back towards the casket, where Davenport was miming sliding the lid to one side while Guy shook his head. As she moved the torch, the light caught something. A movement. At the edge of the beam, in amongst a pile of jars. Cobwebs shimmered as something passed underneath. A draught? Or...

A dark shadow scuttled across the floor.

'Did you see that?' Sarah said. Her voice was tight with nerves. Muffled by the gas mask, it didn't carry. No one answered.

Probably a trick of the light, she thought. Or one of the others had moved their torch, dispelling the shadows in an illusion of movement. Probably. She made her way cautiously over to where she had seen the movement. Sure enough, there was nothing there. Just a few broken jars made of dark pottery. Dust and cobwebs.

And a sound. A scraping rattle from behind her. She spun round – and again, nothing but shadows. She was staring into the dark opening of a doorway. Sarah shone her torch into it, and saw a stone-walled passageway leading off. The sound came again – was it her imagination? Was it the gas-mask strap catching on something as she moved her head?

She glanced back, and saw the others were still busy at the casket. Guy and Sergeant Green were pushing at one side of the stone lid as Davenport pulled from the other side. They obviously hadn't seen anything. She called out to them again. But her words coincided with a loud grunt of effort from Green and the scrape of stone on stone as the lid shifted slightly.

Sarah shook her head, and turned to the passageway. She'd just go down it a few yards, and see where it led. Just a few yards – no further.

Behind her, the others focused all their attention on the stone slab covering the sarcophagus. Another effort from Guy and

Green, and the lid slid back, revealing the dark space beneath. Davenport made sure that the stone lid was not about to slip off the casket, then satisfied that its own weight was holding it securely angled across the top, he shone his torch inside.

The three of them stared down at the figure inside.

'My God,' Green breathed. 'What *is* that?'

The Y Station at Felixstowe picked up the signal less than three seconds after the lid was pushed aside. Several amateur radio hams also detected it, and made notes. These 'voluntary interceptors' sent in their reports along with the official interception stations.

The data from Felixstowe was given more urgency. The signal was like nothing they had intercepted before, and the direction-finding experts were pretty sure it came from inland. An approximation of the warbling screech of sound was recorded in Morse code, along with a handwritten description from the Signals Intelligence Officer.

It was despatched by motorcycle, along with several other intercepts collected that evening, to Arkley View. The house on the edge of Barnet, north of London, was where all signals intercepts were collated before being passed on to Station X – the Government Code and Cypher School at Bletchley Park.

'One for Dr Wiles, by the look of it,' the young female analyst decided. She stamped it 'HUT A' and put it in the out-tray. It would be with Wiles and his team before dawn...

The floor was made up of rough stones laid unevenly. It sloped down slightly from the main chamber. Just a few yards, Sarah had decided. But she found herself going further than that, picking her way carefully in the pale glow of her torch. The passageway began to narrow, until she felt her shoulders brushing against the sides. If it got any narrower she would have to go back.

But she couldn't shake off the feeling that she was following something. Something that kept just ahead of the torch beam, hugging the shadows and scuttling through the darkness. She could barely see as it was – her field of view restricted by the scratched and smeared lenses of the gasmask. Tunnel vision in every sense. A few more yards...

Just as she was about to turn back and fetch the others, the passageway opened out. The area was not as large as the main burial chamber, but every bit as dusty and cobweb-strung. More of the rotting material clung to the walls where it had once hung in, Sarah guessed, colourful splendour. Now it had faded to a dull uniform grey, hanging in ancient tatters. There was no other doorway that Sarah could see as she swept the torch round the area. Her foot connected with shards of broken pottery and she stumbled. The torchlight danced across the walls and ceiling – coming to rest as she regained her balance.

Another light shone back at her.

Sarah blinked, moving her hand instinctively to shield her eyes, and the other torch disappeared. She stood for a moment, uncertain.

'Hello?' Her voice was a nervous rumble in her ears, echoing inside the gas mask. She felt suddenly very hot. Couldn't breathe. The smell of the rubber seal round the edge of the mask almost made her retch. She fumbled with the strap, trying to loosen it slightly, torchlight bouncing round the enclosed space.

The other torch shone out again, blinding her for a moment before disappearing. Something glinted in the darkness ahead of her. Movement – she was sure of it. A shadow moving across in front of her. She tried to follow it, but the glass eyepieces were steaming up. Her chest heaved, breathing became ragged. She would suffocate if she didn't get the mask off.

But if she did – the gas...

Never mind the gas. Davenport had said it was probably all gone. Anything – even choking on the pale mist – was better than the clammy feel of the mask, the stuffy, claustrophobic heat of it against her face. Sarah tore it off.

The seal stuck to her skin, and she was afraid for a moment

that she was tearing her own flesh away with the mask, that it had fused to her – she'd heard that could happen if your plane caught fire. Head down, hands on her knees, she gulped in the stale, musty air of the tomb. How long would it take her to die if there was still gas around, she wondered? From what Davenport had said it was fairly quick.

Her breathing settled into a more normal rhythm and she was still alive. Sarah straightened up. Swallowed, told herself to stay calm. Stay. Calm.

She pushed the gas mask back into its small satchel which she carried over her shoulder. As she began to feel better, Sarah slowly raised the torch, shining it at where she had seen something moving.

There *was* something there – a figure, staring back at her. A figure holding a torch. Distorted, misshapen... A reflection, she realised. She had scared *herself*, and she laughed out loud, a pathetic, nervous, dry laugh.

A stone shelf jutted out from the back wall of the chamber. Something on the shelf had reflected back the torchlight. Sarah brushed away the hanging cobwebs. The light intensified, reflected back from a row of glass containers. Cylinders with open tops – like huge jars. There were five of them, in a row along the shelf. A sixth was a pile of shattered fragments at the end.

There was something else, in among the fragments of broken glass. Sarah carefully lifted it clear – a bracelet, caked with dust and discoloured with age. She was surprised how heavy it was. She rubbed it gently, and the dust and grime fell away – revealing the sparkle of silver tracery beneath.

Looking along the shelf, Sarah could see now that there was a bracelet in front on each of the containers. She slipped the bracelet into the small satchel with her gas mask, and reached for another. It seemed identical – just as heavy, and when she rubbed off the dust it sparkled in the torchlight as if it was new.

Closer to the jars now, the beam of torchlight penetrated the dusty surface. There was something *inside* the jars. Liquid.

That and the curvature of the glass distorted Sarah's reflection as she put down the bracelet and wiped at the side of one of the jars with the back of her hand. The jar was heavy, but shifted as she pressed on the glass. Did they have glass back in the Bronze Age? Something stirred inside, disturbed by the movement.

She couldn't tell if the content of the glass jar was animal or plant matter. It was dark, almost black, as if it had been burned. A bulbous main body the size of a small football, with six legs or branches extending beneath it. Branches or possibly roots, they were gnarled and twisted, textured like the bark of an ancient tree, but segmented and jointed. The creature was a dry husk, brittle and desiccated, like a giant curled-up spider. Dead for centuries.

Sarah peered closer at the other jars, and saw that they held similar contents. It was difficult to make out the details through the discoloured, stained glass. There was a scum of green liquid in one of the jars, like brackish water. The liquid stirred. Movement. The vague image of her reflection was like a ghost in front of her. Staring back at her. But the eyes were not her own.

The eyes that stared back out of her face were those of the creature behind the glass, suddenly open. Black hollows within the oily, bulbous form. Empty and dark. Then the creature seemed to tense, legs drawing inwards towards the centre before shooting out again – smashing hard against the glass.

Sarah screamed and stepped back, hand to her mouth as the jar shuddered. The liquid sloshed round inside. The creature stared out at her, its eyes dark pits of hatred.

She took another step backwards, eyes fixed on the contents of the jar. Torch wavering nervously. If she had looked down, if she had lowered the torch, Sarah might have seen another creature. Dark as a shadow, eyes glinting hungrily, the creature watched Sarah from several feet away.

It seemed to compress down on its stick-like legs as she stepped back towards it. Two of the legs reached out, like tentacles. Small claws snapped at the ends of the tentacles as they edged closer to Sarah. As the creature prepared to leap.

Guy could barely make out the features of the figure lying inside the casket.

'Can we take these off yet?' he asked, pointing at his gas mask.

By way of answer, Davenport pulled his own gas mask off. 'If the gas doesn't get us, the lack of air certainly will,' he joked.

Green and Guy took their masks off too. Together they looked down into the stone casket. The figure lying inside had its hands crossed over its chest. The last vestiges of decaying robes clung to it. The body itself was almost a skeleton. The hands were stripped of flesh, the face sunken with the skin stretched tight against the skull. There was no hair. Pale lips had receded from broken, discoloured teeth. The hollows of the cheeks were lined and wrinkled.

'Looks like he'd crumble to dust as soon as you touch him,' Guy said. 'Is this the same as the one in France?' He reached down towards the hands. There was something on the figure's wrist, obscured by the tattered remains of the sleeve.

'I didn't see the one in France, not the body. But the casket is very similar,' Davenport said.

'Well he's dead,' Green said. 'That's for sure.'

Guy brushed away the material covering the wrist. It flaked into powder, like burned paper as he touched it, revealing an ornate bracelet. Lines of silver tracery gleamed in the light of their torches.

'What do you make of this?' Guy asked. He looked round for Sarah, but she wasn't there. 'Sarah?'

'I'll see if I can find her,' Green said, stepping away from the casket.

'A bracelet,' Davenport said. 'I have seen something similar, I think...' He reached down into the casket.

A scream echoed round the chamber. Distant, but loud – filled with both surprise and fear.

'That's Sarah!' Guy said.

At the same moment, Davenport gasped in horror, his eyes fixed on the casket.

Guy looked too.

The eyes of the dead man blinked open. Dark, shadowy sockets stared up at them. The mouth twisted into a snarl of anger. The arms lashed out, smashing into the lid that lay at an angle across the lower half of the body, forcing it from the top of the casket. It fell to the floor and shattered with a deafening crash of stone on stone.

Guy and Davenport leaped back from the casket.

The nightmare figure inside sat up, dark eyes fixed on them as a skeletal hand gripped the side of the casket and the corpse hauled itself out.

CHAPTER 28

Eyes open, staring at the whitewashed ceiling. A hand scratching at the sheet.

Kruger almost missed it. He was checking each of the dreamers, making sure they were sedated. He made a note that Number Seventeen needed turning – the man was getting bedsores.

The girl's eyes were open, wide but unfocused. She stared up at the ceiling.

'Nurse!' Kruger called. The level of sedative must be wrong. Then he saw the hand, twitching and scratching on the plain sheet that covered her body.

The nurse hurried up, pale with worry that she was in trouble.

'Get pencil and paper,' Kruger ordered. 'Quickly.'

She hurried off, relief obvious in her step.

'And someone find Hoffman,' Kruger shouted after her. 'Tell him Number Fifteen is drawing.'

By the time Hoffman arrived, they had the girl sitting on the side of her bed. A small table had been placed in front of her, with a pile of blank paper. As she completed each drawing, the nurse took it, turned it over, and moved it to a separate pile on the bed.

Hoffman dismissed the nurse and Kruger took over from her. They watched as the girl drew the next picture, shading the sheet almost completely graphite grey. Just a triangular patch of white left across it.

'Light,' Kruger said. 'See – there is a progression.'

He turned over the complete sketches and riffled through them. The first few were almost entirely grey. Then gradually, the patch of white grew.

'How can she be drawing?' Hoffman demanded. 'She has no bracelet. No link.'

Kruger shook his head. 'It happened before. With the first Ubermensch, you remember?'

Hoffman did. 'Like a bad connection. Indistinct.'

'There obviously *is* a connection of sorts. If she is on exactly the right... frequency, wavelength, whatever it is – if she is tuned to the transmission then she is able to receive without a bracelet.'

Hoffman looked at the drawing she was working on. Shapes in the white area now, but vague and indistinct.

'We speculated about radio waves. She's like a badly tuned receiver,' he said, thinking out loud. 'She's getting the impression, not the details. What about the others?' he asked suddenly as a thought occurred to him.

Kruger shook his head. 'She's the only one.'

'And Number Nine?'

'No. I sent one of the nurses to check. He is still in London so far as we can tell. The bombed-out streets.'

'Following people. Assessing and assimilating.'

'If that's what Nine's Ubermensch is doing.'

'And what is this one doing?'

The girl pushed the paper aside and started on the next picture. Hoffman lifted the discarded sheet and inspected it.

'These could be faces. People looking down at it.'

'Light in the darkness,' Kruger murmured, leafing back through the previous sheets.

Hoffman watched the next picture taking shape. Definitely figures – three of them. Head and shoulders in silhouette. On one shoulder three shallow 'V' shapes – an insignia, perhaps? A uniform?

One thing was certain though.

'Another Ubermensch is waking.'

The dark, gnarled creature tensed on its bent legs.

But before it could leap at its prey, the woman was already moving. The sound of shattering stone shocked Sarah back to reality. She turned and ran back down the narrow passageway.

A shadowy form, bulbous like a huge spider, turned to watch her go. Small, deep-set eyes glinted malevolently before it scuttled back into the darkness.

The desiccated figure took a lurching step towards Guy and the others.

'I don't like the look of this,' Davenport said quietly.

'What's it going to do?' Green asked. 'Should we talk to it?'

'Do you speak Bronze Age?' Davenport asked.

The figure stopped. The beams from the three torches picked out the emaciated features, the bare bone sticking through the decaying robes. The mouth moved awkwardly, head lolling sideways as the figure took another difficult step.

'Possibly a good time to get out of here,' Davenport said.

'Not until we know what's happened to Sarah,' Guy told him, surprised at how calm his own voice sounded. He transferred the torch to his left hand, reached down with his right and carefully unbuttoned the flap over his holstered revolver.

'Miss Diamond!' Green's parade-ground shout echoed round the chamber.

'Here,' a nervous voice replied.

Guy swung the torch. He saw Sarah standing on the other side of the casket, beside a dark area that must be a passageway. Her own torch was pointing at the ground, but he could see the horror and fear in her face.

'Just come towards us – quickly but carefully,' Guy said.

Davenport moved in the opposite direction, drawing the figure's attention. It turned to follow his movement, and Sarah ran.

At once the Ubermensch swung back, alerted by the sound of her running footsteps. A withered arm reached out. The grotesque figure moved quickly, the awkwardness of just moments earlier gone as it clutched at Sarah.

She ducked and sidestepped. Bony fingers tangled in her hair, dragging her back. Another gnarled, ancient hand closed over Sarah's face, cutting off her scream. She struggled wildly, trying to wrench herself free.

Green stepped forward, swinging his fist at the Ubermensch. It connected with the creature's face. Dust and fragments of brittle bone showered out from the point of impact. But the figure did not loosen its grip on Sarah. It lowered its hand from her mouth to her throat. Her cries were fading. Her eyes widening. Chest heaving as the breath was choked out of her.

'Get her away from him,' Davenport shouted.

Guy pulled out his revolver. But the Ubermensch was holding Sarah in front of itself, and Green stood in front of Guy.

For a moment it looked as if Green was going to try another punch. But he feinted, then kicked out – not at the Ubermensch, but at Sarah.

His foot curled behind Sarah's calf, dragging her legs out from under her. She fell, her whole weight suddenly pulling her away from the ancient figure's grasp. She sprawled on the ground with a cry of pain. Green grabbed her under the arms and pulled her clear.

The Ubermensch stood watching, no discernible expression on its withered face. Strands of blonde hair were caught in its hand.

The gunshots echoed off the stone walls, floor and roof. The sound was incredibly loud in the enclosed space – two shots in rapid succession. They ripped into the grotesque figure's chest, driving it backwards, tearing holes through the remains of its robes and smashing into the bone and sinew below.

In the light of his torch, braced against the gun so he could aim both together, Guy clearly saw the wounds. Tendrils of orange shimmered and rippled in the light, licking out of the holes torn by the bullets. As he watched, the thin filaments knitted and bound, stretching over the bullet holes and drawing the translucent skin back together. Pulsing, binding, repairing...

The Ubermensch looked down at its chest, as if in surprise. Then it turned back towards Guy, the dark pits of its eyes seeking him out. It strode across the chamber towards him, snarling in rage.

'Out!' Green yelled. 'Everyone out of here. Back to the passageway.'

Guy went last, backing away from the oncoming figure. He fired two more shots. The impact of the bullets drove the Ubermensch back. But it staggered to a halt, then started forwards again.

As soon as he was through the broken wall, out of the antechamber, Green shoved his torch in a pocket and put his shoulder to the metal door. The pale glow of the bare bulbs strung across the ceiling seemed bright after the torchlit gloom of the inner chamber.

The door swung ponderously back towards the frame. Then it stopped.

Skeletal fingers curled round the edge of the door, forcing it open again.

Davenport and Guy put their shoulders to the door beside Green. Sarah stood watching, knuckles pressed to her teeth.

'My God that thing's strong,' Guy gasped. There was no way they were going to get the door shut. Even if they did, how could they keep it closed?

'Roof supports,' Green gasped. 'We had to shore it up when we widened the passage.'

Guy saw what he meant. Wooden struts were wedged against the wall, braced against wooden boards to hold the ceiling in place. The boards were fixed into the ancient stone roof of the original, narrower passageway.

'Sledgehammer, or pickaxe,' he shouted to Sarah. 'Anything!'

His feet slipped on the muddy floor, skidding back as the

door opened another inch. A rotting arm reached round the door, scrabbling and clutching – reaching for them.

'This any good?' Sarah had a pickaxe.

'Let's hope so.' Guy nodded at the nearest support. 'Knock that away, and the roof should come down. With luck it'll jam this door shut.'

'That does sound a bit risky,' Davenport said.

'You got a better idea?' Green asked him, his teeth gritted with the effort of trying to force the door shut.

'Not as such.'

'On three, Sarah. Rest of us – be ready to jump out of the way.'

'Oh, I'm ready,' Davenport assured them.

Guy braced himself against the door, preparing to leap back as he counted out loud. 'One... Two... Three!'

He leaped back. Green was right beside him. Davenport jumped too, but without their efforts to keep it closed, the door sprang open, catching his leg as he leaped clear. Davenport fell, landing on his back. He stared up at the roof as Sarah's pickaxe connected with the support.

The wooden strut shifted. Dust and earth showered down on Davenport. But the strut didn't give way.

Davenport rolled aside as the door opened fully. The Ubermensch stood framed for a moment by the darkness of the chamber behind. It stared down at Davenport.

At the same moment, Green grabbed the pickaxe from Sarah and swung again at the strut. It splintered under the blow. Another, and the strut was knocked sideways, out from under the wooden board it supported.

The Ubermensch reached down for Davenport, who was frantically skidding himself backwards. Guy fired another shot, driving the creature upright. He dropped his torch and reached down, grabbed Davenport's arm with his free hand, dragging him back. Just one bullet left...

Then the board gave way under the weight of the earth above, and the roof came down. Soil and rubble crashed over the Ubermensch. It staggered, and fell. More rock and soil cascaded over it, filling the area with dust and debris.

Guy retrieved his torch. He shone it at the pile of earth and rubble. The top half of the doorway to the burial chamber was a dark silhouette above. A single hand, more skeleton than flesh, protruded from the mound.

'Well, that's that,' Green said, coughing away dust from his throat.

'Don't be too sure,' Davenport said quietly.

Sarah gasped, grabbing Guy's arm for support as she almost fell.

The hand clenched and unclenched. Slowly the wrist and forearm emerged from the heap of fallen debris. Another hand punched through beside it. Rock and earth fell away as the Ubermensch forced its way out.

She couldn't have been twenty yet. Hoffman watched her draw, staring into space, her life suddenly somewhere else. Her blonde hair was matted and dark with sweat, falling over her shoulders. The loose hospital smock clung to her body, damp with perspiration.

Another sheet finished and pushed aside. Hoffman picked it up and examined it. One of the figures was definitely in uniform. A British sergeant's stripes on the shoulder – but that didn't mean the Ubermensch was in Britain. There were allied troops across the world. Even now, the British Empire still covered more territory than Hitler had managed to acquire.

The next sheet was shaded grey again. Possibly some texture, but no detail. A single white strip left down one side. Light shining round a door, perhaps.

Then another figure – seen from above. The Ubermensch looking down at a man sprawled on the floor. He didn't seem to be in uniform, but the detail was vague.

A closer view. The man's face. The clearest image so far. Hoffman watched fascinated as the features were shaded in – a round face, with bushy eyebrows and dark eyes, hair slicked back. Early middle-aged, if Hoffman had to guess. He took the drawing as soon as Number Seventeen had finished it.

231

'The Reichsfuhrer is on his way,' Kruger announced breathlessly as he entered the room. 'He will be here directly.'

Number Seventeen was drawing again – shading the page completely. Total blackness.

Kruger stared down at the paper. Hoffman turned away slightly, masking his actions. He folded the sheet he was holding, and slipped it into his jacket pocket.

CHAPTER 29

The grotesque figure forced its way out of the earth and rubble. Its robes were torn and muddy. Soil trickled from the hollow eye sockets like black tears. It took a lurching step forwards, dragging itself free of the fallen debris.

'Shoot it!' Davenport yelled.

'I've tried that!' Guy was acutely aware he had only one shot left. There had to be a way to make it count.

Green stepped in front of the Ubermensch, swinging the pickaxe he'd used to bring down the roof. The creature brought up a hand to parry the blow. But the heavy metal head of the tool knocked the hand aside. The end of the pickaxe slammed into the creature's emaciated body, biting deep.

The Ubermensch staggered back, pulling the tool from Green's grasp. It stood for a moment, staring down at the pickaxe sticking out of its chest. Then it gripped the metal blade, and dragged it out. Thin tendrils licked out of the wound, twisting and rippling like grass in a breeze. The Ubermensch threw the pickaxe aside and advanced on Green.

'How do we stop that thing?' Sarah demanded, her voice taut with fear.

'Only one way,' Green said as he retreated. 'Fire. Like at Shingle Bay.' He was back with the rest of them now. Together they were backing away as the Ubermensch walked slowly towards them.

'Back down the tunnel?' Sarah said. 'Maybe we can seal the end of it.'

'He'd just dig his way out,' Guy said. He took another step backwards, and his foot collided with a tin mug, sending it skittering away.

'Offer it a cup of tea,' Davenport suggested.

Guy stumbled slightly as he trod on a billy can. He was standing right where the soldiers had been brewing up on the primus stove. 'Actually…'

'What is it, sir?' Green asked.

'We need him in a confined space. Back into the chamber.'

Green grabbed the nearby spade. 'Right you are.'

'You got a plan?' Sarah said.

'Of sorts,' Guy admitted. He had an idea – or rather, half an idea… 'Just keep him back, buy me a little time.'

Davenport grabbed another shovel. He and Green both charged at the Ubermensch. They crashed into it – knocking the creature backwards. It staggered away.

'Again!' Green ordered.

They caught the Ubermensch still off balance, and knocked it back further. It stumbled onto the edge of the fallen roof. The creature's shrivelled lips parted and it let out an unearthly cry of rage. Green jabbed with his shovel and the Ubermensch took another step back – up the slope, towards the half-blocked entrance to the burial chamber. It bent forward, arms stretched out towards its attackers, and roared again.

'Doesn't look like he wants to go back home,' Davenport said, breathless.

'Good enough,' Guy said. 'So long as he's well clear of us. When I say, you two get back over here pronto.'

'What are you going to do?' Sarah said. Her face was deathly pale in the unforgiving light from above.

Guy held the small primus stove. As Davenport and Green drove back the Ubermensch, he had been pumping up the pressure inside. He hoped there was enough paraffin. He hefted the weight of the brass in his left hand. It was about seven inches in diameter, and could probably hold about two pints of fuel. With his other hand he drew his revolver.

'Right – now!' he yelled.

Davenport and Green ran back.

Guy stepped forwards. Just one shot... He lobbed the primus stove towards the figure standing halfway up the pile of rubble, and took aim.

The sound of the shot echoed off the walls. A split second later, the bullet tore into the primus just as it hit the Ubermensch in the chest. The pressurised metal container exploded, spraying paraffin across the monstrous creature. It ignited in an instant, transforming the figure into a mass of flame as dry robes and brittle flesh caught fire.

The Ubermensch was hurled backwards by the blast, falling down the pile of rubble into the burial chamber. Guy ran forwards, gun raised even though it was now useless. He was in time to see the Ubermensch stagger back to its feet. Its eyes were dark pits amidst the flames, staring malevolently. Fire dripped from its body and choking black smoke filled the air.

Guy thought the creature was about to come back at him. But the nearest of the material draped round the walls caught a spark and exploded into flame. Guy felt the heat on his face as the fire leaped from one wall hanging to the next. In seconds, the whole chamber was a mass of flame. Somewhere in the midst of it a figure of fire, engulfed in smoke and heat, toppled forwards and crashed burning to the ground.

The picture of four indistinct figures was pushed aside. The next image was very different. Number Seventeen was scribbling in circles, a mass of dark pencil like thick black clouds. A faint reddening discoloured her cheek, like she'd been slapped.

Himmler examined the previous sheet, peering at it curiously through the small round lenses of his spectacles.

'Do we know who these people are?'

'No, Reichsfuhrer,' Kruger admitted.

'Or where the Ubermensch is located?'

'Possibly underground,' Hoffman said. 'Perhaps another tomb.'

Number Seventeen dropped the pencil. It clattered to the desk top, then rolled on to the floor. Her mouth opened in a silent scream. Her eyes widened and she fell backwards, across the bed. She had flinched before, cried out soundlessly when she drew the men with shovels and pickaxe, just before her cheek went red. But this was more extreme.

'She has lost the connection,' Kruger said. He felt for her pulse.

'Then she is no longer of any use,' Himmler said. 'Get rid of her.'

Hoffman glanced at the girl. She was staring up at the ceiling, calm now. She might be asleep – so young, so peaceful. He cleared his throat.

Himmler glanced at him. 'Yes, Sturmbannfuhrer?'

'The... subject connected without a bracelet. She may have lost this connection, but we don't know what has happened to the Ubermensch.'

'With a full connection, the physical experiences of the Ubermensch are also relayed,' Kruger said. 'If they are damaged, so is the watcher.'

'But that might not happen with a weaker connection like this,' Hoffman pointed out. 'And she might connect again, either to this Ubermensch or to another.'

Himmler stared back at Hoffman unblinking, devoid of expression. Eventually, he gave a curt nod. 'Very well. You will keep me informed.'

'Of course.'

Himmler turned and walked briskly from the room. Hoffman helped Kruger turn the girl so she was lying lengthways along the bed. As Kruger turned away, Hoffman placed his hand gently against the girl's cheek. It was smooth and warm, damp with sweat. But there was something else too... He looked up as Kruger turned back.

'Her hair smells of smoke,' Hoffman said.

*

They waited another twenty-four hours after the smoke stopped billowing out of the tunnel entrance to be sure the fire had burned itself out. Elizabeth Archer came down from London to supervise the removal of any artefacts that had survived the blaze.

'I should have been here in the first place,' she complained.

'And faced the walking corpse?' Sarah asked.

She sniffed. 'I've seen enough of those in my time.' She didn't sound like she was joking.

Lady Grenchard was certainly not joking. She was appalled when she came to investigate the smoke, and spent the best part of twenty minutes railing at Davenport without pause for breath. Elizabeth, however, seemed to be able to charm her into submission. Perhaps the fact they were more similar ages helped, Sarah thought. Or maybe she'd claimed to be Howard Carter's mother.

The tomb was almost entirely burned out. The air was heavy with the residue of smoke. The floor of the burial chamber was littered with the charred remains of wall hangings, pottery, and other detritus. Close to the stone casket, there was a blackened shape, the silhouette of a man burned into the stone floor. All that remained of the Ubermensch.

'Like he was trying to get back inside,' Davenport said.

The stone lid of the casket lay in shattered pieces where it had fallen nearby.

Sarah showed them the second chamber. But the glass jars were twisted and broken. The remaining fluid had escaped or evaporated in the heat, and whatever had been inside was charred beyond recognition. She reached out a tentative finger to prod at what looked like the last remnants of a gnarled tentacle sticking out of one jar, the surface like the burned bark of an ancient tree. It crumbled to black dust when she touched it.

'There were bracelets, or something,' she told Elizabeth.

'Not any more.'

Where bracelets had been, there were now fused lumps of carbonised metal. Shapeless and welded to the stone shelf.

Elizabeth sighed. 'I'm afraid we've learned nothing. Well,' she conceded, 'almost nothing. You and the others need to describe exactly what you saw, everything you can remember. We'll get one of the Museum's draughtsmen to draw it up as best he can. And I'll ask Penelope to arrange to photograph everything that's left before it's moved.' She meant Miss Manners, Sarah realised.

They were halfway back to the promise of daylight and fresh air when Sarah remembered. She shrugged off the satchel that held her gas mask. Holding her breath, hoping she was right, she opened it and felt inside.

'We do have something,' she said, taking out the bracelet she had stuffed in the bag earlier, before the Ubermensch had woken.

Carefully, Elizabeth lifted the bracelet from Sarah's hand.

'It's heavy.' She weighed it in her palm.

'Is it important?'

'I have no idea. But it's better than nothing. It might take a while, but I'm sure this will tell us something.' She smiled and nodded. 'Well done. At least someone kept their wits about them.'

CHAPTER 30

It was several weeks before the bracelet revealed any of its secrets. While Elizabeth Archer painstakingly catalogued what had been salvaged from the burial mound, the rest of Station Z continued as usual. For Guy Pentecross and Sarah Diamond that meant going through more reports and accounts.

'It would help if we knew what we were looking for,' Guy said as they started another day of searching through files.

Sarah leaned over his shoulder to see the cover page of the file he had just opened. 'That could be worth looking at.'

Guy was aware how close they were, her head almost touching his own as Sarah pointed to a line in the contents listing.

'You're not even interested,' she said when he didn't answer.

'Oh, I'm interested,' he said quickly.

Sarah straightened up, glancing at him before going back to her own pile of papers and reports. 'Really?'

He was tempted to tell her just how interested he was. But she was already at work, going through the file in front of her with what he knew would be meticulous care.

He felt he ought to say something, though. 'It's just that everything seems to be moving away from us, does that make sense? Not just us, but the whole country.'

Sarah looked up. 'Yes, I know what you mean. The focus

of the war has shifted. I guess we shouldn't complain there are fewer air raids. The Germans are concentrating on Russia.'

'And the convoys. They're taking a pounding. But we'll make it.'

'What about Russia?' Sarah asked. 'You think the Nazis will defeat Stalin as quickly as they did Poland and France?'

'I don't know,' Guy confessed. 'They've laid siege to Leningrad and they're getting closer to Moscow. But Russia is a huge country, and the winter will be cruel when it arrives. As Napoleon found out to his cost.'

Davenport entered in time to hear this last remark. 'Those who do not learn from history are doomed to repeat it,' he said. 'Let's hope Herr Hitler is not an historian.'

Davenport had taken it upon himself to indulge his interest in archaeology and look further back in history – not just British and European history but the myths and legends and stories of other lands and cultures too. He came up with some fascinating tales of gods from the heavens, or who lived in fiery chariots in the sky. But all of them, he was forced to admit, were at best tenuously linked to UDTs and the Ubermensch, and probably simply fictitious.

There were bursts of activity and excitement whenever a report of a UDT came in. Sarah found herself hoping it would be from somewhere distant enough to mean they had to fly to interview any witnesses. Brinkman had commandeered a rather rackety Avro Anson and, while Sarah objected loudly and frequently at having to drive her colleagues round the Home Counties, she never complained about acting as their pilot.

In the air, Sarah felt at ease and relaxed. She was in her element, in control. Even when she once found herself flying towards an incoming German bombing raid, she didn't panic or feel real fear. But at night, alone at her flat, she was very afraid. Every light outside during the blackout was a UDT singling out her street in Hammersmith. Every shadow in the flat hid a walking corpse ready to lurch towards her, sunken eyes seeking her out – watching her as she slept, as she read or wrote to her father, as she ate. As she undressed...

For weeks after her experiences in the burial mound, whenever she closed her eyes she saw the Ubermensch reaching out for her – hands burning. She'd wake suddenly, convinced she could smell the dry, brittle, dusty stench of ancient death and feel its hand on her throat. Desperate for Guy's comforting arm round her shoulder, pulling her close to him – so close she could feel the warmth of his body tight against her own.

If he kept busy then Guy didn't have time to think about how long it seemed to take to achieve anything. He didn't have time to think about whether he would be making more of a difference to the war effort if he'd stayed in the Foreign Office. He didn't have time to think about the fact there was still an Ubermensch somewhere in London, despite the efforts of the police. There were occasional reports of sightings, occasional deaths that could perhaps be attributed to the creature.

And he didn't have time to think about the way Sarah Diamond looked away when he glanced at her, or lapsed into moments of awkward silence when they were together in a car or the plane.

An unexpected benefit of the desire to keep busy manifested itself at the British Museum. Elizabeth Archer had mentioned her frustration at not being able to keep up with the news while she was working in the vault beneath the museum's Great Court. Davenport had got her a wireless set, but so far below ground it couldn't receive a signal. Having spoken to an expert at one of the Y Stations that had detected a UDT transmission, Pentecross determined to make the wireless work.

He spent the best part of a day running a cable from a radio aerial above ground to the vault below. Elizabeth watched with a mixture of anticipation and amusement as he finally made the connection and turned on the wireless.

They waited for the valves to warm up, Guy ready to play with the tuning and hoping his efforts had not been in vain.

Elizabeth had been working on the bracelet Sarah had

found. It lay on her desk close to the wireless. Now cleaned of dust and cobwebs, it looked as good as new, the tracery of silver catching the light.

A burst of static crackled from the speaker, and Guy twisted the dial. The static faded, then came back – was that a good sign? Finally, a voice, faint but decipherable, emerged from behind the crackling.

'Could be Alvar Lidell,' Guy said. 'I'll see if I can get it clearer.'

'No, go back. Turn the dial the other way, back to where it was.'

Guy did as she said. 'But, why? I almost had the BBC then, I'm sure.'

'Stop!' Elizabeth's tone was urgent. 'Other way, just a touch.'

'You want to listen to this?' The wireless was popping and crackling incomprehensibly.

Elizabeth pointed to the desk. 'Look.'

The bracelet was glowing. The silver was brilliant white, pulsing in time to the rise and fall of the static from the radio. As Guy watched, thin red tendrils edged out from inside the ring of metal – exploring the air around.

Elizabeth picked up a fountain pen and gently prodded the blunt end into the middle of the bracelet. She moved it to one side, into the mass of tendrils. At once, they wrapped themselves round the pen, gripping it tightly.

'What's it doing?' Guy said, watching with anxious fascination as the filaments continued to curl round the pen.

'Something to do with the radio waves,' Elizabeth said. 'We know the UDTs emit radio transmissions. This is the first confirmation that there is a direct link between the UDTs and the burial sites, the Ubermensch.'

She let go of the pen, and it stayed in position, held upright by the thin fingers of red. Then suddenly ink spattered across the desk, running along the thin tentacles, staining them blue.

'They've burrowed through the barrel of the pen,' she said. 'Interesting.'

As she spoke, the tendrils withdrew. Ink dripped out on to the desk as the filaments disappeared back into the bracelet.

'Seems they have no appetite for ink,' Elizabeth observed.

'What were they after?' Guy wondered.

'Oh I think we can guess. Just imagine if one of us had been wearing that.'

Guy looked down at the bracelet. The glow had faded and it lay still and inert in a spattered mess of ink.

In a vaulted chamber in Wewelsburg, one of the sleepers cried out. He sat up suddenly, eyes snapping open. An old man, face the texture of worn leather, he stared straight across the room.

By the time the nurse reached him, he had slumped back on the bed, eyes closed, asleep once more.

In a large house in Jermyn Street, the man the press had once called 'the wickedest man in the world' was holding a séance. Four people sat at a round table. A ring of lighter wood inside the rim of the table was inlaid with the letters of the alphabet and the numbers 0 to 9. In the centre of the polished wooden surface stood an upturned glass. For the moment, no one was touching it.

The two men and two women sat with their hands on the edge of the table, outside the letters and numbers. Heads down, eyes closed, quietly murmuring the incantations necessary before they took hold of the glass. The sound grew slowly from a murmur to a whisper, then from a whisper to a chant.

Another sound was added as the glass rattled against the wood. Gently at first, then more violently as if some unseen figure was shaking it roughly.

The four people looked up, exchanged puzzled looks. Their leader rose slowly to his feet.

Then the glass exploded, scattering fragments and splinters across the table.

*

Elizabeth was absorbed in the bracelet, re-examining it in every detail. Guy had turned off the wireless, not wanting to provoke another reaction.

'I'll put it inside an observation tank and try the radio again later,' Elizabeth decided.

She didn't look up, and after several minutes, Guy decided she had forgotten he was there. When he excused himself, she nodded without comment.

On the way out, he met Miss Manners coming in. 'You'll be lucky to get much response,' he warned her. 'The old lady's rather preoccupied.'

'I was looking for you, actually, Major Pentecross. Colonel Brinkman asked me to catch you. He wasn't sure if you were coming back to the office this evening, and there's a meeting tomorrow he'd like you to sit in on.'

Guy hadn't realised it was getting so late. Evening was already drawing in as he left the museum with Miss Manners. She gave him the details of the meeting – more boring discussions about priorities and funding. He could see why Brinkman didn't want to go.

'Are you all right?' Miss Manners was asking as they reached the road. 'Guy?'

Her use of his Christian name pulled him back to reality. 'Sorry. Had a rather... strange afternoon, that's all.'

She listened patiently and without comment as he described the incident with the bracelet. When he was finished, Guy was breathing heavily. The whole thing had unsettled him more than he realised.

As Guy was talking they had walked back towards Oxford Street. At the corner of the Tottenham Court Road, Miss Manners said: 'There's a pub just up there that I used to go to with some associates. A long time ago, but I would hope it's still standing.'

Guy smiled. 'Are you asking me for a drink?'

She peered at him seriously over the top of her spectacles. 'You look and sound as if you need one. But if you'd rather not...'

The pub was indeed still standing, although several of the buildings nearby on Windmill Street had been hit and were boarded up. Miss Manners led the way to a secluded booth towards the back of the main bar.

'I can't stay long,' she said when Guy returned with her gin and tonic and a pint of bitter. 'I need to get to the YMCA this evening.'

'You staying there?' Guy asked. As he said it, he remembered what Sarah had told him when they first met – about Miss Manners' trip to the YMCA and her photography.

'Heavens no. I need to collect some photographs they've developed for me.'

'The YMCA? Not the local chemist's?'

'Yes.' She raised her eyebrows at his bewilderment. 'Before the war I used to photograph gardens mainly. Plants and flowers. Landscapes. Old houses too, especially if...' She hesitated, and took a sip of her drink. 'I like to think I became quite good at it,' she said.

Guy nodded. 'I should have guessed from the way you looked at those pictures of Suffolk that Sarah got taken from the air.'

She sipped at her drink. 'Now I mainly photograph people.'

'People? You mean, just anyone who looks interesting?'

She smiled. It wasn't something Guy had seen happen often, but it transformed Miss Manners suddenly from stern, efficient secretary into an attractive young woman. 'The YMCA organise a thing called "Snapshots from Home", perhaps you've heard of it? When you were away on service?'

He shook his head. 'So what does it entail?'

'After your time perhaps. Servicemen abroad can fill in a form to ask for photographs of their loved ones. Family – wife, children. Even pets. The YMCA sorts out the forms and allocates them to local amateur photographers, like me.'

'And you photograph the loved ones. Or pets.'

'That's right. The YMCA develop the films, and then I send the photographs back to the troops.'

Guy thought back to his own time away from home. You

certainly made good friends from the people you were with, but that was no substitute for home life. 'I bet they really appreciate it,' he said.

'Oh they do,' she agreed. 'I get letters of thanks from all over the world. I keep them all,' she added. 'It's so hard being away from the one you love.'

Guy wasn't sure how or if to respond to this. But before he could decide, Miss Manners frowned. She seemed to stiffen, looking past Guy towards the bar.

'We shouldn't have come here,' she said quietly. 'And now it's too late – he's seen us.'

'What?' Guy turned to see who she meant. A large man was making his way towards them. He was broad-shouldered and bald, with a long face and cold, deep-set eyes. He wore a light grey suit and a bow tie which provided an elegance at odds with his thuggish demeanour.

Another man was with him, younger with a curl of dark hair hanging over one eye and a cruel set to his mouth. Two women watched anxiously from the bar. One was middle-aged and overweight, wearing a dress that might have suited her when she was younger and slimmer. The other was about the same age as the younger man – perhaps in her late twenties, wearing a plain grey skirt and jacket. Her dark hair was cut short like a schoolboy's.

'Who are they?' Pentecross hissed as the two men approached – quite clearly heading for the booth where he and Miss Manners were sitting.

'The young man is Rutherford. A very unpleasant character,' she said quietly. She didn't have time to tell him more before the men were within earshot.

'If it isn't the lovely Penelope,' Rutherford said. His voice was a nasal twang that instantly irritated Guy.

'Mr Rutherford,' she replied calmly. 'Not been called up yet, then?'

'Flat feet,' he said, grinning at the evident lie.

'We have missed you, my dear,' the older man said. His voice was surprisingly cultured, matching his suit rather than his face.

'I can't honestly say the same.'

The man nodded to acknowledge the remark. 'A new beau?' he asked, looking at Guy.

'We're colleagues,' Guy said. 'Not that it's any business of yours.'

The man ignored him, saying to Miss Manners: 'Aren't you going to introduce us?'

'No,' she said.

The man smiled. 'How is life as an underpaid office assistant?'

'I wouldn't know,' she countered. 'How is life as the wickedest man in the world?'

'Between you and me, there's a lot of competition these days.' The man stretched his neck out, turning his head first one way then the other like a giant, bald turtle. 'But before we leave you in peace, I just wanted to warn you, Penelope.'

'Warn me?'

The man leaned forward, speaking in a low voice. 'Don't meddle with things you don't comprehend. Don't try to understand the sacred artefacts or rites. The Vril will not be trifled with, young lady. Remember that.'

'The Vril?' Guy echoed. 'What do you mean?'

The man turned his head towards him, not moving the rest of his body. It should have looked awkward and clumsy, but there was something unpleasantly sinister about the movement.

'I'm sure I don't need to explain to *you*, Major Pentecross.' He smiled at Guy's obvious surprise at the use of his name. 'I'm sorry, Miss Manners never did introduce us, did she?'

He straightened up and offered his hand. Guy instinctively shook it – the man's grip was firm but his skin was cold and moist.

'Aleister Crowley,' the man said. 'At your service.'

CHAPTER 31

They sat in silence for several moments after Crowley and the others had gone.

Miss Manners drained the rest of her drink. 'Even his own mother called him "the Beast". And she meant it.'

'How did he know us?' Guy wondered. 'How did he know we were here?'

She stood up, reaching for her coat. 'We should go. It may have been coincidence that he found us. Or maybe he's having me watched. I wouldn't put it past him.'

Guy followed her out. 'I didn't see anyone following us.'

'He doesn't have to follow people to know what they're doing.'

'And why would he want to know what *you're* doing?'

The evening was drawing in and it was noticeably cooler. There was a hint of rain in the air.

'I knew him,' Miss Manners admitted. 'I was one of his "set" for a while. Not a happy time. Not something I'm proud of.'

They had reached the corner of the Tottenham Court Road when a figure hurried up to them. It was the younger, short-haired woman who had been with Crowley. She looked round nervously as she approached.

'Penelope – can we talk?'

'Of course, Jane.'

The woman, Jane, gestured for them to follow her into a side street. She looked round again, obviously afraid they were being watched.

Miss Manners introduced Guy. 'You can trust him,' she added.

Jane smiled nervously. 'Thank you.'

'Why don't you tell us how we can help,' Guy said. 'Jane, was it?'

'Jane Roylston. Penelope and I know each other from... a while ago. Only she managed to escape.'

'Oh?'

'I left,' Miss Manners said. 'You can leave too, Jane. Just go.'

'Oh no.' She shook her head rapidly. 'No, I could never do that.'

'Then why are you here?'

'To warn you. He's getting worse, Pen. I didn't think it was possible, but he is. That's why I can't leave. He'd never let me, and that brute Ralph...' She pronounced it 'Rafe'.

'Ralph Rutherford,' Miss Manners told Guy. 'I told you he was a bad sort.'

'I have to get back,' Jane said. 'But, be careful. I don't know if it helps, but Crowley is in touch with something, some force. It takes over the séances, and he claims it speaks to him. Today a glass...' She shook her head again. 'Never mind. I just thought you should know.'

'What force?' Guy asked. 'What can you tell us about it?'

'I don't know, not really. He tells me nothing. But he calls it the Vril. You know, like in that book.'

'*The Coming Race*?' Miss Manners said, glancing at Guy.

'Yes. It was fun at first, all this...' She sighed, glancing round again. 'You were right to get out of it, Pen.'

'Call me,' Miss Manners said. 'It's been too long, Jane. Far too long. Call me if you discover anything, anything at all.'

Jane was shaking her head. 'I... I can't. If he found out.'

'He didn't before. You helped me last year. That was important, it really did help – more than you can ever know.'

Jane frowned. She took a deep breath. 'I'll do what I can.'

'Don't take any risks,' Miss Manners warned. 'But anything you can tell us about the Vril, about what they're up to – it *will* help.'

'I have to go.' Jane hurried out of the side street and disappeared among the people making their way down Tottenham Court Road towards the tube station.

'You think she'll tell us anything?' Guy asked.

'She did before. It was Jane who warned us about Shingle Bay.'

Brinkman summoned Guy, Sarah and Davenport to a meeting in the Conference Room the next afternoon.

'Miss Manners has told me all about your run-in with Crowley,' he told Guy.

Guy had already recounted the event to the others. 'He did seem rather concerned about our work,' Guy said. 'Though how he knows about it...'

'A lot of it is bluff, I imagine,' Davenport said. 'He has many friends in important places. And he may also have some genuine mystical or occult ability.'

'Miss Manners is convinced he does,' Brinkman said. 'And he knew about Shingle Bay before it happened.'

'Could he be a German spy?' Sarah asked.

'Unlikely,' Brinkman told them. 'He seems dedicated to the war effort. He's offered to help the intelligence services, which is partly why MI5 told me I was wasting my time and theirs when I suggested they keep tabs on him last year after Shingle Bay.'

'Didn't he organise a group of witches to go down to Beachy Head and put a curse on the Luftwaffe or something?' Davenport said. 'For all the good it did.'

'You say that, but we did beat them,' Guy pointed out.

'I think we can agree that Crowley knows something of the Vril, and may even be in communication with them somehow,' Brinkman said. 'Although it doesn't sound as if he was terribly forthcoming, he may know more about them than we do. He's warned us not to interfere, and not to study their artefacts. I take that as an indication that we should do both. We're clearly making some progress, perhaps even on the brink of a breakthrough, or he'd not be warning us off.'

'So what do you suggest?' Davenport asked. 'Keep buggering on, as the great man says? I gather from Guy that Mrs Archer has made some interesting progress with that bracelet Miss Diamond found.'

'I'll try to get Crowley under surveillance,' Brinkman told them. 'I'll ask Special Branch rather than MI5 – Alban's still angling to get us closed down. Witch-hunting might give him more ammo.'

'And the rest of us?' Sarah asked.

'It sounds like the artefacts could be key. There's nothing more to be learned from Suffolk. But Streicher's team might still be excavating the French site, don't you think?'

Davenport nodded. 'It's on a bigger scale. Streicher seemed to be a stickler for procedure. They shipped out everything they've recovered so far, as we know. But even if they're not still working there themselves, I would think there's more to be found.'

'Good.' Brinkman stood up. 'Then you'd better get back there. At the very least you can take a look at the layout and construction of the place, even if they've cleared everything out. Miss Diamond can drop you off.'

'Drop me off?' Davenport was aghast. 'Are you seriously suggesting I parachute into occupied France?'

'You'll be fine. Major Pentecross will be with you.'

This was news to Guy.

'You speak French, don't you?' Brinkman said. 'And German?'

'Well, yes.'

'There you are, then.'

'I've never made a parachute jump, though,' Guy protested.

Brinkman was unimpressed. 'You'd better hope Miss Diamond can find somewhere safe and convenient to land.'

*

They flew through the night. Guy found himself volunteered to sit in the cramped, cold dorsal turret and man the rear machine gun. The only other armament in the Avro Anson was the front machine gun, another .303 which Sarah promised she could manage herself.

'I guess you've been trained to defend yourself against an enemy attack when delivering planes for the ATA,' Guy said.

She laughed. 'There's a very real possibility of attack, but if it happens you just get the hell out of there. If it's one of the girls flying, then they don't arm the guns.'

'You're joking,' Davenport said. But she wasn't.

'Don't worry,' she assured them. 'Part of the act in the flying circus was shooting at a target. I was quite good at it. That and dropping flour bombs into a circle painted on the grass. But you shouldn't be so surprised I know how to shoot,' Sarah added. 'I'm half American, remember?'

'But which half?' Davenport murmured to Guy as they boarded.

Davenport made himself comfortable in the cargo bay. He'd brought a book on Greek mythology and a torch together with several blankets.

'You've done this sort of thing before,' Guy realised.

'Several times. Still makes me feel sick though.'

'I didn't mean flying.'

'Neither did I.'

They had an escort of two Hurricanes to see them over the channel. But as the dark mass of France appeared on the horizon, the fighters banked away and headed for home. Guy twisted in his tiny seat to watch them go. They were on their own now.

The plane seemed incredibly slow, incredibly noisy, and incredibly cold. Guy kept his hand nervously on the gun housing, and after several hours he began to wonder if he would ever be able to remove it. He was wearing gloves, but even so his fingers were so cold they might have frozen in place. He wasn't sure he could even press the firing button.

'All right up there?' Davenport yelled from below.

'No,' Guy called back. 'I'm cold and cramped and desperate for a piss.'

'Well see if you can hang on a bit longer. The pilot says to tell you we'll be over the landing zone in about ten minutes. So let's hope we can find a big field.'

'They usually send me over in a Lysander,' Davenport said. 'It can land on a sixpence. Well, not actually on a sixpence, but it needs rather less space than that old thing.'

'I wasn't given the option,' Sarah told him. 'Now I've got to turn this thing round and get airborne again before anyone comes to see what the noise is.'

'You got enough fuel to make it back?' Guy asked.

'It's a bit late now if I haven't.'

She left the engine running and went back with them to the cargo door. Davenport jumped out first, landing with practised ease on the grass below. Before Guy could follow, Sarah pulled him into a sudden unexpected but welcome hug.

'Be safe,' she said.

'You too.'

Guy wanted to stay like this, feeling the heat of her warm his own chilled body. But almost at once she let go and stepped back.

'I'll see you soon,' Guy said.

Sarah gave a quick nod. 'Go on. Leo's waiting. And I need to close the door.'

Guy watched as the Anson turned awkwardly in front of them. Sarah waved from the cockpit, then the engine roared and the plane started across the field, gathering speed until at what seemed like the last possible moment it lifted ponderously into the air. They could still hear the engine long after it disappeared into the darkness.

'I hope she'll be all right,' Guy said.

'She's good,' Davenport assured him. 'The way she handles that thing she could give a one-oh-nine a run for its money.'

'Let's pray she doesn't have to. So, what now?'

'We find somewhere to hide until morning. Even with

decent identity papers we don't want to get stopped.'

'Are they decent papers?' Guy asked. He had memorised the French name he'd been given together with some basic background information. He was Maurice Renan, an academic who was accompanying the American professor Carlton Smith.

'Only one way to find out, and that's to put them to the test,' Davenport said. 'Which is a bit drastic. Especially if they're not much cop after all.'

'Great. And what do we do tomorrow? Look for your German?'

'Not sure how pleased he'll be to see me, but yes we'll head for the dig and see if Standartenfuhrer Streicher is still in evidence.'

They found a barn and settled down inside for what was left of the night. Guy didn't think he'd get much sleep.

'Are we far from the excavation site?'

Davenport sighed. 'My dear boy, I have no idea where we are. I'm hoping the lights we saw as we came in to land are Ouvon, but we could be almost anywhere in France. Let's wait till daylight then go and ask someone.'

'Isn't that a bit risky?'

'Depends who you ask. Good night.'

The next day was windy and wet. Guy wished he had a thicker coat, but he was stuck with the one Sergeant Green had managed to persuade SOE to provide. All his clothes had to be French, or at least not discernibly British. The weather and the undulating rural landscape conspired to make it seem they could still be in Britain.

Davenport's strategy was just to walk down the road until he saw something he recognised or someone they felt they could ask for directions. It sounded haphazard and doomed to failure to Guy. But he'd reckoned without Davenport's impressive memory which seemed to extend to places as well as text.

'Those trees,' Davenport announced after about half a

mile, pointing to a smudge of green on the horizon. 'They border the field next to where Streicher's men were digging. We should reach a gate in about a mile, and there's a farm track we can take.'

He was right. The track brought them round the trees, along a hedge, and to a point where they could look down on the burial mound. Except, it wasn't there. The whole area was a sunken mass of churned up mud.

'What the hell have they done?' Davenport said.

'You're sure this is the right place?'

'Oh yes.'

'They've levelled it,' Guy said. The whole area reminded him of the descriptions he'd seen in his father's letters of the hellish devastated no-man's-land of the last war. 'So what do we do now?'

'I know a good bar not too far from here,' Davenport said. 'And I don't know about you, but I could do with a drink.'

They took a small table at the back of the bar, in a curved brick alcove. On Davenport's instructions, Guy asked the barman for two strong coffees. The man wiped down the table with a flick of a napkin, then tucked it back into his belt.

'And we're looking for someone called Jacques,' Guy said.

The barman pursed his lips and shook his head. 'No one called Jacques in these parts.'

Guy was surprised. 'No one at all? I find that hard to believe in a place this size. It's not an uncommon name.'

'It's not a name I have ever heard, monsieur.'

The coffee was the consistency of syrup and the strength of tar. The barman placed three small cups on the table and left. A few moments later, Jacques joined them.

'It is good to see you again, my friend,' he said to Davenport, shaking his hand.

Guy introduced himself, and Jacques smiled.

'Two things you need to know. First, my name is not Jacques.'

'And second?'

'Your French is a lot better than his.'

By the time Jacques had finished his coffee, he had given them a full description of events after Davenport left. Streicher's men had cleared everything from the dig, filling another train with boxed-up artefacts to follow the one that Davenport and Jacques had robbed.

'After that, they mined the whole excavation with explosive charges. Blew it to Kingdom Come.' Jacques clapped his hands together and then pulled them rapidly apart again by way of demonstration. 'Boom! You could hear it in here.'

'So what do you think?' Guy asked after Jacques had gone. 'Get your friend to send a message to London asking for Sarah to come and pick us up again?'

Davenport turned his cup slowly on its saucer as he considered. 'It's the artefacts we need. That's why we came here.'

'But they're gone. You heard him.'

'Then we follow them.'

Guy leaned across the table. 'You're joking. They'll have been sent to Germany.'

'To Wewelsburg. Himmler's castle of darkness.'

'There you are, then.'

'You speak German, don't you?'

'I do,' Guy admitted. 'Like a native. But that doesn't mean I can pretend to be one.'

'I'm sure you can. Jacques can organise appropriate papers.'

'No, no – this is madness.' He struggled to find some argument that would convince Davenport it was a rash and impulsive idea doomed to failure. 'Do *you* speak German?'

'Hardly a word, old boy,' Davenport said happily. 'But I don't need to, do I? I'm American.'

'But you're not,' Guy said, desperately.

'I sure as hell am. Streicher will vouch for me. In fact, he might even get us in to see the artefacts if I offer my expert help.'

'You *really* think that's likely?'

Davenport shrugged. 'No harm in asking. I'd guess they'd

257

welcome informed opinion about what they've found if it's half as interesting as that bracelet.'

'But from an American?'

'You worry too much,' Davenport said.

'Well you don't seem to worry at all, so I'm doing it for both of us.'

'Look,' Davenport said, his voice calm and reasonable. 'Germany is not about to declare war on America. And the US is not, unfortunately, about to declare war on Germany either, so there's no problem. I'd say we've got a couple of years before that happens and Professor Carlton Smith with his carefully established Nazi sympathies becomes persona non grata in the Fatherland.'

Guy just stared at him. He felt numb inside at the thought of going into the heart of Germany. He drained his coffee, not even tasting it.

'That's settled, then,' Davenport said. 'I'll talk to Jacques and make arrangements. Hopefully we can leave in a couple of days. And with luck we'll be home for Christmas.'

CHAPTER 32

Two Spitfires banked and turned in a sky streaked with pale cloud, elegant but deadly. They had been sent up to intercept an unidentified aircraft that had shown up on the RADAR over Kent. Pilots Billy Glossop and Ken Franks had made good time to the intercept coordinates, only to find there was nothing there.

'False alarm,' Billy said over the radio.

Ken had to agree. 'It might have headed back out to sea. Want to take a look?'

'Why not?'

The throaty rumble of the Spitfires' Merlin engines became a roar as they accelerated out towards the coast.

They never came back.

Brinkman was livid. The report he was holding added to his anger, but it also put his feelings into perspective. Perhaps Davenport and Pentecross were right after all. His first thoughts on getting the message from the French Resistance, relayed via a grudging and puzzled SOE, had been that they were being bloody fools. He couldn't afford to lose either of them on what was so evidently a dangerous and ill-considered waste of time.

Reading the report of the encounter over the Kent coast, he realised that things had changed. Not that Pentecross and

Davenport knew that, and there was no way to tell them. But events now made it clear that any information they could bring back was vital. Their mission might be rash and foolhardy, but it might also provide the only way to begin to fight back.

He read the main part of the brief report for a third time. If there had been any doubt before that the UDTs were hostile, there was none now.

```
Two Spitfires were scrambled
from Thorney Island to intercept
the Unknown Detected Trace at
11:37 GMT. Radio contact was
maintained during the initial
search phase of the operation,
but no contact was made with
the suspected Raider.
   Squadron Leader Glossop made
the decision to extend the
search to the coastal area. No
further contact with Glossop
was made. Flight Officer Franks
radioed in a garbled report at
11:52 GMT, transcribed below.
   It's big, and all lit up.
Never seen anything like it.
No markings. How does it stay
in the air? (BREAK) streak
of light right at him. Billy?
Billy? Nothing from Billy.
Think he may have (BREAK) It's
turning. God it's fast. Taking
evasive action. It's firing
again (BREAK) to base. Damage
to tail section. Losing height.
Going to have to bale. (CONTACT
LOST)
```

Witnesses on the ground report two loud explosions several seconds apart (see Police Report SECon 41-11-0906/4 for statements). Wreckage of both Spitfires was found scattered over a wide area of Walland Marsh. Both aircraft appear to have been fully armed when downed, meaning that neither got off a single shot at the Raider.

Miss Manners was at Bletchley when she got the call. Sergeant Green re-routed it from the Station Z offices to the Station X switchboard, who in turn relayed it to Hut A.

'It's for you,' Wiles said, holding the phone out to her.

She expected it to be Green or Brinkman. It was neither.

The voice at the other end of the phone was a nervous whisper. 'Pen?'

'Jane – is that you? Where are you? Are you all right?'

'I'm fine, but I'll have to be quick. Since I spoke to you and your friend the other week, they've been watching me all the time. I think they know. Rutherford rarely lets me out of his sight. I managed to slip away, but I haven't got long.'

'Oh, Jane,' Miss Manners said sadly. 'Just leave. Get out of there as soon as you can.'

'You know it's not that easy. Especially now. There's something going on, everything's sort of more intense, you know?'

'Can you tell me anything specific?'

'Not much. But I wanted to talk to you, to let you know I'll do what I can.'

'I'd rather you were safe.'

'I'll be all right.' She gave a little gasp. 'Sorry, thought someone was coming. I'm in his study.'

'Whose study? Not Crowley's? Jane!'

'It's no problem, he's out. But his diary's here. Let me give you some dates. I don't know if it will help, but – have you...' She gave a nervous giggle. 'Have you got a pen, Pen?'

Miss Manners scrabbled around in the papers on the nearest desk until she found a pencil and a blank sheet of paper. She wrote down the dates and times that Jane Roylston gave her.

'Thank you, Jane. Now get out of there. I'll talk to some people I know, we can help you.'

But Jane sounded suddenly calm and in control. Worryingly so. 'No,' she said. 'I don't think you can. Not now.'

Then the line went dead.

Jane put the receiver back on its cradle and turned round. She had heard the door open, and she could guess who was there.

'I was just making a call,' she said. 'My mother...'

'But you know we never make phone calls, don't you, Jane?' Rutherford said. 'Not without asking permission. And never from in here.'

'It was the most convenient place.' She couldn't help glancing down at the diary, still lying open and angled so she could see it on Crowley's otherwise tidy desk.

'Was it now?'

He was leaning against the doorframe, hands in his pockets as he watched her. His mouth quivered, as if he was trying not to smile.

'I'm sorry. It won't happen again.' She crossed the room, and was relieved that he stepped aside to let her through the door.

But as she passed him, Rutherford grabbed Jane's wrist, holding it tight, twisting her arm up painfully behind her back.

'No, it won't happen again,' he whispered close in her ear. 'I think you've been a very naughty girl. And we know what happens to naughty girls here, don't we?'

The pain was dispelled by the sudden fear. 'Please, let me go. You're hurting me.'

'No I'm not,' he said, tightening his grip. 'Not yet.'

*

'Jane? Jane!'

There was no answer. Just the tone. Miss Manners put down the phone.

'Problem?' Wiles asked, looking up from his work. Neither of the other two men in the room seemed to have noticed anything.

'I hope not.'

He frowned and got up. 'You've gone awfully pale, you know. You want some water or something? I'll get Debbie.' He helped her to a nearby chair.

'Her name is Eleanor,' she told him.

'Whose name? Well, of course it is. What are you talking about? Here, let me.' He took the paper she was still holding and put it down on the desk. 'What is this?' he asked as he glanced at it. He picked the paper up again. 'Did you just write this?'

'It's just some dates and times. Probably of no use, but she was trying to help. And now... I just hope she's all right. She sounded...' Miss Manners couldn't really describe it. But she had a terrible feeling something was wrong.

Wiles didn't answer. He hurried over to one of the other desks and rummaged through the papers piled there. The man sitting at the desk made no comment, but turned slightly so he could continue his work uninterrupted.

'Secondary data, Edmund,' Wiles said to the man. 'Where's that list?'

The man didn't look up from the sheet he was studying, but pointed to a wooden document tray that was almost buried under more papers. Wiles sorted through and finally found the sheet he was looking for. He brought it over to put down beside the dates and times that Miss Manners had transcribed.

'I thought so. Where did you get these?' He picked up both sheets and handed them to her.

The sheet Wiles had found also had dates and times on it. They were typewritten, and there were more of them. But she could see at once what he had spotted.

'They're the same,' she said. 'Or some of them.'

'The times are very slightly different, but yes. Your list is a subset of this one.' He took it back from her and peered at it, brow creased in thought.

'But – what is that?'

'You know that the Y Stations pick up what seem to be transmissions from the UDTs?'

'Of course.'

'Those transmissions are quite distinctive. They're not like Enigma or any of the other enemy codes, so they're easy to filter out and send straight to us. They record the dates and times of each interception, of course.'

'And that's what's on the list?'

He looked up from the page and smiled at her. 'No.'

'Oh.'

'No, this is what we call "secondary data". It's transmissions of the same distinctive type that a Y Station has picked up, but which doesn't correlate to a UDT sighting. Now sometimes that's almost certainly because no one spotted the UDT. But some of these, we've been thinking, might originate from another source.'

Miss Manners stared at him. 'Oh my God in Heaven,' she breathed.

'This list of yours,' Wiles went on. 'It only goes back to the beginning of September of this year, but it matches some of these secondary data for the same period. So whatever you have listed here, whatever these dates and times correspond to, could be that other source of transmission, do you see?' His smile faded into a frown. 'Unless these are more UDT sightings you've just come across? That would make sense, but it's rather disappointing.'

'No, they're not UDTs.'

'Oh good.' He saw her expression and hesitated. 'Not good?'

'I don't know. But I can tell you what's transmitting the signals that you've intercepted.'

She stood up and handed him back the notes she had

written from Jane's phone call.

'These are all the dates and times in the last three months that Aleister Crowley has held a séance.'

CHAPTER 33

The huge castle dominated the landscape, rising above the leafless trees and standing stark against the darkening winter sky.

Guy could scarcely believe they had made it this far. Davenport seemed to take good luck in his stride. But he did confide to Guy one night that going on stage terrified him.

'You'd think it'd get easier with practice, but not a bit of it. Give me a movie any day. Just the camera to worry about and if you mess things up you can do it again. Theatre with a live audience? Makes me shiver just thinking about it.'

They'd been staying in a chateau when they had that conversation. Guy was new to the dangers of keeping safe in occupied France. Davenport was an old hand, and seemed to have contacts across the country. A few were from resistance groups, but most were people he knew from before the war and trusted to keep them safe. The Countess d'Auverne was one of these.

'We filmed some scenes for *The Princess and the Woodcutter* on the estate. She's got quite an impressive woodshed, you know.' Davenport had apparently played the handsome prince who arrived at the end to capture the heart of the princess.

'A while ago, was it?' Guy asked, suppressing a smile.

'Not so long that the countess has forgotten me.'

He was right, she made them welcome and insisted they

take both French and German money with them when they left the next day.

When they crossed into Germany, things actually got easier. In the occupied countries, the Germans were wary of resistance groups and possible spies and saboteurs. Within Germany itself, the whole atmosphere seemed more relaxed. Jacques had provided Guy with French and German papers. The French ones were forged. The German papers were quite genuine although Jacques assured them the original owner no longer had any use for them.

Wewelsburg was to the west of the country, the village lying in the shadow of the enormous castle. The stone was pale in the evening light and you could believe the place had only recently been built – which, according to Davenport, most of it had. They found a secluded place at the edge of a field and sat down beside a large elm tree, leaning back against the trunk.

'So what's the plan?' Guy asked. 'Go and knock on the door?'

'We could try that. Ask for Streicher. It might work.'

'It wouldn't work,' Guy told him. 'This whole thing is ludicrous, as I keep telling you.'

'Got to give it a try, though.'

Guy sighed. He'd long ago concluded that Davenport saw life like one of his movies. 'There are no second chances here, Leo. This is real life. It's theatre, not the flicks. And if we mess up, they'll shoot us. Never mind dying on stage, this is for real.'

For once, Davenport had the good grace to look chastened by Guy's outburst. 'You're right, of course. What do you suggest? Apart from turning round and going home?'

'Bit late for that. I'm not convinced we should ever have come here at all. But here we are, so let's make the most of it. I don't think we're likely to get inside that place. So the question is, what's the next best thing?'

They sat and watched the early December sun dip below the distant edifice. Davenport said nothing for a long time, and Guy began to wonder if he was sulking.

But finally, Davenport said: 'All right, back to basics. We came here to learn whatever we can about the artefacts that Streicher recovered. Streicher himself may be here, or he may be off on another of his escapades. Question is, who would know and how do we get them to talk to us.'

'Without knocking on the front door and asking,' Guy reminded him.

'At the risk of sounding as if I'm about to burst into song – which I promise you I'm not – there's a tavern in the town. Streicher mentioned it. He told me a bit about this place, how impressive it is and how Himmler's spent God knows how much time and money restoring and extending it.'

'You think we might find Streicher at this tavern?'

'Possibly, though I'll have to convince him I've had a shave. He knows me with a rather impressive beard that wasn't entirely my own. But more likely we can find someone who has worked with Streicher, or who is involved with examining the artefacts he's brought back.'

Guy nodded. 'Makes sense. We hang around at the tavern and get talking to some of the soldiers when they come in. They might let some information slip as they'll be off duty.'

'They're SS, don't forget. I don't think they're ever really off duty. And we'll have to be careful they don't guess what we're up to. If we start with the locals we might have more luck.'

'Any of them work at the castle?'

'I don't know. But they'll have the latest gossip, if there is any. They'll know who's important, who's got a loose tongue, and who can't hold his drink.'

'So long as they don't report us just for asking.'

'We'll be subtle,' Davenport assured him. 'Or you will, anyway. My German's a little rusty, I'm afraid. Not as good as my French.'

'Your French isn't good at all.'

'What?' Davenport was scandalised. 'Nonsense. I understand French perfectly.'

'It's the speaking of it I was meaning.'

*

The tavern was getting busy as the evening turned to night. Guy and Davenport found themselves a table from where they could watch the door. They made sure they knew where the other exits were located in case they needed to leave in a hurry.

'Say nothing,' Guy whispered to Davenport. 'Let me do any talking.'

'We're here to listen anyway,' Davenport murmured back.

It was getting noisy so there was little chance of them being overheard if they kept their voices low. But equally, it was hard to discern any other conversations. A group of several SS soldiers in their distinctive black uniforms sat at a table on the other side of the bar. But getting close enough to hear what they said would only draw attention.

Guy attempted to strike up a conversation with the girl who brought their drinks. She was young and pretty with her fair hair in long plaits. But she didn't smile, and hardly spoke. As well as being busy, Guy guessed she was well used to having to fend off unwelcome approaches from locals and SS alike.

'We're getting nowhere stuck here,' Guy decided. 'I'll go to the bar and get us more beers. Maybe I'll overhear something useful. Keep your head down in case anyone recognises you.'

'You mean Streicher or one of his team?'

'I mean anyone who goes to the movies.'

'Ah,' Davenport conceded. 'Good point.'

The tavern got more crowded the closer Guy got to the bar. He pushed his way through, apologising and excusing himself. But it meant he got to overhear several conversations. A group of soldiers off to one side looked promising and he changed his course slightly to make sure he passed close to them, lingering and listening. But they were making lewd comments about local girls and boasting about how many people they'd killed. Guy wished he hadn't heard. He decided to forget about the drinks and just return to Davenport. The sooner they got out of here the better. They needed another strategy.

The return was easier as the density of drinkers thinned out. He muttered 'Entschuldigung Sie bitte,' as he squeezed

270

past a young couple too interested in each other to notice him anyway, and glanced across to where he'd left Davenport.

His heart skipped a beat.

An SS officer – a major – was standing at the table, talking to Davenport who smiled and nodded in response. What did the fool think he was doing? Maybe it was an unavoidable encounter but the damage was probably already done. Guy glanced round. Should he get out? There was no point in them both getting caught. But he couldn't just abandon Davenport to his fate.

He compromised, stepping back into the crowd and watching what happened – ready to head for the exit, or to help Davenport, whichever seemed best. He could see Davenport was saying something, and the officer was nodding. Then, to Guy's utter surprise, the officer snapped a Heil Hitler salute, turned briskly on his heel, and left.

He waited a full minute to be sure the major wasn't coming back with reinforcements. But nothing happened. Warily, Guy returned to his seat.

'No beer?' Davenport accused quietly.

'Who was that?' Guy hissed. 'What did he want?'

'Didn't catch his name. Not sure quite what he said, actually.'

'He wasn't suspicious?'

'Who knows. As far as I could tell he needs to talk to me urgently and wants me to meet him in an alleyway at the back of the tavern in ten minutes. "Zehn" is ten, isn't it?'

Guy closed his eyes. 'You realise this is a trap, don't you?'

'It does seem likely. But why not arrest me in here? Far easier and safer than arranging a meeting in some dark, deserted alleyway.'

'Assuming you understood what he was saying. And if it is deserted. It's probably stuffed full of soldiers waiting to do something other than arrest you.'

Davenport shrugged. 'You're right, it probably is a trap, but it's a rather bizarre one. And if I don't go and meet him, he can just come back here and find me anyway.'

271

'You're not thinking of going?'

'I don't see what we have to lose.'

'Well, our lives for one thing.'

'My life, possibly. He doesn't even know you're here.'

'We hope.' It was possible, though. Perhaps they could turn this round and ambush the German major.

'Got to be better than just sitting here,' Davenport added. 'With no drink.'

The alley at the back of the tavern was, as Guy had predicted, dark and forbidding. The SS major was leaning back against the wall, smoking a cigarette. He flicked it away and straightened up as Davenport approached.

He had been through a tough regime of Commando combat training when he joined SOE, but Davenport reckoned his greatest protection was his acting ability. Could he bluff his way through whatever was going on? He could have done without Guy's reminder that this was live theatre at its most critical and cruel. His stomach was tightening into the familiar and unpleasant knot of fear.

But he knew from experience that his expression and demeanour would betray none of that fear. He took some comfort from knowing that the SS major would expect him to be alone, whereas in fact Guy was watching from the darkness at the end of the alley. What Guy would be able to do to help him if it came to the crunch, Davenport didn't know. But at least he wasn't alone.

One of his lesser fears was expelled immediately the major spoke. 'I assume you would prefer to conduct this conversation in English?'

'Please.'

As soon as he had spoken, Davenport realised his mistake. That was the trap – it had to be. And now he'd fallen right into it. The major's thin smile seemed to confirm this.

'Don't worry,' the major said. 'I'm not going to shoot you.'

'Ah,' Davenport said. 'Well, that's a relief. So what do you want?'

'To talk. I think we have things in common, things to discuss. Important things.' The major looked round, perhaps sensing that someone was watching them. An iron cross with oak leaves and swords glittered at his throat as it caught the light. 'But not here, not now,' he went on.

'Then where?'

'I have to get back to the schloss. It was fortunate for both of us that I happened to pass through the tavern and recognised you.'

'You know who I am?' He supposed he shouldn't be surprised.

'Not your name, no.'

'Oh,' Davenport tried not to sound disappointed.

'There is an area of woodland to the west of the village. Through the trees, about a quarter of a mile in, you will find a quarry. It is worked out now, but it provided stone for the schloss. There is a wooden hut at the edge of the trees – old and falling down. No one goes there. It used to be a storehouse for tools and equipment. I will meet you there tomorrow morning. Ten o'clock. Yes?'

'Yes, all right. I'll be there. But what's this about?'

'Tomorrow.'

'And if you don't know who I am, how did you recognise me?'

In answer, the SS major drew a folded sheet of paper from his pocket and handed it to Davenport. It was a drawing, crude and blocky – a portrait of a man's face staring out, eyes wide with fear.

'But that's me,' Davenport realised.

'Exactly.' The major took back the paper and refolded it carefully. 'Tomorrow – I shall explain then.' He returned the paper to his pocket and turned to go. Then he paused and turned back. 'Out of curiosity, what *is* your name?'

'I'm not sure you need to know that,' Davenport said warily.

The other man smiled suddenly. He raised his gloved hand and snapped his fingers. 'But I do. Yes, of course, you are

273

Leo Davenport. I see it now.' He clicked his heels and bowed his head briefly. 'Sturmbannfuhrer Werner Hoffman, at your service.'

CHAPTER 34

All light seemed to have been leached from the room. The walls, floor, ceiling were all black. The table in the centre of the room was ebony in colour although the wood was from a lesser tree. Even the candles that provided what guttering illumination there was were as black as the smoke that curled up from their flames. The upturned glass in the centre of the table was made from crystal with a high lead content. The cards around the edge of the table were hand lettered in Gothic script – a single letter or number on each.

'I'm still looking for suitable chairs,' Miss Manners said.

'Are the chairs important?' Wiles asked.

'Everything is important,' she told him.

Henry Wiles nodded. 'I suppose so.'

This was the first time he had been to London for quite a while. The first day he had spent away from Bletchley this year, he realised – and it was 8 December. But he had wanted to see the room. They were standing either side of the table. The surface was lacquered, reflective black. Another set of mirrored flames danced on its surface echoing the candles placed on small shelves round the edges of the room.

The flickering uncertainty of the candles was interrupted by stark electric light from outside as the door opened. Colonel Brinkman stepped into the room, looking round.

'Getting there?' he asked.

'Getting there,' Miss Manners confirmed.

'Still need some chairs, apparently,' Wiles said. He felt he ought to say something to remind Brinkman he was there.

'Good.' Brinkman hesitated on the threshold. 'You're sure this will work?'

'Well, there's nothing certain in this world or the next,' Miss Manners told him. 'But I certainly think it's worth trying.'

Wiles cleared his throat. 'The dates and times of Crowley's séances conform almost exactly to Y Station intercepts of Vril transmissions. The correlation's so high there's a statistical certainty that the two are related. If Crowley can communicate with the Vril in this manner, then we should be able to eavesdrop on the conversation, so to speak.'

'And initiate our own communication?' Brinkman wondered.

'In theory. Though we don't actually know how the communication works. I mean,' he gestured to the table, 'we've assumed a language based on letters and numbers, rather like we've tried to equate the sound of their transmissions to Morse code or an alphanumeric sequence. But we don't know that's how Crowley communicates.'

'How else?' Brinkman asked.

'The communication might be a voice,' Miss Manners said, 'transmitted through a medium.'

'Or he may have a set of cards that show pictograms of some sort.'

'Like ancient Egyptian hieroglyphs?' Brinkman said.

'Or runic symbols,' Miss Manners replied. 'Himmler is apparently very interested in runes. There may be a reason for that.'

'And we have no way of knowing?'

'Not unless Miss Manners' friend gets in touch again,' Wiles admitted. 'Unless you'd care to ask Crowley himself.'

'Not just for the moment, but it may come to that.'

Sergeant Green appeared in the doorway behind Brinkman. 'Excuse me, sir.'

'What is it?'

'Alban,' Green said simply.

'I said I'd give him some figures for the funding meeting that's coming up this afternoon.' Brinkman turned. 'I'll take the call in my office.'

'He's not on the phone, sir,' Green said. 'He's here. In person.'

'Alban?' Wiles asked quietly.

'MI5,' Miss Manners explained. 'He seems to have made it his personal crusade to get us closed down.'

'Does he know what we do?'

'Of course not.'

A voice from the corridor outside cut across her answer: 'Brinkman, there you are. I've been chasing for those figures all week now, and the damned meeting's this afternoon...'

'Christ,' Miss Manners muttered. 'He's here.'

'I've got them in my office, back this way,' Brinkman said quickly.

But he wasn't quick enough. A round-faced man with red hair stepped into view in the corridor. Miss Manners hurried across to the door.

'What are you all up to down here, then? Wasting more time and money?'

Alban smiled at his comment. The smile froze as he glanced into the room, past the closing door. The door stopped, Alban's foot suddenly jammed against the frame as Miss Manners tried to close it fully. He pushed it back open again.

'What the hell?'

'That's a restricted area,' Brinkman said. 'You can't go in there.'

'I said "hell" and it looks like I was right.'

Alban looked round in fascinated horror, taking in the table and letter cards, the upturned glass, the black candles.

'Green – get him out of there,' Brinkman insisted.

'Come along, sir,'

But Alban shook off Green's hand. 'You are completely mad, the lot of you. What in God's name do you think you're doing?'

'Out!' Brinkman snarled.

'You hoping the devil and his hordes will give you some supernatural insight into enemy plans, is that it?'

'You have no idea,' Miss Manners said.

Alban wasn't listening. He looked at Wiles. 'And who's this? High Priest of Darkness? You haven't a clue, you lot, have you?' His voice rose as Green practically shoved him out into the corridor. 'Don't you understand? We're fighting a war, not playing some bloody parlour game! You're unhinged – the lot of you. I'll shut you down.' His voice faded. 'I'll see you never get funding for anything ever again...'

'Can he do it?' Wiles asked nervously. 'Can he really get us closed down?'

'He can try,' Miss Manners said. She looked away. 'And yes, there's a chance he could succeed. He has powerful friends.'

Alban grabbed the sheet of paper Brinkman gave him without a word. His mind was reeling from what he had just seen. What were they doing? What could they possibly hope to achieve? He was well aware of the value of unconventional thinking, but Brinkman's Station Z was something else. Did they seriously think they could defeat the Nazis by *magic*?

Not for the first time he wondered who these people were and what their mission actually was. He couldn't imagine that they'd retain their funding once he'd told the committee what he'd seen today. Couldn't for a moment believe that it was covered by whatever remit they had.

He was outside, gulping in fresh, cold air before he knew it. He didn't remember even coming down the stairs. The car was on the other side of the road. He crossed over, acknowledging Hedges his driver with a nod as the man opened the back door for him.

'You all right, sir?' Hedges asked.

'What? Oh, yes.' He stuffed the sheet of paper into his coat pocket.

'Had they heard?'

'Sorry?' He could still see the black candles burning in

that room. The flickering light reflected in the facets of the upturned glass tumbler.

'I was wondering if Colonel Brinkman had heard the news.'

'No, no, I don't think so. He didn't mention it.'

Hedges started the car. 'Did you tell him?'

Alban was staring out of the window at the door to the offices where Station Z was situated. 'No. He'll find out soon enough.'

As the car pulled out, he saw the woman hurrying along the pavement. Sarah Diamond, half American and in a hurry, he thought. She was almost running, mind elsewhere – he could guess what she was thinking about. She didn't seem to notice the car as they passed her.

'In fact, he'll find out in about half a minute from now,' Alban said. 'Because she's obviously heard.'

CHAPTER 35

Even at night, the Kremlin was an awe-inspiring sight. The Spasskaya Tower gleamed in the moonlight. A red star, added to the top of the spire in 1937 was still the colour of blood, even though it was now two years old.

Mikhael had seen enough blood. He knew he would see a lot more yet, and the thought sickened him. Three days ago, his best friend, Alexei, had been shot dead right beside him. Alex didn't die at once. He spent an agonising hour coughing up rich, ripe, foaming blood and screaming. That was the first time Mikhael had seen death. 20 September 1939 – the day that Mikhael's life changed for ever.

Now, three days later, Mikhael had been brought to the Kremlin to die.

They escorted him in through a side entrance. Two soldiers on guard duty barely spared them a glance. Down a narrow, ill-lit passageway and out into a wide corridor. Their boots rang on the marble floors. Such opulence – Mikhael had never seen anything like it. He struggled to keep looking straight ahead, but his eyes were seduced by the glittering chandeliers, the paintings, the panelled walls...

The General Secretary sat at a large desk at the side of a huge office. He did not look up when they came in, giving no acknowledgement that he knew Mikhael and the three men with him had arrived. The four of them stood to attention in front of the desk, waiting.

After several minutes, the Secretary put down his pen, and looked up. He fixed his deep, dark eyes on Mikhael, his stare so intense he might be looking into the man's soul. Still he said nothing.

Finally, the Secretary turned to the man standing beside Mikhael – the only one of the four not in uniform. 'Is this the man?'

'It is.' The reply was strained with nervous anxiety.

'His rank?'

'He is a corporal.'

'Then promote him.' The Secretary turned his attention back to Mikhael. 'They tell me you speak perfect German.'

'They tell me that too.' He tried to smile, but the Secretary's expression did not change.

'But is it true?'

'It is. My mother was German, though her own mother was English. She worked at the—'

The Secretary waved a hand to cut him off. 'Are you a good Soviet? You know where your loyalty lies?'

'Of course.'

The Secretary beckoned to Mikhael. 'Come closer.' He pointed to the other side of his desk, where several piles of papers were laid out neatly. 'Take a look.'

Mikhael tried to ignore the rest of the desk. There were other stacks of documents. A pile of photographs lay on the blotter – beside the note the Secretary had been writing when they came in. The photographs showed what looked like an aerial view of a forest, except that all the trees were lying down, radiating out from a dark area in the centre like broken matchsticks. The whole landscape blasted across. What weapon could do that?

He forced himself to concentrate on the papers the Secretary had indicated. They were crumpled and old. Identity papers with photographs, letters, a blood-stained page torn from a journal.

'Please, take them with you. All that remains of the lives

of three men. Study them carefully,' the Secretary went on as Mikhael gathered up the papers. 'See which is the most like you, which will be the easiest life to slip into. Not the most comfortable, but the one you can become most convincingly. Names are important,' he added. 'Make sure you like the name of the man you will be when we send you back to Poland.'

There was silence for several moments, then the Secretary leaned forward to study the photographs again. It was obvious that the meeting was over. Mikhael waited for one of the others to move first, then followed them from the room. At the door, he glanced back at the man at the desk – still absorbed in his work. He could see why he had adopted the name 'man of steel' – Stalin.

Hoffman's fingers brushed against the Iron Cross at his throat. 'They gave me this. As the only survivor of an entire unit killed by the last remnants of the Polish army, they thought I deserved it. Whereas in fact, there were no survivors.'

'And the unit was ambushed by the Russians,' Davenport said.

They were speaking in English, sitting on dusty wooden chairs in the hut at the edge of the woodland beside the quarry. The plan had been for Pentecross to stay hidden in the woods, but the first thing Hoffman said to Davenport was:

'Tell your friend to join us. If I'd wanted you killed or captured I'd have done it in the bar last night. I watched the two of you for a good ten minutes before I spoke to you.'

Now they sat round a rough wooden table – none of them the nationality they claimed to be.

'You seriously expect us to believe all that?' Guy said. 'That you're really Russian?'

'Mostly Russian. My mother had some German blood in her.' Hoffman smiled. 'But that wasn't really her fault. Some English too, which is how I know your language.'

'So when the Soviet Army liberated, as they call it, Eastern Poland – you became German.'

'From the sets of papers I was offered I picked out Werner

Hoffman. The candidates were chosen because none of them had any living relatives so far as we could tell. I was decorated, promoted, applied to join the SS.'

'And you're a Russian spy.' Guy shook his head. 'I don't believe a word of it,' he said in fluent Russian. 'I don't know what you're really up to, but you're no more Russian than I am.'

Hoffman laughed. His reply was also in Russian. 'Your accent is very good. I'd guess that you learned your Russian from someone who spent most of their life in Moscow, am I right? It's very formal.'

'What are you two rattling on about?' Davenport asked.

'Just establishing our credentials,' Guy said. 'All right, suppose we accept that you're Russian and you've successfully infiltrated the SS. Why are you talking to us?'

'Please, we're all allies together now.'

'You're risking your cover,' Davenport said.

'I need your help.'

'In what way? You looking to escape, back to Russia?'

Hoffman shook his head. 'There are things happening here. Things I have to tell you about.'

'Have you told Moscow?'

'They wouldn't believe me. I have told them some of it, and had no response. Not even an acknowledgement of the signal.'

'How do you communicate?' Davenport asked. 'Under the circumstances, I can't believe you have colleagues in the village.'

'I have a radio. It's risky. I use it rarely, and only when I can be fairly sure that there is a distraction.'

'Where is this radio?' Guy asked.

'You are sitting on it. Under the floorboards. Buried in the sand beneath.'

'All right,' Guy said. 'Everything you've told us is improbable but I guess it's not impossible.'

'You haven't explained how you knew we were coming,' Davenport said. 'You haven't explained how you come to have a drawing of me in your pocket.'

'I didn't know you were coming,' Hoffman replied. 'The drawing... Well, I can explain that later.'

'And what makes you think we will believe you if your own superiors don't?' Guy asked.

'Because you don't have to believe me. I can show you the evidence. And I know from this –' he drew out the picture of Davenport and unfolded it on the table '– that you already know some of it.'

'From a drawing?' Davenport sniffed. 'And not a very flattering one at that.'

'I don't know what you call these creatures,' Hoffman said, 'but we know them as Ubermensch.' He nodded as Guy and Davenport looked at each other. 'I see you are familiar with the term.'

'You have one of them here?' Davenport demanded. 'At Wewelsburg?'

'No. Not any more.' He smoothed the picture out, hesitating before looking up again. They could both see the fear deep behind his eyes. 'What we have here is much worse.'

'You can get us into the castle?' Guy asked.

'I've brought uniforms. If necessary, I shall vouch for you, although that could cause problems for me later.'

'No need,' Davenport announced. 'Standartenfuhrer Streicher already knows me, assuming he is here.'

'He's here. Although he's organised an expedition to North Africa in a couple of weeks. But how does that help?'

'Because he thinks my name is Carlton Smith, an American archaeologist.'

Hoffman laughed. '*You're* Smith? Oh that is good. Yes, I like that. And a week ago – even a few days ago – that might have worked in our favour. But not now.'

'Why ever not?'

'You haven't heard the news?'

'Tell us,' Guy said.

'Yesterday the Japanese attacked an American base in Hawaii. Pearl Harbor.'

'Never heard of it,' Davenport said.

'As far as we can tell, the attack was without warning, and the US Pacific Fleet was practically destroyed.'

'Christ,' Guy muttered.

'President Roosevelt has asked Congress to declare war on Japan,' Hoffman told them. 'And I think we can safely assume that it will only be a short time before the United States and Germany are also at war.'

CHAPTER 36

She was so angry she didn't trust herself to speak. To Sarah, it seemed the most obvious thing in the world to get the Americans involved with Station Z. They should be setting up briefing meetings through the embassy – she'd offered to talk to Whitman, without letting on quite how well she knew him.

But Colonel Brinkman was adamant. Even now he was still not willing to talk to the Americans. Discussion over.

So Sarah stormed out of his office, grabbed her coat off the back of her chair and left. She clattered down the stairs, swearing under her breath, barging past a startled man heading up to the offices above. By the time she reached the street, she'd made up her mind. If Brinkman wasn't going to talk to the Americans, then she was. She set off towards the embassy, praying that Whitman was there today. Chances were everyone was there. Just so long as she could persuade him to see her. They'd be busy, but as the Japanese attack had taken place thousands of miles away it was unlikely they could actually do anything. He'd see her, she'd make sure of that.

Focused on the pavement ahead, mind full of anger and nervous anticipation, Sarah didn't notice the man in a light grey raincoat. He had been leaning against the wall at the corner of the street, smoking. Now he flicked his cigarette away, and followed Sarah down the road.

*

287

The opportunity to derive information from a new source was too good to miss. The confusion and disarray that the Ubermensch was watching afforded him that opportunity. His latest target was from a very different group of people, and could provide very different data – social, political, tactical… The target would tell him everything.

Rather than simply observe as usual, the Ubermensch followed the target into the building. He walked close behind, matching the man's stride, apparently following him – a friend or colleague. In the confusion, no one stopped him.

Once inside the building, the Ubermensch dropped back. He did not want to be seen until the target reached his office or another quiet place where they could talk. If the target realised he was being followed, that might cause problems.

The first problem was the soldier. Coming the other way down the corridor, the uniformed man nodded in greeting to the target. But frowned as he saw the Ubermensch.

The soldier opened his mouth to speak, hand reaching for the pistol in his holster. But he was too slow. The Ubermensch's own hand was over the man's face, covering his mouth, choking off his shout. At the end of the corridor, the target turned out of sight. The Ubermensch slammed the soldier against the wall. The man's head hit it so hard that the plaster cracked. The soldier slumped forwards, and the Ubermensch hoisted the dead body over his shoulder.

Further down the corridor, he found an unlocked door. A storeroom. He dumped the soldier's body inside. There was no key, so he broke off the door handle.

There was no sign of the target when the Ubermensch turned the corner. There had not been time for the man to get to the end of this corridor. Therefore he was in one of the rooms. The Ubermensch started with the first door. The room was an office – empty.

In the second room a man was working at a desk. Not the target. The Ubermensch murmured an apology and moved on.

The man in the third room asked questions. When the

Ubermensch didn't answer, he reached for a telephone on his desk. As the man glanced down, the Ubermensch grabbed the telephone receiver from him.

'What the hell?'

The heavy Bakelite made a good bludgeon. The Ubermensch weighed the receiver in his hand, then smashed it down on the man's head. He pushed the corpse into a cupboard. The space was small, not designed for the purpose. The Ubermensch had to break several of the man's bones to fit the body inside.

In the fourth room, the Ubermensch found the target. He closed the door behind him and approached the desk.

The target looked up. 'And what can I do for you?' he asked warily.

The Ubermensch sat down opposite the man. 'You can tell me everything,' he said.

Hoffman backed up Guy's insistence that Davenport should not speak a word.

'I managed all right in the bar,' Davenport protested.

'You didn't,' Hoffman told him. 'Your vocabulary is basic and your accent is awful.'

'Just let us do any talking,' Guy said.

Hoffman had brought the SS uniforms of a captain – a hauptsturmfuhrer – and a lieutenant – an obersturmfuhrer. Guy became the lieutenant, as the uniform was a better size. Even so, it was tight and the trousers were slightly short. But the boots were a good fit. Davenport squeezed his slightly fuller form into the captain's uniform.

'I've had worse-fitting costumes,' he said.

He put on the uniform cap and turned to Guy. The transformation was instant and complete – Davenport's expression hardened, his eyes seemed deeper and darker. His features were somehow thinner and he exuded an air of callous indifference. Then, just as suddenly, it all vanished as he grinned. 'What do you think?'

Guy and Hoffman exchanged glances. Hoffman too had been surprised and impressed.

'Very good,' Guy said.

'But still say nothing,' Hoffman added.

'Anything we need to know about saluting and stuff?' Davenport asked.

'If I do it, you do it,' Hoffman said. 'If I don't, you don't.'

The castle was huge – much larger than it had appeared from a distant view. Up close it was also obvious just how much of it was of recent construction. Guy couldn't help feeling that it was an expensive and impressive waste of effort. In an age where the most deadly attack was likely to come from the air in the form of high explosives, building a stone castle was of limited military value.

But the purpose was primarily to impress, and in that it excelled.

They passed along a wide causeway and into the main courtyard without incident. The guards recognised Hoffman, and that seemed to be enough to allow Guy and Davenport unhindered access. Once inside, Hoffman led them through corridors and down winding stone steps.

Eventually he stopped, and said quietly: 'We've come a rather roundabout route as I wanted to be sure no one was following or saw where we are headed.'

'And where are we headed?' Davenport asked.

'There is a restricted area in the cellars, deep underground – below Himmler's Crypt.'

'His what?' Guy said.

'A nickname, but don't worry about that for the moment. Where we are going is far more dangerous and unpleasant.'

He led them down more steps, and along a wide passageway to a set of double doors. Through the doors was another world. Guy blinked in the sudden bright light. They seemed to have stepped into a hospital ward. Rows of beds were arranged under the vaulted ceiling, most of them occupied. All the patients – if they were patients – seemed unconscious or asleep, covered only by thin sheets despite the chill in the air.

'Who are these people?' Guy wondered. 'Are they ill?'

'Sedated, that is all,' Hoffman explained. 'Some are

volunteers, others were brought here from across the Reich. From Germany and Poland, Italy and France. Even Russia.'

He led them through the room, pausing beside the bed where a young woman lay sleeping peacefully. Hoffman paused, looking down at the girl. He brushed a stray strand of fair hair from her forehead.

'They are here because they have certain... abilities,' Hoffman said.

'What abilities?' Davenport asked in a whisper.

Hoffman raised his eyebrows, looking pointedly across to where a nurse was checking the beds. 'I will show you,' he murmured.

They descended again. The lights seemed dimmer the deeper they went. A single electric bulb, imprisoned behind a metal cage, illuminated the small area at the bottom of the steps.

'This is the oldest part of the castle,' Hoffman said. In front of them was a wooden door, banded with metal.

'This part is original, then?' Davenport asked.

'Oh yes. That may be why... We seem to get better reception down here.'

'Reception? You mean, like for radio?' Guy said.

'Perhaps. See for yourselves.' Hoffman turned the heavy iron ring that served as handle on the door and pushed it open. He paused to point at Davenport and then put his finger to his lips. The meaning was clear – they were not alone.

The room was lit by burning sconces of oil. It gave the chamber a smoky, heavy atmosphere. Arched alcoves were black smudges in the gloom, perhaps leading to other areas.

Several stone tables stood down the middle of the chamber, a stone bench beside each. At one of the tables, sat a man. He was staring straight ahead, but his eyes seemed unfocused. His right hand held a pencil that scratched over the top sheet of a pile of paper on the desk in front of him.

A woman stood beside the desk, dressed in a dark skirt and jacket – the female equivalent of an SS uniform complete with jackboots. Her fair hair was twisted into a single plait. The man lifted his pencil from the paper for a moment and she pulled the sheet away. She carried it to the next desk, wrote something in the top left corner, then placed it face-down on another pile of similar pages.

'Anything of interest?' Hoffman asked, walking over to the desk where the man sat.

The woman clicked her heels together and stiffened to attention. 'No, Sturmbannfuhrer. He killed several men, but nothing that seems important.'

Guy looked at Davenport, who shrugged. Did they mean the man at the desk? He looked broad and strong, but emaciated and tired. He continued to stare into space, pencil moving swiftly over the paper.

'You may leave us,' Hoffman told the woman. 'Wait outside. I will tell you when we are done.'

She nodded, and marched briskly from the room, closing the door behind her.

'What is this place?' Guy asked as soon as they were alone. 'What's he doing? Who did he kill?'

'Not him,' Hoffman said. 'Come and see.'

They watched as the man drew. A sketched drawing of the top of a desk appeared. A blotter, papers, notebook, filing tray – sketched approximations of the real things.

'This is Number Nine,' Hoffman told them. 'They all have numbers. I have no idea of his real name.'

'And he draws pictures?' Davenport asked, with evident amusement.

'All the time.'

Hoffman lifted away the finished drawing, and the man immediately started again.

'At least,' Hoffman went on, 'whenever there is a change of view that is significant.' He led them over to the stone table where the woman had stacked the previous drawings. Hoffman lifted several sheets to show them. Each had a number neatly written in the top left corner. 'These will be filed, along with all the others. We have them photographed too, as a precaution.'

Davenport took the sheets from Hoffman and riffled through them. They showed a progression – a view of a door; a view through the open door of a man; several pictures of the man, apparently in conversation across the desk. Then a change – hands around the man's throat; a confused blur of motion; a knife stabbing forwards; a body lying on the floor, a dark stain forming around it. Then the top of the desk; a closer view of the notebook – a diary; the desk again...

'He draws what he sees,' Hoffman said. 'Or rather, what someone else sees.'

'This is the same sort of paper as that picture of me was drawn on,' Davenport said. 'Are you telling us that he draws what the *Ubermensch* sees?'

'They are linked somehow,' Hoffman said. 'Of course the draughtsman – or woman – needs to have some innate talent. It seems to work with fortune tellers, mediums, people with some psychic ability.'

'A mental link then?' Davenport suggested.

'It seems so. But there has to be some affinity between the viewer and the Ubermensch. We tested several of the candidates before we made this particular connection.'

'Candidates?' Guy said. 'You mean the people in the beds?'

Hoffman nodded. 'Anyone who seems to have the right ability is tested, and if they pass the test they are brought here.'

'What sort of test?' Davenport asked.

'Simple things – predicting the next card in a sequence. Identifying a symbol chosen by another psychic. That sort of thing.'

'But – how does it work?' Pentecross said. 'How is the link established?'

'The bracelet,' Davenport told him. 'Don't you see – that man is wearing a bracelet just like the one Sarah recovered from the burial mound. Just like the Ubermensch was wearing.'

'That's right,' Hoffman agreed. 'The bracelets seem to come in pairs. Although we have had instances of a connection forming without the bracelet. It is never as strong or reliable, but if the two – Ubermensch and viewer – are extremely compatible…' He shrugged. 'Kruger is in charge of the project and he pretends to have answers for the Reichsfuhrer, but he doesn't really understand. None of us does.'

The place was in turmoil. People were running – not just hurrying, but actually running – across the main concourse. Sarah pushed her way through to the reception desk. The woman at the desk recognised Sarah. She probably didn't remember why, but it was enough for her to wave Sarah through as soon as she asked for Mr Whitman.

'It's urgent,' Sarah said.

'Isn't everything today? He's in his office. You know the way?'

Sarah nodded.

'I assume he's expecting you?' the woman called after her.

'Of course,' Sarah called back, without turning.

She hurried up the stairs and made her way down the corridor to Andrew Whitman's office. She knocked, not waiting for an answer before she pushed the door open.

'Andrew – we have to talk.' She paused in the doorway. 'Oh.'

It wasn't Whitman. The man in the office was older. He half stood as he saw Sarah, beckoning her in.

'It's all right.' His voice was a lazy drawl, not unlike Whitman's. 'Andrew has been detained, you know what it's like. But he should be here soon.'

'Perhaps I'd better come back.'

'Nonsense. Miss Diamond, isn't it?' He gave a short laugh at her surprised expression. 'Andrew's told me everything about you. Come on in. Take a seat.' He gestured to the chair opposite.

'Everything?' Sarah asked, trying to make light of it. He'd better not have.

'So what brings you here, Miss Diamond?' He ran his hand over his bald scalp.

'I have to talk to Andrew. There are things I need to tell him. Things he should know.'

The man leaned back, swinging gently in the swivel chair behind the desk as he considered this. 'Is that a fact? You can talk to me, you know. Andrew and I work together. Jeff Wood,' he said. 'Call me Jeff. Andrew will be here soon, but if you want to make a start?'

Perhaps because Jeff Wood seemed so casual about it, perhaps because his accent and his tone reminded her of Andrew Whitman, perhaps because she had come here determined to tell her story, Sarah nodded.

'All right,' she said. 'Have you ever heard the expression UDT?'

Jeff shook his head. 'Tell me,' he said. 'Tell me everything.'

'When they brought it here, the Ubermensch knew nothing,' Hoffman said. 'That was well before I arrived. Before I even existed.' He smiled. 'But it had to learn, and it learned quickly.'

'Where did it come from?' Davenport asked. 'A burial site, like the others?'

'I don't know, I'm afraid. I have heard talk of it being unearthed in Tibet, but the circumstances are shrouded in secrecy. I don't like to ask too much, best not to draw attention.'

'What did it learn?' Guy asked.

'Everything. How to speak, how to read... And in return it taught Kruger and the others. It told them how to use the bracelets.'

'Why would it do that?' Davenport wondered. 'Surrender its privacy.'

'I think it had to, in order to win some freedom. They wouldn't let it go to England without being able to see what was happening, and be sure it couldn't escape them.'

'And why did it go?' Guy said.

'You know why. As soon as it could, it tried to recover more of its own kind, its own artefacts. It gave details of several possible sites, including the one in England. It said it wanted to help, that its only ambition was to help Germany win the war.'

'You didn't believe it,' Guy guessed.

'I've deceived enough people for long enough to know when someone – or something – is trying to deceive me,' Hoffman said. 'But what its real motives were, I don't know. Perhaps it just craved company, wanted to find another of its own kind. Or perhaps it thought it could recruit enough Ubermenschen to fight back. Now it is gone, and we shall never know.'

'So all you have now is this link to the Ubermensch from France,' Davenport said.

'Not quite,' Hoffman said. 'If that was all, I'd be less concerned.'

'Then what?'

'You'll see.'

They stood watching Number Nine as he completed another picture. A view across the desk towards a door.

'Where is the Ubermensch this man is linked to?' Guy wondered.

'We don't know. London somewhere. But how he got there from the burial site in France where he was discovered, we have no idea. Do you?'

Davenport gave a short laugh. 'Modesty forbids.'

'I see.' Hoffman took another completed drawing – the office door was swinging open. He numbered it and placed it on the pile. 'We should go.'

'Is this what you wanted us to see?' Davenport asked.

'Part of it. Not the most important part.'

'You coming?' Guy asked Davenport, who was still standing beside Number Nine. He was staring down at the next drawing.

'I think you should look at this,' he said.

'Why – what is it?'

Guy could feel the blood draining from his face as Davenport replied:

'He's drawing a woman. And I think it's Sarah.'

CHAPTER 37

The new picture showed a view across the desk. Sitting on the other side was a woman. It was unmistakably Sarah Diamond.

'You know her?' Hoffman asked.

'Where the hell is she?' Guy said. 'What's she doing?'

'More to the point, what can *we* do?' Davenport demanded. He turned to Hoffman. 'Well?'

Hoffman shook his head. 'Nothing. We can watch, but there is no way that we've found to communicate or interfere.'

Hoffman removed the page as soon as it was complete. Immediately, Number Nine was drawing again. A closer view. Sarah's face – the thin features, the slight curl to her collar-length hair... But her expression was contorted, her mouth open in a cry or a gasp.

They watched in silent horror as the pencil moved down from the face. To the neck. Drawing the hands clasped round Sarah's throat. Throttling the life from her.

She was desperate to talk, to tell someone about Station Z and all that had happened over the past few months. But as she started her story, something about Jeff made her uneasy. He was charming, attentive, sympathetic. But...

'Where's Andrew?' she asked.

'He'll be here shortly.'

'I've never told anyone about these things before.' Not that she had said anything much yet – just that there were unidentified traces showing up on RADAR.

Jeff nodded amicably. 'Is that a fact?'

The way he said it made her even more nervous. The same intonation as Andrew Whitman used. The same phrase. In fact, now she thought about it, the whole way he spoke, right down to his accent, was very similar.

Sarah shifted on the chair. Her foot nudged against the leg of the desk, and she drew it back, glancing down.

It was all she could do to keep from leaping to her feet. She struggled to keep her expression neutral, looking straight back up again. Had he seen her reaction?

The floor was bare boards. No rug or carpet. And across the floorboards a dark stain was spreading slowly from under the desk. Viscous, and blood red.

'Where *is* Andrew?' Her voice was strung out with nerves.

Jeff smiled. His pale lips seemed to crack as they drew back from discoloured, broken teeth.

'I think you know where he is.' Jeff got slowly to his feet. 'Now, you were about to tell me everything.'

Sarah stood up too, backing away from the desk towards the door. 'Not a chance,' she murmured. She turned to run.

But the man was already moving, blocking her path to the door. He grabbed her, shoving her across the desk, hands gripping her throat, forcing her back. She gasped for breath as his thumbs bit into her windpipe. Tore at his hands, scratching and scraping and digging in her nails. But the grip didn't loosen. She scrabbled behind her on the desk top, hands searching for something – anything – to use as a weapon. He forced her down across the desk.

Sarah managed to twist her head. It was over the back of the desk, so she was looking down at the floor behind. At Andrew Whitman's body bleeding out across the wooden boards. The thin blade of a letter-opener had pierced his chest, ornate gilded handle projecting upwards.

Her fingers grazed the top of the handle. Couldn't reach.

Sarah pushed herself back across the desk, the man's hands still tight round her throat. His face was close to hers. She could see the thin maze of lines etched across his skin, like ancient cracked porcelain. The emptiness of the deep, dark eyes. Misting over as her brain was starved of oxygen.

Further back. The musty stench of death seemed to emanate from the Ubermensch as he bore down on her, his weight pressing her to the top of the desk. Stretching down, her hand finally grasped the thin knife, pulling it free with an unpleasant sucking noise. She twisted her hand as she jabbed upwards, blade first.

The grip slackened, for just a moment. For just long enough to enable Sarah to push herself backwards again. The bulk of her weight was over the edge of the desk and she fell – breaking free finally from the creature's grip.

She crashed to the floor, landing half across Whitman's body. Her palm pressed down on his chest, blood oozing half-clotted between her fingers. She screamed, throat already burning and sore. Rolled off the cooling corpse, and staggered to her feet.

The image showed Sarah from above, staring up wide-eyed at her attacker. A single drop of red splashed to the middle of the white sheet. It landed on Sarah's neck, close to the hands grasped round it, blotting into the paper.

Number Nine was crying blood. A thin trickle from his left eye, welling up and dripping as he drew. Then the whole eyeball exploded. Gelatinous debris spattered across the picture followed by a gush of blood.

Guy took a step back. Davenport swore. Hoffman seemed unperturbed.

'Perhaps your friend will be all right. She is fighting back.'

'What the hell just happened?' Davenport demanded.

Number Nine kept drawing, the pencil moving through blood and flesh.

'The affinity between the viewer and the Ubermensch is more than just communication,' Hoffman said. 'They are linked somehow. Physically.'

Guy stared at the bloodied, empty socket. Blood was congealing round the edges already. 'You mean, whatever happens to the Ubermensch is also visited upon this poor man?'

'It seems so.' Hoffman carefully pulled the stained sheet of paper across the table. Number Nine kept drawing, oblivious, as Hoffman folded it. He kept the grisly contents inside, and dropped the paper into the nearest sconce of burning oil. At once the sickly-sweet smell of burning tissue filled the air.

'An eye for an eye,' Davenport murmured.

Sarah didn't look back until she reached the door. She pulled it open, glancing over her shoulder as she fled into the corridor outside.

The Ubermensch was coming across the room. The letter-opener jutted out from its left eye. It reached up, grasped the handle and pulled it out. There was no blood. Just an empty hole – darkness. Then thin orange filaments licked out from the eye socket, feeling their way round the Ubermensch's cheek as if seeking for air.

Sarah pulled the door shut behind her and ran. She needed to get out, needed air. There was a fire escape through the door at the end of the corridor – she'd used it before when she'd wanted to leave quickly and unseen.

The cold chill of the outside air was like a knife after the warmth of the embassy. Her coat was still over the back of the chair in Whitman's office. The fire escape was attached to the back of the building, little more than an iron ladder with a small platform at each floor level. She clambered down, fast as she could, hands almost freezing to the cold metal.

Above her another figure stepped out onto the ladder and started down. It moved quickly and easily, with none of the awkwardness of the creature in the burial chamber. Still a dozen feet off the ground, Sarah jumped. She kept hold of the sides of the ladder, letting the handrail slip through as she fell, slowing her descent. The cold of the metal was burning now, tearing the skin from her hands.

The impact jarred right up through her legs as she hit the ground. One ankle buckled. She ignored the pain and ran.

The image was blurred and vague. It showed Sarah's back as she ran. As the Ubermensch pursued her down a narrow alleyway.

'Perhaps it's getting dark,' Guy said.

'It only has one eye,' Hoffman said. 'This is how it sees now.'

'That should help Sarah escape,' Davenport said.

'I wouldn't put money on it,' Hoffman told him. 'Even severe injuries don't slow them down for long.'

A similar image. But closer to Sarah now. Her terrified face looking back as she ran.

There was a road at the end of the alley. There would be people. She could lose herself amongst them. Just round the next corner. Sarah glanced back – the Ubermensch was gaining on her. But she'd make it, she was far enough ahead. She reached the corner.

And the world changed.

The wall down the side of the alley was gone, bitten off abruptly. Where there had been a busy street, there was nothing. An empty wasteland of rubble scattered over mud. The ground dipped unevenly into the crater the bomb had left.

On the other side, the remains of a shattered building stood precariously against the darkening sky. Joists from the floors stuck out like enormous broken matchsticks. The wall of an upper storey protruded awkwardly over the empty space below, sagging under its own weight.

There was a road on the other side of the building. If she could get there, get through the ruins, she might still be safe. Sarah slipped and slid down the incline. She didn't dare look back. She knew that if she did she would see the Ubermensch gaining on her, orange tendrils like lichen erupting from the empty eye socket and spreading across one side of its face.

Her ankle caught the edge of a blackened brick and gave

way, pitching her forwards. She landed painfully, hardly noticing that the ground where she fell was the front of the building, laid out where it had fallen. Almost intact.

She dragged herself to her feet and staggered on, foot shattering through a window. Broken glass scythed into her shin and calf. Warm blood was running down her leg. Thank God she hadn't bothered with stockings, she thought – they'd be ruined. She gritted her teeth against the pain, limping on, cursing how mundane her anxieties were compared with the horror stalking after her.

She did look back. She had to know how close he was.

There was no one there.

Crying tears of relief as well as pain, she staggered to the edge of the crater and reached the shelter of the building. Where had the creature gone? Had it given up? Looking back across the bomb site, drawing in painful ragged breaths and rubbing her bruised neck, she could see that the edge of the crater was level. The paving was still there. If she'd been less panicked, less scared for her life, she'd have realised it was quicker to skirt round the edge of the crater than try to get across the middle of it, negotiating the uneven ground and debris.

With that realisation came another. Slowly, she turned. She hardly dared look. Hardly dared to hope she might be wrong.

A figure stepped out of the shadow of the bombed-out building, right behind Sarah. A single eye stared back at her, the other a mass of curling orange tentacles.

'Oh no,' Guy breathed as the drawing took shape.

In the background, Sarah – hand pressed to her mouth in terror. In front of her, a black circle – the end of a tube... A barrel. A gun, pointing straight at them out of the paper.

'It's going to shoot her.'

CHAPTER 38

The sound of the gunshot echoed off the ruined building. The bullet impacted on the chest, tearing its way through flesh and bone.

Sarah staggered back, light-headed and confused. The man had come from nowhere, stepping between her and the Ubermensch and firing at point-blank range into the creature. He must have followed it round the crater.

The Ubermensch was knocked backwards by the shot, crashing into the end of a broken wall. Its chest was torn open, orange and red spattering out – blood and tendrils and the pale glint of exposed bone.

'That won't stop it!' Sarah heard herself shouting. She grabbed the man's arm. 'We have to get away from here.'

She had recognised his thinning red hair, but only when she saw his face did she realise it was Alban, the MI5 man.

'What the hell is that?' Alban gasped.

The creature was already pulling itself upright again. Already coming back at them.

'You can't kill it,' Sarah told him as they backed slowly away. 'It isn't really alive.'

Number Nine cried out, thrown back by the invisible impact. He fell backwards, and lay still for a moment before hauling himself back to his feet, pencil twitching in his hand as if he

303

was still drawing in the air. The front of his gown was plastered in sudden blood. Then the man slumped down again. Pencil again met paper.

'The gun was pointing *at* him,' Davenport realised. 'Sarah may be all right.'

'For now,' Guy agreed grimly.

Number Nine gave a grunt of pain, his head knocked suddenly sideways. Blood trickled from his ear.

'What the hell's happening?' Guy wondered.

The drawing was erratic, a confused mess of what might be rubble – fallen stone, shattered wood, and broken bricks.

She hurled the broken brick as hard as she could. It caught the Ubermensch on the side of the head, glancing off. The creature tilted its head to one side as it stared back at Sarah.

Alban fired again. The bullet hit the upper arm, going right through and ricocheting off the brickwork of a broken wall. The Ubermensch barely slowed, running at the two of them across the broken ground.

Blood was seeping from Number Nine's shoulder, as if from a bullet wound. His breathing was ragged. The drawing barely more than scratches across the paper.

'It's killing him,' Guy said. It was horrific to watch.

'He won't die unless the Ubermensch is destroyed,' Hoffman said.

'Surely he can't go on,' Davenport said.

'They heal. But it takes time. There is pain.'

'No,' Guy decided. 'He can't even draw, it's inhuman to let him suffer like this.'

'You want me to put him out of the pain?' Hoffman asked. 'I can shoot him. It might even kill him.' He seemed indifferent.

But Guy wasn't. 'No! The bracelet – you said that was what connected them.'

He didn't wait for an answer, but grabbed the man's wrist. He prised the bracelet open. It resisted. Tiny filaments attached the inside of the bracelet to the man's skin like spikes. Guy could see them stretching and breaking as he pulled harder. The filaments had dug deep into the man's flesh, into his very being. But finally, the bracelet came away, ripping the skin with it, leaving a raw, red shadow of itself around the wrist.

Number Nine's remaining eye widened in sudden fear and surprise. He screamed, and fell forward, slumped across the stone table.

'He's still breathing,' Davenport observed. 'But we've lost any way of knowing what's happening to Sarah.'

'She'll be all right,' Guy said.

'You can't know that for sure,' Hoffman told him.

Guy glared at him, fist slamming down on the hard stone table. 'She'll be all right!'

They had circled round so that they could get into the ruined building, and through it to the road.

'There's got to be some way to stop it,' Alban gasped as they clambered over fallen beams and a collapsed wall.

'Fire,' Sarah told him. 'Don't know what else.'

He jumped down the other side of a pile of rubble, turned and reached up to help her. 'You've done this before,' he realised.

'Not quite like this.' She grabbed his hand, allowing him to steady her as she jumped down. She grimaced with pain as her damaged ankle took her weight. She was limping badly now.

Behind them, the Ubermensch leaped easily up on to the rubble.

'We won't make it to the road,' Alban said.

'You could. Leave me.'

He didn't answer, looking round desperately for any way of escape, anything to use as a weapon. 'This way,' he decided.

He half dragged her across the shattered remains of a room, ignoring her gasps of pain. A picture lay on the ground, a painting of a boat pulled up on a beach. The canvas was ripped through, the frame split. Even so, Sarah felt bad about stepping on it as she staggered on.

They were right under the overhanging wall. Sarah heard it creaking and protesting. She was glad to stagger out from under it. Alban pushed her to one side.

'Wait here.'

He darted across what had been a small courtyard. A long splintered beam lay on the ground, one end snapped off, the other blunt and rotted. He struggled to lift it, swinging it upwards.

The Ubermensch paused, watching from just beyond the broken wall. The dying rays of the afternoon sun enhanced the orange-red of the growth spilling from its eye socket, the blood across its chest and down its arm. Tendrils clawed like impatient fingers out of the wounds.

'Come on, then!' Alban yelled at it. 'Get it over with. Kill us if you're going to.'

The Ubermensch took a step forward.

Alban grunted with the effort of lifting the wooden beam. He held it out in front of him, like a lance, and charged at the Ubermensch. The creature didn't move, didn't flinch.

Sarah hardly dared to watch, waiting for the end of the beam to smash into the thing's chest. It wouldn't stop it – she knew it wouldn't stop it.

But at the last moment, Alban angled the beam upwards – driving it hard into the underside of the wall jutting out above.

A scattering of mortar, then a trickle. A brick fell, dislodged by the impact of the beam. Then another. They crashed down beside the Ubermensch, rattling across the rubble. It looked up.

And the whole overhanging wall creaked, groaned, tore away from the rest of the building. The brick, stone, plaster and wood collapsed, cascading down in an avalanche of broken masonry. The Ubermensch was enveloped in a cloud of dust. Through it, Sarah saw the creature driven to its knees by the falling debris. Collapsing, buried under the rubble. Still more fell.

The next wall of the building was shifting, pulled out of kilter by the collapse. The whole edifice was crumbling, crashing down. Despite the pain in her ankle, Sarah ran forward. Alban was rooted to the spot, watching the wreckage piling on top of the Ubermensch. She grabbed him, dragging him back as the next wall fell, bricks and concrete scattering like shrapnel across the area where Alban had just been standing.

'Were you following me?' Sarah demanded as the noise and the dust died down.

Alban still stared at the rubble that buried the Ubermensch. 'Yes.'

She slapped him across the face. It was an impulsive reaction, and she regretted it at once. But he didn't comment. He barely seemed to notice. Somehow, that made her feel worse.

'One of my men reported you'd gone into the embassy. I decided it was time for a few words about national security and careless talk.'

'You were going to arrest me?'

'Perhaps.'

'And now?'

'What?' He turned to look at her for the first time.

'Are you still going to arrest me?'

'I don't think so. But you've got some explaining to do. And you should get that ankle looked at.'

At three different Y Stations, operators monitoring radio transmissions in the London area pulled off their headsets as a burst of loud static drowned out the signals.

In the candle-lit basement of a house in Jermyn Street, Jane Roylston cried out. She lay on a red velvet sheet on top of a stone altar. Her legs were splayed apart, arms outstretched, tied at ankles and wrists to iron rings set into the stone. Her body was filmed with sweat despite the chill of the cellar.

'Pain!' she gasped. 'Darkness. Crushing weight...'

'What else?' Crowley asked. He leaned over her, licking his bloodless lips hungrily. 'Death?'

She didn't answer. Her head lolled to one side on the velvet and her eyes slowly closed.

She had lost track of time, had no idea how long she had been sitting there. The room was lit only by the black candles. Perhaps it was her imagination or perhaps a trick of the light, but the upturned glass in the centre of the table seemed to tremble.

Penelope Manners leaned forwards, concentrating on the glass, focusing all her attention and mental energy on to it. Was it moving? Was it trying to tell her something? Was she receiving a psychic signal, even without a full séance?

She could hear it rattling on the wood as it shuddered. Then the glass shot across the table, off the edge – slamming into the wall on the other side of the room and exploding into fragments, ice-like splinters that glimmered in the flickering light.

CHAPTER 39

Hoffman sent the woman who had been watching Number Nine to get Kruger.

'He can sort things out and report to Himmler,' Hoffman decided.

He led them through the chamber, away from where Number Nine lay slumped across the stone table. 'Kruger is in charge of the project,' he explained. 'Or this aspect of it at least.'

'There are others?' Guy asked.

'Oh yes. There is much more. That's what I need to show you,' Hoffman said. 'Then you both have to get as far away from here as possible.'

'That sounds like an excellent suggestion. But what do you expect us to do about what you show us?' Davenport asked.

'I don't know. Perhaps knowledge will be enough. The more people who know...' He shook his head. 'I honestly don't know if anyone can do anything, it's gone so far. But apart from the technology that they are deriving from the Vril Project, the whole thing is...' He struggled to find the right word in English. 'Unnatural,' he decided. 'Evil, even. These things should not exist. Yet here they are examined and perpetuated. What is learned is passed on to other parts of the Reich.'

'Such as?' Davenport asked.

'Hitler wants to develop what he calls Vergeltungswaffen.' He looked at Guy for help.

'Weapons of vengeance,' Guy translated.

'What we have learned from the Vril Project is fed into that. There are other developments too, things that even I do not know about. But I hear Himmler talking with Speer and Heydrich and others. I know they are planning the most terrible things.'

'Then we have to stop them,' Davenport said. 'Simple, eh?' He smiled. 'But as you say, forewarned is forearmed, knowledge is power, information is strength. And other clichés too, probably. Whatever you can tell us will help, but you're right – we're probably in this for the long haul.'

The corridor sloped slightly downwards as they approached the Vault. Hoffman was taking a risk bringing them here. It had been dangerous enough already, but if Kruger or Himmler or one of the most senior officers or scientists found them actually *in* the Vault...

They were almost there when they ran into trouble. Hoffman heard them before he saw them – the click of jackboots from round the next corner of the passageway. The shadows of two officers cast on the side wall, jagged and distorted in the harsh light of the unshaded bulbs strung from the corridor ceiling. It was too late to go back, and there was nowhere to hide. Their only chance was to brazen it out.

'Say nothing!' Hoffman whispered. 'Leave this to me.'

The two officers strode towards them. A major and a captain, he saw as they approached. At least the major didn't outrank him, but equally Hoffman couldn't ignore someone of the same rank as himself. He recognised them as they got closer. He didn't know their names but he had seen both of them around the castle.

He thought for a moment that they were going to be all right. The two officers strode past with barely a nod. Hoffman allowed himself a silent sigh of relief.

Then the major called after them: 'You are going to the Vault?'

Hoffman stopped. Switched on a thin smile and turned. He could demand what business it was of theirs, but that would just antagonise. Instead, he nodded. 'We are.'

'You know that Standartenfuhrer Streicher has ordered that no one enter the Vault without specific orders until further notice.'

Hoffman didn't. He wondered why such an order had come from Streicher rather than Kruger, or Himmler himself.

'Sturmbannfuhrer Schmidt and the hauptsturmfuhrer have come from Berlin at the express orders of the Fuhrer,' Hoffman said. If he was going to bluff, he might as well do it properly. 'Sturmbannfuhrer Schmidt is one of the Fuhrer's personal guard.'

The major regarded Davenport and Pentecross with interest. 'It is good that our work is being taken so seriously. So, what is the news from Berlin?'

'I hardly think—' Hoffman started.

But the major cut him off. 'I was addressing the sturmbannfuhrer.'

Davenport was facing away from the major, watching Hoffman's reaction. His eyes widened as he realised that he was being addressed. He raised his eyebrows briefly, then turned.

Hoffman's heart was thumping in his chest. If Davenport spoke, they were finished. But if he didn't answer...

Davenport regarded the major for a few seconds, then turned to Guy. He said nothing, but gave a curt nod.

Guy coughed. 'The sturmbannfuhrer would like you to know that although you outrank him technically, we are here on the express orders of the Fuhrer. Our visit is classified, and you are to tell no one that you have seen us.'

The major frowned, glancing at the captain beside him, who gave no reaction. 'Can the sturmbannfuhrer not speak for himself?' he asked. There was an edge to the question, a hint of a challenge. Distrust.

Guy made to reply, but Davenport raised his hand to stop him. He walked slowly towards the major until he was standing

311

right beside him. The nearest light was shining directly on to his face as Davenport looked up at the slightly taller man.

Hoffman was surprised at the transformation. Davenport's soft, avuncular features seemed to have hardened to granite. His eyes were dark as he glared at the major. He held the other man's gaze for a long time, unblinking. Then his mouth curled slightly into a thin, cruel smile. The major looked away.

Davenport stepped back, still staring at the major. With an abrupt click of his heels he raised his hand. 'Heil Hitler!' he barked.

The major and the captain immediately responded. A second later, so did Hoffman and Guy.

Davenport turned and marched back towards them. His face cracked open into a self-satisfied grin. Behind him, the two officers turned and walked away.

'You think they'll tell anyone?' Pentecross asked.

'Would you?' Davenport replied.

'We can't be sure,' Hoffman said. 'So we had better hurry.'

The corridor ended in a metal door. It was thick and solid – gunmetal grey with a locking wheel in the middle. It reminded Guy of the airtight hatch of a submarine. A sentry stood on guard outside the door. He snapped to attention as Hoffman and the others approached.

Hoffman gestured for the soldier to open the door. He turned the locking wheel, and had to lean back using his whole weight to pull the door open. Guy was surprised how thick the door was – a foot or more of solid metal. Whatever was behind it was valuable.

Inside was dark. Hoffman reached for a switch, and lights flickered into life overhead, casting a harsh luminance over the chamber. The heavy door swung shut behind them, closing with a metallic clang that echoed off the stone walls and floor. The ceiling was like the roof of a cathedral, high above. Shadowed alcoves stretched into the distance, ending in another identical hatch-like metal doorway.

The end of the long chamber where they were standing

was like an operations room. Wooden tables were covered with papers and plans. Diagrams and blueprints that meant nothing to Guy. Maps were hung on the walls, marked with coloured pins and pencilled annotations.

'These are interesting,' Davenport said quietly, nodding at the maps.

'We should have brought a camera,' Guy said.

'I can memorise them,' Davenport assured him. 'It'll only take a minute. This is the burial site in France, look.' He moved on to the next map. 'Shingle Bay – rather an old map. Italy, North Africa… And several Greek islands. That's Crete.'

'What's the significance?' Guy asked.

Hoffman shrugged. 'Streicher is always on the hunt for more artefacts. Sometimes he is right when he predicts where they might be found. Usually he isn't. He claims he is on the track of a huge cache of Vril material but…' He waved the notion away. 'I'll believe it when I see it. And I hope that's never. But this isn't why I brought you here.'

He led them through the chamber towards the other door. But before they reached it, Hoffman stepped into one of the alcoves. He pulled a small lever attached to an electrical box on the wall beside the alcove and more lights came on. The alcove was an arched opening into another chamber, as big as the first.

A heavy wooden workbench ran down the length of the table. It was covered with artefacts – pottery, glass, metal, ceramic. Neatly written labels gave each artefact or collection of similar artefacts a number. Guy saw that there were more, similar tables against the walls, all laid out in the same way.

'What are these things?' he wondered out loud.

'Most of them – we have no idea,' Hoffman said. 'They are all artefacts that Streicher or his colleagues have recovered. They are examined and catalogued. Kruger and his team work on some of them. Experts in various fields are brought in to analyse certain components. They call them "components", but components of what I do not know. Perhaps no one does.'

At the end of the chamber, metal shutters covered what

might be a window or an opening. Beside them was another wooden workbench. On it were the Vril.

One was in a cracked glass jar. A scum of fluid stained the bottom of the jar. The creature lay curled on its back, inert. Dead. One of the stick-like legs had shattered, another was bent backwards. It was a dried up husk, desiccated, like an enormous ancient spider.

Another of the creatures was pinned out on a wooden board, like a school dissection project. The legs were splayed away from the body, held in place by staples as if it had been manacled in position. It was as dry and dead as the first.

A third Vril was standing at the end of the workbench. Guy gasped as he caught sight of it, thinking the creature was still alive, preparing to leap at him. But it didn't move, and he saw that it was held up by a thin metal armature like a stuffed animal in a museum.

On a shelf behind this Vril, large specimen jars held fragments of other creatures in green-tinged liquid – a leg, part of the main body, a single dark eye...

'Recovered from the Black Forest in 1936,' Hoffman said. 'Or so I am led to believe.'

'Were they dead when they were found?' Davenport asked. He was staring at the upright creature with a mixture of fascination and revulsion.

'These ones were.'

'These ones?' Guy echoed.

In answer, Hoffman turned a small handle at the side of the metal shutters. The shutters drew back slowly, revealing glass behind – a window looking into a tank of grey-green liquid. For a second, Guy thought the tank was empty. But then the liquid stirred. Green slime swilled round inside. Something slammed against the glass – a long, dark limb. It left a slimy trail as it whipped away again. A hideous face appeared out of the murky depths. Dark eyes stared malevolently out at Guy and Davenport and Hoffman. The grotesque twisted maw of a mouth opened and closed, snapping shut so violently that the liquid churned again.

'My God,' Davenport said. 'What a vile, hideous thing.'

From behind them came the click of a pistol being cocked.

Guy saw their reflection in the glass before he turned – the major and the captain from the corridor. The captain was holding the pistol. The sentry from the door stood beside them, rifle unshouldered and aimed.

'I had some more questions to ask you,' the major said stepping forward, hands clasped behind his back. 'But hearing you speaking in English just now – well, I think I have my answers.'

He walked slowly to the side of the room, never taking his eyes off Guy and the others.

'I can explain,' Hoffman said.

'No, you can't,' the major told him.

'Sir?' the captain asked.

The order when it came was dismissive. The major turned away, apparently bored with the whole scenario. 'Shoot them.'

CHAPTER 40

Guy dived for cover, hoping that Davenport understood what was going on. Hoffman was already going the other way, and Davenport was close behind him as the captain's Luger pistol fired two shots in rapid succession at the space where the three of them had just been standing.

The first shot ricocheted off the floor, chipping stone before slamming into the wall. The second shot was higher. It cracked into the middle of the glass tank containing the Vril creature. A spider's web of fine lines splayed out from the point of impact. But the glass held. Behind it the creature's dark eyes watched coldly. A single thin tentacle caressed the inside of the glass, searching out any damage.

Hoffman had taken cover behind the workbench and drew his own Luger. His first shot went wide, but sent the captain scurrying for cover. The sentry was slower. He struggled to bring his rifle to bear, and Hoffman's second bullet caught him in the forehead. The man froze, as if he'd been startled. Then he simply crumpled at the knees, and collapsed face down on the floor. Blood pooled round his head.

'You'll die for this – traitor!' the major yelled from where he was sheltering in the shadow of the alcove. He couldn't get to the main door without stepping out into Hoffman's line of fire.

The captain was shooting again. Guy reckoned he and

Davenport were safe enough in the recess of an alcove. But they were pinned down with no means of fighting back.

'Only a matter of time before someone else comes down here,' Davenport said.

Another shot blasted past. Chips of broken stone stung Guy's face. Hoffman appeared above the level of the workbench, just for long enough to fire a shot of his own. Behind him, the Vril watched through the cracked glass window. Tentacles reached round the edges of the damage, as if the creature was bracing itself. Then the main body slammed forward, crashing into the weak point where the bullet had hit.

'Look out!' Guy shouted to Hoffman.

Hoffman turned to see what was happening – just as the whole of the front of the glass tank shattered under the impact of the Vril's assault. Dark, viscous liquid poured out, sweeping away the remains of the glass which crashed to the floor, smashing into fragments.

The creature leaped from the tank. It hit Hoffman in the chest, knocking him backwards – just as a bullet roared past. It lay on top of Hoffman, bulbous body pulsating, legs twitching. Hoffman gave a cry of pain as one of the rough tentacles ripped across his leg, drawing blood.

Then the Vril was gone – scuttling across the room, splashing through the puddle of liquid and disappearing under a workbench.

'That's what I saw,' Davenport gasped. 'In France – I'm sure of it. As I was escaping from the burial chamber with Streicher. There was one of those things there.'

Hoffman dragged himself back into cover as the captain shot again. The major had drawn his own gun and joined the battle. Under cover of the distraction of the breaking tank, they had both moved forward to better positions. Guy realised that they were trapped – the captain was almost on them. He called for Hoffman to help, but the German's gun clicked on empty.

The captain stepped into the alcove, gun raised, mouth

curled into a smile of eager anticipation. His finger tightened on the trigger.

With a yell of rage, Guy leaped at the man, driving him backwards. The captain's gun went off, the bullet drilling into the ceiling high above them. A scattering of dust fell back. The captain swung the gun savagely, catching Guy on the side of the head and knocking him back. He raised the pistol again. And screamed.

A dark scaly tentacle wrapped round the side of the captain's head, across his mouth. Another appeared from the other side, jerking his head back. There was an awful cracking sound as the man's neck broke and he collapsed. The Vril sat perched like some grotesque gargoyle on the man's back, pulsing and twitching. Then it scuttled off into the shadows.

A split second later, the major's bullets ripped through where the Vril had been, shredding the captain's body and spattering blood and tissue across the floor.

Davenport grabbed Guy, pulling him back into cover. 'Just one of them now,' he said. 'We can rush him.'

'And get shot?'

'Or get our necks snapped by that creature. Take your pick.'

Guy glanced across to where Hoffman was lying. He hoped the major didn't speak English, and called out: 'You up to distracting him?'

Hoffman was massaging his leg where the Vril had scratched it open. But he nodded at Guy. He retrieved his pistol from where it had fallen, and checked the ammunition. He shook his head and shrugged.

'I am out of ammunition,' Hoffman called in German. 'And that creature will kill us all if it gets the chance. We should fight it together.'

'Fight with a traitor to the Reich? To the SS? To everything I believe in?' the major yelled back. 'Never.'

'I am sorry you feel that way. But in that case...' Hoffman stood up, hands clasped behind his head. 'I surrender.' He stepped out from behind the workbench.

The distraction was enough. As the major watched

Hoffman, Guy and Davenport charged from the alcove. Guy rugby tackled the major, his shoulder crunching into the man's legs just above the knee. Davenport slammed into him higher up. The major was knocked sideways. His pistol clattered to the floor. He struggled back to his feet, but Guy grabbed one of his arms and Davenport held the other fast.

Hoffman walked slowly over to them, glancing round to make sure the Vril creature was nowhere in evidence. He paused to scoop up the major's fallen pistol.

'You will never get away with this,' the major said. 'Someone will have heard the gunfire.'

'The creature escaped and killed the captain,' Hoffman said. 'We were shooting at it.'

The major shook his head. 'No one will believe that. And anyway, someone must have allowed the creature to escape.'

'I shall tell them it was you.'

'Yet you are the one with the British friends. No one will listen to you, not when I tell them the truth. I shall tell them everything.'

Hoffman considered for a moment. 'I don't think so,' he said at last. He raised the major's gun.

The sound of the shot seemed louder than all the others, right next to Guy's ear. The arm he was holding became a dead weight as the major's lifeless body slumped.

Davenport looked pale as he too let go and the body fell to the floor, blood mingling with the scummy liquid from the tank. 'Was that necessary?'

'You know it was,' Hoffman said. 'And now you'd better get away from here.'

'Come with us,' Guy said.

Hoffman shook his head. 'I can sort out this mess. And someone needs to deal with that creature. Now get out before the guards arrive.' He winced. 'Anyway, that bastard thing ripped my leg open. I doubt I can run, but you may have to.' He held out his hand. 'Good luck.'

'And you.' Guy shook Hoffman's hand.

Moments later, he and Davenport were hauling open the

heavy metal door to the Vault. They passed soldiers running the other way in the passage outside.

'Quickly,' Guy shouted in German. 'Sturmbannfuhrer Hoffman needs your help – and fast!'

The metal rod was attached by a cable to batteries in the soldiers' backpacks. Three of them had the rods, which worked like cattle prods. They held them out in front of them, sweeping back and forth as they progressed slowly across the chamber, like blind men feeling their way through the darkness of life.

Kruger watched, frowning heavily. 'How did it happen?'

Hoffman shrugged. 'It was so fast. The captain just went berserk. He shot the major at point-blank range. Not pretty. The sentry heard the shot and came in...'

'Hauptsturmfuhrer Reizl always struck me as rather level-headed.'

'Not today,' Hoffman said grimly. 'Perhaps he has some history with the major?'

'He shot the sentry too?'

'And tried to kill me when I intervened,' Hoffman said. He nodded at the cut across his leg. The lower half of the trouser leg was soaked in blood. A makeshift tourniquet was tied tight round his thigh. 'The bullet grazed my leg, as you can see. Then it hit the tank.'

'The glass should have withstood that.'

'It did. But it was weakened enough that the creature...' Hoffman broke off as there was a shout from across the chamber.

'Don't harm it unless you have to,' Kruger called. 'We should keep well back,' he said more quietly to Hoffman. 'It's a vicious brute. I lost two men getting it into that tank in the first place.'

'Like Hauptsturmfuhrer Reizl,' Hoffman said, remembering the crack of bone as the creature snapped the man's neck.

Two white-coated scientists were holding a large glass jar between them, ready to place it over the creature as soon as it was exposed and in the open. They never got the chance. One of the soldiers with the electric prods jabbed under the workbench where they had spotted the Vril. There was a crackle of electrical discharge and a flash of sparks. A smell like charred wood permeated the chamber.

With a screech of pain, the creature shot out from under the workbench. The scientists struggled to lower the bell jar as the dark, spindly creature blurred past them. But too late. The Vril hammered into one of the scientists, knocking his legs from under him. The jar fell, smashing to pieces, fragments of glass flying across the room.

The other scientist shouted a warning, but too late. The creature's gnarled tentacles whipped across the fallen man's face and neck. Then the thing was gone, leaving a bloodied mess behind, a red trail across the stone floor.

The soldiers backed away. The remains of the fallen scientist spasmed, spluttered, and stuttered into silent stillness.

'What is going on here?' a voice asked calmly in the silence that followed.

The harsh light glinted on Himmler's spectacles as he looked first to Kruger then to Hoffman for an answer.

'The creature is out,' Hoffman said.

'There was an... an accident, Reichsfuhrer,' Kruger blustered. 'It wasn't our fault. The tank was strong enough—'

'Excuses waste time. How many men are dead?'

'Four,' Hoffman said. 'So far.'

Himmler's forehead creased. 'Then why haven't you killed it?'

'Killed it, Reichsfuhrer?' Kruger stammered.

'You know what those creatures are like,' Himmler snapped. 'What they do.' He turned to Hoffman. 'Destroy it, Sturmbannfuhrer – before it kills us all.'

Hoffman clicked his heels and nodded, ignoring the stab of pain in his wounded leg. He drew his Luger and walked down the chamber towards where the soldiers had again cornered the creature, this time in an alcove. He was aware of Himmler walking close behind him.

'Drive it this way,' Hoffman ordered.

'But, sir – it'll kill anything it touches.'

'Do it.' Hoffman braced himself, gun aimed at the empty air in front of him. 'Now.'

Two of the soldiers prodded forwards. Another explosion of sparks, and the hideous creature was moving again, racing towards Hoffman. It launched itself towards him, tentacle-legs splayed to reveal vicious barbs arranged on the inside edge, tiny pincers snapping at the ends. He waited until he could see every detail, until the dark, cold eyes were fixed on his own.

Then he fired.

The first shot missed completely, ricocheting away. The second caught the creature full in the bloated main body. The force of it hammered the Vril across the chamber and it crashed into the wall. It slid down, leaving a sticky green trail down the stonework. Hoffman fired again.

The other soldiers were firing too now. A blizzard of bullets ripped into the creature tearing it to pieces, scattering its brittle flesh and bone and its glutinous innards across the floor.

Finally, the guns fell silent, leaving only the drifting smoke and the smell of cordite mingled with a musty, ancient stench of death.

'Leave us,' Himmler said in the sudden silence. 'All of you, out. You can clear up later, Kruger.'

'I'm sorry, Reichsfuhrer,' Hoffman said, holstering his Luger. 'I'm sure the creature would have been more use to us alive.' He gave a brisk salute and turned to leave.

'Stay a moment, Hoffman,' Himmler said.

'Reichsfuhrer?'

Himmler waited until everyone else was gone before he spoke again. 'There is something I want you to see, Werner.'

Hoffman couldn't recall the Reichsfuhrer addressing him by his first name before. He wasn't aware the man even knew it. He followed Himmler across the chamber, past the scattered remains of the Vril creature, to the heavy metal hatch-like door beyond.

'Do you know where this leads?'

'I have only ever entered through the other doorway,' Hoffman said.

Himmler nodded. 'You were right, of course. A live Vril creature is of infinitely more value than a dead one. But we cannot take the risk that it might escape from here. Never mind how many it might kill on its way out, there is always the possibility – the very real and very frightening possibility – that it might come back.'

Himmler regarded the doorway thoughtfully as he went on: 'We controlled the Ubermensch through threats. You train an animal by teaching it to fear you and rely on you. With fire and food. More intelligent creatures you have to tame in other ways. Your threats must be more sophisticated. You agree?'

'Absolutely, Reichsfuhrer.' Hoffman had no idea where this was leading.

'You threaten its comrades, its friends, its family. But if they escape, or if you simply push it too far... Well, the cornered tiger is as nothing to the man who seeks revenge and believes he has nothing left to lose. That he has already lost everything. Yes, please – open it.'

Hoffman turned the locking wheel, and swung the heavy door open. He moved aside to allow Himmler to step into the darkness beyond.

'But what that creature did not know, what you do not know, is that it had not lost everything. Not yet. And neither have we. What you killed,' he said as he pulled the lever to turn on the lights, 'is easily replaced.'

The overhead lights thunked on in sequence down the long, narrow chamber. Hoffman gasped in astonishment. It was like a wide corridor, with windows down both sides. Except that each window was covered by shutters just like the tank in the main chamber.

Himmler turned another switch, and with a grind of gears and motors, the shutters all slid slowly back. Revealing the tanks behind them – each one filled with pale green liquid. The dark, hate-filled eyes of the Vril stared out from each tank, watching Hoffman as he followed Himmler through the chamber. The muffled thump of tentacles hammering against the glass echoed in Hoffman's ears as he saw there was another identical metal door at the other end of the chamber.

CHAPTER 41

Still in his SS uniform, with Davenport standing silently nearby, Guy had little trouble commandeering a Kubelwagon. They drove from the castle as fast as they dared, leaving the small vehicle hidden at the side of the road at the edge of the woods. Despite being only a two-wheel drive, it was surprisingly manoeuvrable.

'Ugly-looking things though,' Davenport remarked as they continued on foot.

'Kubelwagon translates as "tub truck",' Guy told him, 'because it looks like an iron bathtub on wheels.'

'German humour?' Davenport gave a snort of disapproval.

Once back at the hut, they collected their civilian clothes and fake papers, but stayed in the uniforms. It took a few minutes to lift the boards and find the radio that Hoffman had told them was concealed in the sand under floor. Davenport had a one-time code sheet printed on silk rolled up inside the hollowed-out shell of a pencil. Guy was impressed at how proficient the man was at sending Morse code.

'Though whether anyone will pick it up and pass it on remains to be seen,' Davenport said as he packed the radio set away again beneath the floorboards.

'There are Y Stations monitoring radio traffic throughout the Empire,' Guy told him, sounding more confident than he felt. 'You can bet one of them heard us.'

They made their way back to the Kubelwagon, and drove off into the gathering gloom of the afternoon.

The deciphered message was delivered to Station Z less than two hours later. Miss Manners read it through, her frown deepening with every word. She passed it to Sergeant Green whose eyes widened. He handed it back.

'You'll have to tell him. And he's not in a good mood.'

Miss Manners knew that. Brinkman was about to leave for the last of a series of meetings discussing special operations funding.

The colonel read the flimsy message paper in silence. He refolded it, tapping the paper against his palm as he thought. 'Well, we can't just leave them there. It would be useful to know what it is they've discovered.'

'Something they couldn't trust to a radio message.'

'Well, it may not matter anyway after today. By the time we get them back here this place may well be shut down and cleared out.'

'You really think that's a possibility?'

Brinkman nodded. 'The Prime Minister is too occupied with the Americans to be giving us the support we need. Pug Ismay is just as unreachable right now. At the last session, SOE and MI5 were both after our blood – or rather our funding. If they remain adamant that we're a costly irrelevance then it doesn't really matter what anyone else thinks.'

'But – our work,' Miss Manners protested.

'We can't tell them what we do. You saw how Alban reacted to your séance room. We've still got precious little we can show them.' He checked his watch. 'I have to go.'

'And this other matter? Guy and Leo?'

Brinkman handed her back the message. 'Sort it out. Do whatever it takes to get them back.'

Miss Manners nodded. 'I shall have to send—'

Brinkman raised his hand. 'I don't want to know. Not until after it's done. Because I suspect I can't agree to it.'

'Where's Diamond?' Miss Manners asked Sergeant Green

as soon as the office door had closed behind Brinkman.

'She went off in a huff. Demanded the colonel bring the Yanks in on things.'

'That's all we need,' Miss Manners muttered. 'Is she coming back?'

'God knows.'

'Well, call the ATA and see if she's gone there. Send someone to try her flat.'

Green got the chance to do neither. The door slammed open and Sarah Diamond came in. She was limping, dishevelled, her clothes and face spattered with dust and blood.

'Good God, what happened to you?' Green said. 'I'll get some tea. Universal remedy. Hot, strong and sweet – if we have any sugar.'

'Come and sit down.' Miss Manners helped Sarah to the nearest chair. 'Tell us what's happened.'

'I found the Ubermensch,' Sarah said. 'It damned near killed me.'

The representative from MI5 was biding his time. After a few sarcastic comments early on in the meeting, the man sat back and folded his arms. Brinkman didn't know him, but he knew the type – young, impetuous, confident, and full of himself. He was also overweight and sweaty, constantly dabbing at his forehead with a handkerchief. His dark hair was slicked back but looked forever in danger of flopping forward again, out of control.

SOE was going for the jugular. Their man had already laid into Brinkman for 'poaching – yes *poaching* – one of our most valuable agents.' He meant Davenport, of course. Now he was itemising the daring and invaluable missions that SOE could fund with their share of Station Z's budget if Brinkman's 'jokers' were closed down.

The man from the Secret Intelligence Service – also known as MI6 – said nothing, content to let matters take their inevitable course as he watched and smoked his pipe. Occasionally he nodded, never speaking and almost invisible in a fog of his own making – appropriately enough. If it came to a vote, Brinkman couldn't predict which way SIS would go – they might support Brinkman just to spite SOE, who they regarded as a bunch of amateurs encroaching on their own territory.

Brinkman was hampered by the fact he had been ordered not to tell any of these people what Station Z actually did. But as he'd already mentioned to Penelope Manners, telling them might make things worse – they'd never believe it.

The meeting was drawing to a close, and the chairman – Sir John Rampton from the Treasury – was beginning his summing up, when the door opened and another figure entered the room. David Alban caught Brinkman's eye before walking up to the MI5 representative and tapping the man on his substantial shoulder.

Come to gloat, no doubt, Brinkman thought angrily as the MI5 rep reluctantly relinquished his chair to Alban and left the room.

'Have you quite finished, Mr Alban?' the chairman asked. 'It's good of you to grace us with your presence. I assume you've come to hear the summing up and conclusions.'

Alban smiled, his eyes fixed on Brinkman. 'Thank you, Sir John. If I'm not too late, there was one small thing…'

'Yes?'

So not just gloating, but hoping to stick the knife in and deliver the *coup de grâce*. Brinkman clenched his fists so tightly his knuckles whitened.

'I'm not sure that our man made the Security Services' position quite clear. I've just come from the head of SIS…' He paused to look for approval to the pipe-smoking MI6 man. There was a nod of acknowledgement from within the smoke. 'The heads of both our services are of the same opinion and have asked me to communicate that opinion to this meeting.'

Again his eyes were fixed on Brinkman. 'Get on with it,' Brinkman muttered.

'It is our belief,' Alban said slowly and clearly, 'that the work Station Z is doing under the command of Colonel Brinkman is absolutely vital to the defence of this country and our allies.'

Brinkman felt the blood drain from his face. Sir John Rampton frowned. The SOE man spluttered incoherently.

But Alban wasn't finished. 'We know that given the clandestine nature of the work of Station Z that this committee may feel it has insufficient information to continue with the unit's funding. We believe that would be a mistake of the worst kind and are prepared to support Colonel Brinkman in any way he deems useful in making his case. For the record, and please do minute this, personally I would recommend that the Station Z budget be increased.'

The man from SOE was staring in horror, his face turning a shade of puce.

The MI6 man wafted his pipe smoke away with his hand. 'Perhaps under the circumstances, we should agree to leave the current funding levels in place,' he said. 'For all departments. Anyone against?' He didn't wait for an answer but stood up, knocking his pipe out in an ashtray on the table in front of him. 'Good. Because I have another meeting to get to. You'll circulate minutes and confirm our decision, Sir John?'

Again, he didn't wait for a reply, but strode from the room.

In something of a state of shock, Brinkman gathered his papers together. When he looked up again, the room was emptying. Alban still sat opposite, watching Brinkman across the table.

'I think you and I need to have a few words,' Alban said.

Fire cleansed everything, scalding its way down through the rubble, finding the smallest gaps and rushing through in orange and red fury. Green supervised the two soldiers as they made their way methodically across the bomb site behind the American embassy, flamethrowers spitting out liquid fire.

Sarah had shown them where the Ubermensch was buried, and there was no sign of it digging its way out. But Green was taking no chances. When they had scorched the whole area, he ordered one of the soldiers to help him shift the top layer of rubble while the other stood ready with his flamethrower.

When the next layer was exposed, the process was repeated – fire eating down into the ground.

Green was surprised to see Colonel Brinkman watching from beside one of the ruined buildings. He was even more astonished to see that David Alban was with him.

'Is Miss Diamond all right?' Alban asked as soon as Green approached. 'I was with her.'

'She didn't mention that, sir.' Green glanced at Brinkman, who nodded for him to continue. 'But yes, she's fine. Just working out a flight plan. Says being in the air will calm her down.'

'Not the air she's flying into,' Brinkman said, but he didn't elaborate. 'Have you found anything?'

Green shook his head. 'I'm hoping we won't to be honest. If the flamethrowers do their job, there'll be precious little left of it.'

They spoke in the back of Alban's car, screened from the driver by a glass shutter.

There seemed little point in holding back now, so Brinkman told Alban everything they knew. UDTs, Hess, Shingle Bay, everything.

'I imagine you have a lot of questions,' he said as the car reached its destination.

'And I'm guessing you don't have many answers,' Alban replied, getting out to follow Brinkman. 'I wish I could help you find some.'

'You've helped already.' It was as close as Brinkman was prepared to get to saying thank you. He led the way up the steps and into the British Museum.

Alban didn't push it. 'Any chance my people can look at Wiles' UDT data?'

'None.'

'They wouldn't need to know what it is or where it came from. A few fresh sets of eyes might help, and I have some pretty bright sparks on hand who are trained to spot patterns in information, make deductions.'

It was sensible, Brinkman supposed. 'All right, but as few people as possible. Anything they come up with—'

'I shall report back to you, and only to you. Deal.'

Mrs Archer was waiting for them, leading the way down to the area where the Ubermensch body from Shingle Bay was stored. She slid it out of its refrigerated drawer and uncovered it for Brinkman and Alban, giving a similar brief description to the one she had given Guy Pentecross and Sarah Diamond several months previously.

'This lichen-like stuff,' Alban said, pointing to the orange growth that permeated the limbs.

'Yes?' Brinkman said.

'It looks as though it's grown there. I mean, like a plant or a fungus. A cancer.'

'I agree,' Elizabeth Archer said. She prodded at it with the end of a pencil. 'It must have been very resilient, giving the body strength. From what Green and the others said about the Sussex dig...' She hesitated. 'You know about Sussex?'

Alban nodded. 'Not the details, but yes.'

'Well, it seems this material heals over wounds. Basically it keeps the human body alive and functioning after death should have occurred by natural causes. The trouble is, there's no central intelligence so far as I can see. It's a nervous system rather than a brain.'

'So?' Brinkman asked.

'So how does the infected body know what to do?' she asked.

'How does the Ubermensch get its orders, you mean?' Alban said. 'And from where?'

'Exactly.' She prodded experimentally at the orange growth again. It was blackened and charred from the fire that had engulfed the body, but the stunted ends of tendril-like filaments were still visible.

'Here's another question,' Brinkman said. 'You called this an infection. So how is that infection transmitted? What turns someone into an Ubermensch?'

*

By the end of the day, his head was pounding – from what he had been through and from what he had seen. Hoffman felt numbed by it all. He was amazed he had survived, and astounded that Himmler now seemed to regard him as even more trustworthy. The things the Reichsfuhrer had shown him...

It was a shame that the British agents were long gone, and Hoffman had no way of contacting them again. He had intended to establish some sort of system of keeping in touch, but their hasty departure had put paid to any hope of that.

Alone in his small room in the barrack block, Hoffman took off his uniform cap and jacket then unbuckled his holster. He slumped down on his bed, staring up at the ceiling, unable to think clearly about anything. The pain in his leg had subsided to a dull ache. He probably needed sleep. Tomorrow he would be fine. Tomorrow he would decide what to do. He drifted into sleep...

More than anything, Hoffman realised when he woke the next morning, he wanted to get away from this ungodly place and go home. Surely he knew enough now that his superiors would understand that?

Unthinking, he swung his legs off the bed and got up. He crossed to the corner of the room and levered away a loose tile at the back of the small washstand. Behind it was a small piece of cloth, the size of a handkerchief. Hoffman unrolled it, and took out the photograph concealed within. It curled up in his hand, and he had to bend it backwards to see the image.

A young woman with long dark hair. She was sitting on a stone step outside a small house. Her head was tilted slightly to one side, her hand running through her hair. She wasn't beautiful by any means, but she had a pretty smile. Was she even still alive, Hoffman wondered. She'd said she would wait for him, but he had no illusions about that.

He rolled the picture back inside the cloth and hid it again, pressing the tile back into place. He didn't deserve waiting for. He didn't deserve Alina. He turned on the hot tap and let water run into the sink. It was probably a good idea to bathe his wounded leg.

The wound had crusted over. Frowning, Hoffman ran his fingers over the long, thin scab where the cut had been. It wasn't like a normal scab of crusted, dried blood sealing the wound. It was spongy and soft. And orange. Tiny filaments rippled under his fingers.

He took a pair of trousers from his wardrobe and put them on. Then he sat down on the bed, staring across at the small desk against the opposite wall. What should he do? His mind was a blank.

After a while, he got up and went over to the desk. He took a pad of paper, tearing sheets into small squares about four inches along each side. On each he wrote a letter or a number. A to Z and 0 to 9. With a sweep of his arm he cleared everything else from the top of the desk, and arranged the squares round the edge. Then he went back to the washstand and removed his toothbrush from where it stood inside a small glass tumbler.

Hoffman placed the upturned tumbler in the centre of the desk, surrounded by the letters and numbers. He sat down and watched the glass. Waiting for it to move. Waiting for orders.

CHAPTER 42

They managed to refuel the Kubelwagon at a supplies depot. Intimidated by their SS uniforms, the soldiers manning the facility hurried to obey Guy's orders while Davenport looked on with studied disdain from the back of the vehicle.

With a full tank, they managed to get back into France. If Davenport's friend the Countess was surprised to see them again, and in SS uniform, she concealed it well. The coded Morse message Davenport had sent from Wewelsburg gave little more than an acknowledgement that their mission had been successful, followed by a pick-up location and a time two days later.

That night, back in their civilian disguises, well rested and nourished, Guy and Davenport said their goodbyes to the Countess. They made their way through the estate to a large field where they had already arranged piles of hay from one of the barns. They waited until they could hear the plane's engines, then Davenport used his cigarette lighter to set fire to the bundles, forming a line down the side of the field.

'Just so long as we're not lighting up a landing strip for a German night fighter,' he told Guy cheerily.

The plane bounced and slewed to a halt close to the end of the field. It was the same Avro Anson that had brought them to France several weeks previously. A line of ragged bullet holes was stitched along the fuselage.

Guy held his breath as they waited for the pilot to emerge. Would it be Sarah? Was she all right?

'Well, come on if you're coming,' a familiar voice called.

He could hardly contain his relief. 'Thank God you're OK.' He went to embrace her, but Sarah was already disappearing back inside the fuselage.

'Oh don't worry about the bullet holes,' she called back.

'Let's hope we don't pick up any more on the way back,' Davenport said as they clambered into the aircraft.

But the bullet holes did nothing to dent Guy's mood. He felt light-headed, though his euphoria dimmed slowly as they made their way back through the cold night. With Sarah piloting the plane, and Guy once again acting as gunner should the need arise, he was left alone with his thoughts. Desperate to ask her what had happened, but unable for the moment to do so.

The flight back was mercifully uneventful, but Guy breathed a long sigh of relief when he recognised the wide dark expanse of the English Channel. He knew they weren't safe yet. In fact it was more dangerous to come down in the December sea where the cold would kill them in minutes than to crash-land in occupied Europe. But they were nearly home. And despite what they had seen at Wewelsburg, despite what he had never admitted to himself he feared, Sarah was all right.

He sat for hours, unmoving, mind blank. The glass didn't move. But gradually a thought formed in Hoffman's brain. A shape, an image – something he needed.

He finished dressing and made his way briskly through the castle, back down to the Vault.

Streicher was supervising the clean-up. The floor had been scrubbed and the artefacts replaced in their positions on the workbenches. Bullet holes in the tables and up the walls were the only signs that anything had happened here. The shutters over the shattered Vril tank were closed.

'Are you all right?' Streicher asked as Hoffman walked

slowly through the chamber, attention focused on the main workbench.

'I'm fine.' His voice was flat and uninflected.

Streicher reached out and caught his arm. 'You are sure?'

Hoffman looked down, and Streicher quickly removed his hand. But not so quickly that Hoffman had not seen the glint of silver from the bracelet on his wrist.

'I am now,' he said.

Further along the workbench was a collection of several of the heavy metal bracelets. Hoffman looked round to check no one was watching. Streicher had moved away and there was no one nearby. Hoffman reached out for one of the bracelets, his bare wrist emerging from the sleeve of his jacket. It would take only a moment to put on the bracelet. That was what he had to do. That was why he was here.

But somewhere in the back of his thoughts, he could remember the pain on the faces of those who wore them, as the bands of metal bit into their flesh. He could remember the smoking ruin of Number Five, the sickly stench of burning flesh. Number Nine's scream as the bracelet was torn from his wrist...

Hoffman's hand closed on the nearest bracelet. Held it for a moment. He knew what he had to do.

Christmas was little more than a date on the calendar. Guy went to his mother's for lunch, both having attended the local church in the morning. Davenport disappeared for a couple of days without giving any hint of his destination. Sarah spent the day alone in her flat. She wrote a long letter to her father, which actually told him little of what she had been doing. She mentioned that she'd been sorry to hear that Andrew Whitman had died in some sort of accident at the embassy.

Sergeant Green enjoyed an army Christmas lunch, which was heavy on vegetables but light on meat and served with thin gravy. Brinkman spent the day in the office, only realising that it was actually Christmas when Miss Manners brought him a home-made minced pie that was almost all pastry.

'Don't you have somewhere to go?' he asked her.

She looked at him sternly. 'Of course I do. The same place as you. So here I am.'

The war barely paused. But Christmas brought some good news. The Russians were counterattacking the advancing Germans outside Moscow and finally driving back the Panzers. Churchill spent Christmas in the USA, and addressed Congress on Boxing Day. His confidence and rhetoric were tempered by the knowledge that the Japanese were advancing almost unchallenged through the Pacific region.

Station X at Bletchley Park allowed itself little respite for the festive season. There was some levity – even homemade crackers at Christmas lunch. But generally the tireless work of interception, decryption, and analysis went on uninterrupted.

That suited Henry Wiles. He hated interruptions. His personal opinion was that Christmas, and any other public holiday whether religious or secular, was a complete waste of time and opportunity. He was pleased when the brief 'holiday' period was over, and predictably irritated to be summoned to London for a meeting.

'I hope this won't take long,' were his first words as he entered the Station Z offices. He declined Miss Manners' offer to take his coat and hat, emphasising his ambition to be finished and away in as little time as possible. He did allow her to take his newspaper.

'Only half finished?' she asked, raising an eyebrow and indicating the uncompleted *Times* crossword.

'The rest of it was easy,' Wiles said dismissively. 'Not worth filling in. Now what do you lot want?'

The walls of the conference room were covered with maps. Davenport was adjusting the position of a chart of the Mediterranean as Miss Manners led Wiles in. He took a seat at the table, next to Guy Pentecross and opposite Brinkman and Sarah Diamond.

'I think we can start,' Brinkman said. 'Sergeant Green will

listen out for the phones, if you could take minutes please, Penelope?'

Miss Manners nodded, and took a seat close to where Davenport was now inspecting a map of North Africa.

'Thank you for joining us, Henry,' Brinkman went on. 'I know you are extremely busy.'

As a concession to this admission, Wiles removed his hat, placing it on the table in front of him. He lifted his briefcase and put that beside the hat. 'So why am I here?'

'Two reasons. First, you suggested on the phone that you had some information for us.'

Wiles sniffed. 'True. Supposition and theory, but it might get us somewhere. Second reason?'

'A fresh pair of eyes. Expert eyes. These maps...' He waved for Davenport to explain.

'These maps are arranged precisely as they were in the Vault beneath Wewelsburg Castle. They were obviously significant to Himmler and his team, so we need to know why, and what they show.' Davenport pointed out features on the various charts as he explained. 'I've marked them up in the same way as they were marked there, though obviously I can't guarantee I've reproduced everything exactly. And of course we don't always have access to exactly the same charts or maps. Where we do, I've fixed the map at the top, and put an English-language equivalent underneath.' He lifted one of the maps of Europe to reveal a similar one behind it.

Wiles nodded. 'I see, I see. Interesting.' He stood up abruptly and took his coat off, dumping it over the back of his chair before hurrying round the table to inspect the maps at close range.

'We've all examined them,' Guy told him.

'And drawn a few rather obvious conclusions,' Brinkman added.

'Like the fact that the crosses inside circles...' Sarah began, pointing to the nearest map – which showed southern Italy.

'Are all archaeological sites, yes,' Wiles finished for her. 'As you say, obvious.'

'So obvious it took us three days,' Sarah muttered.

'These lines..?' Wiles asked, moving along the row of maps. He traced one of the lines drawn on several of the maps with his index finger. 'They were on the German originals?'

'Significant?' Brinkman asked.

'Undoubtedly.'

'Any idea what they are?' Davenport asked.

'Possibly. It's one of the theories I mentioned.' He turned, taking in the other maps and charts. The wall opposite where he stood had a large map of the British isles, with the bigger map of the Shingle Bay area pinned to one side. 'Yes, this will do very well,' Wiles said. 'I'll need a few minutes. And drawing pins obviously.'

Miss Manners got to her feet. 'I have plenty of those. Anything else?'

'Reels of cotton. As many different colours as you can find. Thank you.'

Wiles worked quickly, but it was still almost an hour before he was done. He pulled a sheaf of handwritten notes from his briefcase, referring to them constantly as he pinned lines of cotton over the map of Britain. Then he turned his attention to the other maps. He pinned fewer threads on these. Finally he sat down and looked round at his handiwork.

'You want to explain?' Brinkman asked.

Miss Manners and Sarah handed round black tea. There was no sugar and they were out of milk.

'The lines show the paths of UDTs,' Wiles said. 'Sometimes we only have a few points, so I've extrapolated. We don't know where they come from, as they just appear. We don't know where they go as they just disappear. Hence the lines start and stop at the first and last confirmed points of contact.'

'Appear and disappear?' Guy said. 'That's impossible surely.'

'I'm talking about RADAR traces and observations. It could be to do with their speed, if they travel too rapidly to be tracked. It could be their height if they move above or below the detection field. Or perhaps they have some intermittent way of jamming the RADAR and only appear when they want to.'

'Why would they want to?' Davenport asked.

Wiles shrugged. 'I didn't promise you any answers. Just supposition.'

'So what do the threads tell us?' Sarah asked.

'I think I know,' Miss Manners said, staring at the map of Britain. 'I've seen lines like this before, drawn out across ancient sites.'

'They do seem to go through some interesting archaeological areas,' Davenport agreed. 'Is that significant?'

'Possibly,' Wiles said. 'You see, I think these UDTs of yours follow Ley Lines.'

Guy shook his head. 'Sorry – what lines?'

'They're ancient paths and tracks,' Wiles said, 'I think that's right isn't it, Miss Manners?'

She nodded. 'There is a theory that ancient sites are joined by paths – some of them still used, others hidden or lost. They are generally straight lines, as we have here,' she indicated the map. 'A man called Alfred Watkins coined the term, after he noticed that many ancient sites seem to be in alignment – wayside crosses, burial mounds, churches, standing stones.'

'Some of those would be rather more modern though, surely,' Guy said. 'Churches don't date from the same era as ancient burials and standing stones.'

'But most churches are built on ancient sites that have a religious or ritualistic significance that predates the church,' Davenport told him.

Miss Manners nodded. 'There's also a theory that these paths have some mystic quality or power. Perhaps that they follow magnetic lines of force on the earth. Dowsers claim to be able to detect them. Someone even suggested that homing pigeons use them for navigation.'

'Seriously?' Brinkman asked.

'It does all sound rather improbable,' Davenport agreed. 'Though I suppose the Romans were able to build straight roads so the paths and tracks theory might be on the nail.'

343

'I should tell you something else that's interesting,' Miss Manners said. 'And that is that our friend Rudolf Hess had all the Ley Lines in Germany mapped out several years ago. Perhaps we should ask him if that's significant?'

'Assuming he's talking to us again,' Brinkman said. 'Or that we can believe a word he says.'

'Something to look into, I suppose,' Guy agreed. 'How close a correlation is there between the UDT paths and these Ley Lines?'

'Well, that's difficult to say,' Wiles admitted. 'Ley Lines are theoretical, so we don't really know where they all are, or even if they actually exist at all. But let's just say that a significant number of the UDT tracks follow generally accepted Ley Lines. And a good many of the remainder can be extended to cover other ancient sites. Take this short line section, for example.'

Wiles pointed to a short green thread on the map. 'It doesn't follow a Ley Line that we know of, and it doesn't pass over any significant ancient sites. But extend the line in this direction, and it goes through Hereford Cathedral. Extend it this way and we find it passes over Tewkesbury Abbey.'

'Could be coincidence,' Sarah said.

'Could be,' Wiles agreed.

'Or,' Sarah went on, 'they might be navigation markers. When you're flying you look for waypoints, things you can recognise from the air that give you your position.'

'Ah, that's very good,' Wiles said. 'So these UDTs perhaps navigate by ancient sites. Or, conversely, ancient sites could originally have been navigation beacons. Points at which to change course, perhaps emitting some signal that we cannot receive or have misinterpreted to give the site some religious or ceremonial significance.'

'Flight paths,' Guy said. 'This is a lot to think about.'

'Then let me give you something else to think about.'

Wiles pulled a folded sheet of squared paper from his briefcase and unfolded it on the table. The paper had a grid marked in letters down one side of the page, and numbers along the other. Some of the squares were shaded black and others left empty.

'You have to squint a bit, but you get the idea.' Wiles held the paper up for everyone to see.

'It's a picture,' Davenport said. 'Yes, if you squint it blurs the squares and makes it easier to make out the image. Looks like a face.'

'So what is it?' Brinkman asked.

'Your MI5 chap said that one of his bods suggested some of the intercepted data we shared with them could be a radio-fax signal. It's a way of transmitting an image by sending a series of instructions about how to reassemble that image at the other end. Basically you break it down into dots, like these squares only smaller, then indicate whether each dot is black or white. This data seems to use a coordinates system rather than just a linear sequence, but even so – we get an image.'

Guy looked at Davenport. 'Like that poor man was drawing.'

Davenport nodded. 'That must be it. The transmissions, some of them anyway, are the images that those people see and interpret.'

'They're transmissions from an Ubermensch?' Sarah said.

'It would make sense,' Brinkman agreed. 'Is it possible to triangulate where these transmissions come from and go to?'

'Most of the data we have is in a different form, and comes from the UDTs,' Wiles said. 'It may be navigational, or progress reports, or observations or even comments on the local cloud cover for all we know. These images... Well we have relatively few because we've not been looking for them. There are undoubtedly others waiting unidentified amongst the radio traffic that hasn't been decrypted. There's a lower priority given to anything that's not from one of the known Tunny lines.'

'The what?' Sarah asked.

'Oh sorry, enemy communications lines that we've successfully penetrated. We name them after fish and sea creatures for some reason – so Jellyfish is the link between

Berlin and Paris. Anything outside those lines, or where we know there's significant enemy presence, could turn out to be local wireless stations broadcasting the weather forecast, or some amateur with a crystal set. So a lot of it is ignored or discarded. Most of it is probably never picked up at all. We can try to triangulate what we have, but really we need more data. The more the better.'

'And that will tell us where there's an Ubermensch?' Davenport asked.

'Might do more than that,' Wiles said. 'From what I can tell, the people the Germans have who pick up these image signals are merely intercepting the data, just as we are.'

Brinkman frowned. 'You mean it's actually being *sent* somewhere else?'

'Oh yes.' Wiles started stuffing papers back into his briefcase. 'Get me more data, and we can find out where your Ubermensch fellows are sending it, and probably where the UDTs are transmitting to as well. Get me enough data and we can find out who they're really transmitting to.'

CHAPTER 43

After Wiles had gone, the rest of them spent some time discussing how they could get more data.

'We've been collecting and collating reports of UDT sightings,' Brinkman said. 'That gives us dates and times when there are likely to have been transmissions. The Y Stations will have reported some of them, but probably not all.'

'You think they discarded them as just background noise or interference or something?' Guy asked.

'It seems likely,' Davenport agreed.

'Great,' Sarah sighed. 'So now we have to go through all the Y Station intercepts.'

'At least we have dates and times to check,' Miss Manners pointed out. 'We're not just working blind like before. Ah!' Her eyes widened behind her glasses in realisation.

'What is it?' Brinkman asked.

'Dates and times – that list I got from Jane, of the dates and times that Aleister Crowley held séances.'

'I thought Wiles already had the intercepts for those,' Guy said. 'Isn't that how he knew they were related?'

'There was a match for some of them, but not all. We can check the other dates and times.'

'How serious is Crowley about this occult mumbo-jumbo?' Davenport wondered.

'Deadly serious,' Miss Manners said. 'Given his reputation,

347

I'm surprised you need to ask.'

'No, no – I mean is he meticulous? Or is it all in the moment, as it were?'

'In what sense?' Brinkman said.

'Does he keep records?'

'He is absolutely meticulous,' Miss Manners told them. 'He views it as a science, so he records everything.'

'Including the information that comes through at these séances?' Davenport asked. 'Because if he does, then maybe we don't need to go hunting through pages and pages of Y Station intercepts. Maybe Crowley already has it all recorded.'

There was a brief silence while this sank in.

'It would be in a very different format though, surely,' Guy said at last.

'A different form of transcription,' Miss Manners agreed. 'But the same data, nonetheless.'

'I'm sure Wiles would be able to interpret it,' Brinkman said. 'And it would give us a complete list of dates and times. Good thought, Leo. Very good.'

'There is a rather more intractable problem, however,' Miss Manners said. 'We seem to be assuming that Crowley will happily hand over his notes and observations.'

'I wasn't intending to ask,' Brinkman said. 'But I think Crowley is the key here. Not only will he have additional information we can pass on to Wiles, but he may be able to shed some light on how he intercepts the Vril transmissions. Our own efforts so far have met with limited success.'

'But we have had some success,' Miss Manners pointed out.

'Maybe he has some artefact,' Sarah said. 'Something to focus the transmissions, like the bracelets.'

'He certainly seems to have some link with them,' Guy agreed. 'Possibly even a way to contact them – in which case we could use that to generate more data by provoking further transmissions.'

'By somehow goading Crowley into contacting the Vril,' Davenport said. He gave a short laugh. 'Trick him into giving us what we want? I like the notion of that.'

'Can't we just raid his place?' Sarah asked. 'Go and take what we need?'

'There are rules about that sort of thing, despite the war,' Brinkman said. 'We're not the police. We could work with them to get a warrant, but that takes time.'

'What about the Emergency Powers Act?' asked Guy. 'We could invoke that to justify going in heavy.'

'Either way might tip Crowley off,' Brinkman said. 'He has friends and contacts in pretty high places, you know.'

'Perhaps our friends in MI5 could assist?' Davenport suggested.

'You're right. Alban is a good person to ask,' Brinkman said. 'He can probably help us get into Crowley's place.'

'I'll go,' Guy said.

'I'm game,' Davenport agreed.

'Not this time,' Brinkman said. 'He's met you, Guy, remember. Same reason why Miss Manners can't go in – you'd both be recognised at once. You too, Leo.'

Sarah started to speak, but Brinkman cut her off immediately.

'I'm not sending you into that den of depravity, Miss Diamond. Don't even think about it. I shall go myself.'

'You?' Sarah said before she could stop herself.

'You think I like driving a desk? Anyway, I'll take Sergeant Green with me. Between us, I fancy we've more frontline experience than anyone else here – even you, Major Pentecross. Unless anyone has any better ideas?'

'Just a suggestion, Colonel,' Miss Manners said. 'If we can wait for New Year's Eve, Crowley will be having a party. The place will be packed, lots of people who don't know each other. You should be able to get inside while it's busy. Crowley himself will be... distracted. So you can bet he won't be in his study. I can tell you exactly where he keeps all his records and notes.'

'Thank you. That's a good suggestion.'

'Only...' Miss Manners hesitated. 'I should warn you, however experienced you are, prepare to be shocked.'

*

'There's no need for you to come,' Brinkman assured Alban. 'If you can just give me something to pick the lock to Crowley's study and his filing drawers…'

'Certainly I can, but not the three-week course you need to know how to use it,' Alban insisted. 'I'm coming too – no argument. I'm sure it won't surprise you to know that I do have some experience of getting into houses that don't belong to me.'

'Did you get authorisation?' Brinkman asked as Green drove them to Piccadilly.

'Not as such,' Alban replied.

Brinkman frowned. 'I thought they knew all about Station Z, now that you've briefed them.' There was no reply. 'That *is* what you said at the funding meeting.'

'Well,' Alban said slowly. 'Perhaps I gave slightly the wrong impression. I'm afraid I was rather vague with my superiors. Didn't think they'd believe the whole story, to be honest.'

'So how did you convince them to continue our funding?'

'I went to see the heads of the Secret Intelligence Service, as I said,' Alban told him. 'And I told them that MI5 would appreciate their support in agreeing to maintain your funding. Then I told my own bosses at Five that SIS had told me they'd appreciate MI5's support in the same deal.'

Brinkman laughed. 'So they each think the other one owes them a favour. You're a cunning bugger, I'll give you that. But it might come home to roost.'

'I'll worry about that when it happens. For the moment, let's get on with the job in hand, shall we?'

Green stayed in the staff car, parked out of sight in the next street. He had strict instructions to come and assist if Brinkman and Alban were not back by midnight.

The combination of darkness and noise never ceased to amaze Brinkman. It was even more pronounced as they neared their destination. Walking along blacked-out Jermyn Street, they heard the noise of Crowley's festivities long before they made out the dark silhouette of the tall town house that was number 93. Edges of light spilled round the side of the door as it opened in front of them and two people stumbled out – a man and a woman, locked in an embrace so tight that they might have been a single entity.

Alban grabbed the door before it shut. He and Brinkman stepped inside and closed it behind them.

Immediately, they were accosted by a young woman. She was very drunk, and almost naked, wearing only a simple velvet cloak, tied by a gold cord at the neck. Brinkman could feel the colour rising in his face. Alban seemed indifferent, but perhaps he was merely better at controlling his embarrassment.

'More lovely people!' the woman slurred. Champagne slopped out of the glass she held. 'Whoops. We're all through here. Come along.'

The cloak fell away as she walked down the hall. She turned back, totally without shame. 'Come along, boys.'

'We'll be right with you,' Alban assured her. 'Jesus Christ,' he muttered under his breath as she turned away again. 'My New Year's party was going to be a pint in the pub followed by a couple of hands of bridge. Do you play?'

'Sadly not,' Brinkman told him.

They let the woman turn out of sight into a room further down the hall. The sound of talking and laughter, accompanied by a gramophone, spilled out.

'She's left the door open,' Alban said. 'That's a pity. We'll have to be quick up the stairs and hope no one sees us.'

'They probably won't care if they do,' Brinkman said.

'True. But better safe than sorry.'

Brinkman hurried after Alban, taking the stairs quickly and quietly. He couldn't resist glancing back down into the room below. There were maybe a dozen people in the room all in various states of undress. A mass of writhing, intertwined bodies. He doubted any of them would notice two people hurrying up the stairs.

Alban knew the layout of the house from a rough plan that Miss Manners had drawn them. He led the way to the study on the first floor. The door was locked, and Brinkman waited impatiently while Alban set to work. It seemed to take for ever, but finally the door clicked open.

At the same moment, there was the sound of heavy footsteps on the stairs coming down. They slipped inside the room, Alban closing the door quietly behind them.

'Empty,' Alban whispered. 'Thank God. Not sure how we'd explain what we're doing here otherwise. I suspect there are people hiding all round the house for various reasons, but we're hardly a couple.' He grinned suddenly. 'Though here, maybe we could be – what is it Crowley says? "Do what thou wilt shall be the whole of the law"?'

'There's enough of that going on downstairs,' Brinkman told him. 'Let's find the files and get out of this place.'

They started with the desk, Alban easily unlocking the drawers and checking the contents of each quickly and thoroughly. It was obvious he had done this sort of thing many times before. The desk yielded nothing of interest so they moved on to a large filing cabinet on the back wall of the room.

'Ah now we're getting somewhere,' Brinkman said as Alban pointed out a set of hanging files labelled 'Séances – Transcriptions'.

The noise from downstairs was suddenly louder. A female voice was shrieking – though whether in pain or pleasure was impossible to tell. Over the noise there was a dull, metallic click. It was a sound both men recognised at once. They turned quickly.

To find a young man standing just inside the door. He wore dark trousers and an open-collared white shirt, the front of which was flecked with what looked like blood. His dark hair was slick with sweat, a curl matted to his forehead. His thin lips were set in a cruel smile, and in his hand was a revolver.

He walked slowly over towards them, until he was standing right in front of Brinkman, the revolver inches from Brinkman's face.

The man's voice was slightly nasal, upper-class and affected. 'Do you have one good reason why I shouldn't shoot you both here and now?' he asked. 'I thought not,' he went on before either of them could speak.

His finger tightened on the trigger.

CHAPTER 44

Alban's hand snapped out in a blur, grabbing the other man's wrist and twisting it so the gun was pointed upwards. A bullet cracked into the ceiling. Brinkman reacted at once, hammering his fist into the man's midriff. He doubled over, crying out in pain.

Alban was still holding the man's arm, still twisting it. He brought up his knee as he slammed the hand down on it. The gun clattered away across the floor. Alban finally let go, and the man crumpled to the ground in a painful heap.

'I'll kill you for this,' he gasped.

'Yes, well, good luck with that,' Alban said. 'Next time I'd suggest you don't stand so close to the person you're hoping to shoot.'

'Get the files,' Brinkman said, 'and let's get out of here.'

Alban scooped up the revolver and stuffed it into his jacket pocket. Then he stepped over the prone figure on the floor and joined Brinkman at the filing cabinet. They both glanced round at the sound of the man stumbling from the room.

'You should have hit him harder,' Alban said.

'Next time,' Brinkman promised. 'Is there a briefcase or something we can put all these in?'

'I'm sure I can find you something suitable.' The voice came from the doorway. The young man they'd disarmed was with an older man which Brinkman recognised at once as Crowley.

'Perhaps if you tell me what you want, I can help?'

'We should just kill them,' the younger man said. His face was still contorted with pain.

'Oh please, Ralph – go back to the party and see if you can't enjoy yourself,' Crowley said. 'Preferably without hurting anyone else for once.' He dismissed the man with a gesture.

Doubly humiliated, Ralph glared at Brinkman and Alban before turning and striding away.

Crowley crossed to his desk and sat down. He motioned for Brinkman and Alban to be seated too. 'I'd offer you drinks, but I suspect you're on duty. Am I right? Is this some sort of official visit?'

'I'm not at liberty to say,' Alban told him, sitting down.

'So it is, then. I'm flattered.' Crowley glanced at the open filing cabinet. 'You think I'm a spy?'

'Nothing so mundane,' Brinkman assured him. 'We think the transcripts of your séances might hold vital information.'

'Vital for the war effort?'

'Of course.'

Crowley nodded. He ran a hand over his bald scalp. 'Then, by all means, take them. I'd be grateful if my files could be returned when you've finished, but you should know that whatever else I might be, I am a patriot.'

As Green drove him up to Bletchley first thing the next morning, Brinkman wondered if he should have asked Crowley about the Vril. Should he have insisted the man tell them everything he knew? But Alban's advice had been not to trust the man, however patriotic and cooperative he might seem.

'In any case,' Alban had said as they left the house in Jermyn Street, 'I doubt if he can distinguish between myth and reality. He doesn't know what's actually true and what's his own warped imagination.'

'I guess we can always pick him up later,' Brinkman had agreed.

It didn't occur to Brinkman until they arrived at Station X that Wiles might have taken New Year's Day as a holiday.

'I don't think he knows what a holiday is, sir,' Green said when Brinkman voiced his thoughts.

He was right. Wiles and, so far as Brinkman could tell, his entire team were already hard at work. Or what passed for work – one of the men was asleep in his chair, snoring happily.

'Just ignore Douglas,' Wiles said. 'He's been here all night.'

'Doesn't he have a home to go to?' Green asked.

'Oh yes. I think that's why he stayed, actually.'

Crowley's files took up two large cardboard boxes, which Wiles accepted with delight rubbing his hands together. 'Ah, now we're getting somewhere.' He pulled out a file at random and leafed through the pages. 'I imagine it's a simple case of substitution. These people use letters and numbers where we equate the signals to Morse code or image data.'

'Can you rationalise the two?' Brinkman asked.

'Just a matter of finding a decent-length transcript in here that matches a transmission we already have. That will give us our Rosetta Stone, as it were. Child's play after that. Bit of a slog, but easy enough. Did you learn any more about how Crowley makes contact?'

'Sadly not,' Brinkman said. 'He was willing to let us borrow these records – he wants them back, by the way – but not very forthcoming about his activities. Just said it was all down to the rituals and arts as laid down from time immemorial, or some such guff, channelled through an empathic medium.'

Wiles snorted. 'So Crowley probably doesn't know how it works either. Just that it does. Luck, more than science I suspect. This empathic medium will be an individual tuned into the Vril frequency, I would think, rather like the German psychics.'

He started emptying out the files onto his already cluttered desk. After several minutes of sorting through, he glanced up at Brinkman and Green. 'Are you still here? There's no need to wait. I'll call you as soon as we find anything interesting.'

Wiles was already lost again in his examination of the files as Brinkman and Green let themselves out of the hut.

*

It was not until the middle of January that Wiles called. 'I think I may have something' was all he would commit to on the phone when he did eventually call. He promised to be more forthcoming in person the next day.

Guy and Sarah welcomed the relief from ploughing through lists and transcripts of Y Station intercepts. Davenport was called back from recording the commentary for a documentary film about how bravely the Allied forces were resisting the Japanese in the Pacific. 'Bloody disaster' was his personal take on the situation as they gathered in the conference room.

'The situation in the Pacific, or the film?' Guy asked.

'Both, if you want the truth.'

As usual, Miss Manners prepared to minute the meeting, while Green remained in the main office to man the phones and field any visitors.

Wiles was late. But the others used the opportunity to update each other on their progress, or lack of it.

'I've been wondering,' Guy said. 'Do you think these UDTs only started coming recently?'

'We know one crashed in the Black Forest in 1936,' Davenport reminded him.

'True, but has their activity increased? And if so, why?'

'To do with the war, maybe?' Sarah suggested. 'Perhaps the upheaval, the fighting, the bombardments and troop movements have woken something up.'

'*The Coming Race* talks about a civilisation under the ground,' Brinkman said, 'so that's possible I suppose.'

'There are all sorts of legends about underground civilisations, or sunken societies,' Miss Manners agreed. 'From Atlantis to Agarthi, which is thought to be in Tibet.'

'More likely UDTs have been around for a long time,' Davenport said, 'and it's only because of RADAR that we're picking them up now. That and the fact we're on the lookout for aircraft that we can't account for. There are all manner of reports of strange things flying about in antiquity, usually put down to gods or monsters.'

'And don't forget it's only in the last few years that we've had aircraft up there ourselves,' Brinkman said, checking his watch. 'Perhaps Wiles will have some answers for us.'

When Wiles finally arrived, he was armed with rolled up maps and a stack of handwritten notes. He proceeded to pin up the maps alongside and sometimes over the ones already on the walls. He rearranged the cotton threads, still in place from the last time he'd been.

Finally, happy with his handiwork, Wiles slumped down in a chair. 'Well, there you go,' he said, gesturing at the walls as if this explained everything.

When this was met with silence, he sighed and went on: 'Using the dates and times from Crowley's séances, together with the data contained in the transcripts, we managed to trace most of the Y intercepts. Thanks for your help with that, by the way. Anyway, to cut a long story short, if a transmission was picked up by more than one station, and using the varying reported signal strengths, we managed an approximate triangulation for quite a few of them. We also extrapolated the lines of flight for the UDTs, though that was less conclusive. The reason being that the craft can evidently change course, whereas a radio wave cannot.'

'And you've found – what?' Brinkman prompted.

'A point of origin. Well, actually several possible points of origin, but one in particular seems to be a focus. Almost like the transmissions are searchlights pointing it out to us.'

Jumping to his feet, Wiles pulled a wooden ruler from his bag. It was hinged and doubled over, and he unfolded it into a straight length a yard long. He placed the extended ruler over one of the maps and drew a line. After repeating the process several times, he turned. 'You get the idea. In fact, to save the effort of drawing all the lines in, Douglas and Eleanor produced this for me.'

Wiles unfolded another map. It showed most of western Europe and north Africa. A web of lines was drawn over the top of the map – most of them originating in different parts of Britain, but others from different places too, mainly within territory controlled by the allies. Most of them converged on a single point on the map.

'North Africa?' Davenport said. 'Where is that – Libya?'

'Someone over at the War Rooms was saying that we took the Halfaya Pass yesterday,' Brinkman said. 'Is that anywhere near?'

'That's here.' Wiles pointed to a location to the east of where the lines converged. 'We're looking at somewhere much further south, in the middle of the desert.'

'But Allied territory, yes?' Sarah asked.

'At the moment,' Brinkman said. 'But I doubt we'll push Rommel back much further.'

'There's a real danger he may launch a counterattack,' Guy said. 'From what I've heard from my friends at the Foreign Office, German supplies are getting through again. The Mediterranean fleet isn't in great shape, and now the Seventh Armoured Brigade along with a couple of Australian divisions have been moved out to the Pacific.'

'Still won't be enough to stop the Japs,' Davenport said. 'They'll be in Australia before we know it, if we aren't careful.'

'Whatever is here...' Brinkman leaned over and tapped his finger on the convergence of lines. 'We have to find it. Find it, assess it, and if necessary neutralise it. Certainly we must make sure Himmler's people don't get to it.'

'And if Rommel really is about to launch a second offensive,' Sarah said, 'we're up against a deadline.'

'Oh no, hang on,' Guy said. 'I've just remembered something.' He turned to Davenport. 'Didn't Hoffman say that your friend Streicher was off to North Africa soon?'

Davenport nodded grimly. 'I believe he did say that, yes.'

'You think there's a connection?' Wiles asked.

'Streicher is an archaeologist, or so he maintains,' Davenport said. 'It'd be a huge coincidence if he just happens to be going to North Africa now. More likely, they've assessed their own data and come to very similar conclusions.'

'Then we have to get there first,' Brinkman said. 'Miss Manners – you and Sergeant Green organise troops on the ground. And I mean that literally. Guy, Leo – be ready to leave. Miss Diamond, you'd better sort out the logistics of getting us all there.'

Wiles passed the map to Brinkman. 'I'll leave this with you. And I'm assuming you won't want me traipsing off to the middle of nowhere with you.'

'I doubt I'd be allowed to take you,' Brinkman said. 'I doubt I'll be allowed to go myself. But we'll see. I need to clear this with the Prime Minister, just as soon as I can get to see him.'

'I wonder,' Wiles said, 'might I make a phone call? There's something I'd like to get checked out.'

As Brinkman had suspected, there was no way that he would be permitted to go to Africa.

'Can't take the chance of losing you,' General Ismay said. He had managed to find ten minutes to speak to Brinkman, and he wasn't a man to waste time. He came straight to the point. 'Can't afford to lose any of you really, but certainly not you, Oliver. So how important is this really?'

'Honestly? We won't know until we go and look.'

'We could send some of the locals.'

'With respect, they won't know what they're looking for. Or how to deal with what they might find.'

'And you think it's urgent?'

'I do. Dr Wiles checked with Station X, and there is Ultra material that suggests a special group of the Afrika Korps, supplemented by an SS unit, is being sent to the area. The deployment makes no military or strategic sense, so we have to assume they're after the same thing we are.'

'Whatever it is.'

'Whatever it is. We've no details of the enemy's schedule or route, so we can't intercept. We can only hope to get there ahead of them.'

'Recommendation?' Ismay demanded.

'Major Pentecross to take command of local forces, whatever can be spared, with Sergeant Green assisting.'

'Very well.'

'I'd like Davenport there too. He has experience of the archaeological side of things, and Mrs Archer is obviously not up to the trip.' This was probably not true, but Brinkman knew she was even more vital to the continuing effectiveness of Station Z than he was himself.

'Agreed. And how will you get them there in a timely manner?'

'I'm sure we can arrange something, sir.'

Ismay gave a short laugh. 'I'm sure you can. But whatever happens, I don't want Miss Diamond involved in frontline operations. She's not some SOE agent, she's not trained for combat situations. She's a pilot. Understood?'

'Understood, sir. Transport only.'

Ismay nodded. 'Then you'd better get on with it. I'll inform Winston. Report back to me as soon as you have any information. And good luck.'

'Thank you, sir,' Brinkman said. He had a feeling they were going to need it.

CHAPTER 45

The landing strip was little more than a short length of concrete across the sand. They flew in over the Jalo Oasis as they approached. Only as they got lower could Sarah make out the tents and camouflage netting against the undulating desert. There were planes and vehicles concealed under the nets. A narrow road snaked between sand dunes, clogged with military vehicles – trucks, Jeeps, and a light tank – waiting to move out.

A soldier waited at the end of the landing strip to usher the Avro Anson to where more soldiers were waiting with nets ready to cover it.

'Good landing, sir,' the soldier called as Sarah opened the door and jumped down. 'Er, ma'am,' he corrected himself.

Guy and Davenport jumped down after her. Guy was in a lightweight major's uniform. Davenport wore khaki shorts and shirt with a Panama hat that set him apart from the military. Sarah shrugged out of her flying jacket, the dry desert heat a contrast to the British winter they had left behind.

'We'll get this crate under cover and look after her for you,' one of the ground crew assured Sarah.

'Thanks.' She looked round at the other planes under netting at the end of the makeshift runway.

'Kittyhawks and Tomahawks, mainly, miss,' the crewman told her. 'American. Got a bit more bite to them than the old

363

Hurricanes. Rather have Spits though.'

'I thought I saw a Hurricane as I came in,' Sarah remembered.

'Got a couple of Hurri-bombers. They're Hurricanes converted for ground-attack. Pack quite a punch as a fighter-bomber, actually. I'll, er, I'll show you one later if you like,' he added with sudden diffidence. 'Just ask for Jimmy.'

Sarah smiled her thanks. 'I'd like that, Jimmy. But I'd best be getting on now.'

Their contact was Lieutenant Mike Maguire. Tall and thin, with a messy thatch of hair bleached blond by the sun and blotchy skin, he was waiting for them in one of the tents, where a map of the area was laid out across several packing cases that served as a table.

'Not a lot of detail,' he apologised. 'Most of the area hasn't been mapped yet. We make charts as we go along, really. They set up a Survey Section last year to sort it, but they've barely made a start.'

'So where are we?' Guy asked.

'Right here, sir. By the oasis. This whole area to the east is called the Great Sand Sea, appropriately enough. As I understand it, you want to be heading down this way.' He pointed to the area south west of their location.

'And this is the closest landing area?' Sarah asked.

'It certainly is. From here it's truck, which is where we come in.'

'Long Range Desert Group,' Davenport said. 'So what do you do, exactly?'

'Much of the time, transport. Like now. As you can imagine it's not as easy as it looks navigating round this empty space full of sand, especially if you're heading behind enemy lines.'

'Does that happen often?' Guy asked.

'Often enough. But you're better asking Captain Henderson about that. He's a bit spiky, if you don't mind me saying, sir. But he's all right. Good at what he does.'

'And what does he do?' Guy asked.

'On this occasion, you tell me.' The man who had entered the tent as Guy was speaking was shorter than Lieutenant

Maguire, but broader. He had dark hair and a moustache above several days stubble.

'Henderson?' Guy asked.

'That's right, sir. With L Detachment of the Special Air Service Brigade.'

'Air service?' Davenport said. 'You're paratroopers?'

'If we need to be. But to be honest the name's nothing to do with our role, it's just to confuse the enemy if they hear about us. L Detachment suggests there are other detachments, which there aren't. Air Service, well – it doesn't really mean anything. Think of us as North African Commandoes. And may I ask who you are?'

'Oh, I'm a civilian.'

'So I see.' Henderson looked Davenport up and down, then sniffed. 'Maguire here doesn't take joyriders. No excess baggage.'

'Mr Davenport is an essential member of my team, Captain,' Guy said. 'And let's get one thing clear before we start.'

'That you outrank me, and you're in charge, you mean?' There was a noticeable lack of 'sir'.

Guy met the man's confident stare. 'Both those things are true. But what I was going to say is that your job, together with Lieutenant Maguire, is to get us safely and swiftly to where we need to be. Then secure the area, and bring us back again together with whatever material we recover from the site.'

Henderson made to reply, but Guy cut him off.

'You will see things that you don't understand. You will be in as much danger as you have ever been – if not more. You will not speak of this mission to anyone ever again. Now, having said all that, you and your men are the experts here, you have the experience. How you do your job is entirely up to you and I won't interfere unless I have to. Davenport and I are new to the area, and have no idea of the conditions here. So in all operational and tactical matters, you are in charge.'

Henderson nodded. 'Sir.'

'But if I do have to interfere, or if Mr Davenport has to, you listen to what we say and you obey without hesitation. It may seem that we're being obtuse, or that the orders we give are strange. But I promise you, it will be essential that you follow them. Are we clear?'

Henderson nodded. 'Crystal clear, sir.'

'When do we leave?' Davenport asked.

'Tomorrow, first thing.'

'Why not today?'

'With respect, sir,' Henderson said, 'we've only just got back from a raid on enemy airfields this morning. It will take the rest of the day to get everything sorted, re-armed, and packed for another expedition.'

'Fair enough,' Guy said. 'A successful outing, I hope?'

'Destroyed sixty planes on the ground with no loss to ourselves. So yes, I'd call that a success, sir.'

'Excellent.' Guy nodded. 'Seems we're in good hands, then. Carry on, Captain.'

Davenport and Guy shared a tent on the edge of the small camp. Sarah was given a tent to herself close by. They ate an evening meal of canned stew straight out of mess tins from a camping stove. Guy suggested they should get an early night, as Lieutenant Maguire wanted to leave at dawn.

The light was fading when Sarah summoned up the courage to go and find Guy. When she reached the tent, she almost bottled out, and went back to her own. There was nowhere to knock, and she couldn't just go inside – they might be getting ready to bed down for the night.

'Are you decent in there?' she called finally.

'More than decent, my dear,' Davenport's voice replied. 'We are superb.'

She took this as a yes and pushed through the tent flap. Davenport was standing in front of a pile of crates on which he had laid out his shaving kit and hairbrush, apparently checking his hair in a shaving mirror. Guy sat perched on the edge of his low camp bed, untying his boots.

Having got this far, Sarah wasn't going to back away. 'Are you avoiding me?' she asked.

Guy looked up. 'What? No. Why do you ask?' He didn't meet her eye.

'I've hardly seen you since you got back from Wewelsburg,' she said.

There was an awkward silence. Then Davenport said: 'You know what? I think I'll take a short walk down to the oasis. I could do with the air.' He paused in the entrance to the tent. 'Unless you'd rather I stayed here and you two went for that walk? I thought not,' he added when there was no reply.

'All right,' Sarah said when Davenport had gone. '*Why* have you been avoiding me?'

'I haven't.' He still wouldn't look at her.

'Don't lie, that just makes it worse. We have files and records to go through, and you take the ones you're looking at off to another room. We used to go for a drink when we left the office, but not recently. Not even over Christmas. You just leave, without asking.'

'I didn't like to ask you. I...' He did look up now, staring across the tent at Davenport's makeshift wash stand. 'I didn't think you'd want to.'

She couldn't believe that. 'Don't be stupid.'

'I'm not – I just assumed. You never asked me for a drink, or came to find me if I was in another office.'

'Because *you* were avoiding *me*. Why? Tell me, Guy – just tell me, that's all I ask. Do you really dislike me so much? Can't you bear to be with me? You won't even look at me.'

'No.' He stood up, looking right at her now, deep into her eyes. 'No, how can you think that? Don't ever think that.'

'Then *what* should I think?'

'Do we have to talk about this now?'

'Yes,' she told him. 'Yes we do. Because tomorrow you're going off into the desert. And I don't know how long you'll be gone, or even if you'll ever come back again. I hope to God it isn't, but this *could* be our last chance to talk. Ever. So yes, we have to do this now.'

Guy nodded. He rubbed his hand across his eyes before he spoke. He sounded tired, wrung out. 'When I was in the cellar at Wewelsburg and that man drew your picture... When I saw that you were with the Ubermensch... I was so scared. I felt cold and numb and empty, and I couldn't *do* anything. I was useless. Just watching. I thought you were going to die – I thought I'd be stuck there watching as that thing killed you. And there was nothing I could do about it. Then, when I knew that you were all right, I just thought – how could I have failed you so badly? You needed me, and I wasn't there.' He shook his head. 'How can you bear to look at me after I let you down like that? You're my friend, and I wasn't there.'

He slumped down on the bed again.

After a moment, she sat down beside him.

'I've lost so many friends,' he said quietly. 'I can't lose you too.'

'You're not losing me,' she said. She took his hand, holding it between both hers. 'And you *were* there for me when I needed you. You did what you could in Wewelsburg. And just hoping I'd see you again helped get me through. But we have to trust each other to survive. You look after yourself and you come back from this safely.' She stood up. 'I have to go now.'

He stood up too. 'Why?'

'Because Leo will be back in a minute. Because it's been a long day and I need some sleep. And because I promised myself I wouldn't let you see me cry.'

He caught her arm as she turned, and pulled her back round into an embrace. They held each other tight for several moments. So tight Sarah could feel her heart beating against his chest. Then they stepped away from each other.

'I'll see you tomorrow,' Guy said. 'I'm glad you came.'

'Me too.' She wiped at her eye with the crook of her index finger. 'Stay safe.'

'Did you kiss her?' Davenport asked next morning as they loaded up the Long Range Desert Patrol Group's trucks and said their goodbyes. Sarah had kissed Davenport on the cheek, before shaking hands with Guy then hurrying away to 'check on the Avro'.

'What?'

'Last night – did you kiss her?'

'Of course I didn't kiss her,' Guy retorted.

Davenport shook his head sadly. 'You should have kissed her.'

'Well, thanks for the advice.'

'I don't know, I leave you alone for ten minutes and you can't even misbehave yourself.'

The thirty-ton trucks were loaded and they were ready to go. Guy and Davenport were in the lead truck with Maguire. The second truck carried Henderson and some of his men, together with the radio operator. A third truck was empty apart from the driver and one SAS soldier – ready to be packed with whatever Vril artefacts they could recover from the site. The rest of the SAS travelled in the fourth and final truck.

The trucks were Chevrolets, which Maguire had explained were being phased out in favour of four-wheel drive Fords. 'But these are two-wheel drive so they're lighter and use about half the fuel. For the distance we're going that's a major factor.'

The doors and all excess weight had been stripped off, and the vehicles were fitted with enlarged radiators and condensers to cope with the desert heat, though in late January that was less of an issue. The only other extra weight, apart from the passengers, and extra tanks of fuel and water, was a .303 Vickers machine gun mounted on the back of the radio truck.

Captain Henderson hurried up to the lead vehicle for a final check with Maguire and Guy before they started off.

'We should be all right,' he said, 'but word's coming through that the Afrika Korps are on the move. Rommel's advancing from El Agheila towards Agedabia.'

'How close is that to where we're going?' Guy asked. The names meant nothing to him.

'Way over to the east,' Maguire said. 'Nothing to worry about, except that we might get called back if things get hairy.'

'And you can probably forget about any chance of reinforcements being sent after us,' Henderson said. 'Right, let's get the show on the road.'

He banged twice on the bonnet of the truck and waved Maguire's driver on.

'That should be my line,' Davenport said as they pulled away, kicking up a plume of sand and dust from the low-pressure desert tyres.

They didn't stop when night fell, the navigator sitting beside the driver in the front truck switching from using the sun compass to astronomical position tables. To Guy, the desert all looked the same. But Maguire assured him they were making good progress and would reach their destination the next day.

His confidence was well placed. It was mid afternoon of 23 January when the driver suddenly slammed on his brakes just as they crested a rise. The Chevrolet slewed to an abrupt stop. The navigator was standing up and waving to the vehicles behind to halt, as the driver reversed rapidly, wheels spinning and sand spraying out from under them.

'What the hell?' Maguire demanded from the back.

'Sorry, sir,' the navigator said. 'But the target location is just over the ridge. And we've got company. Someone's got there before us.'

Guy swore. 'Did they see us?'

'Harry reacted pretty fast, so hopefully not. Just a spray of sand, maybe. They're quite a way away.'

'Let's take a look,' Davenport suggested.

Captain Henderson joined Guy, Davenport and Maguire as they crawled to the top of the ridge. The ground sloped gently away, forming a large basin. In the middle was a huge mound, like a small hill. Lined up in front of it were several half-tracked vehicles and smaller wheeled vehicles attended by soldiers in desert uniform.

'That must be it,' Davenport said. 'Bigger than the site in Suffolk.'

Guy trained his field glasses on the troops.

'Afrika Korps uniforms,' Henderson said. 'But I don't recognise the markings on the vehicles.'

'I count about twenty soldiers,' Davenport said. 'They've dug their way into the mound, look.'

Guy moved his glasses to focus on the mound of sand. Sure enough, there was a dark hole dug into it, shored up with wooden props, sheets of corrugated metal lined the floor as it dipped away into the depths of the earth.

'That's our objective?' Maguire asked.

'Think of it as a weapons cache,' Davenport said. 'Though you should know that the weapons inside are like nothing you could imagine.'

'Nazi weapons?' Henderson asked.

'No,' Guy told him. 'But they're after them too. Our primary objective is retrieval, but failing that we destroy them rather than let the contents of that mound fall into enemy hands. Clear?'

'Crystal.' Henderson continued to survey the scene below. 'They know we're coming?'

'I'd hope not, but we have to assume the worst,' Guy said.

'We should be able to take them, assuming they're not expecting us. They don't seem too heavily armed, probably equipped for rapid movement like us rather than heavy fighting, and they're just regular troops.'

'You might want to reconsider that,' Davenport said slowly. 'Take a look at the figure standing just outside the entrance to the mound.'

'Officer,' Maguire said. 'Colonel by the look of him. What about it?'

'I've met him before, that's what.'

Guy felt himself tense, gripping the field glasses tightly as he focused on the tall standartenfuhrer. 'Streicher?'

'The very same. Which means,' Davenport went on, 'that those aren't regular troops at all. They've been sent here by Heinrich Himmler, and they're Waffen SS.'

CHAPTER 46

Two of Henderson's men kept watch from the ridge, while Henderson himself together with Guy, Maguire and Davenport discussed the options.

'It's no different from an airfield,' Henderson said. 'We used to think sneaking up under cover of darkness, planting bombs, and then getting the hell out of it before they exploded was the best deal.'

'And it isn't?' Davenport asked.

'We discovered it's more effective to drive in at speed and make no secret of our presence. Jerry's nothing if not orderly, and they line the planes up neatly – just like those vehicles down there. We drive between them, machine gunning and chucking grenades both sides and we're away before they know what hit them.'

'Take out the vehicles and they can't come after us,' Lieutenant Maguire said. 'We can pick off any survivors from the ridge with the Vickers gun.'

'Unless they retreat inside the mound,' Guy pointed out.

'We can cover that from up here,' Henderson said.

'How long do you think they've been here?' Davenport asked.

'They look well established,' Maguire said. 'A day at least. Does it matter?'

'Probably not. I'm just surprised they don't seem to be in

a hurry to bring out artefacts. If I was Streicher, I'd want to recover everything I could as quickly as possible and get the hell out of here.'

'He doesn't know we're coming,' Guy pointed out.

'Even so – he's hardly in his own back yard. It's only a matter of time before someone spots him.'

'Well,' Henderson said, 'perhaps you'll get the chance to ask him.'

The radio truck stayed on the ridge, its Vickers gun trained on the entrance to the mound. The other three trucks hurtled over the crest and down the incline as fast as they could go. Sand kicked up behind them like smoke. The sound of the engines was a throaty roar in the still desert and the air tasted of diesel.

It took several moments for the SS soldiers to react. They turned towards the sound and saw the vehicles racing towards them. Streicher shouted orders, his voice lost in the sudden rattle of gunfire from the SAS men's submachine guns as they fired from the backs of the Chevrolets.

The leading vehicle, with Henderson in the back, drove between the lined up German vehicles. Grenades rolled under them, detonating as the small truck passed. One after another, the half-tracks and wheeled vehicles exploded in flame behind them. Dark smoke gathered in the sky above the mound.

Guy was in the second of the three vehicles, Davenport keeping his head down beside him as Guy brought his own submachine gun to bear. They headed straight for a group of German soldiers. Several of the SS men fell immediately – bodies juddering as bullets hammered into them. Others managed to unshoulder their weapons and return fire. But they were aiming at fast-moving targets.

The other Chevrolets were weaving through the remaining SS troops, picking them off. A soldier was slumped in the back of Henderson's vehicle. There were casualties in the third truck too.

In front of Guy's vehicle, Streicher stood his ground, raising his Luger and aiming straight at them. A bullet impacted in the side of the vehicle close to where Davenport was sitting. A second pinged off the bonnet. The vehicle was almost on him as Streicher fired his third shot. It caught the navigator in the shoulder, knocking him sideways.

Then the bonnet thumped into Streicher, lifting him off his feet and flinging him sideways. He landed in a crumpled heap. Guy fired at the prone figure, bullets stitching across the back of the uniform as they sped past. But then, incredibly, Streicher got back to his feet.

The Chevrolet swung round, passing Streicher again. This time he was on Maguire's side of the vehicle and the lieutenant fired a long burst into the officer's chest. Streicher stumbled backwards under the impact, but remained on his feet. His cap fell away and sunlight fell across his face – revealing the sunken eyes and hollow cheeks.

'Why won't the bastard die?' Maguire yelled above the sound of the engine.

The Chevrolet was pulling away now, but Streicher was running after it. The wheels spun on churned up sand. The driver swerved round the body of a German soldier, blood seeping out from beneath the corpse and soaking into the desert. It slowed their progress. Not by much, but it was enough.

Streicher launched himself at the back of the truck. His hands closed on the tailgate and he hauled himself up. His deep, empty eyes fixed on Guy. Tiny orange tendrils clutched and rippled in the bullet holes across his chest.

'Ubermensch!' Davenport yelled.

Streicher's reply was a guttural snarl, just audible above the sound of the engine and the distant percussion of more grenades. 'Humans,' he said in German. 'You think you can defeat us? Even destroy us?'

Maguire raised his gun again, but Guy held his hand up to stay the man's fire.

'What are you?' he shouted back, also in German.

'You call us Vril. We are the coming race, the supermen. The inheritors of your world. We were here before your civilisations discovered gunpowder. Nurtured you, watched you learn and progress. Watching and waiting until you were ripe. Ripe and ready to pluck. And now we will emerge from our resting places and descend from the skies to harvest what we have sown.'

Guy stared back horrified. He barely heard Davenport asking what Streicher had said. He nodded to Maguire.

The Lieutenant jammed his gun up against Streicher's chest and fired. The German was thrown back, off the truck. But as he fell, he grabbed the hot barrel of the machinegun, pulling Maguire after him. The lieutenant fell with a cry.

'Back – we have to go back!' Davenport yelled to the driver.

The Chevrolet swung in a wide arc and headed rapidly back to where Maguire was grappling with Streicher. But his blows were ineffective. The Ubermensch had its hands clasped round Maguire's throat, throttling him. Maguire clutched and tore at the hands, gouging out skin – revealing the inhuman orange growth beneath. Weakening, Maguire's hands fell away, reaching instead for something on his belt.

'Keep going!' Guy shouted.

'We can't leave the lieutenant,' the driver yelled back.

'We're too late,' Davenport said. He too had seen what Maguire had at his belt. 'Keep going!'

The Chevrolet shot past the two figures. Guy caught a confused glimpse of Maguire, with the last of his strength, bringing the grenade up between them, jamming it against Streicher's chest. The explosion was a deafening roar. The blast wave shook the vehicle as the two figures disappeared in a sudden ball of smoke and flame.

The vehicle slewed to a halt. The other two Chevrolets drew up beside it. The German vehicles were burning wrecks. The bodies of the German troops littered the ground. Dark smoke hung over the desert like an improbable thunder cloud. The sudden silence was broken by an explosion as one of the German gas tanks blew in the heat.

Then came the chatter of the radio truck's big Vickers machine gun. Two surviving Germans had made a run for the entrance into the mound. The .303 rounds tore their bodies apart in seconds.

'Tend to the wounded,' Henderson snapped.

'Sorry about Maguire,' Guy said quietly.

'He was a good man,' Henderson said. 'But we keep losing good men in this war.'

'Is that it, sir?' The driver of Guy's vehicle asked. He looked pale. Beside him the navigator had his hand clamped over his bloody shoulder.

'No,' Davenport said. 'I don't think this is over by a long way. Look at the ground.'

The desert was moving. The sand around the vehicles rippled, as if a strong wind was blowing. But the air was still. Something emerged from the sand – a dark, gnarled length of what might be a tree root. Except it was jointed, clutching at the air, scrabbling for a purchase on the sand.

Another tentacle thrust through beside it, clawing and pushing. A shower of sand was thrown up as the creature forced its way up to the surface. A dark bulbous shape about fifteen inches across supported by spider-like legs squatted over the desert floor. Black hollow eyes stared up at Guy and the others. A thin slit of a mouth gaped suddenly open.

All around the vehicles, more of the creatures were erupting from the sand.

CHAPTER 47

There were cries of horror and shock from the soldiers, followed almost immediately by gunshots. The Vril creature closest to Davenport exploded under a sudden storm of bullets as Guy opened fire.

Another of the grotesque creatures hauled itself up on to the back of the Chevrolet. A whip-like limb lashed out, catching the nearest SAS man and knocking him sideways. He was already standing up, staring out across the rippling sand. The blow pitched him over the side of the vehicle. He dropped his rifle and fell to the ground.

At once another Vril was on him. Its long limbs clamped round the man, tearing through his uniform. Blood spurted from a ruptured artery, spraying across the side of the vehicle and staining the sand.

Davenport grabbed the fallen man's rifle, reversed it, and slammed the butt into the bloated body of the Vril at the back of the Chevrolet. The creature was knocked back, but lashed out again. Davenport ducked under the flailing limb, and rammed the rifle into the creature again. With an ear-splitting screech, it fell away. It lay on the ground, limbs curled above it, clutching at the air. Then they seemed to curl back on themselves, as if the joints were suddenly inverted, and the creature raised itself up once more.

As it braced, ready to leap back up at them, Guy fired

379

several shots into it. The bulbous body exploded in a mess of green and orange.

Close to them, Henderson's vehicle gunned its engine and roared across the sand. The soldiers inside were shooting at the Vril around them. Several of the creatures clung to the sides of the Chevrolet, and another was clutching the bonnet. The front driver's wheel crunched over one of the creatures. It exploded in a glutinous mess.

The third vehicle was further away – right in the middle of the area where the Vril had erupted from the desert. It was covered with the creatures as they swarmed over it. The whole vehicle was engulfed by a seething mass of gnarled, inhuman shapes. The sounds of firing from inside were muffled. So, mercifully, were the screams. A side panel was ripped away. The bonnet discarded. The vehicle lurched forward several yards then stopped abruptly.

'They're tearing it apart,' Davenport realised.

'Get us moving,' Guy ordered, shooting another Vril off the side of their truck.

The truck jolted and bumped forward, then stalled. The engine coughed back into life, and they lurched forwards again.

'Which way?' the driver yelled.

'Whichever way is clear of those things,' Davenport shouted back.

'Follow Henderson,' Guy ordered.

There were fewer of the Vril closer to the mound, and Henderson's Chevrolet was heading at speed for the entrance cut into the landscape. It was almost there when the ground seemed to explode under it. More of the Vril erupted from the desert, right beneath the vehicle. It crunched and bounced over them, but then slewed violently to one side.

The Chevrolet skidded, rolled, ended up on its side. Henderson and the surviving soldiers were thrown out. One of them was immediately covered with Vril. A line of the creatures scuttled hungrily towards Henderson and the last three soldiers. They fired shot after shot, but still the creatures kept coming.

Guy yelled at the driver to accelerate. But they could all see there was no way they would reach Henderson before the Vril overwhelmed them. One of them was already clawing its way over the end of the truck. A sharp tentacle skewered into the back of one of the soldiers – erupting from his chest in a shower of blood and tissue. Henderson stuck his revolver into the creature's body before it could withdraw, and fired three shots. The Vril collapsed in a deflated heap, dragging the man it had impaled with it.

Then the creatures exploded, one after another. The desert sand was strewn with suddenly visceral slime and severed limbs. The deep roar of another engine made Davenport turn – and see the radio truck racing towards them. Its big Vickers machine gun was trained on the advancing Vril, the heavy .303 bullets ripping them to pieces.

'They're giving us covering fire,' Guy realised. 'Get to Henderson!'

They skidded to a halt beside Henderson and his men, who quickly clambered into the vehicle. The driver accelerated away as a Vril leaped at them, slamming into the side of the truck. One of the soldiers rammed his submachine gun into the dark body and fired. The Vril shrieked, and exploded into pieces. A single twitching limb remained hooked over the side of the Chevrolet. Davenport prised it loose with the end of the rifle he still held, and it fell away.

'Head for the entrance,' Guy said. 'It's the only cover.'

'Unless there are more of those things inside,' Henderson told him. 'What *are* they?'

'I wish we knew,' Davenport told him. 'But apart from "nasty" we don't have a lot to go on.'

'And what's this place?' Henderson said as they raced towards the dark hole cut into the desert.

It was easily wide enough for the Chevrolet. There seemed to be no Vril close to the mound, and they drove inside, the radio truck close behind. Its Vickers gun swung to cover the desert outside as it slowed to a halt behind Guy and Davenport's vehicle.

'This place is why we came here,' Guy said. It seemed eerily quiet after the sounds of the battle outside. 'We're hoping to find answers to your question in here.'

The Vickers gun was ready to blast away at any of the creatures that came close. But for the moment they seemed content to keep well back.

'They know we'll have to come out again at some point,' Davenport said.

'We should call up air support,' Henderson decided. He looked to Guy for agreement, and he nodded his consent.

Henderson's suggestion that there might be more of them inside made Guy and Davenport cautious as they left the surviving soldiers with the trucks and made their way along the tunnel. Guy had a rifle slung over his shoulder and two grenades hung from his belt. Davenport wore a handgun in a holster, his hand never straying far from it. Before long they were out of sight of the entrance, and their torches gave the only light.

'Streicher didn't make this tunnel,' Davenport said. 'He cut a hole into the end of this passageway, like a door. Like he knew it was here.'

'Maybe he did,' Guy agreed. 'He was an Ubermensch.'

'But how? He was human enough when I met him in France, I'd swear to it. Unless...'

'Unless what?'

'When I pulled him out of the burial mound,' Davenport said. 'Maybe something happened to him then. He breathed in the gas or whatever it was. Or perhaps he was bitten or stung by one of those creatures. I did see... something. Something in the tomb, just from the corner of my eye.'

The passageway sloped down into the ground. There were openings off, each of them giving into a large chamber. The first few were empty.

'It's a different layout to the other sites,' Davenport said. 'But we should be careful. There may still be traps.'

'Look at this.' Guy shone his torch through another opening. 'This is more like it.'

The pale light picked out broken glass and pottery strewn across the floor. A pile of bracelets, like the one Sarah had found in Suffolk, lay close to one wall. They picked their way through the chamber, and Guy stuffed one of the bracelets into his pocket.

'We should gather up as much of this stuff as we can,' he said.

'Best check what else is down here first,' Davenport cautioned. 'We want to make sure we take the most useful things. Who knows what's further inside?'

'Nothing good, I suspect.'

They found a chamber of empty glass jars, identical to the ones that had housed Vril creatures at the other sites.

'The ones outside, do you suppose?' Davenport said. 'You think maybe they burrowed their way out of here?'

'No,' Guy said. 'Look at this.'

At the back of the chamber, two small circular openings were cut into the wall, close to the floor. Guy shone his torch into one of them, revealing a round tunnel. There were grooves cut into the sides, like small steps.

'That's how they get out,' Davenport realised. He shone his own torch into the second cylindrical tunnel.

A dark tentacle lashed out from inside the tunnel, whipping across in front of Davenport's face. He cried out and leaped back, fumbling for his gun.

'Christ – they're coming back in!'

Guy stepped in front of him, dropping his torch as he unslung his rifle from his shoulder and brought it to bear. The Vril was right in the opening now, gaining purchase from the narrow step-like ledges inside to pull itself up and out. Its dark eyes glinted in the erratic light from Davenport's torch.

The rifle shot tore through the creature's outer skin. It deflated, screeching – falling back into the hole. Tentacles scrabbled round the lip of the tunnel. Then Guy fired again, and the bulbous body exploded. He grabbed a grenade from his pocket, pulled out the pin and threw it into the tunnel opening. It rattled down the shaft.

He repeated the process with the second tunnel, then turned and ran. Davenport was right with him as they charged out of the chamber and took shelter to the side of the doorway. There were two explosions in rapid succession. A blast of heat swept past them. Smoke drifted out into the passageway.

When the sound had died away, they cautiously made their way back inside. The two small openings were blocked with rock and debris, the tunnels collapsed.

'Let's hope there's no other way for them to get back inside,' Davenport said.

His words were punctuated by the distant rattle of gunfire.

'Sounds like they're trying the main entrance now,' Guy said, leading the way back out into the main passage. 'We'd better get a move on. Let's see what we can find, then organise getting the hell out of here.'

There was a glow coming from further down the passageway. Pale light spilled out from an entrance into another chamber. Guy and Davenport warily stepped into the light, peering into the vast space beyond. The walls were covered with strange equipment – lights glowing, dials and readouts giving information in runic symbols that neither of them could decipher.

'What's it for?' Guy wondered aloud.

'Buggered if I know,' Davenport replied. They were both speaking in hushed voices.

'You think Streicher found this?'

'If he did, then why didn't his men remove anything?' Davenport asked. 'They found their way in here and then... Nothing. If it was me, I'd have been loading up the trucks outside. There's something wrong about this place.'

Guy laughed. 'You can say that again.'

'No, I'm serious. I mean...' He shook his head. 'Ignore me, I don't know what I mean.'

Thick metal mesh hung down like spiders' webs from the arched roof. Guy's torch picked out the bulbous shape of a Vril hanging motionless in the netting.

'It's dead,' he realised.

The body was a pale, withered husk.

Davenport had a small camera. Neither of them thought the pictures would come out in the dim light with no flashgun, but he took pictures anyway. They worked their way through the cavernous chamber, and finally pushed past the last of the hanging metal mesh, to discover what lay beyond.

'My God,' Davenport breathed. 'Is that what I think it is?'

'We'd need to ask someone who's seen one,' Guy replied, equally awestruck. 'But yes, I think we've found a UDT.'

The craft hung suspended below the roof of the cavern – though it was impossible to see what held it in place above the floor. It was as big as the Avro Anson that Guy and Davenport had arrived in, but unlike a conventional plane it was circular, like an upturned soup bowl. The only wings were stubby fins that projected from one side of the disc. The underside was patterned with circular recesses that gave off a faint, yellow glow which was just enough to blur the shape of the disc and make it hard to discern its colour. It looked like a dull silver or possibly gunmetal, but it could really have been anything.

'Engines?' Guy wondered.

Davenport shrugged. 'It's almost like it's on display, isn't it. This whole place could have been designed to lead us through to this finale. The great reveal at the end of some bizarre freak show.' He raised the small camera and snapped two pictures. 'A couple more for the family album.'

'How do we get that out of here?' Guy asked.

'Short answer is, we don't. Though – how did *they* get it out of here I wonder?'

'They flew it.'

'Yes, but where? Streicher made the entrance hole, and anyway that thing's too big to fit down the passageway... Unless the roof opens up somehow?'

'No sign of that,' Guy said. He raked his torch across the roof. The light barely touched it, but the whole structure seemed to be solid.

'We should get back,' Davenport said. 'See if Henderson has any ideas.'

'Let's see what we can take back with us.'

As Guy was speaking, there was a loud scraping sound from somewhere behind them, followed by a dull thump that echoed round the chamber.

They ran to see what had happened – and found that a screen had slid into place across the opening into the passageway. It was textured like stone, but warm to the touch and slightly spongy.

'Someone shut the door,' Davenport said.

'Maybe it was automatic.'

'Doesn't much matter, does it? However it happened, we have to get it open again.'

They put their shoulders to the huge door, but it refused to move in the slightest.

'There's a panel here with some sort of markings on it,' Guy said.

The panel was set into the frame of the doorway. It was made from the same material as the shutter, and there was a pattern inlaid into it, like the silver tracery on the bracelets. A spiral pattern of intersecting lines.

'Looks like a maze,' Davenport said.

Guy traced his finger across the panel. The lines glowed as he touched them.

'You suppose we solve the maze and the door opens?' he said. 'Or is that too obvious?'

'Got to be worth a try.'

It took three attempts before Guy – encouraged and distracted by Davenport's constant advice – solved the puzzle. They both looked expectantly at the door. Nothing happened. In frustration, Guy thumped his fist into the panel. It juddered under the blow, skewing sideways slightly.

'Hang on,' Davenport said. 'Let's see if we can lever it off.'

Together they were able to ease their fingertips behind the panel and ease it away from the wall. Behind was a recess, filled with filaments like the tendrils that emerged from the wounds of an Ubermensch, only thicker. The panel remained attached by one of the filaments, which split into narrower fibres just before it reached the plate.

'Big help,' Guy said. 'Now what?'

'No idea,' Davenport confessed. 'But if these tendrils are like wires in an electrical circuit, maybe we need to connect them up in a particular way to open the door.'

'Or maybe none of this has anything to do with the door.'

But Davenport was already pulling out strands of the spongy, organic material and touching the ends together. He was rewarded by a sudden hiss and a flash of sparks. Guy shone his torch into the recess to give more light over and above the ambient glow from the equipment around them.

'Try that one,' Guy said, pointing to one of the strands. 'It's the same shade as the one you're holding.'

Another flash of sparks. Then the panel across the doorway slid slowly back.

'Well done!'

Guy's relieved congratulations were curtailed by a wail of high-pitched noise. The control plate was suddenly pulled back to the wall by the tendril, snapping into place. The silver tracery on the surface had shifted into another shape, like a Celtic cross. The wail died away, then started again, falling and rising regularly. And with each burst of sound, the runic pattern on the plate changed – to a similar symbol but with one of the arms of the cross shorter. A second later, it changed again, the arm shortening still further.

'We have to get out of here,' Guy said, staring at the plate. 'Now!'

'You can read those runes?' Davenport said, surprised.

'No. But I know a countdown when I see one. Come on!'

They ran, torchlight dancing round the walls and floor as they raced back up the passageway.

'You could be wrong,' Davenport gasped.

'Then we can come back and salvage that equipment.'

From deep behind them came a low rumble. The ground began to shake.

'All right,' Davenport shouted above the growing noise. 'You're not wrong.'

A dark figure was coming towards them. A silhouette in the dim light now visible from the end of the tunnel. It slowly resolved itself into Henderson, running towards them.

'Thank God,' he said. 'What's going on? It sounds as if the whole place is going to blow.'

'I think you're exactly right,' Guy told him.

'Did you get through to base?' Davenport asked as they ran back towards the two trucks parked inside the end of the tunnel.

'We did,' Henderson told him.

'And you called in air support?' Guy said. 'Because God knows we're going to need it.'

'There is no air support,' Henderson said.

'What?'

'Rommel's heading towards Benghazi. They've got the whole of the Desert Air Force on standby to support our troops. The DAF can't spare anyone to come and help us against... against whatever it is out there we're fighting.'

They reached the trucks. The Vickers gun opened up, its violent chattering echo adding to the deep rumble growing inside the tunnel. Abruptly it cut out again.

'That's it, sir,' the gunner shouted to Henderson. 'That's the last of the ammo.'

'They're coming!' one of the other soldiers shouted. Outside the tunnel, a dark mass was swarming and scuttling across the sand towards them.

From deep down the tunnel, there was a violent roar of sound. A huge detonation. A rush of hot air blasted over them.

'We've no air support and we've lost the Vickers,' Henderson shouted above the increasing noise. 'But believe me, sir – we have to get the hell out of here now!'

His face was glowing in reflected light. His eyes widened as he stared past Guy and Davenport. They both turned to see a huge ball of flame and smoke roaring up the tunnel towards them.

CHAPTER 48

With nothing else to do, Sarah spent a lot of her time in the radio tent. Whenever the set crackled into life, she hoped it would be Guy and Davenport calling in. But the news from further west and updates on Rommel's advance consumed the airwaves.

She was about to leave and get herself a cup of tea in the mess tent when Henderson's signal finally came through. She listened in horror to the message sent back by the DAF commander – that no help would be coming. She could see from the faces of the soldiers and airmen that it wasn't a decision they liked, but outside the planes were already being fuelled and readied for reconnaissance and possible action over the Afrika Korps.

From experience, Sarah knew there was no point in arguing. So instead she slipped away to look for Jimmy the ground crewman. Speed was vital, so she asked the first Desert Air Force man she saw. And kept asking until someone directed her to a maintenance area.

'How about you show me that Hurri-bomber?' she said when she found him.

'Sure.' Jimmy grinned. 'Maybe this afternoon if they're not needed. There are a few of them.'

'I only want to see one. But I want to see it now.'

'I'm kind of busy.'

'Oh.' She deployed her best disappointed pout. 'That's a pity. Still, maybe one of the other boys can show me. There's a few who have offered. Just a quick look, mind, because I know everyone's got a lot on.' She undid the top button of her blouse and shook the material gently. 'Hot, isn't it?'

It wasn't especially warm, but Jimmy didn't contradict her. He wiped his hands on an oily rag. 'All right, all right. But we'll have to be quick.'

There were half a dozen planes arranged at the end of the main landing strip, concealed under camouflage nets. They passed several Kittyhawks before reaching a Hawker Hurricane. It didn't have the elegance of the Spitfire, but poised on the sand the harsh military menace of the aircraft was unmistakeable. The only difference that Sarah could see from the normal Mark II model were the bombs, one slung under each wing.

'Two two-fifty pound bombs,' Jimmy pointed out.

'Cannon or machine guns?' she asked.

'On this one, twelve .303 machine guns in the wings.'

'Very impressive.'

'We keep them fuelled and armed ready, like all the planes.'

It took Sarah a few moments to persuade Jimmy that she should be allowed to check out the controls. Just to see if they were like a conventional Hurricane, even though he assured her they were.

'Just be quick,' Jimmy warned, making the most of giving Sarah a leg-up into the cockpit. 'If anyone sees you, I'll be in real trouble.'

'No,' she said. '*Real* trouble is what you'll be in if I steal the plane.'

He gave a nervous laugh, shielding his eyes from the sun as he looked up at her. 'You seen enough yet?'

'Nothing like enough. Sorry, Jimmy. Tell them I'll be back as soon as I can.'

Whatever reply Jimmy had was lost in the burst of power from the Merlin engine as the aircraft stuttered into life.

*

The two Chevrolets shot out of the tunnel. A wave of flame exploded out behind them, the blast punching the vehicles forwards, across the sand – straight at the sea of advancing Vril.

The back tyres of the second vehicle were burning, black smoke pouring from them as it bounced along. It crunched over one of the creatures, shattering it and spreading glutinous debris mixed with burned rubber in a trail behind. Most of the Vril were still ahead.

The SAS men in the front vehicle fired at the creatures swarming towards them, converging on the two trucks bouncing across the undulating sand.

'We're never going to make it through that lot,' Guy realised.

'Can't we go round?' Davenport shouted.

'They're too quick.'

One of the burning tyres ruptured with a dull popping sound. The Chevrolet slewed sideways and skidded to a halt. Guy waved to Henderson in the front vehicle to keep going, to save himself and his men. But Henderson was having none of it, and the vehicle turned in a wide arc. A dozen Vril scuttled after it.

The radio truck drew up beside Guy's crippled vehicle. The driver and other soldiers leaped across, Guy shoving Davenport ahead of him. As soon as they were all crammed into the vehicle, the driver gunned the engine. Sand spewed up from the back tyres. The vehicle lurched and juddered. But it didn't move.

'We're too heavy,' Davenport realised. 'We're stuck in the sand!'

The Vril were fifty feet away, scuttling across the sand like enormous, malevolent spiders. Behind the stranded vehicles, fire roared from the mouth of the tunnel. Even if they could outrun the creatures, Guy realised, there was nowhere to go.

The sound of the straining engine seemed to deepen to a throaty roar. The Vril were so close now that Guy could see the dark glistening pits of their eyes. Then as he watched, the nearest Vril exploded into fragments. The body was a sudden visceral mess, the tentacles blasted clear.

The roar of engines was coming from above them. A dark shape blotted out the sun, silhouetted against the pale sky – a Hurricane. The plane swept round, charging back across the landscape. Emerging from the dark smoke gathering above the tunnel mouth. The forward edges of the wings spat fire as the machine guns opened up again.

'Down!' Henderson yelled above the noise as a dark shape detached from the underside of one wing.

Guy leaped out of the vehicle, Davenport beside him. As he ducked down, he saw the bomb slam into the ground, right in the middle of the mass of swarming Vril. There was a massive 'crump'. The ground shook beneath them, and sand showered down from the sky.

'Choose your targets,' Henderson shouted.

Together with the few surviving soldiers, he was aiming his rifle over the top of the vehicle, bracing it on the side struts. A rattle of rifle and submachine gun fire split the air, counterpointing the distant sound of the Hurricane as it banked and turned.

Several Vril exploded. One got close enough to leap up on to the radio truck before a soldier jammed the end of his submachine gun into the glistening body and blasted it to pieces.

They all ducked again as the second bomb crashed down into the last remaining Vril. The explosion was even closer, even larger. Shrapnel hammered into the sides of the vehicles. One of the soldiers cried out as hot metal grazed his leg.

A single Vril staggered from the wreckage of the crater, one tentacle-leg snapped off, another quivering ineffectually. Then a burst of fire from the hurricane sent it skidding and rolling across the sand, ripping it to pieces.

Slowly, cautiously, Guy and the others peered over and round the vehicles. The landscape was a broken, blackened mess strewn with the shattered carcasses of the Vril creatures. Smoke drifted across the sand. Nothing else moved.

The Hurricane came in low. The pilot raised his hand in a wave of victory. Or rather, Guy realised, *her* hand. For the briefest moment, his eyes met Sarah's. Then the plane was turning again, and disappearing into the distance. It gained height as it cleared the ridge, spinning slowly in a victory roll.

CHAPTER 49

Mercifully, the radio truck was relatively undamaged. They managed to dig it out of the sand, which had been softened by the Vril as they dug their way out of the mound. Back on the ridge, the ground was firm enough for the truck to continue with all the survivors on board. Before they left, Henderson and his men buried the dead Germans as well as their fallen comrades in the sand.

It was a strange journey back – the euphoria and adrenalin of victory tempered by the sense of loss. Jammed between Davenport and Henderson, Guy's mind was numbed – by what they had been through and what they had seen.

The camp by the oasis was a shadow of its former self. Most of the troops and the equipment had been deployed in the desperate battle to stop Rommel's advance.

But Guy didn't care. There was only one person he wanted to see at the base, and he was sure she would still be there waiting for him.

They said nothing when they met. Guy enfolded Sarah in a tight embrace, barely feeling Henderson's pat on the back as he led his men away to recover and prepare for their next mission. Finally, the two of them pulled apart, and walked slowly to Guy's tent.

Davenport was already inside, tipping sand out of his boots. He glanced up as Guy and Sarah came in. 'Funnily enough,' he said, pulling his boots back on, 'I was just going for a walk.'

'Thank you, Leo,' Sarah said. 'It's good to see you too.'

'Of course it is.' Davenport put his hand on Guy's shoulder as he passed. 'And this time,' he said quietly, 'get it right.'

'There are sure to be other, smaller centres of Vril operations,' Brinkman said. 'Like the burial sites in Suffolk and France.' He looked round at the others – Guy Pentecross, Leo Davenport, Sarah Diamond and Miss Manners. 'But it sounds as if we've put their main base out of operation.' He nodded and smiled. 'Well done.'

One set of the photographs that Davenport had taken inside the Vril base were pinned up on the conference room wall alongside the map of North Africa. A duplicate set was on the table in front of them. Miss Manners had supervised getting them developed by MI5, who had made a pretty good job of clarifying the vague, dark smudges. In some of them, the detail was discernible. A blurred lightshow constituted the only decent shot of the UDT.

'We didn't learn much,' Guy confessed.

'Except that the Desert Air Force can't court martial a civilian for borrowing one of their planes, apparently,' Davenport said, grinning at Sarah across the table.

'I'd have named you as an accessory,' she told him.

'At least we got another bracelet,' Guy said.

As he spoke, the door opened to admit Elizabeth Archer and Sergeant Green. Mrs Archer sat down and tossed something onto the table.

'You mean this?'

The bracelet spun to a halt in front of Guy.

'It's useless,' she said.

'What do you mean?'

'Maybe it's damaged. Or maybe it never worked. But it doesn't react like the other one to radio impulses. In fact, the whole construction is rather less robust.'

'Is that important?' Brinkman asked.

Mrs Archer shrugged. 'Possibly. Who knows.'

'I've just taken a call from Dr Wiles, sir,' Green said to Brinkman. 'He's still receiving UDT transmissions from the Y Stations. And Fighter Command tracked another one this morning.'

'You said there are likely to be other bases,' Sarah pointed out.

'Yes, miss,' Green said. 'But according to Wiles, the traffic and sightings haven't diminished. If anything, they've increased.'

'So what was that place?' Guy said. 'If we haven't set them back...'

Davenport cleared his throat. 'I do have an observation,' he said. 'But you're not going to like it.'

They all watched as he spread the duplicate set of photographs across the table.

'It struck me at the time that there was something amiss, but we were rather too busy for me to dwell on it. I think Guy was worried too.'

'Go on,' Brinkman prompted.

'Well, it just seemed rather neat, that's all. Everything laid out ready for us to find. A central passageway. No traps or defences as such, not like in France or at the site in Suffolk.'

'Until we got trapped in that final chamber and the whole place blew up, you mean,' Guy pointed out.

'True. But until then, it wasn't set out like a military base, was it? The whole place seemed to be arranged for our benefit, not for the Vril. I mean, why was their chamber so far from the main entrance if they wanted to get out? Come to that, why come out at all – why not wait inside for us?'

'That would make more military sense,' Guy agreed.

'They don't think like we do,' Miss Manners said. 'Who knows what purpose they had.'

'Bear with me,' Davenport said. 'But think about it, Guy – that whole place seemed to be leading us to the UDT. To the most impressive sight of all, right at the end. Behind a screen of hanging mesh, waiting to be revealed, and with no obvious way for it to be flown out.' He picked up the indistinct photo of the UDT. 'I know some of you think I live my life like it's a film anyway, but this really was like a film set, or a theatrical display. Not practical, but spectacular.'

'But what would be the point?' Sarah asked.

'Ah, now there you have me.'

There was silence for several moments, then Miss Manners said: 'Tell us again about when you were locked in, how you opened the door.'

Guy described what had happened and how they had escaped.

'Is it just me, or does that sound rather like some sort of initiative test?' Miss Manners asked.

'As if the Vril were assessing you,' Mrs Archer agreed. 'Yes, that would make sense. In fact...' She and Miss Manners were staring across the table at each other. 'It all makes sense then, doesn't it.'

'Not to me,' Brinkman said.

'They were testing us all along,' Miss Manners told him. 'You said that Streicher and his men hadn't disturbed anything. That's because it was all ready for *you* to find. Then they wanted to know if having found it you could solve the puzzle and escape again. Even locating the base in North Africa and getting there was a test.'

Guy leaned forward, suddenly anxious. 'Are you suggesting they were assessing their enemy's strength?'

'Or perhaps just deciding if we are worth fighting,' Sarah said. 'If we are intelligent and advanced enough to be worth their efforts.'

'Then the whole place,' Guy said slowly, 'even down to the Vril creatures that were there, it was all expendable.' He picked up the bracelet that Elizabeth Archer had brought back. 'That's why this doesn't work. Maybe the UDT itself was a dummy, a copy, a diversion.'

'Remind you of anything, Elizabeth?' Davenport said.

'Possibly two things,' she replied. 'But I think you're right. It was their version of the Suicide Exhibition.'

'Which means that everything they really value, everything that's truly irreplaceable is concealed somewhere else,' Brinkman said. 'We've wasted our time and effort.'

'To say nothing of those soldiers' lives,' Sarah murmured.

'You said it could be two things,' Miss Manners prompted.

Elizabeth Archer nodded. 'They've been here a long time,' she said. 'Perhaps it was also an alarm clock.'

'In which case we just set it off,' Guy said.

'And in some style, I'm ashamed to say,' Davenport added.

'If you're right, then this isn't the end of the Vril,' Brinkman said grimly. 'If you're right, the real war is just about to start.'

The story continues in:
The Blood Red City